I'M GOING TO DIE!

It's a charge. The NVA are yelling, screaming, running toward us and shooting—hundreds of them.

Suddenly I'm no longer an advisor watching the war. It's aimed directly at me. I sight in on a running figure's head and squeeze the trigger.

His head explodes and he drops.

I sight in on the one next to him. Thirty meters, nearly pistol range. Sight picture, trigger squeeze. He goes down.

I keep firing, but there's no end to the enemy. They keep coming.

I shoot rapidly, sight picture, trigger squeeze. In ten seconds or less I've emptied another magazine. Frantically, I reload. They're right *here*. I flip to auto and spray upward, lying on my back. For God's sake, one's right on top of me. He's wild-eyed, panicked. His AK is spraying high. I pull the trigger back and hold it, hitting him in the guts and letting it ride up under recoil. It cuts up a red swath, and his wild-eyed expression becomes permanent. I'm empty again. I grab for another magazine and shove it home. It's harder this time. I'm shaking too much. *My God, I'm going to die!*

THE ADVISORS

CURT RICH

ZEBRA BOOKS
KENSINGTON PUBLISHING CORP.

ZEBRA BOOKS

are published by

Kensington Publishing Corp.
475 Park Avenue South
New York, NY 10016

First printing: November 1985

Printed in the United States of America

DEDICATION

Contrary to popular belief, John Wayne never fought in Vietnam. Real live men went to Vietnam, men who were scared, tired, brave, cowardly, strong, and weak. I tried to write about these men, specifically, about the MACV advisors, the first combat soldiers in Vietnam, and the last to leave. Being an advisor was a particularly thankless task. It was also hairy. It took me twelve years to be able to write about it with the bullshit removed (assuming I have).

The United States Army gives only one badge to signify combat experience in a combat arm, the Combat Infantry Badge. There is no Combat Armor Badge, or Combat Artillery Badge. The reason is obvious to one who has endured combat in all three forms. Infantry combat is the most harrowing experience on earth.

Consequently, this book is dedicated to the individuals who wore the MACV crest on their left shoulder, and who earned the CIB.

As for the REMFs, fuck 'em.

Curt Rich
August 1983

20 July 1969 — 24 July 1969

Neil Armstrong and Buzz Aldrin landed on the Moon today. The Moon! Americans walked on the Moon. I saw it on a little black and white TV in the BOQ at RVN Training Center, Fort Lewis, Washington.

The irony is obvious. I am going to a pitiful, painful, dirty jungle war, and they walk on the Moon. It figures. I will leave beautiful Washington on July 25th for Vietnam, A.P.O. San Francisco 96222, that's MACV, Military Assistance Command, Vietnam. MACV means being an advisor. It figures. I very much want to command American troops, so I'll get a bunch of Vietnamese. (No, that's not right. I don't want to lead American troops in combat, I want to stay in the U.S. and say to my grandchildren, "I missed the Vietnam war. Gee, I would have liked to go, but . . .")

It beats, "This is my first husband's grave. He died in Vietnam at the age of twenty-three. Such a waste."

Jerry A. Harris, first lieutenant, U.S.A.R., born 9-6-45 in Fort Worth, Texas, an only child. Parents divorced 1950. Mother moved to Texas City to work at the chemical plants there. Jerry was an honor student at Texas City High School, played cornet in the school band. Graduated tenth in a class of two hundred and fifty-six. University of Houston — ROTC scholarship. Graduated 1967 biology (pre-med) major. Commissioned second lieutenant, U.S.A.R. June 6, 1967, active duty July 26th. Married Carole Anne Stacy, October 13th, 1967. Served one year First Battalion Thirty Second Armor, Friedberg, Germany, one year ground liaison officer to Fifty-Third T.F.W., RAF Lakenheath, England.

I wonder if that'll be the extent of my obituary.

Rather than get mired in self-pity, I grab Mike Clarendon, and we go to the Officer's Club for dinner. Mike graduated from U of H about one semester ahead of me. He was one year ahead in ROTC, one of my senior TAC officers during my rough junior year. He used to run me to death. I never could run worth a damn. Now we're almost equals. We're both scared silly.

Mike tried on his newly issued jungle boots. They didn't fit. He read the instruction card and found out you need to get one size bigger and wider than you normally used because they have inserts in them and to allow for swelling of your feet.

I tried mine on. They hurt. I tried Mike's on. They didn't. I tried to get Mike to trade since he was going to have to turn in his anyway.

"No, what if I get stuck with them?"

So we both went back to supply and got larger boots. Apparently a lot of people do what we did. They were ready for us.

RVN (Republic of Vietnam) training is a joke. They fitted us in jungle boots and jungle fatigues and gave us lectures in VD, TB, VC, MPC, etc. We got to go through a mock Vietnamese village and learn the difference between a hamlet and a village. The mock village is made of old ammo crates and C-ration cans, for Chrissakes. How accurate can that be? And if it's inaccurate, how good is the rest of this training?

It's boobytrapped in supposedly typical ways. If that's true I'll get killed for sure. No one can avoid all these fiendish devices. No, I won't get killed. I'll get my nuts blown off. That'll be my luck.

Sergeants show us a mean collection of killing devices, punji stakes, foot mines, claymores, nail mines, tiger pits, etc. They're all Vietnam vets. It must be hell having to relive it all as an instructor after you get back. Worse, some of them have been there two or three times. I don't know if I could take that. But then I don't know what I could take. I don't think I want to find out. I doubt if I am hero material. I'll probably wet my pants in combat.

We got jungle fatigues and made the local seamstress rich sewing on our patches. We don't have too many patches—MACV on left sleeve, subdued, name over right pocket, and U.S. Army over left pocket, rank and branch for collar. No right sleeve insignia. You get that after one tour, the shoulder insignia of the last unit in which you were in combat. I am considered weird by Mike because I leave off Ranger and Airborne patches. Those get one respect by senior officers who like people who have gotten their appropriate tickets punched. On the other hand I do not want a ranger or airborne job. I want a desk, a

9

nice safe dog robber's job. Not bloody likely.

The jungle fatigues are a great improvement — rip stop material, four patch pockets on the shirt, which is more bush jacket than shirt, room for a ton. The pants have six pockets, very functional for the boonies. Even I, a virgin to all this, can see that. I find a black belt buckle, replacing a rear area brass type. One does not need brass to reflect in the bush. All my insignia are black where they used to be living color. They call it subdued.

T-shirts and underwear are O.D. (olive drab). Now that looks strange.

We do ambushes from trucks. We look at disgustingly real-looking wounds for first aid. A lot of good we'll be in a situation needing first aid. Most of these kids can't stand to look at the phony wounds, much less the real ones to come. A sergeant tells us how to comfort the wounded. "If he's hit, say, in the face, he'll want to know how bad it is. 'How much do I have left?' they say. He may have half his face blown off. You've got to change the subject. Tell him he'll be okay. If it doesn't show on your face, he won't know."

"Swell. If I'm ever shot in the face and some guy says I'll be okay, I'll know my jaw's blown off, and I'll die from the shock," said Mike under his breath.

"I've seen a lot of cases at Madigan General, the hospital over here, and you'd be surprised how much the human body can take and still live. You can live without a lot."

We "qualify" on the M-16. This bugs me. I qualified expert on the M-1 rifle and .45 pistol. My tank crew was all expert. I shot on the battalion and brigade pistol teams. I take the weapons seriously.

Here they don't. The weapons orientation is hurried. I don't think I can disassemble an M-16 and get it back together in a hurry. Since I've heard all the horror stories about the M-16 jamming in combat because of dirt, I am bothered by this. Of course, the official story is that the marines weren't good at cleaning their rifles. This is an easy story for the army to throw out, but I don't believe a word of it. Marines are even more fanatic about clean weapons than soldiers. Of course the fact that their cleaning kits were for .30 caliber weapons and wouldn't go down the bore of the .223 caliber M-16 barrel might have had something to do with it.

Of course, in Europe the infantry troops carried M-14s, great weapons for a jungle war if you happen to be 6'7" and weigh 276 lbs. Otherwise they're *heavy*. We tankers, of course, carried fifty ton weapons with .45s as backups. If a tank doesn't do the job, I doubt a .45 pistol or submachine gun will, but they made good security blankets.

Then we go out and fire and "qualify"—all at once. They call it "emergency" qualification. I believe it. Jesus, I've had no practice with the little Mattel toy. I do not shoot it well, especially on full automatic fire. I am beginning to think automatic fire from a hand-held weapon belongs in the movies. An M-60 on a bipod or tripod is devastating. This little sucker just wastes ammo.

The qualification is not too realistic. We load up eight rounds at a time, even though the weapon holds twenty rounds. This, of course, is left over from M-1 days. When loading two eight-round magazines I decide to improve my chances by loading nine rounds in each. Naturally there's a screwup, and each guy uses four magazines, so I have to give them to the guy ahead.

But after all is said and done, Mike talks to a scorer in the pits. They didn't even try to score them. They didn't have time.

"Don't worry, sir," says a PSG. "Officers do well. They have rank on the scorecard."

But scores sheets are not collected, and orders come down with all of our names on it. We have all qualified.

I hope I can get a .45 in Nam. Some of the officers have pistols in their luggage. I did not think of such a thing. I would be afraid of getting caught with it if I did. (So what? What would they do? Send me to Vietnam?) I don't own any guns, so I'd have to buy a commercial .45 or a little snub-nosed .38 like these guys have. Surely I'll get a .45 in Nam. I do not trust Matty Mattel, here. It's Mattel, it's swell.

Mike and I call our wives and see a movie at the post theater. We're in civvies and a drunken GI hits us up to go AWOL with him. We don't.

One of the other inmates of the BOQ, another silver bar, Bill Dawson, tells how he had his passport and almost took his wife and ran to Canada while on leave. That I could not do.

While I was still in college one of my classmates went to prison rather than be drafted, and I remember Mom saying she didn't know how the boy's parents could live in our town after that. She would just die if I did something like that. Of course, the kid became a cult hero, and she's the one having trouble with townspeople. I haven't even left the country, and she has received a phone call accusing her of raising a killer.

The BOQ is a temporary type building, probably built during World War Two, the kind you find army wide. It's drafty, hot, a firetrap, two guys in a room. One of the guys is a chaplain major. He took the M-16 "training" as seriously as I did. We mention it, knowing he didn't have to take the training at all.

"I wanted to. Most chaplains spend their time in the rear where they're not needed. I intend to stay with the combat troops as much as I can. I may need that rifle someday."

Amazing, I think, knowing that most Protestant chaplains are the bottom of the barrel. I am impressed, but still, I think, "Hmmm, how will you explain that to God, chaplain?"

For that matter, how will I?

A verse from a "Jody" marching cadence:

> Jody, Jody stole my girl,
> An' left me all alone in this world.
> Lord, I feel so all alone,
> Guess I'll go an' play with my bone.

25—27 July 1969

We are divided into flights. Mine leaves last. Mike goes another way. I am going to Tan Son Nhut—Saigon. Mike is going to Da Nang. I figure I won't see him again. I am on a "diversionary" flight through San Francisco to Travis AFB to Vietnam. First we take buses to Seattle-Tacoma International Airport, then a commercial flight to San Francisco, and busses to Travis.

If you're goin' to San Francisco, be sure to wear your class A uniform . . . runs through my mind to the tune of "If you're goin' to San Francisco."

On the bus in Seattle I notice Pete Lovely Volkswagen. Pete was driving a private entry Lotus Formula One car in England when I was there. Briefly I'm transported to London and Brands Hatch where Carole and Mark Rambo and I were watching the Race of Champions. The drivers have life expectancies similar to infantry advisors. I was in Hockenheim when Jimmy Clark got killed in a meaningless Formula Two race. I watched them tell his girlfriend and Graham Hill.

15

Get your mind off death, Harris. Remember the London Racing Car Show, the topless girl at the Lotus display, the Castrol bird with the miniskirt that didn't cover her crotch.

I listen to the conversations in the bus behind me.

"Do you know what my life expectancy is?"

"Tell me."

"From the time I flick the safety off until I almost pull the trigger."

"I don't wanna work for MACV. Being an advisor sucks."

"No, it's okay. A lieutenant friend of mine was an advisor to an ARVN captain, and the guy used to get him dates, take him to Saigon on the weekends."

"Screw 'em all but ten, six pall bearers, three to raise the flag, and one to salute."

"It's not a bad job, a hard job, but not a bad one."

Someone in the back begins to sing. Several people join in:

A cruel war is raging.
Johnny has to fight.
Tomorrow is Sunday.
Monday is the day,
That your captain
will call you,
And you must obey.
Johnny, oh Johnny,
it grieves my heart so,
won't you let me go with you.

16

No, my love, no.

I'll tie up my hair.
Men's clothing I'll put on.
I'll pass as your comrade;
No one would ere guess.
Won't you let me go with you?
Yes, my love, yes.

Then in the silence after it ends, someone says, "Lyndon Johnson told the nation, 'have no fear of escalation. I am trying to please. Though it isn't really war, I'm sending fifty thousand more to help save Vietnam from the Vietnamese.' "

Someone else says, "How many Vietnamese fought in our Civil War?"

Then we get on the commercial flight. I'm the senior officer. My God, aren't they sending anyone but EM (enlisted men) and lieutenants? I am Lieutenant Fuzz, for Chrissake. Senior officer? The NCOIC before the group boarded the bus gave the stock lecture about anyone getting drunk or hopped up will get time in the stockade in Nam, and it will be bad time—time added to their tours.

I grab the two most senior NCOs and tell them I do not want any trouble, and I certainly do not want any of the men on my flight arrested. Take care of it. Keep the drunks in line and don't make me look bad.

See, I have learned something in two years active duty.

On the commercial flight there are eight seats in

17

First Class. Naturally the NCOs and I take them. We are all in greens for this part of the flight. The NCOs are all second or third tour men with rows of ribbons and hash marks. Korean War, even a World War II vet. Jesus, three wars.

I, of course, have one measly National Defense Medal, issued to every schnook on active duty for some silly reason. They look silly all by themselves.

In First Class there are free drinks. The stewardess gives me a bourbon and water. Then she gives me a little bourbon bottle, then another on the next pass. Nine in all. I don't know if she likes me or feels sorry for me. I must look petrified and about eighteen years old.

I *am* petrified. I know I am going to die or be horribly maimed. Death is the preferable alternative of the two, of course.

In San Francisco we take another military bus to Travis. There we stay overnight. In the VOQ I am exhausted but sleep is not easy.

The next morning I get up, have breakfast, and hump luggage. Why can't I pack lighter? Aerosol shaving cream cans are forbidden on MATS flights. There is a collection of left shaving cream and spray deodorants in every bathroom enroute.

"Are they afraid I'll stick a can of Right Guard in the pilot's ear and say 'Fly thees plane to Cuba'?" asks one lieutenant.

Braniff flight B2A3 leaves Travis AFB at twenty-three fifty hours going to Hawaii and Clark AFB Philippines, then to Tan Son Nhut. I don't know

18

what to expect at TSN. Incoming? Snipers? But no, it is like any other MATS flight, part airline, part military cattle car. We land at about thirteen hundred on the 28th of July. We walk to waiting busses and sweat. God, it's hot.

The busses are armored with wire mesh. I wonder why.

I have lost a day, a Sunday. We jumped ahead one day by our westward high-speed journey. Somehow I am depressed by that loss of one day. Will I ever get it back? Or will I die on this side of the international date line?

We are sorted and processed. I go in one of the armored, chicken-wired busses to MACV HQ. The street scenes are straight out of Terry and the Pirates. I am petrified. Do they have the wire over the windows to keep grenades out? Is it that bad?

I see people of both sexes wearing coolie hats. Women wear high-necked, long-skirted outfits called *ao dais*, usually white tops, black skirts, slit up the side. Apparently they have a thing about underwear as they'll have black bras under white tops. Some of the women look pretty good: long, straight black hair down to their asses. There are a lot of children running around, teenagers and subteenagers, some teenaged hoodlums, Saigon *Cau Bois* (cowboys). I even see a rickshaw, a real foot-powered one in addition to some motorcycle engine-powered ones. The streets are incredibly crowded with foot, bicycle, motorscooter, motorcycle, and military traffic.

U.S. Military Assistance Command Vietnam Adjutant General Processing Center says the sign flanked by a MACV crest and an adjutant general crest. The MACV crest is a red crest with a yellow border and a stylized yellow wall with a gate in the middle and a sword standing vertical, guarding the gate in theory. The A.G. crest is blue stars over red and white stripes. It should be, of course, bullshit wrapped in red tape on a field of assholes. I like soldiers, guys who wear uniforms, use weapons, get dirty and exhausted, give and take orders, fight battles and occasional wars, and tell lies over beers or Jack Daniels.

The Adjutant Generals Corps, on the other hand, is made up of old maids, bureaucrats, and the aforementioned assholes, dedicated to a man (or whatever) to preventing soldiers from getting paid, promoted, or treated properly. I.e. they push paper. I've never seen paper kill an enemy soldier or protect one of our tanks from armor piercing shells.

We get billets for the night. We won't be in the trenches tonight. It's sightsee and get over jetlag tonight. Sightsee? I'm afraid to leave the area. Some of the guys in the MACV Visiting Officers' Quarters with me want to get laid. I'm afraid of getting VD or my throat slit from just looking at the women, so I pass. A couple of us have dinner at the mess hall and go to a movie. Guess what's showing. *The Green Berets*.

Naturally.

The bunk next to me is occupied by a captain going on R and R. He has a tan beret – ARVN Infantry. Beret? Does everyone get a beret of some kind? I thought they were for elite units, but I see all kinds, black, green, red, khaki. It's meaningless.

Graffiti on the men's room wall, stall three on the left, at the VOQ:

> The VC is like a sore dick,
> Not worth a shit, but you can't beat it.

More graffiti:

Fighting for peace is like fucking for chastity.

I like that.

28 – 31 July 1969

Inprocessing, processing, and more processing.

We get to fill out forms — again, telling where to send our G.I. insurance money, etc. etc. Theoretically it is set up so we'll get paid. I send most of mine home, with one hundred dollars a month given to me here. Carole needs it more than I. She pays the bills while I'm gone — I hope.

First timers do not get a choice of assignments. Second tour guys get to choose corps areas. Third timers get carte blanche.

I will go to Bien Hoa at Third Corps H.Q. for further assignment. Swell. How about PX officer at MACV HQ?

We get ration cards and MACV I.D. cards and Geneva Convention cards. I'm overloaded already.

We get field equipment, M-16s, pack, canteens, big two-quart flexible plastic ones much better than the old aluminum one-quart ones, and some plastic versions of the one-quart one, pistol belt and harness, compass, first aid kits, a lot of disgustingly field-oriented stuff. No .45, though. It is suggested I try the black market. A .45 is three hundred dollars. A .38 is two hundred dollars. I pass on the black market.

I do buy a small camera, a Pen FT 35 mm half frame camera to stick in an ammo pouch. Naturally, with the F/1.8 lens it doesn't quite fit, so it'll go around my neck instead. They make it with a thinner F/2 lens that would fit, but does the PX stock it? Of course not.

We go by chicken-wired bus to Bien Hoa. On the way a Vietnamese throws a rotten melonlike fruit at the bus. Now I know why the chicken wire is there. Gee it's nice to be the loved liberator.

God, what a place. The streets are crowded, and sidewalks are covered with little booths selling everything. I get the feeling you could not only buy somebody's mother or sister or marijuana cigarettes with filter tips or ninety-seven percent pure heroin, but M-16s, grenades, and maybe a tank or two.

Last night I couldn't sleep because of the pounding of distant guns. I and the other FNGs (Fuckin' New Guy) don't know that. We can't tell how far away it is. We have visions of Tet of '68 and street fighting and Hue. But Saigon is safe after a fashion if one stays out of bars or whorehouses and off the streets after dark. Bien Hoa I don't know about.

I am assigned to Advisory Team Seventy at Lam Son to an armored cavalry advisor's job. At least it isn't infantry. I will go there tomorrow. Tonight I get a bunk in a building with a machine gun and observation post on the balcony. The guy manning the OP says a Vietnamese whore comes every afternoon between four and four-thirty to a shower stall about fifty yards out and showers herself in sight of his post. He has binoculars with which to watch her. Today she doesn't come.

A captain is in another bunk after some time in the bush. He speaks of firefights and dinks, whatever they are.

The Officer's Club is labeled The Last Resort. A Vietnamese woman is standing in the doorway making one think of a whorehouse. I take a picture, of course. Drinks at The Last Resort are simple, with water, tonic, soda, Coke, 7-Ups, that's about it.

Sleep comes only from fatigue, and I awake early, unsure of where I am when the observation post changes the guard.

1 — 3 August 1969

I take a helicopter to Lam Son, over beautiful green and blue terrain, with flooded rice paddies glistening in the sun. The sky is incredibly blue, and the country quite beautiful. The irony is obvious. People are dying below.

Lam Son looks awfully permanent, Quonset huts almost equal to temporary BOQ at Fort Knox, a swimming pool (!) It's almost stateside.

I process in and go through the long line of people to process through. One gets a list of people to see. Everyone initials the card. When the card is full, one is fully qualified to go out and get killed. When one leaves, unless one does so in a body bag or a Dustoff, one does the same thing. I have a feeling I'll be much more eager to get all those initials.

Advisory Team Seventy "advises" the Fifth ARVN (Army of the Republic of Vietnam) Infantry Division, which consists of Seventh, Eighth, and Ninth Infantry Regiments (based on the French Regimental system rather than the U.S. Brigade system), First and Fifteenth Armored Cavalry Regiments, and Fifth Divisional Recon Company.

An infantry regiment consists of four infantry battalions, in practice smaller than U.S. battalions, about five hundred men in working strength, give or take a few deserters and LCDBs, and a recon company. An ARVN armored cavalry regiment is equal to a U.S. squadron, and is made up of three squadrons equal to a U.S. troop, one tank squadron of seventeen tanks, two ACAV squadrons of fifteen modified armored personnel carriers (APCs) modified to ACAV condition (armored cavalry fighting vehicles) through the addition of armor shields around the machine gun mounts. In practice one tank troop (platoon) is attached to each of the other squadrons and vice versa so that each squadron has five tanks and ten APCs, plus command and control vehicles and such delightful targets as flame-throwing APCs.

The armored units plus the recon units are considered to be "elite" units.

Elite ARVN unit, that's comparable to a respectable whore.

Colonel Pink is the commanding officer for Advisory Team Seventy and senior advisor to the Fifth ARVN Infantry Division. He does not command the Fifth Division.

Organization of Team Seventy is, therefore, screwed up to an American military mind. The staff functions, normally screwy, are really screwy here. S-1 becomes administration, so that what would normally be an S-1 officer is called the admin. officer like in the Air Force. The admin. officer is a jolly fat

28

Captain Adjutant General Corps with less than thirty days to go. His replacement is due. He is hoping I am him. He sees the tanks and crossed sabers on my collar and curses.

"Goddamn, fuckin' army can't send what we really need. I'm short. I've reached my P.C.O.D. and they send us more fuckin' prima donnas. We need a good A.G. captain, not another combat arms Boy Scout. You can't get this paperwork straightened out. You can't believe how much paperwork you field assholes fuck up. Why this morning Lieutenant Calahan got himself wasted. Fuckin' next of kin notification, mandatory Silver Star to phony up, insurance forms, morning report, casualty report, you wouldn't believe."

"War is a motherfucker," I say. "Ah, Calahan? Killed? How?"

"Shot. Shot in the chest. Was by himself, silly shit. Can't get by yourself. ARVNs can't call you a medevac when you get hit."

"Thrill. What unit was he with?"

"Three—Eight. Eighth Regiment has the worst U.S. casualty figures in the division."

"Too bad. Must really screw up your reports."

He lights a cigar and says, "You wouldn't believe."

What would normally be S-2 (intelligence) is the G-2 advisor. A tall, stocky major gives me an unintelligible briefing on a map rattling off VC and NVA unit names and place names far too fast for me. Of course, I don't vocalize the logical thought. If they know where the enemy is, why don't they kill the cocksuckers and go home?

29

The G-3 (operations) advisor gives me more of the same. He rattles off friendly unit names and locations as though I could tell one place from another or one unit from another in a place with names like Phuc Long, Dong Xoai, and, for all I know, Phuc Yew.

Finally I meet the sergeant major, the assistant senior advisor, and Colonel Pink. Colonel Pink is grey-haired, red-faced, nearly bald, fifty pounds overweight, and sweaty in his air-conditioned office. He is an infantry officer, usually a disadvantage to us armor types. But then that's the least of my worries.

His sergeant major is a prissy prick, fussy, too neat. He points out things in my records to Col. Pink, things I don't need pointed out. Pink apparently does anything this prick says.

"Good," says Pink. "Armor, ranger, airborne, air-ground operations experience. Good. Unfortunately we have no openings in air-ground operations right now, but you need command time anyway, don't you?" He doesn't wait for an answer. Of course I don't need command time. I need survival time, PX officer in Saigon would be good, lifeguard supervisor at the MACV pool, something really worthwhile and important.

"Maybe after six months we can give you the G-3 air. We'll have an opening in armor in a month, First Armored Cav. Want it?"

"Yessir." I'm lying. I want a dog robber's job in Bien Hoa or Saigon.

"Good. Meantime we'll have to send you to Eighth Infantry. They're short a lieutenant."

Oh, Jesus, not infantry. God help me. I hated everything to do with infantry, all the ROTC bullshit, the summer camp, ranger school at Benning, airborne. It all sucks. Armor is rough enough, but infantry, Mother. In infantry you live in the mud, and what's worse, you die in the mud.

"Just temporary. When are you due to make captain?"

"Last week, sir."

"Oh, orders haven't caught up with you yet, huh?"

"No, sir."

"Okay, Eighth Infantry it is. Lieutenant Colonel Pride is very good. Tough. You'll have to be sharp."

Swell, I have George Patton's spiritual descendant to work for.

I get to spend one night in Lam Son before going to Ben Cat, Eighth Infantry headquarters.

At the mess hall I sit between an artillery captain and a quartermaster lieutenant.

"Where ya goin', Harris?" asks the artillery captain.

"Eighth Infantry, sir. Temporarily, I'm told. First Cav. eventually."

"If you make it."

"Sir?"

"Did they tell you about Calahan?"

"Just that he got killed," I say feeling silly.

"First Lt. Robert A. Calahan, staff advisor with Three-Eight for eight months. Got killed yesterday. Shot in the chest at close range. Through and through wound through right chest. Bled to death because he was by himself—no other Americans around. Damn little people let him die. Ignored him. In fact, I'm not sure they didn't shoot him themselves. Colonel Pride is nuts. He'll order you spread out if you don't watch it. Four man team. S.A. stays with headquarters, lieutenant with the lead company, a sergeant with each of the other companies till you run out of sergeants. Real dangerous. Strictly against orders. Whenever the shit hits the fan, the battalion S.A. gets the blame. Loses more advisors than the other teams put together."

"Great. You know you could've talked all night without sayin' that."

"I know. I just wanted to shake you up. Are you worried now?"

"Are you kiddin'? Me? No, I'm terrified."

The next morning I take a jeep to Ben Cat. The road is paved, with cemeteries and oxen and rice paddies beside the road between villages. I have my M-16 loaded and am constantly wary. The sergeant who picked me up, a tall, lanky country boy, thinks I am nuts. "This is civilization, Lieutenant."

Like hell, I think.

Ben Cat is a dreary, forboding place, white Quonset huts with screened windows and doors. The ARVNs I see do not impress me as the type of people upon which I want to depend for my life. They look slovenly and underfed.

Colonel Pride is something else. A smart-aleck young captain is his staff advisor, and he introduces me.

"Lieutenant Harris will be with us temporarily, sir."

"I don't want anyone temporarily. Send him back. Tell Pink to send someone permanent. No, I'll call him. Wait outside, Lieutenant."

Welcome to Vietnam, Lieutenant Harris, I think.

I wait outside half an hour. Then the smart-aleck captain ushers me back in.

I salute and stand in a brace, the whole cadet bit. He returns my salute contemptuously.

"At ease, Harris, I do not want you in my unit. I do not want a tourist. I only want serious, long-term infantry officers, airborne rangers."

"Sir, I did not ask to be here."

"I know. You were forced down my throat. You do not deserve to be in a first class infantry unit. I don't need any little armor wimps. I want hard, career infantry officers who are here to kill VC. You might think we're here to advise. Some politician made that up. We're here to kill VC. Kill VC! Kill all the VC! That'll win the war, not Vietnamization! Not pacification! Grab 'em by their balls and their hearts and minds will follow! Kill VC! Kill VC! Kill VC!" He is yelling at the top of his lungs, a mode he uses often. He catches his breath and calms down. "I can't send you back, so I'll send you to Third Battalion. You'll replace Lieutenant Carnahan—ah, Calahan, whatever the little Irish bastard's name was. Let me tell you, Lieutenant. Don't *ever* let me catch you unarmed. And armed means with an M-16, not a .45. You can't kill VC with a .45. You can't defend yourself with a .45. Anyway, the NVA knows officers wear .45s, so they aim for

33

them. You will carry an M-16 at all times."

"Yes sir."

"I'll tell you, I'd rather do without than have a virgin for two or three weeks, a fuckin' tourist. Major Brown will feel the same way. But while you're in my unit you will remember that being an advisor is the most difficult job in the United States Army. You must work harder than your counterpart. You must be without fatigue. You must have infinite patience. You must have absolute physical courage, absolute moral courage. You must be an example for your counterparts and your troops. You must be absolutely correct in everything you do, from military courtesy with your counterparts to calling in artillery fire to map reading. Any mistake you make can and probably will be fatal. In short you must have all the attributes of Jesus Christ. Dismissed."

Jesus.

Major Brown is a jolly, chubby, thirty-five-ish black man, round face, balding, with a perpetual, wry half smile. The first thing I notice is that all the uniforms are a little darker green than mine. The ARVN uniforms, not jungle type, but simpler, copies of U.S. regular fatigues in smaller Asian sizes, are Lincoln green, too. They must dye them. That's it. I've joined Robin Hood, but he's Oriental and five feet tall.

Major Brown welcomes me cordially, tells me he needs all the help he can get, and not to worry about Lieutenant Colonel Pride except when he's around.

He introduces Sergeant Cross and Sergeant Morton. Sergeant Morton is the one who drove me up. He is an Oklahoma native. Sergeant Cross is younger, built like a small football player, and a little crazy. He carries a CAR-15, I think it's called. It's an M-16 but shorter, with a short barrel with a large flash suppressor/noise suppressor on the end, a different foregrip, and retractable stock. He also carries a big bowie knife with a stag handle worn on his load-bearing vest. Instead of a harness, he has a locally made vest with a pack built into the back and pockets and hooks for the normal impedimenta of an infantry advisor, smoke grenades, frags, ammunition for the CAR-15.

He speaks of his body count. He has been in Nam for five years and has been refused another extension. He does not want to go home!

That's why I say he's crazy.

Three—Eight is in Bo Dai, which, as best I can tell, is nowhere. We have a flagpole and a bunch of bunkers on a flat plain with razor wire, claymores, and the whole bit on the perimeter.

The flag is yellow with red stripes. Yellow for the way the ARVNs fight, red for American blood.

The Co-Vans (advisors) get an in-ground concrete bunker, with bunks. It looks like hell to me, but they're proud of it. They got the Seabees to build it. They had to give up several cases of scotch. I don't ask where the scotch came from.

Their interpreter is a goofy little ARVN named Tran. Major Brown gets an LCDB to carry his pack.

LCDB—*Lau Cau Dau Binh* I think—are soldiers who have deserted and been caught. They serve a sentence, but not in prison, out of combat. They

35

serve it in their unit. They're unarmed. They carry mortar rounds, the C.O.'s pack, etc. For this they get twenty-six dollars per month, which won't buy their food. Ours is in rags. It's not considered good form for advisors to clothe them. At the end of their sentence they get their old rank back. All is forgiven—if they survive.

At the camp I see women and children. I'm stunned. ARVNs get to take their wives and kids along when in bivouac. Children run around naked or only with shirts until they're toilet trained. No diapers.

The place stinks.

We're expected to eat Vietnamese food.

Thrill.

The first meal is not outstanding, rice with horribly cooked chicken. They've taken a chicken and a cleaver and just chopped every inch down the bird, ignoring bones and structures. I can see hollow bones with bloody marrow visible. Also the chicken has not been gutted. I try to eat rice and green leafy vegetables and a little chicken. Of course, it would gag a maggot.

They have a sauce. *Nouc maum*, I think. It's rancid fish oil and hot peppers. Tastes awful if the smell doesn't kill you.

I get my first mail from Carole. Only the applicable parts of letters will be printed.

My Dearest Darling,
    Did you see the men walk on the moon?

Wasn't that just wonderful? Aren't you proud to be an American at a time like that? I got to see it on a color TV at Mary Alice McTavish's. Her husband is a Green Beret sergeant. He has an awful job, lives in the jungle with awful Vietnamese, eats their food, sleeps on the ground. It's terrible. I'm so glad you have a nice, safe desk job. I worry about you so . . .

All my love,

Carole

4 — 6 August 1969

We move out in the early afternoon on a search and destroy mission. I've read about search and destroy missions for too long. I'm not excited about it. I'm terrified. At dark we bed down in deep woods, sleeping in hammocks that the sergeants call "VC hammocks." They're very small and strong, rolling up to a ten inch by four inch by four inch bundle. I'm just too big for the average Vietnamese one, such as the one I have borrowed until I get one made. I never considered myself big. I'm only five feet ten inches tall and one hundred forty pounds, but the average Vietnamese is very small.

On the morning of the fourth, Major Brown and *Dai-Uy* (Captain) Tranh, the battalion C.O., go to an awards presentation and party at regimental head-quarters, leaving one terrified Lieutenant Harris "in charge" as the only American there, as if I knew what I was doing. I have to coordinate with a nearby U.S. unit, but on a whole the day is a bore. Staff Sergeant Morton comes out in the afternoon.

On 5 August Major Brown and Sergeant Cross

come out. We cordon and search a village of sullen people with dead eyes. Major Brown and I accompany the *Dai-Uy* on a roundup of suspects and a tunnel-searching and blowing expedition. I think I am given my test of manhood. Tranh asks me if I would like to search a tunnel.

I look at Brown with obvious fear in my eyes. "What do you think, sir?" I ask.

"Sure. Good training."

"Training for what?"

"Searching tunnels."

"Great. Sure, I'll do it." What am I saying?

I've been carrying a little vial with earplugs in it since AOBC. I open it and put them in. *Dai-Uy* gives me a .45. I pull the magazine. It has seven fairly clean rounds in it. I put it back in, pull the slide back and chamber a round, then check to make sure one is in the chamber by pulling the slide back a quarter of an inch. I do not engage the safety. As a security blanket it beats the hell out of a St. Christopher.

"Left-handed, huh?" says Brown with a half smile.

"Yes sir."

"How'd you qualify on the .45 being left-handed?"

"Expert, sir. And I shot on the battalion pistol team while in Germany."

"Well, in a tunnel," he says chuckling, "you don't have to be an expert to hit a guy two feet away. Don't stick the gun out too far, as he can take it away from you. He'll probably use a knife. They don't have too many handguns. Mostly K-54s, little bitty bullets. A .45'll stop a truck."

A knife. I've been here a few days and I'm going into a fucking tunnel to fight a motherfucker with a knife? This is a bad dream. I'm a brainy underweight kid who never won a fight in his life. What the fuck am I doing here?

The tunnel is inside a hooch, a narrow hole. I can drop down four feet. Then it goes off at an angle, and I go on my hands and knees, flashlight in the right hand, .45 in my left hand. I flash the light then move in the dark, then flash it again. Then I find the M-26 grenade in an old C-ration can with a trip wire across the tunnel at about three inches above the ground. Then I leave the light on. The wire would pull the grenade out of the can, and the spoon would open, and four seconds later the dumb son of a bitch in the tunnel, me, would look like a spaghetti explosion.

Shaking like a leaf I cut the line with my Swiss Army knife. Then I continue, cursing Tranh and Brown silently. The tunnel goes down at an angle then levels off, with twists and turns and pockets in it big enough for a small man to go into the fetal position and either hide or survive a grenade explosion nearby.

I see something move and fire instantly.

The flash is blinding, but all motion stops. My eyes readjust to the lack of light.

I've just killed a rat the size of a small cat. I hear Brown calling to me.

"I'm okay!" I yell back. Then I throw up. I sit there and shake for a minute or two, feeling stupid. I'll obviously never be mistaken for John Wayne. I'm so goddamned scared I couldn't stand up if I had room.

What a mess. I crawl past carefully.

Thank God the tunnel starts up pretty soon. At the other end there's another booby trap like the first. I'm shaking so much I can't cut the line for three or four minutes. Then I come up in heavy jungle. I'm outside the perimeter. I head back and a goddamned sentry takes his M-16 off safety.

"Co-Van! Co-Van! Toi la Co-Van My!" I yell frantically. I don't want to be shot by one of my own troops by accident, for God's sake.

He replies *"Du Ma!"* from a concealed position. Then I hear laughing and he motions me back in.

Inside Brown says I look a little peaked and asks me what I shot at.

"A rat. But I have reason to believe it was a VC rat."

"What makes you think that?"

"He didn't have a government I.D. card."

7 — 10 August 1969

We're on the move. An Loc is getting rockets. I don't know what the hell's so important about An Loc, or even where it is, other than a place on the map, but we're going up there. Intelligence says there are two NVA regiments ready to attack the town if they get the chance, so we're going up to reinforce. We come by jeeps and trucks and then dismount to do sweeps around the northern side of the city. It's all hot, open fields of something almost head high, cultivated at least at one time, not jungles like I expected. We walk and walk. I am exhausted. I thought I packed light, but now I can think of several things I need to leave behind. Each item weighs more and more the further I go.

I'm sunburned. I do not tan, being fair and freckled. My neck is burned, my lips parched. I develop a strong attachment to my Chap-stick. I will write to Carole and ask her to send one a week if I can't find them at the PX.

On the second day I get worse. It is not just the heat and exertion anymore. Bac Si (the medic) takes my temperature and shows it to Major Brown.

The next morning I am taken into An Loc and left with the Air Force doctors at the compound there. Why Air Force doctors are on a MACV compound fascinates me. When I ask they say that because of a shortage of army doctors and a surplus of Air Force doctors (for obvious reasons), they were requisitioned—i.e. drafted.

"Dengue fever," says one of my condition. "FUO," says the other. They give me medicine and an unused cot with a CORDs (Civil Operations Revolutionary Development) sergeant in the room. I don't care. I can hardly sit up. I am burning up. I can't eat. I vomit everything up. The CORDs sergeant tells war stories. His troops are all former VC who came over to "our" side. Consequently, he has a bodyguard. I just wish he would shut up.

Then the rockets start. A medic comes and takes me to the medical bunker.

"This is where you've got to go when you hear the siren, sir. Everybody runs to a bunker. This is yours."

"Can't run—barely walk."

"I'll come and get you, sir. If I can. But try to go yourself."

In the medic bunker I must lean against a wall or sit on the floor. More serious cases have the two bunks. I'd rather listen to the CORDs sergeant. Finally the all clear. I go back to my bunk.

I don't know how many times this happens, three, four, five? I am delirious finally, and it all blends into one nightmare.

Two, three days are spent in this special hell before the fever leaves. Now I am okay but weak. I am eating pretty well at the mess hall here. It's starchy, high calories, but probably good for the activity. I meet Dufus. Dufus is a small monkey, a spider monkey I believe, "belonging" to a country-boy sergeant with a First Infantry Division patch on his right shoulder. Apparently he inherited Dufus from his predecessor and is trying to figure out how to take Dufus to the U.S. when he rotates.

The doctors release me and tell me to go back to my unit and get killed.

We do more sweeps with no action. I don't want any action, though. Just walking along is a struggle. I'm lightly loaded by Nam standards, just a pistol belt and harness with a compass, first aid kit, and two ammo pouches with three magazines in each, one hundred twenty rounds total, a strobe light, and a smoke grenade plus two fragmentation grenades, two one quart canteens with a canteen cup and one big plastic bag canteen that goes on a shoulder strap, plus a pack full of about thirty pounds of rations, messkit, smoke grenades, ammunition, uniform, underwear, soap, towel, socks, etc. not to mention a novel or two since I am cursed with a need to read to keep my mind off this nightmare when I'm not doing anything worthwhile.

I weighed all of one hundred thirty pounds when I left An Loc. I'm skin and bones. An extra five pounds hurt. I finally get my own extra long VC hammock when we make a run into An Loc.

The little shops lining the streets in An Loc are something else, unbelievably cluttered, with all kinds of junk in them. Signs are yellow and red, gaudy, unintelligible gobbledegook. The streets are dusty.

Why the hell are we defending this?

At night we dig in, naturally, expecting mortar fire. I sleep in my foxhole, a restless sleep without comfort or freedom from pain.

11−23 August 1969

The threat to An Loc has evaporated, if there ever was one (so much for military intelligence), so we're going to build a new fire support base. Major Brown goes to a meeting at sector headquarters, so I'm in charge. Boy, they must be desperate. The sergeants go off to handle an operation with Eighth Recon, which is without its advisor temporarily.

We have an American Combat Engineer section from the First Infantry Division, the "Big Red One," so named because their patch is a red *1* on an olive drab patch. A Lieutenant Fisher is in charge. The plan is to clear the hilltop with Rome plows, big bulldozers capable of knocking down trees.

We drive to the hilltop in jeeps, set up a perimeter, and await the plows. Everything seems okay so far. They come up the hill with a convoy of other vehicles, including tanks and APCs. They deploy around the area to be cleared, and the plows start.

The Americans get hot lunches flown in on helicopters! We're eating Vietnamese C-rations, rice and really bad pork, so the American food looks awfully good. We don't get invited.

We register artillery in the afternoon, and the plows continue working.

Whomp!

A plow stops. Several Americans run to it and pull the driver out. He is on a stretcher almost immediately, and a First Infantry Division "Dustoff" helicopter is on the ground picking him up in ten minutes.

That's the good news. The bad news is that the plow ran over a Bouncing Betty mine. A spring shoots the mine to somewhere between groin and head height depending on the spring and your height, where it blows up. In the case of the plow, it is dislodged by the plow blade and comes up behind the plow blade and in front of the driver. The plow blade reflects fragments, and the driver has his forehead peeled back, with a square inch or two of brain visible, and a chunk scooped out. Instant pre-frontal lobotomy, the hard way.

The plows are construction equipment, not combat vehicles. They have roll cages with roofs to protect the drivers from rollover and from dropped items. The sides of the cage are lined with chicken wire. There is no armor to protect the driver. I know immediately why they call them *combat* engineers.

Another chopper comes in a few minutes later, and a lieutenant colonel hops out, the Engineer Battalion C.O. He cusses out Lieutenant Fisher for not protecting the driver, and they lay flack jackets up the sides and around the front of the cab, and the drivers are ordered to wear flack jackets. One wears two, one over his lap.

The lieutenant colonel sees me. "You in charge of these gooks?"

"I'm the advisor, sir. They have a C.O."

"Don't get smart with me, kid. Your goddamned gooks didn't do their goddamned job."

"Sir?"

"Security, you idiot. You're responsible for security, and you fucked up. If you were doing your job, there wouldn't be any mines here. You don't have enough wire up. There should be three rows of concertina wire up three hundred and sixty degrees around."

"Yes sir," I say, very confused. What does concertina wire have to do with mines that are already here?

"Well, if you fuck up again, young lieutenant, I will hang your young ass. When I get back, I expect to see that wire up. Got that?"

"Yes sir."

"Good. I hope you're happy with your performance, you fuckup. You put a fine young man in a hospital."

I remain quiet, with great difficulty.

He gets back on his chopper and leaves.

Another chopper brings dinner to the U.S. troops. We get invited this time. I eat with Lieutenant Fisher and his sergeants. We even have ice cream — a Mermite can of vanilla ice cream!

The next day one of my ARVNs, on a sweep of the area, in front of me and on my left, steps on a Bouncing Betty. It blows off his left shoulder, leaving the arm dangling by strips of flesh and cloth, his right hand, chunks out of his back and legs and, needless

49

to say, kills him. It also wounds the nearest two ARVNs walking behind him. They are dusted off almost immediately by a First Division chopper. The body, wrapped in a poncho, feet sticking out, boots missing, probably taken by one of his buddies, goes with the wounded, on its way to graves registration after dropping the two wounded at a field hospital.

American troops have run out to the scene out of curiosity. But we haven't really moved far from the mine accident.

Click.

I hear it ten yards away. A young engineer has stepped on a Bouncing Betty and kept his foot down. It is a pressure release mine. When he raises his foot, he is dead. His buddies and the ARVNs back away. The ARVNs continue on their sweep, ignoring us altogether, of course, as *Co-Vans* aren't people. Fisher is thirty feet away.

"Norton, you'll have to get out of that by yourself."

"What? How, sir?"

"Jump and roll. Colonel's policy, no help."

"Jump and roll? I'll be blown to bits."

"There's no help for you, Norton. I can't order another man to sacrifice himself to save you."

Fisher walks away.

Norton screams, "Lieutenant, you gotta help me!"

Fisher says nothing, his head down. He doesn't look back.

I'm out of the kill zone backing away from Norton. I realize no one else is looking at him. They are all looking away. An image of myself shaking and vomiting in that tunnel flashes, and another of the mutilated body of my dead troop, but the face is mine.

I am naive and stupid. I remember the "school solution" from MACV or RVN training or somewhere. I walk to an APC nearby. I look up at the sergeant commanding the track.

"G-gimme three flack j-jackets, Sergeant," I say, my voice shaking like a child's.

"Sir, you can't —"

"Now, S-Sergeant."

"Yes sir," he says, anger and contempt in his voice.

He throws them down one by one, almost knocking me over each time.

I take them to Norton. I have one on. "Put this one on, Norton."

He reaches for it.

"C-carefully, Norton, v-very carefully."

"Yes sir."

"I'll be back."

I walk back to the APC. The sergeant is glaring down at me.

"Gimme two fifty c-cal. ammo boxes, Sergeant."

"Lieutenant, they belong to the engineers."

"I — I'll give 'em back, g-goddamnit, Sergeant. G-give me the goddamned a-ammo boxes!"

He pulls them out and throws them on the ground next to me. They dig in and throw up a dust cloud. I pick them up and return to Norton, walking very carefully.

"W-which foot is on the mine, N-norton?"

"R-right." Oh, good, he's stuttering, too.

We're both scared shitless.

"Good. I'm left-handed." I get on the ground on all

fours, ammo cans beside his right foot. I put the other flack jacket over my head. I know it won't help, though.

I feel the eyes of the engineers boring into me. I don't know of what I'm most afraid, those guys or the mine. I don't know why. I know I'm shaking and want very much to run away. I used to run away from every bully in school as a kid. I feel they're bullying me. Maybe that's what keeps me going.

"S-slide your f-foot left v-very slowly. D-don't l-lift it o-or we're both c-cold m-meat."

It must take his foot ten minutes to uncover the edge of the mine, just an eighth of an inch, a nailhead-shaped piece of steel—with my life on it. I am sweating blood. I'm sure my heart can be heard stateside. I'm shaking like a goddamned leaf. Goddamn, I'm scared.

"Stop. Don't lift or lower. Left a cunthair, n-no more. There! That's it! N-now, Norton, I'm go-going to s-slide these am-ammo boxes o-ov-over it. T-then I'm going to slide them and kind of p-push your f-foot out of the way. If I-I fuck up, d-dive left. I'll be g-going right. Got it?"

"Y-yeah."

Norton is maybe nineteen, pimple-faced, scared to death of course. I am sweating and freezing at the same time. I think I might wet my pants. When I was a kid and really got into trouble I had the same feelings. Of course, then, wetting your pants was more socially acceptable than it is here. Here, of course, bleeding is socially acceptable.

The ammo cans weigh two tons easily now. My

52

shaking hands work somehow, and I feel the cans into place.

"Norton."

"Yeah?"

"Very care-carefully—very carefully, left, another c-cunthair."

The boot, two feet from my face and filthy, the scuffs and mud patterns etched in my memory forever, which might be measured in milliseconds for us, move to the left a sixteenth of an inch. I follow it with the ammo cans. "Again."

He moves again, shakily.

"D-don't shake, Norton."

"I'm tryin', Lieutenant," he whispers.

"Me-me, too."

I move the ammo cans again. Now the detonator is covered.

"There. It's on. You're off."

I stand up. He stands back. We stand there staring at it, the stack of O.D. ammo boxes.

Fisher yells at us, "Get back here! It might still go off."

I look at Norton, and he looks at me. We laugh hysterically, nervously. Then we walk back to the APC. I am so weak I can hardly walk. My knees wobble. The world is spinning mildly.

A couple of E.M. catch me and pull me into the APC. One of them takes a rope and goes out and attaches it to the handle of the top ammo can. Then he comes back and, from behind the APC, pulls the rope. The mine goes *pop—bang!* I'd feel better if it were a dud. The APC takes us back to the headquarters tent.

Fisher gives me a look appropriate for a strange bug.

"You're an idiot, Harris. An idiot."

I start to say something, then think better of it. Norton is given a back-slapping reunion with his buddies. He turns and says, "Thanks, lieutenant."

I smile, unable to speak. I nod and whisper/croak, "Yeah."

The engineer's first sergeant sees my white, shaking face, gives me a cigarette and a glass of cold milk. I'm sitting down shaking when the engineer lieutenant colonel comes in.

"What the hell are you doing sitting on your ass, Lieutenant, when there's work to be done. The wire isn't up."

I'm in a daze. "Sir?"

"The wire, Lieutenant. Get up off your dead ass and and go get your *Dai-Uy*."

I realize I am standing up. "I want to talk to him right here!" He points to the ground emphatically. "Now!"

"I'll try to get him, sir, we just had a problem with a—"

"I don't care about that! I want that wire up. Why haven't you gotten that wire up?"

"Sir! I advised my counterpart about the need for it. I don't command these—"

"Go get your, your counterpart. Get the head gook."

I run over and get him, and he comes over at a half trot, thinking it is super important.

"Captain, *Dai-Uy*, I will give you half an hour to get that goddamned wire up, or I will pull my troops out. You are here to provide security for them, and you cannot do it without wire. Do you understand that?"

"Yes, sir. You pull troops out now. We have all our wire up. That all we have."

The lieutenant colonel is fuming. "Is that the normal amount of wire given to one of your battalions, Captain?"

"No, sir. We stole it. It much more than we normally have."

"All right. I'll be back to check on your security. Improve it, Captain."

He gets on his chopper and leaves. Fortunately, he does not come back to check, because the *Dai-Uy* does nothing to improve security. I have about as much influence on him as a fly.

Major Brown and the sergeants return in time for supper.

Another ARVN is wounded by a mine just before dark, and we have to medevac him. Sergeant Cross stands in the middle of the helipad with a strobe light held overhead going *flash . . . flash . . . flash*. The smoke grenades used in the daytime, of course, don't work at night.

At twenty forty-five our ARVN ambush points make contact with five VC. I get out of bed, a bunk in the tanker's tent this night, in the driving rain, and stand around, with little to do while Major Brown calls in U.S. artillery illumination because the ARVNs are running out of mortar illumination rounds. It's a one man job, and Major Brown is pretty self-sufficient and good at it.

The ARVN Third Company make a sweep of the area and bring in two VC, one dead, one dying. We dust off the dying one, and I go back to a fitful, exhausted sleep, soaking wet.

The next morning I see the dead VC. His face is blown off, leaving by now bloodless details of the middle of his skull, with one staring eye in half a socket and brains visible, and his guts hanging out, flies buzzing around them and his head. Several G.I.s are taking pictures. I resolve to never take pictures of the dead of either side. I can only look for a second, then I have to walk away, nearly vomiting. The white, pale, horribly mutilated face haunts me. I see myself there. I know that I am no different than my enemy. I can die that way, and this scares me, makes my stomach almost lose control, my head ache and the world to spin about me.

An American sergeant, Sergeant First Class Fuller, comes to me and tells me that his camera was stolen during the night. I tell Major Brown, who tells Tranh. Three hours later Tranh hands me the camera. It was found during a search of his troops. I give it to Fuller. He's thanking me when I see, out of the corner of my eye, the flash on the Rome plow. Then I hear the *whomp!*

A ball of flame and smoke embroil the plow. The driver tries to get out and falls back. Several people, including me, run to the plow, and the cries of "medic" ring out.

It is not like the movies. The cry is much more

desperate. When we get there we see that the driver has been hit in the face. His lower jaw has been blown off, hanging by a string of gristle. A medic is on him immediately. He is making terrible gurgling noises. His eyes are bloody sockets.

I read the nametag.

Norton.

The Dustoff is quick, and Norton, doomed to a life of mutilated blindness if he survives at all, is carried onto the chopper. The wap-wap-wap-wap of the rotor blades lingers after the chopper is out of sight.

Lieutenant Colonel Pride comes down in a chopper just after Major Brown leaves in his jeep without telling me where he is going. For all I know he is going into the town for a blow job, but Pride gives me hell for not knowing. Then he gives me hell for the fact that the area is not policed. I have no authority over the engineers, and most of the trash is in their area, but that makes no difference to him.

Fourteen fifty-five hours: the Rome plows uncover a buried mortar base plate, some VC food supplies, and blasting caps in a tin can.

While we're looking at them, an ARVN steps on another mine, with predictable results. The man is still alive when we get there, his back full of shrapnel, his right arm blown off at the elbow. The ARVN medic goes to work on him, and I pop smoke for the chopper called in through First Infantry channels because it's so much faster than through ARVN or advisor channels.

The chopper comes in through a swirling purple haze of the smoke grenade.

Fifteen thirty hours: I haven't much more than finished calling everything in when Lieutenant Colonel Pride gets on the radio and gives me hell for being late with my spot report.

"With all due respect, the mine was detonated at fourteen fifty-five hours. I was handling the mede — Dustoff till now. How could I have informed you any faster? Over."

"Three, this is Super Six. Don't make goddamn excuses. That incident was called in through ARVN channels as occurring at thirteen forty-five hours. What did you do in the other hour? Over."

"Six, Three. Your report was incorrect. Incident occurred at fourteen fifty-five hours. I was there, and my watch reads fifteen thirty-nine now. Please correct if my watch off. Over."

"Your watch correct, out."

That son of a bitch wouldn't apologize if his life depended on it.

I am eating dinner with the Americans when the interpreter runs over to me.

"*Trung-uy, Trung-uy*, helicopter."

"Why?"

"Six men wounded."

"What? How?"

He is pointing. I run to where he is pointing. There are several ARVNs standing around a circle of men. One has his feet blown off. One, his head, leaving a ragged stump with his lower jaw attached to his body. He doesn't need a medevac. Four others have bloody arms or chests or faces. Fisher has already called in the medevac through First Division channels, so I ask

58

why the men were hurt.

"They sit in circle," says the interpreter. "One with feet blown off — he play with detonator. Others watch. It go off."

"One killed, five wounded, three badly, because he played with a detonator? Holy shit!"

I am stunned, both that a detonator could do so much damage and at the stupidity of my troops. It is almost dark, so the medevac is directed with a strobe light going *flash . . . flash . . . flash*. I'm beginning to hate the sound of the capacitor charging on the strobe.

24 – 26 August 1969

On the night of 24 August Chan Tanh is hit, hard.
First ARVN Armored Cav is there. Sergeant Cross
and I must drive near there on a run to Ben Cat and
Lam Son, and Sergeant Cross wants to stop by, so we
do.

On the way there is a road junction north of Lam
Son guarded by one of the white mice (National
Police), in this case a cute little girl of eighteen or
nineteen, her uniform two sizes too large. Cross, it
seems, has been stopping and talking to her for
several months. So he does this time while I watch the
scenery, little kids, and deuce-and-a-halves and jeeps
whizzing by. She's the best-looking Vietnamese girl
I've seen, clean, no smallpox scars, hair nearly to her
waist. Cross speaks pretty good Vietnamese. When
we go on I get him to start teaching me Vietnamese.

I visit the guy I'm going to replace, Captain Grimaldi, and Major Dartmouth, the Regimental S.A.
Grimaldi's interpreter has been killed. He was sleeping in an APC which was hit with a B-40 rocket.
APCs are not safe, as they are "armored" with

61

aluminum. Somehow someone decided that if an American company calls it armor it will work. But aluminum will not stop Russian heavy machine gun bullets, much less a B-40 rocket.

Congress investigated the M-16. Congress investigated the Sheridan tank—excuse me, Armored Assault and Reconnaissance Vehicle. Why didn't they investigate this? Of course with ARVN units it's worse, as we use gasoline APCs and tanks. U.S. units get diesel. These things are Zippos. One hit in the gas tank and flames go fifty feet.

They have laid the dead VC in downtown Chan Tanh so the villagers can see them. This attack on Chan Tanh failed. The one before included mortars on the village and involved considerable civilian casualties.

Cross sees one with a belt on the body and cuts off the NVA belt buckle.

I just stand there kind of stunned. The bodies are black and bloated and bloodless.

I say to myself, "These bodies have been burned."

Cross answers me. Apparently I have been thinking aloud: "No, Lieutenant, that's just how bodies look after a few hours."

"Yeah, course," I say, thinking I may look like that soon, vacant, expressionless stare, black, bloated, unhuman, flies buzzing about me.

I do not vomit, turn away and run, or cry. But I want to. It is an act of bravado to stay.

Cross asks me if I want an NVA belt buckle.

"No, thanks." I see an NVA bending over my blackened body. "Ah, an American belt buckle. Want

62

it, Lieutenant?"

After we finish, Cross asks me, "Wanna beer, sir?"

"What's Major Brown gonna say if we come back with beer on our breaths?"

"He won't get mad if we ain't drunk. He ain't no chickenshit."

"Maybe we'd better get on back."

"Ah, come on, sir. Honest to God, Major Brown won't get mad. Come one. I'll buy you a *Bau Muy Bau*."

"What's that?"

"Beer thirty-three. Great stuff. Instead of pasteurizing it, they preserve it with a drop of formaldehyde. Unbelievable taste."

"Think they have any Cokes?"

"Yeah, if you want one. Don't you drink beer?"

"I drink it. I just don't like it."

"I bet you don't fuck the whores here, either."

"Haven't yet. Don't know what I'll do when I get super horny after a few months."

"Boy, I do. Ever' chance I get."

"Come on. Where's the beer?"

"Over there."

We walk to a little open-air cafe. Cross went to the rearmost table. I follow, not too happy at the sea of Vietnamese faces inside, old men and ARVNs.

We sit down and Cross gets a waitress, a very young girl, to bring a beer and a Coke. I sit with my back to the corner, eyeing warily the door and the Vietnamese in the cafe. The smell of *nuoc mam* and rancid meat is overwhelming. The building is thatched walls with some parts built of old C-ration cases.

63

"You eat pussy, Lieutenant?"

"What the hell kind of a question is that, Sergeant?"

"I do. I love to eat pussy. The whores love me. There's some whores workin' here. Want one?"

"Nah."

"Okay if I get one?"

"Ah, Jesus, now I see why you wanted me in here. Haven't you reached your PCOD?"

"I ain't got one, sir. I ain't got anyone at home. How 'bout it?"

"Okay. You've got fifteen minutes, sergeant. At sixteen, I'll drive on."

"You'll have a hell of a time explainin' it to Major Brown."

"Nah. I'll just say the hogs ate ya."

So Cross talks to the young waitress. She points to the back door. A thin Vietnamese woman is leaning against it smoking a cigarette. She sees him and says, "You wan' sho't time, G.I.?"

"Yeah, short time, sucky-fucky."

"Come on, G.I., I give you sucky-fucky. Ten dolla. You got MPC? Piastres?"

"Ten dollars! Number ten! Two dollars."

"You cheap cha'lie, *Trung Chi*. Seven dolla."

They disappear behind the door for maybe a minute before the grenade explodes.

I roll to the ground, my reflexes working pretty well for a FNG. The ARVNs scream and run out the front door.

I crawl under the table and knock it over, giving me a barrier between me and the back door.

"Oh, my God! What the fuck's goin' on here?"

From behind the cafe come screams, women's screams. I'm not quite dumb enough to go back there to find out what's going on until I hear groans.

"Lieutenant!" It's Cross's voice, strangled, high pitched, obviously hurt.

"Shit, shit, shit, shit!" I get up and go in, swinging the M-16 ahead of me, looking for the source of the noise.

"Over here." The voice, Cross's, is choked, weak, and hoarse. I can smell blood. He's in a hallway. There are three doors on the left. I know Cross is in the last one because the door is blown down, and the wall blown open, and blood is running out the door. But I have to check out the other doors or I could be hit from behind. I don't yet know what has happened, whether a terrorist has lobbed in a grenade, or whether the whore has decided to take out a *Co Van* or what.

The first room is empty. The next room has a scared, ugly young woman in it, wearing fancy bra and panties and nothing else, bleeding from several spots, sitting in the corner. She screams when her eyes meet mine. Her eyes seem to be the size of oranges with fear. I put my finger to my lips silently and back out. I do not turn my back on her. The third room has the screaming woman and Cross. She is screaming because her right arm has been blown off at the elbow. The smell of human feces is overwhelming.

Cross is lying on his side in a pool of blood. His intestines are visible.

I panic and back out of the room.

"Lieutenant! Ya gotta — get help."

I gag and almost throw up. I'm sweating and shaking. I go back in. I walk past the whore to Cross. He's too badly hurt for first aid. He seems to be bleeding from several places.

"Medevac," whispers Cross.

"Right." I run to our jeep. I call in a medevac and run back. I realize I haven't helped the woman. I tie a tournequit around her arm and carry her out to the street. She's hysterical, making a terrible, nonstop wail. I can't carry Cross. I try to stop some of the bleeding.

"Goddamned whore . . . pulled the grenade off my belt tryin' to undress me."

"What?"

"Yeah. Accident. Stupid fuckin' bitch."

"Jesus."

I hear the *thwap-thwap-thwap* of the incoming medevac chopper. I run back to the street and pop smoke for them. The Huey lands on the street. The crew chief and gunner come out with a stretcher at my yelling and follow me into the back room. They put Cross on the stretcher and take him. I carry the whore with one arm blown off. The other one, the one in panties and bra, walks out, screaming not to be left behind. The crew chief helps her aboard.

It takes off, blowing up chaotic dust in the street.

By the time I get back to my unit, Cross has died. He was pronounced DOA at ninety-third Evac. I expect to get court-martialed for the fiasco, but Brown just says, "Five years in Vietnam . . . three Silver Stars, a body count of eighty odd, and he gets

66

killed getting a blow job. For Cross it's appropriate."

Of course Lieutenant Colonel Pride is livid. "You are responsible for all your men's actions all the time! If it had happened while Cross is on R and R you would be responsible! I wish you were permanently assigned to me so I could fire you, you incompetent son of a bitch. Dismissed!"

27 – 31 August 1969

Finally the call for First ARVN Cav. comes, no doubt hurried up by Pride. Grimaldi is rotating day after tomorrow, so I fly by chopper to Lam Son and catch a cav. jeep to Go Dau, the cav. headquarters. It is a permanent, fancy base by ARVN standards. Advisors have a big building, with kitchen, rec room, dining room, and rooms for each advisor. We also have toilets and showers — real running water.

First Cav. consists of three squadrons, one of tanks, and two of APCs. In practice, each squadron consists of one platoon of tanks and two platoons of APCs. It is a common arrangement to U.S. units.

The tanks are Korean War vintage M-41s, gasoline burners, with 76 mm guns, .50 caliber Browning Commander's machine gun, and .30 caliber coaxial machine gun. The variety of "special purpose" ammo is available, such as beehive. Imagine a 76 mm shotgun. These'll devastate troops in the open, if we ever find any.

I'm fairly happy about everything in my equipment but the flame-thrower APC. If it blows, we'll all fry.

The APCs have ACAV modifications usually, armor around the .50 caliber machine gun and the .30 caliber machine gun. U.S. units have M-60s instead of .30 caliber machine guns. The M-60 is superior to the .30 caliber, and logistics are complicated by having to get 7.62 mm NATO ammo for our infantry M-60s, and .30 caliber for our tracks.

The CO's and XO's tracks also have two armored seats stolen from Hueys put on the top. No one gets inside an APC who doesn't have to because of the B-40s.

I get one of the chopper seats with a PRC-25 strapped to it. I sit behind the C.O., *Dai-Uy* Tonc. Tonc is a fairly tall Vietnamese, mid thirties, unsmiling, and a good candidate for a part in a remake of *The Purple Heart*.

My interpreter is a little guy, Luong Dinh Du, a sergeant. I have no LCDBs because there are none in Armored Cav. If you desert from the cav. you go to an infantry unit when you're caught. Armor is an "elite" unit — assuming any ARVN unit is elite. Armor is all volunteer, no draftees.

One gets a black beret with an armored unit. I wear one but feel embarrassed by it. I am not John Wayne. I get the biggest size they make for Vietnamese. It is too small.

More importantly, I wangle a .45 from the ARVNs. Finding a left-handed holster is more difficult. Finally I find one in a little shop in Phu Loi. It is a bit too much Gene Autry and not enough George Patton for my tastes, because it is not a flap holster, but it has a strap that'll keep the damn thing from falling out. Army regs state you'll keep a .45 with seven rounds in the magazine and none in the chamber, and you carry it hammer down, safety off. That's fine if you have all day to draw, chamber a round, and fire. Ridiculous, I think. I scrounge three magazines and twenty-two rounds, load one into the chamber, seven into the first magazine, and put the strap between the hammer and the firing pin. The other two magazines, with the other fourteen rounds in them, I put in a U.S. issue magazine holder bought from the little shop in Phu Loi. I feel I could probably get a B.A.R. or an AK-47 from that shop if I flashed enough money. When in the rear I flip the safety on. In the boonies I flip it off and rely on the strap. The safety was designed for a right-hander, not for me. John Moses Browning, the good Mormon designer of the Model 1911A1 as well as the Browning Automatic Rifle, Browning machine guns, Browning Hi-Power, and several other fine military weapons, apparently, did not believe in left-handers. The Model 1911A1 is a truly modern weapon, designed for cavalry officers to use with one hand while they wielded a saber with the other. Reloading an autoloader is easier than with a revolver, and that was the justification for the weapon. No one expected to have to use one in a hurry. Contrary to popular belief, it was not designed to combat Moro tribesmen in the Philippines. Forty-five Long Colt revolvers were brought out of retirement for this when .38s proved to be inadequate.

Of course, this is 1969. The last .45 built to government contract was built in 1945. This one was built in 1942 by Remington Rand. It is three years older than I am. Really gives you confidence, doesn't it?

I expect to be hassled about my carrying habits by senior officers. I'll simply comply with their demands until they leave. The holster goes under my fatigue shirt when I'm in the rear anyway, so maybe no one will notice.

My sergeant, Sergeant First Class Garner is on R and R. He's a bit of a legend with First Cav. He has been here over five years with the unit — seven years in Nam. He's picked up a DSC, three or four Silver Stars, two Purple Hearts, half a dozen Bronze Stars or more. Second Squadron's Sergeant, Sergeant First Class Johnson, is almost as experienced, three plus years here. He and I hit it off well from the first. He gives me a parachute knife, noticing I have no combat knife. These guys all carry Ka-Bars or Randalls or Camillus. The parachute knife is more practical. It's a black-handled switchblade. You can clean your nails with it much better than with one of the big ones. If anyone thinks I'm going to fight with a knife they need to think again if I'm not in a total corner. I order a big bowie/ Air Force survival knife by Camillus from Ken Nolan, Inc. for reasons that are beyond me. Maybe I watched *The Green Berets* too many times.

Gee, a guy at home who carried a concealed .45 and a switchblade knife would have the local Gestapo after him pretty fast. Until they got him, mothers would call him bad company for their sons and would hide their daughters. It is a macho fantasy, but since I checked my macho at the gate, I'm a little bewildered by why I'm getting caught up in it.

Johnson, according to Dartmouth, got a DFC while drunk. During Tet of '68 the First Cav. had been pretty heavily infiltrated by VC. When the shit

hit the fan one night, the VC commandeered several vehicles and tried to fight their way out. Some rusting hulks still stand out front as a monument. Half of First Cav. lay in smoking ruins afterward, with one-third casualties. All the VC-driven vehicles were destroyed except one. It went down the road never to be seen again until a couple of days ago when it was found in a cave. They're still checking it out for boobytraps. Only the machine guns were missing. It's unlikely it'll ever be brought back into service. Who would want to take the chance that a boobytrap or two was missed? Tanks make very messy explosions.

Johnson apparently fought like hell and was, to his own admission, roaring drunk when the battle started, but fought all night. He jumped onto a tank, grabbed a radio, called in air support, and when that was all tied up elsewhere, controlled artillery and finally fired the main gun at rebelling tanks, destroying three. This story really gives me confidence in my troops. How many of them are VC now?

1 – 10 September 1969

The advisors throw a hell of a party for the ARVNs to give Grimaldi a send-off. I discover these guys really like to drink. They sit me between two ARVN officers, my counterpart and his XO. I try to be polite. When they give me a drink, I drink it.

Wrong.

Then they have *Hoan Hoi*. They fill my glass and Tonc's. Then we chug-a-lug. Last one finishing loses. They all shout, *Hoan Hoi, Hoan Hoi, Hoan Hoi*, while we drink and applaud and shout for the winner and clap us on the back. I lose.

Then they pass a bottle of scotch and the lid around. You take the lid, fill it with Johnny Walker, and go bottoms up, then pass it on.

Then things get very hazy. I remember being carried out, throwing up in the commode, and making it to my bunk. I am in awful shape when Garner sees his new C.O. I am in my underwear between my bunk and the latrine. I am green. I do not look brave, intelligent, or leaderlike in O.D. underwear with face to match.

I think the battle's lost already.

The next day we move out to Chan Tanh.

We laager each night in a different place. One night, Major Thuong, the Regimental XO, tells us to laager at coordinates so and so. They look good on the map.

Of course coordinates so and so are in a rice paddy.

Tanks — in a rice paddy. Sure.

Before we get there we gas up just out of Chan Tanh, of course. One always gases up at the end of the day.

Trying to get in his assigned position, one of the tank commanders hits a soft spot, and the left tread digs a deep hole, sticking the tank, and causing it to slip much lower on the left rear than the right front.

Fuel spills out the filler cap and runs down to the left muffler, hits the hot metal, and bursts into flames.

At this point I discontinue taking pictures and back up fifty yards at flank. I figure the son of a bitch is going to blow up.

Two ARVNs pull out fire extinguishers and aim them at the fire. It's like pissing on a campfire. It just makes the fire mad.

They get desperate. They throw mud on the flames, more and more mud. I'm waiting for the explosion.

Son of a bitch, it works. The fire goes out. Everyone congratulates the crazy, er brave ARVNs. I'm impressed. They're nuts.

We hook up an APC to try to pull out the stuck tank.

It gets stuck, of course.

Then we hook up an APC to try to pull out the

stuck APC and tank.

It gets stuck.

Then we hook up an APC and try to pull out the stuck APC, APC, and tank.

It doesn't move.

Then we hook up an APC to try to pull out the stuck APC, APC, APC, and tank.

It doesn't move either.

It works — finally. They all come out. We move off the now destroyed rice field into a bit higher ground. No doubt the owner of the rice paddy will be a VC tomorrow. Destroy a man's livelihood and see where his heart and mind goes.

Sleeping by an APC is fun. For one thing, I'm always soaking wet. I'm wet because of the four o'clock rains. They last long enough to soak me. Then I can't dry out before night. It's semi-miserable, but it beats the infantry.

I have a folding cot. I unfold it and put a poncho over it, hung from the side of the APC to the ground using shoelaces from an RSP pack.

The rain always gets in, though, if it rains at night.

My orders for captain come through dated 26 July.

11 — 30 September 1969

Song Be.

Song Be is the capital of Phuoc Long Province. Its lifeline is a road from Saigon to Dong-Xoai to Bunard to Song Be, QL 14 on the maps. Song Be is in the shadow of Nui Ba Ra, the Black Virgin mountain, a large black peak overlooking a large expanse of flat land with cultivated rice paddies, open areas, and deep forests.

The ARVNs tell me that the legend is during one of the many wars in this godforsaken place, a young soldier married his love and was called away to war before their marriage could be consummated. She went up the black mountain to await his return, a virgin but a married lady, a *Ba*. She is still waiting because he never returned.

There'll be a lot of those, except in modern Vietnam girls won't wait. They'll sell themselves in car washes or massage parlors.

But then, are our women any better? Were I in an American unit how many Dear John letters would I hear about? When will I get mine?

But then are we men worth waiting for? Every man I know here, whether married or not, myself excluded, goes to the whorehouses. Most of them speak of having gotten VD at one time or another. Each has a PCOD, a Pussy Cut Off Date, meaning the date after which they can't get any for fear of giving their wife/girlfriend VD on their R and R or at home. Nine days is the gestation period for gonorrhea, I believe, though some strong forms take less time, so two weeks is apparently safe.

The VC/NVA control Nui Ba Ra from the base almost to the top. On the top is a U.S. commo station. Every once in a while the NVA take the commo station and kill everyone on it until the Air Force levels everything in sight and order is restored.

The road to Song Be must be secured "regardless of cost."

The cost is that we run up the road with a convoy. We almost make it, and the third APC from the front takes a rocket as we round a bend.

The treeline is two hundred meters away on a side. We return fire. I call for choppers, a heavy fire team, and Garner calls for F-100s.

The APC ahead is burning fiercely. Flames shoot fifty feet, black smoke two hundred feet into the clear, blue air.

I feel awfully exposed, sitting on that damn APC in that armored helicopter seat.

"Snuffer Three, this is Cobra Two, over," comes over my headphones.

"Cobra T-two, th-this is Snuffer Three, over."

"Snuffer Three, I am moving east over the road. I see a line of armored vehicles. Please pop smoke at your position. Over."

"Roger, over." I lean forward to Tonc. "*Dai-Uy*, pop smoke, right side, for the Cobra."

He tells one of his minions, and a can of smoke goes out of the APC to the right.

It boils out purple smoke.

"I identify violet," says Cobra Two.

"That is correct. I need fire suppression in the-th-the tr-trees, n-north, zero degrees, of th-that treeline, over."

"Roger. I'll shoot a Willie Pete, and you adjust. Over."

"Roger."

He is so fucking cool up there, a man dryly, discussing plumbing fixtures from his den while I am terrified.

About then the world tilts ninety degrees, and pain fills it.

Oh, shit, I'm on the ground. Why am I on the ground? Grass is in my face. My ears are ringing. I see blurs only. I begin to touch my face to rub my eyes.

Blood!

Oh, shit! I've been hit!

Calm down, Harris, you asshole!

Where is the blood coming from?

Never mind that. If you're hit once, you can be again. Look around. Are you in danger?

I draw my .45 as if it could protect me from B-40s and AK-47s and look around, focusing my eyes. Behind me is the APC. It looks strange. I'm looking down in it.

Oh, shit! It's on its side! The gunner is sprawled

awkwardly in the turret, head down, blood dripping from his nose and mouth.

I look around. The Cobras are flying overhead. Firing must be going on, but I can't hear. I can see only blurs.

I wipe my face. More blood. I am scared. I vomit from fear as much as disorientation.

It's my nose. My nose is bleeding! Shit! I ignore it.

My glasses. Where are my glasses? No wonder everything is blurred. Where was I lying? Over there? Nothing. Hmmm, they have to be somewhere.

There they are. One lens is broken. Still that's better than nothing.

An ARVN is gesturing at me. He is pointing to his radio. I reach for it. He pulls back and shakes his head. Then he points at the APC. Mine is at the helicopter seat, out of reach. Instead I grab his and switch it to my frequency.

"Snuffer Tha-ree, I say again, this is Cobra Two, O-ver."

"Two, Three, over." I can barely hear him with the handset to my ear. I realize my headphones are gone. Of course. They're dangling from my radio. My ears are ringing and roaring now.

"Where the hell have you been? I'm burning a lot of fuel. I need corrections, over."

I look into the treeline. I see his white smoke, almost dispersed, from his W.P. rocket.

"Add five zero. Five for effect. That is, to your direction, go long five zero. Over."

"Roger. We'll do one run each, then adjust."

The ARVN wants his radio back. I point to the helicopter. He runs to the APC and gets me my radio.

By the time the two Cobras have made their run, I have switched to my radio. Surprisingly it works.

Snuffer Six, Major Dartmouth, gets on the radio and berates me. He is in a helicopter.

"There's a jeep five hundred yards ahead of your lead tank. It's been shot up. You should be there. Tell your counterpart and get off your ass, over."

Where is Tonc?

"I can't find my counterpart, over."

"What? Where the hell are you?"

"O-on the g-ground, b-by my track. Over."

"Well, get it up to the front and find him, over."

"It's not-not going a-anywhere. Over."

I turn to the ARVNs. "Where is *Dai-Uy* Tonc?"

They point. He is getting on an APC. I run to it, but it starts off without me. He is in similar bad shape, bloody, disoriented.

"Oh, fuck!" I try to flag down the next APC. Those bastards would just as soon run over me.

I try calling Snuffer Six to get him to tell his counterpart to tell mine to pick me up. He doesn't answer. I then call Garner, and his tank picks me up and gives me a ride. He gives me a look appropriate to one who has just fucked up royally in a life-or-death situation.

He is, by now, controlling, through an airborne FAC in a Bird Dog, four F-100s who are dropping napalm in the south treeline, while my Cobras work the north.

I break my Cobras off so I can move to the new problem. I transfer to an APC with Tonc.

A jeep, the jeep type, not the Ford built M-151, but one you'd find at your jeep dealer, marked

U.S.A.I.D., is off the side of the road with three bodies in it, a Vietnamese driver and rear seat passenger and a tall, handsome U.S. captain in the passenger's seat. At least he used to be handsome.

He was a CORDS advisor in Song Be who wanted to see some action. He did. I stare at his body for some time, too long. I am seeing me in death. This is an American. It is me. It is the first American dead I have seen, no body bag, no nice closed coffin, but freshly dead, grotesque and pitiful.

I am transfixed.

Finally I hear someone yelling in my headset and answer.

"Three, this is Six," comes the angry voice. "Quit fucking off. I need some direction. Over."

"Roger. Over." I turn to Tonc.

"*Dai-Uy*, where do you want Cobras?"

He points. I give stuttering directions. I am a blank to correct terminology. I work in slow motion with much prompting.

I use up the Cobras, and the fight ends. We clean up, pull the broken APC onto its broken track, and strip it. I get my rifle and pack and go with Tonc. The APC is repairable at depot.

I am a virgin no more.

My head hurts. My ears have bled, and I can't hear well. I am dizzy for days. My left eardrum, it turns out, is split. It heals, though, with some hearing loss.

In Song Be we set up in the soccer field. One of the reasons for reinforcing Song Be was the loss of a Chinook one hot day. A Chinook is a big twin rotor helicopter, noisy, ugly, dangerous, vibration-ridden, a monstrosity. The common terminology is "shithook."

I think it's descriptive.

ARVNs decided to use one to move fifty troops and two advisors. Normally thirty-three is a load, but ARVNs are small, right? So they put in fifty.

They lifted off the soccer field and something went wrong. The shithook staggered up, then back down rolling, bursting into flames, exploding. Fifty-two passengers and four crew were burned to death on the soccer field.

Major Dartmouth chews me out for my performance during the firefight. I was off the air, and I lost my counterpart. I also stuttered.

"I stuttered because I was scared shitless," I say. This is not the correct thing to say.

"My advisors are not scared. Ever! They are professional soldiers, love war! It is exhilarating."

Bullshit, I think. I keep my mouth shut.

Anyone who isn't scared is a fool.

I wonder if I will ever get good at this.

For a few days we laager outside Song Be.

Garner carries a Remington pump shotgun on his tank, a long-barreled mother. Is he after geese? I think. Of course, that shotgun is probably more reliable than an M-16.

Tonc gets a week's leave for his "wounds" received when the APC went over the mine. Trung-Uy Van is friendlier. He would've played Kato in *The Green Hornet*.

We set up outside a village. Mail comes, including a *Playboy* for me. Van and his friends get quite a kick out of it. I wonder what these photos of big, buxom light-haired women are like to men in a land of small, dark, flat-chested women with very little pubic hair.

Of course, girls in *Playboy* have no pubic hair at all. If the pose does not hide it, they perform airbrush surgery. The official MACV definition of "pornography" is any photo which shows pubic hair.

Then comes another convoy. We go to Dong Xoai and pick it up. We are hit as we come up a hill. The lead track is hit hard. It blows up. Flames shoot fifty feet into the air. For an instant I see the men inside, bathed in flames. Those on top are thrown off. Small arms fire rakes the area and kills them. It is an effective ambush. We return fire, of course, seeing green tracers come from the trees. I call for helicopters.

We have infantry attached, and their advisor is a first lieutenant in a tan beret. He dives into my APC. I stay on top, of course. I'd rather be shot than burned.

Before my helicopters arrive, a Huey arrives with "Blackhorse Six Mike," General Garry, deputy commanding general of First Cavalry Division, U.S. The First Cav. patch is an oversized yellow shield with a black horse and a black diagonal bar on it. Hence, blackhorse as their call sign. Of course, they've been using it so long every VC with a radio knows when they're coming.

He offers artillery. Garner controls that while I work the choppers. I look around. Mine is the only head up. I feel silly and exposed. I get my head down. I am still stuttering. Funny, I never stuttered "back in the world."

"Snuffer Three, this is Cobra One, over."

"C-Cobra One, S-Snuffer Th-Three, over."

"We have only enough for one more pass, over."

"Roger. W-wait one." I lean forward to Van.

"Only one more pass. Over there, okay?"

"Okay, *Dai-Uy*."

"Cobra One, S-Snuffer Three. Add f-five zero, l-left f-five zero, over."

"Roger, I verify, add five zero long, left five zero left, over."

"C-correct, over."

"Roger. Here we go."

The Cobras scream in shooting ARA and mini-guns. The ordnance goes *whomp-whomp-whomp* right where I want it. The last Cobra wiggles as he pulls out and heads for Song Be, beer, a hot meal, a warm bed, movies, a massage, etc.

When I look back, I see movement. It is thirty yards ahead in high weeds. I raise my .45. I've never shot it at a target thirty yards away with a .45, but I see a head and start to pop off a round using both hands. The APC lurches forward, and I fire rapidly, before I intend to. It is an accidental shot.

The head explodes, and the body drops. Several people are shooting at it. Anyone could have shot it.

After things calm down the infantry goes to the spot, and I accompany them. It is a boy sixteen, seventeen, black pajamas, Ho Chi Minh sandals, and an RPG-2 rocket launcher and two B-40 rockets. He was hit two inches above the left eye, which blew his brains out the top and back of his skull. He also was riddled with bullets entering at a down to up angle, indicating he was hit several times while on his back. His eyes are open, and his mouth hangs open wide. Flies buzz around his mouth and the top of his head.

I am congratulated and slapped on the back. I say

that I don't even know if I hit him. They ignore that. But the face haunts me. Did I do that?

Major Dartmouth lands his helicopter, jumps into the driver's seat of a tank, and pushes the spectacularly burning APC off the road. The shooting is, of course, over, and all is calm, but General Garry's aide writes him up for a Silver Star.

General Garry congratulates me for doing a good job. The infantry brings back more bodies. He looks at them. His aide takes pictures of them for some reason. Garry stops him and makes him destroy the film. Since I hate body pictures, I cheer silently. His aide is a thin, good-looking young first lieutenant in impossibly neat fatigues. He has a notebook in one hand constantly and takes incessant notes. I take an instant dislike for him. Anyone who can remain neat and clean and detached from this chaos I do not trust.

Then Garry and his aide get back in their polished Huey and leave.

I don't think I hit the B-40-wielding NVA. You don't shoot a head-sized target from thirty yards with a rusty, twenty-seven-year-old .45 that rattles when you shake it. If I did, it was luck, sheer luck.

Of course, in another split second he would have turned my APC into a flaming inferno.

Not just luck, it was chance. It's all chance. We live and die by chance.

We set up on the top of the next hill. It had been napalmed during the battle and is blackened. The ARVNs find a charred, burned dead cat killed by the napalm. Incredibly they skin and cut it up and start cooking it for lunch. For three days I eat C-rations to keep from eating with the ARVNs. I get sick every time I think of the cat.

Dearest Jerry,
I've got a job! I'm working for American National Insurance Company. I only make $350 a month, but that's the best I can get. A man would make a lot more, of course, ha ha. Men really have it good compared to women in our society.

As if we didn't have enough animals here, your cousin Freddie brought me another cat. He's a huge, sweet, shaded silver Persian. I named him Sultan. He weighs over 10 pounds. Your mother's awful dog, Poopsie, drives him crazy, but Sultan just tries to ignore him.

Love,
Carole

1 October – 3 November 1969

These road convoys are getting to be a drag. We run down the road to Dong Xoai, spreading out the squadron along the way and lead and trail the convoy back. Every day it rains I get soaked. Then I freeze all night. Meals with the ARVNs consist of rice, green leafy vegetables which taste like grass, and/or some horrible meat, such as a bear killed by claymore mines, fish and *nuoc maum*, or chicken. The advisor gets offered the head or claws as a delicacy. Fantastic. I'm dreaming of steaks, fried chicken, or hamburgers. The best dream is of wiener schnitzel in some neat little German restaurant in Heidelberg or Stuttgart, with, of course, my beautiful blond bride for company.

Never happen, G.I.

I listen to the music of this war on a small portable – anything to soften the sound of Vietnamese music. The station, of course, is Armed Forces Vietnam, a military-run station which plays a little bit of everything the common soldier could be expected to want to hear. "Leavin' on a Jet Plane," "Are you goin' to San Francisco?" get on once in a while, with a lot of rock junk and country and western junk. I suppose it's appropriate for the "common soldier." Most of the soldiers are black (rock and roll) or poor white (country and western). There are few Harvard grads. West Point yes, Yale no. Beethoven and Bach aren't big here. I mention once that I like a tune by Edyie Gourme, and a liaison sergeant, all of nineteen, looks at me as though I'm father time. I listen to Frank Sinatra singing "My Way," and his lieutenant, an old man of twenty, says, "God, he's ancient."

Finally the black bandanas I ordered from Carole arrive. I wear them around my neck. I never tan, so it's necessary, and she can't find green or camou. She made these. They wipe my face, clean my glasses, and one served as a tournequit once. Send freeze-dried camp foods, darlin'. This rice shit is awful.

Only rarely do they play Glenn Campbell singing "Galveston." I mentioned to Carole it's a favorite of mine. She says she hates it because of the line, "I clean my gun, and dream of Galveston." That, of course, is why I like the song. I see myself as the soldier, and Carole as the beauty he dreams about. I can relate to that song.

The NVA hit our convoys at will, just harassment, because they don't stop the convoys, just sap our strength. No convoy has turned back, but they hurt us. They pop out, shoot off a rocket or two and *di-di mau*. Then we fight thin air for two hours.

I keep my M-16 at hand all the time now. I can't expect to get lucky with the .45 again. I shoot at muzzle flashes once when we're taking fire, or at least where I think I see muzzle flashes. When we sweep the area we find four blood trails and five bodies with AKs. I'm rather pleased that the M-16 didn't jam. The ARVN Infantry takes credit for the bodies.

We take the tracks out into the woods looking for them. It's uncomfortable and scary, but is it useful? I doubt it. You can hear a track from so far away you can either run away or set up an ambush.

Then I learn about command-detonated mines.

We're going through heavy brush. Up on top overhanging branches and limbs are tearing us up. We follow the exact track prints of the track ahead. But ours has extra antennas and a *Co-Van My* (American Advisor), so it must be the command track.

This time there's a flash before my eyes, and I tumble to the ground enveloped by pain and noise. I land in a heap, probably unconscious.

It's just as well. The mine gets the gas tank, trapping the driver and gunner inside. Flames shoot up in a billowing cloud of orange and black. The ammo catches and begins popping off. It begins to rain 40 mm grenade rounds. They don't explode, of course, not having gone far enough to arm.

There goes my radio.

Tonc is on the ground beside me. The infantry lieutenant is in a bush. We're all alive.

The gunner is screaming, but not for long.

My ears are bleeding as well as my nose. I see double. I vomit. I stagger on all fours, and so does Tonc.

Cover, cover, find cover. I find a tree and plop behind it, bleeding, disoriented, burned a bit around the edges, and scared. Fuck Dartmouth. I'm terrified. this is hell on earth.

I don't see my M-16, so I pull the .45 out of its holster.

ARVNs come and pick up Tonc. They ignore me until they demand a medevac for him. Garner handles it. I'm useless. I can't hear. I can't see. I certainly can't fight.

I get onto another APC, hanging on a corner, the infantry lieutenant on another, and we just hang on until the rocking, lurching beast stops. We're in a clearing, and Garner has popped yellow smoke for a medevac. They put Tonc and another ARVN on it. By then I've stopped leaking blood. So has the lieutenant. But neither of us feels like John Wayne. In fact, I'm not good for much for three days. I'm just getting over the dizziness when Trung Uy Van murders the kid.

We are setting up positions for night ambushes with the infantry when the infantry company finds a kid following the tracks and dropping foot mines. Foot mines, if you step on them, blow off one foot.

Van screams at the kid, a twelve or thirteen-year-old, and slaps him around. I'm sickened enough by this, but then he whips out a .45. I grab for his arm, and about six ARVNs cover me up, hitting, kicking, and butt stroking me with rifles. One stroke closes my right eye and damn near knocks me unconscious, but something keeps me awake. I'm on the ground on my back, face all bloody, several guys on me, when Van, the sweet-looking ARVN screams something at me in Vietnamese, waves the .45 at me, then turns and shoots the kid in the left ear, blowing his brains out onto the ground in a five-foot oval.

Needless to say, I am no longer of any use to First

ARVN Armored Cavalry. I am relieved and sent to Lam Son for reassignment. I get several chewing outs along the way for interfering with the ARVNs, for failing to properly get along with them, and for not being aggressive enough.

Dartmouth says, "You never influenced that unit anyway. You never earned the respect of Sergeant Garner or your counterpart. You're just an immature kid who never earned his captain's bars and who thinks this is an intramural game with rules. This is a war, and you're too stupid or immature to understand that."

"Sir, he was going to murder a twelve-year-old boy."

"That twelve-year-old boy was crippling your men. If you were worth a damn as an advisor, you could have talked him out of it. I could have, if I'd wanted to. If he'd been my counterpart, I would have done nothing."

I begin to dream of headless men.

My Dearest Jerry,

I'm sorry I haven't written, but I've been working so hard at American National. That drive is a real drag. Your car has been acting up a lot, too. It stranded me just off the causeway yesterday. I wish we had a new one, but I know we can't afford it . . .

This is all a nightmare that'll pass, I know. It won't be long, and you'll be on the plane. I've made the trip to meet that plane several times in my dreams . . .

Just don't get hurt. I know you're in a nice, safe job, but even rear area soldiers get hurt, in

95

jeep accidents and the like. I want you home
intact, my knight in olive drab armor . . .

Love all ways,
Carole

4 November 1969

The new senior advisor of Advisory Team Seventy is Col. John J. Norman. Colonel Norman came to Vietnam as a major in 1964. He is still here — by choice. He was Special Forces for a long time and commanded Project Delta. One does not make General in Special Forces, so he left SF and commanded the 196th Light Infantry Brigade. Conventional army types do not like SF, and after this war ends, I have little doubt the career SF types will be forced out. Norman is no fool. On the contrary, he is brilliant, and an exemplary soldier. He has won two DSCs, five Silver Stars, and nine Purple Hearts. Needless to say, he is airborne, ranger, and West Point.

I am standing in front of him explaining my failure. No one has listened yet when I mentioned the murder of a twelve-year-old boy. I look like a battle casualty, bandage over my closed right eye, black eye and bruises and lumps here and there. I don't walk too well as one of the rifle butts hit me in the groin.

He listens. "Tell me about the boy," he says, before I get to it.

97

"Van murdered a twelve-year-old boy."

"How? Why?"

"The boy was caught putting out foot mines. The interrogation started rough, and the boy showed a little defiance. Van became furious and shot him."

"What did you do?"

"When he drew his 45 I tried to stop him. That's when I got the shit beaten outta me. Then he laughed at me and shot the kid."

"What did you do then?"

"One of his troops hit me in the groin, and I threw up and gagged for fifteen minutes, then I crawled to my radio while the ARVNs laughed at me, and I reported the problem. Major Dartmouth yelled and screamed in the radio for a few minutes then called a chopper to pick me up and bring me here."

"I see. Did you have any warning he would behave that way?"

"No sir. I-we never had taken a prisoner before."

"Why did you try to stop him?"

I stare at him for a minute, stunned at the question.

"I . . . I, er, w-what should I have done, sir? That was murder."

"Foot mines maim and cripple your troops."

"So what? I've maimed and crippled a few VC. That's the job. I'm not an animal. I have to live with myself. I can live with the job. If you want us to condone murder of children, then get yourself another sucker. All the goddamned protesters are right."

"I don't. I would have shot my counterpart if he did that. But I managed to avoid such incidents by reporting capture of a live, unwounded prisoner immediately and telling my counterpart I had done so. It dissuaded him. I would suggest that next time. The killing of prisoners is a problem in any war with any army, including ours."

"Yes sir."

"Do you like working with the ARVNs?"

"No sir, I hate it, every minute of it."

"Do you hate combat?"

"Of course, but that's part of the job, sir."

"Of course. I love it. It makes you appreciate life more. What job would you like now, Captain?"

"Sir, I've been blown off APCs twice. I'm nearly deaf. I'm ready for a desk. I have extensive air-ground operations training. I'd like a G-three air or S-three air type job."

"You think you'll be good at that?"

"Yes sir. I do."

"I don't. I think you need more command time. In any case, there is no opening in G-three air till, hmm, December first. Then if you've proven yourself, we'll talk about it. Captain Ramblin is rotating then. I think you need more field time. You're immature and impulsive. You act before you think. You haven't shown me any physical courage, and an officer without physical courage is a disgrace to the uniform. My staff officers have earned their jobs. You haven't."

I started, "Sir, I —" but I stopped. "Never mind."

"I thought so. I'm putting you with Fifth Recon. You'll get a chance there to prove yourself."

Great, I think. Just what I need. I shake like a leaf, vomit once a day, have bloody hemorrhoids, can't hear, have headaches all the time, see double, and dream horrible dreams. I must prove myself?

Then I think, maybe he's right. Maybe I have no physical courage. I'm terrified all the time. I don't think I want to find out whether I have any or not. I just want to survive.

Fifth Recon is a highly trained infantry reconnaissance company attached to Fifth Division headquarters. It has seventy men with a captain in charge. The advisory team consists of me and a fat, lazy non-infantry specialist, third class, Thurlow. If I'm unsuited for recon, Thurlow is unsuited for the U.S. Army. Change his accent and he would be a good Guatemalan customs inspector, or maybe a cab driver in Chicago. He strikes me as immature, lazy, and cowardly, just what I want to depend on for support. He is twenty. It is a children's war.

Our first operation is through medium rough terrain in Tay Ninh Province. We meet no resistance. My wallet is stolen.

I go to Lam Son for new cards. The HQ company commander won't give me another MACV driver's license because I can't produce a U.S. driver's license. I try to explain that everything was stolen, but I am speaking a foreign language. The guy is a bureaucrat. I tell him he will never have trouble with hemorrhoids and leave. He doesn't figure out what I've said for three days.

I have to go to Saigon for a new MACV I.D. card, ration card, etc. I also go to Saigon so I can complain about not being paid in three months. Carole tells me they're about to repossess the car, and she's flat broke. I barge into MACV finance section with my hand on my .45 on my hip and raise hell with an asshole first lieutenant for three hours until I leave with three months back pay. I send it in money orders to Carole, keeping just a bit. Apparently they can't handle sending most of it home as an allotment and sending one hundred dollars to me each month, so I send it all to her and rely on my checkbook to live off. I'll take a hundred dollars — one fifty per month, and she will get eleven hundred dollars.

Then I make the mistake of going to the commissary. I check my M-16 at the door and go in. Then I get arrested by two MPs for carrying a concealed weapon, my .45. I can't believe it.

"Keep me. Throw me in jail. I won't get killed there." They look too stupid and serious to be joking.

"Excuse me, fellas, but there's a war on. You've read about it, haven't you? Isn't it in all the papers?"

They write a D.R. and eventually release me after calling Colonel Norman's office to make sure I get in a lot of shit when I return.

Colonel Norman has me in his office two days later when the D.R. reaches him. He has to RBI to the provost marshal, of course. Major Gumber, Dartmouth's replacement, is there asking for the .45 back anyway. Solemnly I unload it and hand it to him.

"I could get you for stealing government property for not turning this in," he says.

"Go right ahead, sir. Please."

"Harris, you've got an attitude problem."

"Yes sir, I do. People are trying to kill me, and the bullshit paperwork seems more important than the shooting war."

"No one's trying to kill you, Harris."

"That sounds like the psychiatrist talking to Yossarian in *Catch Twenty-two*, sir."

Norman is beginning to crack a smile through his number three fierce look. He growls, "Get out of here, Captain. Kill some VC."

We go on Navy PBRs up the Saigon River and put out ambushes at good river crossing points. NVA are infiltrating at a terrible rate, similar to the rate they infiltrated before Tet of '68 according to Major Stout, the intelligence advisor. Major Stout is my direct boss, and he gives me no trouble. He just explains the missions and lets me do my job. Obviously he has no future in the U.S. Army.

We do night river ambushes every night for a week, sleeping in the daytime. At least we try to sleep. It's a hundred and ten degrees, and the hooches aren't too cool. Lieutenant Colonel Pomeo, the assistant S.A., Colonel Norman's assistant, catches me asleep and gives me hell for it. I try to explain I'm up all night.

Wrong.

"You sleep on ambushes. Don't give me that shit."

"Whatever you say, sir."

Advisors in Recon units get bodyguards. This mere fact scares the hell out of me. I get a tall, muscular Nung — meaning of Chinese extraction. He carries a machete as well as his M-16 and tries to look fierce. His name is Chen. He speaks pretty good English and reads *Time* magazine when I finish with my copy. We get various U.S. magazines fairly regularly. Reading *Time* is interesting because they're describing some mythical war and calling it Vietnam. They're certainly not describing the war I'm fighting.

I tell Chen I'll give him one hundred dollars for a .45, no questions asked, must be in working condition. He returns the next day and says the best he can do is two fifty. I say one seventy-five, MPC. He says two hundred. I say okay. He returns with one with the serial number removed fairly neatly, a row of Xs stamped over it. I stick a magazine in and kill seven Coke cans at fifteen yards. I tell him I need a hundred rounds of ammunition, then I give him two hundred dollars. It's hard to explain to Carole.

A PBR (Patrol Boat River) is a plywood boat with twin .50s up front and M-60s in back, with a Honeywell 40 mm automatic grenade launcher in the stern.

The C.O. is a navy chief petty officer (sergeant in army-ese), and he has a couple of American crewmen and two or three Vietnamese navy crewmen. None of this advisor shit for the navy, they put U.S. personnel in *command* of Vietnamese. If we had, we might have won this thing in '67 or so. But then considering the quality of leadership I see, Colonel Norman and Johnny East notwithstanding, perhaps not.

We meet them at their HQ on the river. They live in rear area splendor and bitch about it.

Of course.

All soldiers/sailors/marines/airmen bitch. Fact of life number two-six-eight. I would trade easily, as they don't have to eat chicken heads and rice, but I keep my mouth shut.

We go upriver in three boats, one holding the command group, two with ambush teams.

Dai-Uy Khe, the C.O., puts his exec, Trung-Uy Phong, and his first sergeant all in the same boat. The first night I put Thurlow in the command boat with me. Then I come to my senses and suggest Khe split his command group up.

"No, *Dai-Uy*. I command Recon. You get me helicopters, jets, artillery. I want my men here with me."

"Whatever. I think I'll put Thurlow on boat two tomorrow night."

We have a starlight scope. Starlight scopes are devices which electronically amplify available light so that starlight, seen through one, is an eerie green daylight.

They are so secret that only major headquarters and VC know anything about them. We have to take extraordinary security measures to protect them. Losing one is grounds for court-martial. In the Army of the Republic of Vietnam that means probably a firing squad. So usually they stay locked up. Eighth Infantry never used theirs.

Using one is neat, though. You see a green fairyland. Lights linger and trail as they burn out their phosphorescence on the tube. A match turns the whole thing nearly white. We have one on our boat, and we use it to scan the marshes where our ambushes are out.

"Something's moving," I say while watching the scope. My right eye sees someone low crawling.

I close it and look with my left eye into the darkness.

"*Dai-Uy*! Straight ahead." I point. "Two hundred yards out. Two men low crawling toward us."

He consults his map.

"Not mine. Anyway, mine no crawl in ambush. No move. Kill them."

The CPO orders the twin .50s aimed where I point. I use the scope.

They open fire. I see the tracers tearing up bush short of their location.

"Short. Add fifty," I say, as though I were correcting artillery.

The green fairyland gets ugly bright green lingering streaks as they get closer. The men stand up to run, panic in their faces and actions, and they are hit, rolling into the marsh and sprawling hidden by weeds.

"Cease fire."

The gunner turns to me. "Did I get 'em?" he whispers.

"You got 'em," I whisper back. He is elated.

The next morning we go ashore and look at the bodies. I am getting less bothered by looking at freshly killed bodies. They are dressed in khaki, Ho Chi Minh sandals, no hats, two AK-47s, packs just like the ARVNS wear but khaki, even the same brand name inside, with rice, Chinese and homemade grenades, and three magazines each.

We strip the bodies of military stuff, pour gasoline over them, and burn them in place. We don't use enough gasoline or something. The result is very ugly.

We leave and have breakfast.

Recon works out of intelligence. I go back to intelligence and give Major Stout a briefing. He says we'll do it again the next night.

Wrong.

At about zero-two hundred the next morning the exec shakes me awake. I'm propped against a bulkhead somewhere below deck.

"*Dai-Uy, Dai-Uy*. The scope no work. You fix?"

Typical, I think, in my bleary-eyed near stupor. They don't want to know I'm here till the shit hits the fan. Then it's *Dai-Uy, Dai-Uy*. I put on my helmet and pick up my M-16 and go topside.

See how fast I pick up these nautical terms?

At least I'm not seasick.

I have a boil on the back of my right thigh. It is going *throb . . . throb . . . throb*. It is, at the beginning of the evening, dime-sized, an angry, ugly gumdrop.

I look at the starlight scope and fiddle with the knobs. After two minutes I return a verdict.

"The batteries are dead. We can't use it tonight. I'll get it fixed in the morning."

"Okay, *Dai-Uy*."

Khe is asleep. His first sergeant is asleep. The exec and I are wide awake, now. He sits on the port rail, and I sit on the starboard rail silently staring into the dark river. There is no moon. It is a clear, starry night. I think of Carole, her lush body and its delights, how lonely and scared I am. I'll never go home. I'll never see her again, I think. I am hornier than a three-balled tomcat, but only if I let myself think about it. I do not go around with a constant erection and/or stain my shorts every night. The body adjusts. Somewhere in the controlling mechanism a voice says, "Okay, guys, we got enough semen here to float a battleship. Shut down that factory and make muscle. This sucker is killing himself. More back muscles would be good."

At Lam Son in the Officer's Club there is a four panel Snoopy cartoon.

Panel one: Here's the famous war hero on guard duty at exotic Lam Son.

Panel two: The famous war hero walks his post and keeps an eagle eye out for VC.

Panel three: But always, in the heat of battle or on his lonely guard post one thought fills his thoughts.

Panel four: Goddamn, I'm horny!

Amen, brother.

I have my feet over the rail, my M-16, stupidly, for I can't see needing it, slung over my shoulder. I am half asleep already, a lousy person for guard duty because the mind, when not busy, says, "Fuck it, Jerry, I'm shutting down. I'm bored."

Whoosh.

The world turns red, then white. I think I'm dead, or in a weird nightmare.

I am underwater choking, drowning, kicking. I come to the surface and spit out, cough, and exhale half the filthy Saigon River.

The world is red again, a vision of hell with blackness around. I can see nothing. I paddle and turn, for I feel heat on the back of my head.

I shouldn't have turned. The PBR is a flaming inferno, a ghost ship, with flames into the water around it.

Unforgettably I see a figure, I don't know who, in the center of the flame, arms out, a scream unheard in the surrounding noise, a supplication to God or a god to stop the agony. But it does not stop, not immediately.

A .50 cal. machine gun is firing. Tracers go past me. It is from the second PBR.

I go underwater.

That cocksucker is shooting at me!

Panic.

Don't panic. Swim. Survive.

I come up twenty feet away from where I went under. I swim for weeds near shore.

The PBR is already sunk, and the flames diminishing. I don't know how long it's been. Fifteen seconds? Fifteen minutes? Anytime? A lifetime, several lifetimes.

Tracers are everywhere, and flames overhead. The light is unworldly. Ashore red and green tracers cross. More red tracers come from the PBRs.

I realize the PBRs are firing into the source of the red tracers—our ambushes.

"No!" I scream, then I realize no one can hear me, and if they do, they'll shoot me. I shut up. I think I'm crying. I don't know.

Perhaps it's an optical illusion. Maybe they're not really killing my troops from the other boats.

But I know they are.

I hear a scream ashore, then a moan. Then a bang of an explosion near the moan, and it stops.

The PBRs are firing grenade launchers now. The shore does a series of *whump whump whumps*.

I go deep into the weeds. They're shooting at everything that moves, even if it doesn't move. They've gone into total panic mode.

It gets quiet first. After ten minutes or so the firing

dies out. A helicopter is overhead with flares. The eerie light continues for an hour, flare after flare.

I am cold, shivering, now calm enough to be terrified. Things brush past me in the water. I imagine it is eels and snakes and crabs, but it is only harmless fish.

I begin to hurt. My face feels raw. My eyes and eyelids burn. My hands burn. My neck burns.

I stay hidden. Anyone, friend or foe, who sees me, will shoot. Therefore I want no one to see me.

I paddle and float, finally finding something to stand on in the weeds.

I wait.

Finally there's a light, false dawn, then more endless night. Then comes the sunrise and daylight. It would be a beautiful surprise if I weren't in such a mess.

The other two boats are patrolling and picking up our ambush team survivors. Two Cobras are circling. One of the boats glides by slowly.

A medevac goes in ashore and picks up five wounded, three litters.

I see an American in the boat leaning beside the twin 50s.

"*Do not shoot!*" I yell. "*Help! American in the water! Do not—*"

I am cut off by the 50s firing at me. For a mad half minute or eight hours, I'm not sure, I am the center of a circle of fire. Everyone opens up. I dive underwater.

I stay under till I feel my lungs will burst. Finally I must breathe.

"*Don't fuckin' shoot, you dumb cocksucker!*"

The firing stops.

I hear, "Hey, it's an American in the water. Don't shoot."

"Hagerty! It's an American. Don't shoot."

"Cease fire."

Christ, I think. I paddle to the side of the boat, and they haul me in. I look around at a sea of American and Vietnamese faces and see one over a nametag: HAGERTY. It's definitely the guy who shot at me first.

I smile at him.

He smiles back, uncertainly.

I deck him with the grandmother of all left hooks. I think I've broken every bone in my hand.

His face is a new shape there on the deck. His nose is bleeding and points east.

"Whadya do that for?"

"Lousy marksmanship and piss-poor target identification."

I spend an hour trying to make sense of it all.

Two ambush teams of four men are wiped out, one by .50 cal. fire, one by AKs and grenades. Nine men are wounded. Three are critical.

Dai-Uy Khe, Trung Uy Phong, Trung Ta Chen, Trung Ta Huong, and four ARVN enlisted are dead or missing. We find some badly burned bodies floating over the wreck. One is missing both arms. There are no NVA bodies.

I begin my spot report:

"Line one, ARVN, fifteen, U.S. Navy three, VNAV four. Line two, ARVN, nine, over."

The report causes chaos at the TOC, which had, of course, received some kind of report from Thurlow, no matter how garbled and, apparently, ignored the reports from the Navy PBRs.

"Why didn't you call in during the battle? Over."

"I was swimming. Over."

"Swimming? Did you think you were on R and R? Over."

"Not exactly. Over."

"Was your radio inoperative? Over."

"Yes. Very. Along with the entire Papa Bravo Romeo and all hands, over."

"Then . . . ah . . . why are you able to report? Over."

"You would prefer I was dead? Over."

"Oh . . . well . . . ah . . . er . . . report in when you get back. Over."

"Roger. Out."

Before I report in I go to the medic shack and have my neck and the backs of my hands dressed. I also realize that my right leg is in agony and find the boil is now huge, two inches by an inch and a half, very inflamed.

The medic sergeant puts me on a table facedown and goes to work. He taps the center of the boil with a scalpel, and pus hits his glasses.

I'm doing various gyrations and calling forth every obscenity I know while he presses and wipes, presses and wipes.

"Gee, Cap'n, I've never seen so much pus from one boil."

"So call *Stars and Stripes*. It's a record."

I can't see the boil. It's just below my ass on the back of my thigh. I can barely tell what he's doing. I see him fill a pan with pads soaked in pus and blood.

The pain is exquisite. If they give out academy awards for pain, I'll nominate this.

Gee, something to tell my grandchildren about. "Kiddies, I had boils so bad in Nam—"

"How bad were they, Gramps?"

When he finishes my leg looks hollow. I feel as if I've given birth to a bouncing six pound eight ounce collection of pus.

The boil drains for two weeks.

I shower and change and report to Colonel Norman.

"You look like shit, Captain."

"Yes sir, I sure do, sir."

"You lost your command."

"No sir, Captain Khe lost his command. I commanded one man, Thurlow, and he's alive."

"As far as I'm concerned that was your command."

"Then if you'd given me command authority over the ARVNs the situation wouldn't have happened. Khe put his entire command group in one boat against my expressed advice to the contrary. He set out his ambush teams against my advice. You know the result."

"Then you're an ineffective advisor."

"Yes sir. You have grasped the situation firmly."

"You are also a smartass."

"Yes sir. I am a fuckin' smartass. I also just spent the fuckin' night in the fuckin' Saigon River dodging goddamned U.S., ARVN, and NVA bullets. I was a hell of a lot more afraid of the U.S. bullets than the enemy. Blame it on Saigon River water swallowed while dodging 'friendly' fire. It does funny things to the mind. One gets smartassed, exhausted, and pissed

113

off."

He laughs. "Yes, I bet you are. Get some sleep and see me at zero-nine hundred in the morning, and we'll figure out what to do with you. Still, you're in a lot of trouble."

"Yes sir."

A few hours later I am in my bunk in a hot, sweaty, painful nightmare when I'm awakened by, "On your feet!"

My eyelids open. I see a mosquito net. It's par boiling temperature.

"Get your lead ass outta that rack you sorry-assed excuse for an officer!"

I look over toward the sound. It is Lieutenant Colonel Pomeo.

"Get up! *Now!* Stand at *attention!*"

I hit a very shaky brace. I am about to throw up.

"I'm going to court-martial your ass, Harris. Dereliction of duty. Disobeying a direct order."

I stand there sweating, saying nothing.

"You report to my office at zero-nine hundred tomorrow, Harris. You're in a lot of trouble. I'm going to hang your young ass."

"You'll have to take a number, sir."

30 November — 3 December 1969

I am standing at attention in front of Colonel Norman and Lieutenant Colonel Pomeo. I am in starched fatigues with boots spitshined by a *mama-san's* number three girl, one of the advantages of being in the rear for twenty-four hours.

"At ease, Captain," says Norman, looking at a folder.

"Harris, Fifth Recon is going into retraining at Vung Tau. Three months. They'll get new officers. They won't need advisors while they're there. So I'm giving you your wish. You'll replace Captain Ramblin as G-three Air. He's been doing an outstanding job. You have some large shoes to fill."

"I still want to court-martial your ass, Harris," says Lieutenant Colonel Pomeo. "You can thank Colonel Norman for saving you this time. If he hadn't stopped me, I'd have court-martial charges ready for your sleeping on duty yesterday. So I'll be watching you. Colonel Norman has assured me that if you fuck up once, I'll get your ass."

What are you going to do? Send me to Vietnam? I

think. I manage to keep my mouth shut, though. I have turned into a smartass lately.

I meet Ramblin, another boy-captain, two years six months out of ROTC. He works twelve hours on, twelve off, in the TOC. It is a big, underground bunker with all the comforts of home: desks, radios, a refrigerator with Cokes, a coffee machine, maps, telephones, M-16s and .45s; officers, sergeants, ARVNs, the navy liaison officer, and two FACs. FACs are Air Force fighter pilots stuck flying Forward Air Control Cessna Bird dogs.

I train for two days listening to Ramblin and Sergeant First Class Savitch, the G-3 air sergeant, explain their SOP. They've alternated shifts. Now I alternate with Ramblin till he leaves. In any sane world there would be three G-3 air officers, one for each shift, at least two.

Anyone who thinks Vietnam is sane please leave the room.

The third day boredom has just begun to set in when a young Air Force pilot, Lieutenant Reich, says from the front door, "Anyone know how to use a Pentax camera?"

"Sure. I do," I say truthfully. I'm bored, very bored.

Fool, no one ever died from boredom.

"Come on. I need a photographer to get some strike photos."

"Sure. Why not?"

He hands me a camera bag with a Pentax Spotmatic, film, 50 mm and 200 mm lens, and accessories, Air Force issue. The army probably uses Brownie Hawkeyes.

A Cessna Bird Dog looks like any number of small airplanes you'd see at a small airport: fixed gear, tailwheel, no tricycle gear, round, old style Cessna tail, aluminum construction, high wing, single engine, two passengers in tandem like the old Piper Cub, a plane to which it bears too much resemblance for my tastes. Under each wing on the struts are rocket launchers with smoke-marking rockets. A Bird Dog is considered unarmed. A CAR-15 is on a bulkhead, and Reich carries a Smith and Wesson .38. That's unarmed, all right. I stow my M-16. My .45 is on my left hip, my big bowie knife on my right, and a survival vest in between. The survival vest is an Air Force issue item with lots of little pockets with boxes of who knows what in them.

A FAC tells fighter-bomber pilots where to bomb in response to instructions from army troops on the ground. A FAC plane is not meant to fight, though an occasional FAC has earned a well-deserved posthumous Medal of Honor by trying to fight with one.

I hope Lieutenant Reich has no such ideas.

One of the ARVN artillery spotter Bird Dogs has a running Pink Panther on the side of the fuselage.

Reich, a pudgy, placid, good-natured guy, his career no doubt ruined by this assignment, flies quite well, smoothly and accurately. I wonder if FACs are chosen from pilots in disfavor with Department of the Air Force as MACV officers must be chosen from among officers in disfavor with armor branch or infantry branch.

This means I work with a lot of duds. Eleventh Armored Cav., Colonel Patton's unit, seems to get the cream of armor officers, and First Air Cav. seems to get the cream of infantry officers.

I am no Patton. I am one of the duds I have to work with. Only one limitation seems to be put on advisors. They have stopped using artillery officers as infantry advisors because they sustained twice a many casualties as infantry and armor officers in the same slots.

Reich is a maniac. We find the bunker complex easily, mark it, and let the F-100s have some practice.

But all of this can be done from four thousand feet. The bunkers are quite visible due to a fire having burned off the undergrowth. At three hundred feet, to which he descends, it is basically suicidal.

Now I know why Reich is so calm and placid on the ground. He goes nuts in the air.

I'm airsick. I've secreted a paper bag in my stuff just in case it gets the best of me.

It's a long flight back. Every wing waggle is pure agony. I can't throw up. If I do, I'll never be invited along on another one.

But then, why would I want to?

I win the race with my stomach. My face is saved.

Dearest Jerry,

I'm so glad you have a nice, safe desk job. Let the others fight the war. Just spend your time and come home to your (horny) wife.

The Waiting Wives Club met today. Most of the wives have husbands in noncombat jobs like you. We're all so glad our husbands aren't traipsing through the jungles. It looks so hot and miserable in the news. I used to look for you every night. Your mother swears she saw you once, but I told her you command a desk.

Mary Lou McCorkle is not so lucky. Her husband is a warrant officer flying helicopters — Cobras? Is that right? She worries about him terribly because of the high casualty rate among helicopter pilots. Theirs must be a terrible life.

I'm glad yours is so much better.

All my love all ways and always,
Carole

4 — 6 December 1969

I awake with the dawn, with a hard-on that's painful. I'm sure I had some great dreams, but I can't remember them, just faint visions of white, clean skin, blond hair, erect nipples, and breasts you could swim in.

I hear noise, shuffling. I have my hand on my .45 before I realize it's *mamasan* cleaning up. I put the .45 back under the pillow, safety on.

She walks by, saying, "Chao *Dai-Uy*."

"Chao, *mamasan*."

She's probably thirty-five, but Nam is hard on women. Her teeth are bad, and she's pretty dried up. She looks fifty. Of course, she could be, but I couldn't tell the difference. They go to seed pretty early, then stay ageless.

She sees the bulge in my shorts. I am lying on my back wearing only olive-drab briefs, and the head of my cock protrudes from the elastic.

It happens too fast for me to turn over or cover up. *Mamasan* giggles. Then she turns and shuffles out.

I don't need to get up for another hour, so I just lie

there.

They call them piss hard-ons, but, of course, they have nothing to do with pissing, as any man knows who has tried to hit a toilet bowl in such a condition. They're just indicators of R.E.M. sleep in a man with healthy plumbing.

Of course, the fact that I'm hornier than a hoot owl doesn't help.

I had a girlfriend once who thought men had to have erections in order to piss. The absurdity of that occupies my mind for a few minutes.

Mamasan's number two daughter, Co Kim, I think, comes in, giggling, pulls up my mosquito netting and drops her dress.

"Jesus H. Christ!"

She's thin, little breasts, more skin than fat, so they fall and the dark little nipples point up. She is wearing black bikini panties. She drops them, revealing the typical nearly hairless "bald pussy," a few strands of black hair down the middle.

Mamasan is behind her, points to my cock, and speaks rapidly to her in Vietnamese. I'm learning Vietnamese as I go along, but she loses me.

"Jesus! If Lieutenant Colonel Pomeo walks in now!"

Naturally I'm the only man in the empty hooch. I had a choice of an empty one or one with roommates. I could have chosen one with roommates. Either they would be witnesses, or *mamasan* wouldn't be doing this.

I can see what's happening. Mamasan likes *Dai-Uy* Harris because he tips her and gives her fruit from the chow hall. *Dai-Uy* Harris has a hard-on, so she'll have Co Kim cure it.

Co means virgin.

Not bloody likely G.I.

Co Kim is reaching for my cock. I would dearly love for her to do what she wants to with it, but I have visions of Lieutenant Colonel Pomeo coming in on one of his impromptu hooch inspections. One night he did one at 3 A.M., and I almost shot the mother-fucker.

"Oh my God."

Prison.

The Long Binh jail.

But on the other hand she does look a tempting morsel.

Three strokes and I'll probably come, just as Pomeo walks in.

"Ah, no, ah, thanks, Co Kim. Ah, er, no—"

Oh my God. She has her hand on my cock. Jesus that feels good. She's giggling and crawling into bed with me.

"Co Kim! No! *Mamasan!* No!"

Co Kim pulls her hand back. I half wish she wouldn't.

She must be fourteen, fifteen? One of my friends said he spent the night with a girl who turned out to be twelve.

"You no like?" Her hands point to her little tits. "You no like me?"

"Oh, you're . . . you're," I'm sweating profusely, "you're just fine, Co Kim. I'm . . . I'm not allowed to fuck the help. It's a rule. No pussy on base."

"What matter, *Dai-Uy*? She numba one, not numba ten. Nice gi'l. No VD," says *mamasan*.

"I know. I know. Number one girl. Nice girl. I . . . ah . . . I have VD."

Mamasan pushes past Co Kim. She pulls down my shorts. The erection is a persistent devil.

She grabs my cock, looks at it, turns it so she can see the top. "No. No. *Dai-Uy*. You fine. Nice plick. No VD."

"Jesus. *Mamasan*. If I got caught screwing your daughter I'd go to jail. No pussy on base. Only in town. It's Colonel Norman's rule. Sorry. No. I'll pay you anyway." I reach for my wallet.

"No! No money. Goddamn G.I.! Money everything! Co gift! Thought you nice. Need woman. I give. Co Kim good gi'l. G.I. numbah ten!"

Co Kim is crying. She puts on her clothes, and they leave, *mamasan* speaking Vietnamese a mile a minute, most of it cussing me out.

"Jesus."

At dinner I sit with a table of captains and lieutenants. We have girls like Co Kim as waitresses, and one particularly obnoxious, fat captain bitches that they're not fast enough with the tea, our trays, etc.

"We need a Co of the Month Club."

"And what might that be?"

"The worst Co every month gets fired."

"Why? We didn't have Cos in the boonies, and we managed to feed ourselves."

"Don't be barbaric, Harris. These girls keep the place civilized. And they should be grateful for a job. Look at them. Before the French came Vietnamese walked. The French improved the economy enough they could ride bicycles. Now with us here they have Honda motorcyles and three-wheeled trucks. Pretty

124

soon they'll be in Datsuns. All because of us. They should kiss our feet."

"You going to take one with you to the field?"

"Shit, man! This is the field! My air conditioner went out today. This is rough-assed conditions. We earn our combat pay here. We have rocket attacks regularly everytime they show movies."

It goes on like that till I leave, feeling bloated from the high calorie, starchy meal and dessert. I feel guilty. There's a war out there, and these assholes are complaining about air conditioning. They have maids, kitchen help, kids to spitshine boots, and they bitch, bitch, bitch.

I feel like I should be suffering more. After all, I'm in a war. I know how bad it can get, and I'm living in luxury, working in safety, watching the medevacs go over, watching the war on TV at night.

I go out on a Firefly chopper to fight boredom and guilt, a Huey with twin M-60s on the right and a coaxial spotlight. We search for something to shoot at till we run low on fuel, land at Long Binh, refuel, and do it again. When we finish I get a couple hours' sleep and go to another twelve hour shift in the TOC, avoiding Co Kim and *mamasan*.

Everybody in the TOC is complaining. It begins to get to me, that and thinking of Co Kim's little body, her hair down to her waist, friendly little tits, nearly bald pubes.

Harris, you're a married man. You promised to be faithful if she would. She's at home in a miserable existence, working at American National Insurance for a lousy three fifty a month. She tells you how bad it is every letter.

125

But I'm still tempted. I have a hard-on so much now I fear damaging it. Jesus. I never had one in the field.

Goddamned Vietnamese. Imagine that bitch offering me her daughter. Was she going to watch her daughter fuck the *Dai-Uy*?

I do another Firefly and fall asleep on it. Then I fall asleep in the TOC.

Captain Ramblin reports to Colonel Norman that I am not suited to the job of G-3 Air.

Again I find myself standing at attention in front of Colonel Norman.

"Captain Ramblin told me he didn't want you as his replacement. He said you don't take the job seriously enough. Do you? What do you think of the job?"

"It's a fine dog robber's job, sir."

"I thought that was what you really wanted."

"Sir, did you ever work for months to get a real dish into bed, a blonde with big tits and an eighteen inch waist, just to find out she just lies there in bed?"

"What do big tits have to do—oh, I see what you mean. There's an opening in Eighth Regiment, Eighth Recon. You're the only ranger qualified captain available. It won't be so dull. Report there at zero-nine hundred tomorrow. Take the rest of the day off."

"Yes sir."

Harris, you are an idiot.

Dearest Jerry,

I don't understand your last letter. You said you cashed a check for two hundred and fifty dollars rather than the one fifty a month we agreed on. This leaves me pretty broke. What could you possibly need that costs that much? You said two hundred dollars went for a necessity. I don't understand. Don't they give you everything you need?

Your mother and I do not get along. That goddamned dog of hers doesn't let me sleep, and . . .

They put your grandmother in the hospital again. She's okay now, but she asks about you. She knows you didn't go to Washington like we told her.

Love,
Carole

7—11 December 1969

Lieutenant Colonel Pride gives me the "kill VC" lecture, forgetting he has already. He also tells me I am not up to his standards as a senior advisor. Anyway the new T.O. and E. calls for a major as senior advisor and a captain as assistant, so I am to be assistant S.A. of Three—Eight.

Fine. Who gives a shit? At least I have the sense not to wear the .45 near Pride. He hates .45s. Everyone should have an M-16. I wouldn't argue if I thought the M-16 would always go bang when I pull the trigger. When I was a kid I went to war with Mattel toys. Now I still do.

Oh, Jesus, the battalion S.A. is a carbon copy of Lieutenant Colonel Pride, Major Andrews, a tall, thin, burr-headed blond with a Dick Tracy jaw. He's so gung-ho he starches his shorts and spitshines his dick.

Immediately we're split up. I go with Trung Uy Tuy's company. Tuy has been promoted since I last saw him. Ten years in grade as a second lieutenant—proof he's too good.

Tuy I understand. He only enjoys three things: fucking, drinking, and killing VC. Tuy was born in Hanoi. In 1954 when the Communists took over, all the Catholics were run south and/or killed. Tuy's mother and sister were gang-raped to death by Communist forces, and his father was disemboweled and left tied to a post. A person can live for two or three days like that if he's strong. Tuy's father was strong. He lasted from noon Monday till Tuy sneaked into the square and cut his throat in the night on Tuesday. Tuy was fourteen at the time.

Tuy did not tell me that story when sober, naturally.

We're attached to First ARVN Armored Cav. Christ. I'm back with those bastards again. Van is the C.O. now of First Squadron. Oh, shit.

I sit on an APC with Captain Pullen, the guy who replaced me when I was fired from the cav. He gets the armored helicopter seat. I hang on to a spare corner. I certainly won't get inside of the son of a bitch.

We're to provide road security for the Dong Xoai, Song Be road. It's a hard-packed unpaved, smooth-surfaced road with two hundred to four hundred yards on each side defoliated a couple of years ago before they banned defoliants. Maybe they should have defoliated the whole country.

Pullen has a theory:

"We give a polygraph to everyone in the country. The ones loyal to the U.S. side we put in a boat in the South China Sea. The others we leave in Vietnam. Then we move out and nuke the whole fuckin' country. Level the son of a bitch." He pauses for effect. "Then we sink the boat."

130

Pullen has black, black hair, wears Rommel goggles under his black beret, very chic. I learn it's because he's wearing contact lenses.

"Contact lenses in this dust? Wow."

"I don't have any trouble."

"Whatever works. I can't see with glasses. I can imagine the pain with contacts."

Contacts would be nice when the damn rains come. My glasses get covered with water, and I can't see worth a damn.

There's a spot in that road I'm beginning to hate. After three days we get ambushed there, a B-40 into the track ahead of us. Van turns his track toward the small arms fire from the right edge of the jungle. As soon as we leave the road the front of the track lifts and I'm on my ass in the middle of the road, deaf, blind, and groggy.

It's all surreal. Slow motion, silent, blurred focus.

It's hot. I see red, orange, and black in front of me, blue sky, green shapes, and sand-colored road.

What the fuck's goin' on?

I grope around. Aha. Glasses. There they are. I put them on.

Oh, shit. I can see a bit—double. The world's spinning.

Now it's roaring. Every sound is accompanied by pain in my ears.

I see Pullen. He's on all fours, bleeding from the nose, crying.

Come to think of it, I'm bleeding from the nose, too. Hmmm, and the ears. Not again. This is ridiculous.

I look up. The APC is burning fiercely. Motherfucker, not again.

My radio's on my back. I try it.

"Slimy Pitcher Six, this is Three, over."

"Where the fuck have you been? I've been calling you for half an hour. Over."

"Took a slow rickshaw. Ah . . . we . . . ah, Two Alpha Papa Charlies in flames. Small arms fire coming from, ah . . . oh shit, er . . . three-four-six-four-four-eight over."

"What the fuck kinda sitrep is that? How many line ones, twos, size of enemy force? Get your act together. Deacon One-Six (Pullen) has already called for a Dustoff." He doesn't say over. He just clicks off the handset. What is he mad about?

"Roger. Line one and two unknown. I'm in a ditch keeping below ground level because AKs are raking the ground above me. There are several bodies in sight. Now mortars are incoming. Enemy force size is unknown and likely to stay that way for a while. Request heavy fire team, eight inch from Song Be, and a flight of jets with napalm. We can play fiddlefuck with my report procedure sometime when you've just gotten your fuckin' head knocked into your ass, just get the goddamned ordinance. Over."

All my anger is directed not at the NVA killing us but at the asshole with the radio in a safe location trying to play quarterback in the blind.

An ARVN jumps up to fire off a burst and gets a round in the face. In seeming slow motion his face explodes and his arms jerk out straight, flinging his M-16 at me, hitting me in the shoulder.

Tuy jumps into the ditch with me, radio operator right behind.

"*Dai-Uy*, you get helicopters?"

"On the way, Trung-Uy."

Then Song Be artillery calls me, and I give him eight digit coordinates and tell Tuy we have arty on the way.

The spotting round is short.

I double check my procedure for calling it in and make sure I have my shit together and then say, "Add five zero, over."

"Add five zero, shot over — shot out."

Wham. It lands right behind me, fifty yards short of me.

"Negative, negative. You dropped five zero. Add, I say again add. Over."

"Roger. Add five zero to last. Shot over."

"Negative, negative. Over."

"Shot out."

"Oh, shit. Head down, Trung Uy."

The round hits dead on the burning APC. The noise and flash is unbelievable, even though I have both hands over my ears and my head in the dirt. I don't think it kills anyone else.

"Congratulations, you have successfully located my position. Now, from that position, add one hundred. I say again, add one hundred. Over."

"Roger. Add one hundred. Shot over — shot out." The motherfucker is too fuckin' calm. He just dropped an eight inch round on my head, and he's sitting there drinking a Pepsi and screwing up. I want to scream at him that my fuckin' life depends on what he's doing.

The round hits the treeline. By now the NVA have the message and are *di di-ing* the area.

133

"Fire for effect. Over."

"Roger. Fire for effect. Shot over—shot out."

I shoot eight inch artillery till the heavy fire team arrives with ARA and play with that for a while.

A Dustoff arrives. Pullen is controlling that, so I pay little attention except to give a lot of heavy fire team fire while it's there to keep the dinks' heads down.

Then come the F-100s. They're correctly armed with napalm, and they burn up the treeline for fifty yards into the jungle.

A chopper has landed behind me. I'm paying it little attention, though, coordinating with the FAC so we don't get fried.

A man runs out of the treeline. He is on fire from head to foot. In his right arm is a rifle.

I see someone dash out of the ditch.

It is Captain Fitch, an assistant G-3 advisor and Colonel Norman's constant companion. If colonels were allowed aides, he would be Norman's aide. I look around. Norman is standing up in the ditch, Swedish K from SF days in hand, ready to fire from the hip.

Is he going to use that 9 mm popgun against dug-in NVA a hundred yards away?

Fitch runs up to the screaming, burning man, grabs his right arm, and pulls him to the ditch, where he burns. The skin from the man's arm pulls off when Fitch grabs it. Fitch rolls him over and puts the fire out.

"Gee, Fitch, that was really brave, but he'll die anyway," says Norman.

"Ah, fuck him. Did you see this?" he says, holding

134

up the rifle.

He waves it around. "It's a scoped Mauser sniping rifle. I can take this mother home as a souvenir."

"Mother," I whisper. Norman laughs and shakes his head.

In the ditch the NVA dies slowly.

I control the fire support for the rest of the battle, not noticing that I haven't heard from Captain Pullen. When it calms down Deacon Six is calling me asking the whereabouts of Deacon One-Six. He's not around. I can't find him. Finally an ARVN says he got on the medevac chopper and left.

I hear later he's been sent to Vung Tau, the in-country R and R center, and won't be back in combat for six weeks. His nose was bleeding, and his ear-drums ruptured, and he sees double — just like me. He gets a Purple Heart and six weeks in the rear. I spend the night on LZ O'Keefe with the rats and the ARVNs.

I am an idiot.

Dearest Jerry,

Here's the closest I could come to your request. This is a green rain suit from Sears. I don't know where all those stores you mentioned are, and I don't have time to go there. I *do* have other things to do, or did you forget? Sometimes, Jerry, I wonder if you think I have nothing better to do than wait on you hand and foot.

Love,
Carole

135

12−15 December 1969

My company moves to Fire Base Mary. Mary is eight miles from Song Be, in supporting distance of the Special Forces A Team at Bunard. Of course they wouldn't support us if we needed it. Major Andrews, my radio operator Mike "Mad" Hatten and I drop by and visit them.

They sell us beer from a pallet load at twice PX prices, and steaks!

They even have a round-eyed Red Cross girl visiting, but she's also round-butted and wider than an APC, so she doesn't get much male interest. I have no idea what she's doing there. She needs to find a more remote outpost if she's hooking like the one in Saigon who told me her price was one month's combat pay, sixty-five dollars. "That way it's fair to all ranks."

The A Team has concrete emplacements. It's really heavy duty. Just the thing for a mobile, jungle war. While we're there two Chinooks drop pallet loads of stuff. The A Team C.O. is a captain. He does not look like Patrick Wayne. He is my size and has an acne problem. The XO is a second lieutenant. They told me there were no second lieutenants in Special Forces. He looks too young to be a promoted NCO. Maybe they're getting desperate, too.

Captain Baker, the HQ company C.O. from Lam Son moves up to replace Pullen. He's a National Guard retread, forty years old and still a captain. He's very regulation happy. He and I don't get along. After the incident when my wallet was stolen we've not been friendly. I still don't have a MACV driver's license because I couldn't prove to him I had a Texas driver's license because it was stolen, too. So if I crash a jeep, say, over a mine, I buy it. I wonder if they would deduct the price of the jeep from my G.I. insurance.

So they put him at O'Keefe and swap first and second squadrons so as to keep us apart — this is his request, not mine. I can stand anyone and work with anybody.

So I get First Lieutenant Preswick, a gung-ho airborne type who carries a Smith and Wesson five shot snub-nosed .38 in a concealed shoulder holster. He really thinks he is John Wayne.

What, I think, is he going to do with the little .38 — stop an AK-equipped sniper at three hundred yards?

Lieutenant Colonel Pride comes by and asks me why Baker dislikes me so.

I explain that I'm just a rotten son of a bitch. He lets it drop.

16–18 December 1969

Every morning we move out of Mary and set out road security. Then there's nothing to do for a while, so Hatten and I take an ammo can full of ammo, our M-16s, ear plugs, and empty Coke and beer cans and practice shooting. I practice with the .45 when I can get .45 ammunition, which is more difficult. I seriously consider buying some on the blackmarket but decide it might be loaded with C-4, and that would ruin my whole day. Even Johnny East can't get me any .45 ammo.

On 16 December, though, we don't practice, because a big convoy is coming through.

We deploy from Bunard to Song Be. First Squadron is at Bunard, or more correctly, between Bunard and the road. We're at FSB Mary.

When the shit hits the fan, it hits it at First Squadron.

I hear it only over the radio. I'm too far away to see it.

I hear Garner's voice.

"Six, this is Three Alpha. I need two heavy fire

139

teams, a flight of jets, and a medevac. Three Sierra's been hit — urgent — over."

"Roger. What's the situation? Over."

"We've been hit — bad. They B-fortied the command track and raked the top with AK fire. Three counterparts is dead. Two other tracks out, heavily damaged."

I picture Garner on his tank with his Remington pump shotgun. Later I learn he's wounded in the knee.

Major Andrews successfully screws everything up. Instead of getting a couple of heavy fire teams immediately and controlling artillery, he takes his C and C chopper and makes passes over the treeline with M-60s firing. Not smart. Pure John Wayne give-me-a-medal bullshit. But Lieutenant Colonel Pride is in the area in his chopper, and he orders him to cease about three times. Major Strine, the S.A. for the cav. is screaming for the same thing.

This gives the NVA a chance to leave while they play circlefuck.

We sit on our tracks, waiting to get called in. But we never get the call. Garner hangs on to his tank, controls artillery, helicopters, and napalm-dropping jets until all is quiet. Then with much kicking and screaming, he gets on the C and C chopper for medevac. Three real medevac birds have come and gone with dead, dying, and wounded.

Baker is among the dead. He is pronounced DOA at Song Be. They call to tell First Cav. to come and pick up his weapon, thrown on the chopper with him for some reason. Then he is put out into the sun for the next chopper to take to Long Binh for processing

140

the body back to the U.S.

But the chopper misses him, and the next. Two days later someone notices a swollen, stinking, fly-covered body and gets it on a chopper for the rear.

By then the HQ company C.O., a friend of his, has realized, in going through his two-oh-one file, that he hadn't changed his G.I. insurance, and it will go to his ex-wife. His current wife and two children will get zilch.

War is hell, captain. Fuck it and continue to march.

19 — 24 December 1969

I am told to be ready to move in fifteen minutes for an extended stay. I pack. Fuck Lieutenant Colonel Pride, the .45 goes on — under my shirt, though. A chopper picks me up. In it are Colonel Norman and another captain, Bill Grimes.

Norman explains briefly: "Bo Duc is under siege — Ninth Regiment plus a squadron of Eleventh ACR are in the AO. NVA lob rockets, mortars, and artillery from across the Cambodian border. Regimental CP keeps taking hits. The battalions keep getting in skirmishes, enough to tell me if we don't reinforce, the NVA'll come across the border with tanks like they did at Liang Vie. The advisors are getting pretty ragged so we're reinforcing them. You'll take over the TOC, and the regimental advisory team will go into the field."

"Yes sir."

Why me, Lord?

We don't get over fifty feet above the trees the whole trip. Nap of the earth flying is it? It's a roller coaster without the tracks. My stomach rebels but doesn't embarrass me.

Over Bo Duc we see the airfield, A C-123 is burned out at the end of the field, and another is unloading rapidly. We land outside the CP compound and walk in. The C-123 climbs away at full power at a steep angle. How many died in the other?

As we walk from the chopper pad, Colonel Norman says, "I see you have another .45, Harris."

"No, sir. Advisors aren't authorized .45s. I'm carrying an M-16." I hold mine up.

Norman is carrying his Swedish K and wearing a Browning Hi-Power in a shoulder holster. Neither is authorized.

"Right." He laughs.

Somehow I'm not afraid of him anymore.

Advisors are in a long, thin building. We're introduced to the senior advisor, Lieutenant Colonel Singer, by Colonel Norman, who then tells Singer to keep him informed and leaves.

As the chopper leaves a 122 mm rocket round impacts fifty meters down the hill, scaring the hell out of me but doing no damage.

"Okay, gentlemen. You'll be TOC duty officers. We use four men, two officers, two NCOs on two shifts. I'll put you on opposite shifts so you can get acquainted with our procedures. Call it, Captain Grimes." He holds out a half dollar. Grimes calls heads. Singer flips the coin. It's heads.

"Day or night, Captain?"

"Day."

"Good. Harris, you're off till nineteen hundred hours. Then you'll go till zero-seven hundred. You two will use the same bunk, the one over there. All the others are in use. Any questions?"

We have none.

Sleeping is out of the question, of course. I have a feeling I'll be tired by zero-seven hundred for sure.

I wander around the camp. At one "corner" is a large ammo dump, sitting in sand bags but above the ground. I groan at the thought of its blowing up.

One of the NCOs asks if I want to go to the village. I'm surprised that we're allowed, but I go.

In the dirty little typical village are buildings built of ammo crates, C-rations cans flattened out, etc., just like in Fort Lewis. Two or three little boys try to sell me their mothers and sisters.

"You wanna fuck my sister. She virgin. Twelve year old. Sweet. Hey G.I., *Dai-Uy*. You like my sister. She suck big dick."

I don't know whether to laugh or cry. Neither the sergeant nor I buy any women. He buys ice, and I try a strange yellow citrus fruit, very sour, yellow, larger than an orange. Nothing in Vietnam is sweet, the young street urchin notwithstanding.

I make the mistake of giving a Life Saver to a small child. Soon twenty children are begging and fighting over Life Savers. They don't want chocolate, only Life Savers.

We drive away to get free of the mob. They have the same face. It's the face in those "Save the Children" ads with about three dashes of hatred in their dead little eyes.

I guess if I were selling my mother or sister I'd have hate in my eyes, too.

145

The night shift is pretty quiet, very dark. We have used PRC-25 batteries with little light bulbs for light. It's not much. I doze off once or twice. My NCO, an SP-4 kid of nineteen isn't much better.

At seven we brief Lieutenant Colonel Singer, who is grumpy. His situation map isn't done neatly enough. I redo it, have breakfast, and go to bed.

The Co-Van quarters are noisy. People wake me eight or nine times, and I get maybe four hours of sleep. Then it's C-rations and do it again.

Eleventh ACR gets into a firefight at dawn, so I stay on duty till zero-nine thirty. By that time they have forty-two NVA bodies and two tracks lost with all aboard casualties. The troop C.O., a Captain Starr, is given an impact Silver Star on the spot by the regimental C.O., Starr's second.

Our units have moved into position to help during this period. One of them gets hit and takes seven casualties. I relay their call for medevacs and Cobras and turn it over to the day shift. I can hardly see I am so sleepy.

It's another no sleep day, with people going in and out of my cubicle, slamming doors, and yelling in nearby rooms, plus one asshole with a loud stereo. He does not take kindly to my request that he turn it off. I repeat the request with the .45 aimed at the receiver, cocked and unlocked. This accomplishes its intended purpose. Of course, two hours later, I am awakened by Lieutenant Colonel Singer to explain why I pointed a weapon at First Lieutenant

Markowitz.

"I didn't. I pointed it at his goddamned stereo. If he turns it on again, I'll point it at him." I rolled over to go back to sleep.

"Oh. I see." He pauses, then begins: "Ah, er, Harris, you, ah, can't ah, point a weapon at a junior officer."

"Then promote the son of a bitch or tell him to keep that goddamned stereo turned off. If I don't blow the goddamned stereo away, I'll come here at zero-two hundred and turn the volume to full tilt. Where the fuck are we? A goddamned college dorm or a fire base under siege?"

"I, ah, see. Ah, er, don't point a weapon at his stuff again, Harris. I'll tell him to keep it turned off."

"Right. Thank you, sir."

At zero-six hundred the next morning, Singer, an early riser, sneaks into the TOC and finds both of us dozing. He gives me hell about it. I shrug it off, being too tired and sleepy to argue. The radio has been silent for hours or we'd be awake anyway. Breaking squelch wakes us, much less a call.

He runs out of steam and leaves.

Then the world ends.

The noise is unbelievable, God clapping his hands; and I'm on the floor with a terrible headache and stars and fireworks before my eyes.

It's pitch black.

The ARVNs are screaming and whining. SP-4 kid Aldine is crying like a six-year-old. I try to stand up but hit my head. I sit down, unbalanced, dazed. I reach up with my hand.

147

My God, the roof is four feet off the floor. I feel back and forth. It is a level four feet.

The exits at each end no longer exist.

We're trapped.

Oh, shit.

I understand why they're crying.

I try the radios. They're uniformly dead. The generator is above ground.

"What happened, Captain?" asks the kid.

"I guess the ammo dump took a direct hit. They'll dig us up when they get around to it."

"W-what if they're a-all dead?"

"Somebody'll come eventually."

"B-but we could suffocate by th-then. We could be dead!" He's beginning to break up.

I'm so scared it's all I can do to keep from screaming and beating my head against the wall or going into the fetal position and sucking my thumb, and he's worse.

"Oh, shit, Thorsten. It's my turn to break down and cry this time. It's your turn to be strong and brave," I yell.

The incongruity of it causes him to stop and to laugh nervously. We both begin laughing.

An ARVN tells me, "No laugh. Not nice."

"Why?" I ask.

"Thieu-Da Kung dead," he says, and points his flashlight at a body with a twelve by twelve through it grotesquely.

"Sorry. I didn't know."

I feel very stupid.

One of the ARVNS begins to cry, to wail, to moan.

I hear another curse him savagely in the dark. Then he knocks the moaner silly with a heavy blow.

Then it's quiet.

Too quiet, as they say.

No outside noise. No digging sounds. No taps on the beams.

Finally the kid says, "We should be tapping on one of these vertical beams."

I think of the men trapped in the Oklahoma hammering on the bulkhead till they all died, unheard, after Pearl, leaving a pitiful diary.

But we tap on the beam with a piece of a chair for hours, alternating.

Tap-tap-tap . . . tap . . . tap . . . tap . . . tap-tap-tap. S.O.S. Save our souls.

Our souls may all be lost, but I fear for my mind.

I am hallucinating in the dark, broken only by dim flashlights used sparingly.

I see Carole's lush white body, walking to me and then turning and going away, waving good-bye. She is nude, and the detail is perfect, long blond hair, large breasts with large areola and erect nipples, the beginnings of a belly over a lush light brown bush, long legs. She is wearing only jungle boots, filthy, unpolished, mud-covered jungle boots, like Nortons, and a Ka-Bar on a pistol belt.

She waves good-bye and goes away. Then I hallucinate snakes and worms.

It is two P.M. when I look at my watch, I should say, fourteen hundred hours, feeling I should die like a soldier, but under all the facade of terror I am a civilian.

Thorsten has told me his entire life story, all nineteen years. I feel he has done it one year at a time. I am ready to strangle him.

Bang!

The noise is deafening, the flash painfully blinding.

I can see nothing amidst the jabbering and screaming and moaning.

I finally focus under a flashlight's dim glow. One of the ARVNs has put his M-16 in his mouth and pulled the trigger. His head is splattered about the far wall.

The snakes of his nightmares have consumed him.

I wonder how long it will take the rest of us to be consumed by our nightmares.

Then I realize that shooting a rifle might be enough noise to penetrate outside.

I tell everyone to cover their ears and put in my earplugs.

Then I fire my M-16 every sixty seconds, muzzle in a beam, for an hour, sixty rounds pile up on the floor.

Then we hear it.

Clank.

Clank.

Clank. It happens every twenty seconds or so.

We scream and cry. Now Thorsten breaks down completely.

"What if it's VC?" he moans. "They'll take us prisoner."

"Why do you say that?"

"They wouldn't rescue us to kill us."

He's right.

I sit back. Eventually a shovel breaks through.

The ARVNS mob the hole, clawing, fighting. I

150

hear a scream I know is not for nothing. It is followed by a gurgling sound, and a flashlight beam shows a third ARVN dead, his throat cut. We presume the throat cutter is one of the first ones out. Five ARVNs survive to exit. Then Thorsten, then me.

It is late afternoon. The top of the hill looks like a trash dump. The advisors' compound was flattened. Everything is demolished. A jeep is on its side, burned out.

"How bad is it?" I ask the first person I see, a Mexican sergeant, Sergeant Vasquez.

"How, what?"

"Up here. How bad is it?"

Vasquez looks blank. "Ah . . . sir . . . I . . . ah . . . dead . . . lotta . . . dead."

I look past him for another face, a face not lost in shock.

A tall, thin sergeant with a bandage on his left arm who is covered with mud and dirt says, "Captain Grimes was the only advisor killed, sir. Lieutenant Colonel Singer was medevaced urgent. So was Bloom and Deutsch. The building collapsed on us. Lieutenant Colonel Singer won't be back. He lost an arm. We had, best we can tell, seven ARVN line ones, three loads o' line twos. Lost count. I think they made a direct hit on a conex full of C-four. I guess you're th' OIC till Lieutenant Colonel Pomeo comes back, sir."

"Thanks, sergeant. Have we requested supplies, radios, a jeep, ammo?"

"We've been too busy diggin' out, sir."

"Roger. And I'm glad you were. Do we have commo now?"

"Yes sir. Over there that jeep radio works."

"Roger. I'll work up a supply requisition."

I get on the radio and call for Captain Johnny East by call sign at Lam Son. He's the only supply type I can get straight answers from.

"We don't have personnel to give you a line by line equipment requisition. Everything above ground except two jeeps and four APCs is about four feet tall. We need a full compliment of radios and generators as priority one, then a complete resupply of the ammo dump, and rations, then equipment to rebuild, and one Mike one-five-one. Got the picture, over?"

"Got it solid Four Alpha. I'll have a slingload on a shithook in . . . oh, six zero minutes with your highest priority, less if I can make it. Over."

"Roger. Thanks, out."

"Four, this is Sandy Magnet Five. Over."

That is Lieutenant Colonel Pomeo.

"Go ahead, Five. Over."

"That's the worst spot report I've ever heard. Where the hell have you been for six hours? Over."

"Five, Four. I've been buried in the TOC since the explosion. We were dug out less than ten minutes ago. Over."

Now I'm seething. The nerve of the son of a bitch.

"Roger. I will shortly be enroute to provide leadership that is lacking on the spot, out."

And fuck you, too, colonel.

After an hour I hear rotor blades *wap-wap waping.*

A Huey arrives with two Cobra escorts. The Huey sits down on the side of the hill.

Something makes me watch it.

The rear of the skids touch first, with the front still in the air. Then out hops an ARVN, General Ti. The chopper pilot is still searching for solid ground, letting the front settle.

Right behind Ti comes Pomeo, but he's six feet four inches tall, while Ti is five foot three. The front settles and a rotor blade takes off the top of Pomeo's head. He crumples and falls, and we run to him.

The ARVN general doesn't even look back.

Pomeo is on the ground facedown, the top of his head has been almost sliced off still attached at the front, it's open, showing brains and blood.

Vasquez turns him over. The expression on Pomeo's face is unbelievable. The word ghastly comes to mind. I look away as Vasquez tries to put his head back together.

The chopper pilot is shutting down. He is dead white, an older WO-3 on his third or fourth tour, horrified by it all and the certain knowledge his career is over.

Vasquez is crying like a baby. I'm too numb to faint or throw up.

I walk to the jeep with the radio.

"Sandy Magnet, this is Foxfire Four Alpha. Over."

"Foxfire Four Alpha, Magnet control. Over."

Sandy Magnet, Foxfire Four. Spot report. Over."

"Prepared to copy. Over."

"Roger. Accident to Uniform Hotel enroute. Magnet Five is line one. Over."

"Roger, wait . . . out."

I can imagine the chaos at Lam Son. There is silence for a good five minutes. Then I hear Colonel

153

Norman's voice.

"Foxfire Four, this is Magnet Six. Over."

"Magnet Six, this is Foxfire Four. Over."

"This is Six. If you can within security, tell me exactly what happened. Over."

"Roger Six. The Uniform Hotel One landed on bumpy terrain on the hillside because there's a burned out jeep in the Hotel pad. Five's counterpart got out before the cho—ah, Hotel was settled. Five followed and walked into the rotor blade. Over."

More silence. I have a vivid imagination. I can see the scene at the TOC.

"Oh, my God . . . ah . . . I understand you are Sierra Oscar. Over."

Sierra Oscar—oh, senior officer.

"Roger. Over."

"Roger. There must be an inquest. I will send another Hotel for Five. An Oscar Four will be aboard to relieve you. Over."

"Roger. Over."

"Six, out."

The supply Chinook arrives first, with radios and small arms and mortar ammo. Another one with 105 mm ammo for the artillery is next. Then Major Lawlor from HQ arrives with Captain Fitch and three first lieutenants I don't know. Johnny East is on board, too.

I report to Lawlor.

He returns my salute contemptuously.

"Real featherfuck you've got here, Harris. Got anything to add to the briefing I got from Colonel Norman with all the casualty and damage reports?"

154

"We still need some illum for both the mortars and the one-oh-fives before dark."

"Hear that, East?"

"Yes, sir. One more bird is coming with that."

"Good. In that case, Harris, get on board so we can get that chopper out of here."

"Sir?"

"You're going to Lam Son. Get aboard."

"Why, sir?"

"It's Christmas eve, dummy. You get to spend the night in Lam Son. Go."

I do not have to be told again.

In Lam Son I take a luxurious hot shower and get my ragged fatigues washed, starched, and pressed. I wear some drawn from supply in the meantime, with pinned on rank borrowed from East.

We have a reunion with Jack Daniels in the O. Club after he gives up for the day.

The place is very subdued due to the two deaths and one crippling. But Norman doesn't cancel the planned Christmas party.

"Ya know, Jerry," Johnny says, sipping Black Jack as if he got it every night, "we fucked up."

"How?"

"We shoulda gotten orders for January arrival in Nam. Everybody who came here last January is home in the great U.S. of A. getting pussy and good food."

"No shit?"

"No shit. Drops up to fifty days to get the boys home by Christmas. This is my second Christmas here."

"Yeah?"

"Yeah. Sixty-seven. Brand new silver bar—armor. Got a tank platoon in the three-quarter cav. Spent eleven months in the bush. No rotation to the rear, no nuthin'. Field work. You know what I got for it?"

"What?"

"Nuthin'. When I got on the plane and sat down, next to me was a captain with three rows of ribbons. Gee, I thought. Must be a real hero. I asked him how he got so many. I had my one row, the three everybody gets. I thought here was Audie Murphy. Turned out he was a troop leader for Eleventh ACR. He said if you get a troop the air medal and CIB are automatic, so's a Silver Star. Troop leaders were written for a Silver Star or a DSC if they got a good body count and didn't fuck up. Shit."

"Figures. Colonel Patton's glory brigade."

"Yeah. I saw Patton. Wore his father's ivory-handled Colt .45s. Every afternoon, from five to six Patton wasn't to be disturbed. He was hunting."

"Hunting?"

"Yeah. Took a Huey with twin M-60s mounted on the right and hunted dinks. He lost three aides doing it. When they found one dink at a tunnel once, for example, they landed to get him out when he dived in to avoid the twin sixties. The lieutenant tried to protect Patton and went into the tunnel with his .45. *Zap.* But Patton did give out medals!"

We talk about anything but the actions at Bo Duc. He talks about his wife. The pictures of her he shows don't look too appetizing. I wonder how she's handled two goddamned tours with her man gone. Even unappetizing women can get laid if they want to.

They have an R and R coming up in January. Johnny will be here two months after I'm gone, but he get's R and R two months ahead of me, an advantage of being in the rear. Of course, there are ways to speed it up, such as make a trip to Saigon and drop a K-54 pistol casually on the R and R clerk's desk. I have a feeling when/if I get home, and I see some vet with a K-54, I'll know he was an R and R clerk, and I'll punch him out.

I get quietly drunk and sleep on clean sheets in a safe bunk dreaming of brains and snakes and wake up in a cold sweat at three A.M.

25 December 1969

At oh-seven hundred I can't sleep. I go to breakfast. Johnny's there, and he asks me if I want to go to Lai Khe to see Bob Hope. I grab my cleaned fatigues and jump into the jeep. Johnny has filled it with field troops, SP-4 Rodriguez, Sergeant Oliver, SP-4 Hatten, Sergeant Havlicek, and me. Johnny has a fondness for E.M. He used to be one, and he's a good officer. He could have filled the jeep with REMFs and no one would have said anything.

Johnny is all right.

We drive up to Lai Khe and are stopped by an MP roadblock south of the compound.

A very sharply dressed MP comes to the driver's side.

"State your business."

"State your business, sir," says Johnny quietly.

"Sir."

"We're going to see Bob Hope."

"Sir, I can't let you in."

"Why not, trooper."

"My orders are to allow in only soldiers who are

properly dressed. Those men with you are not properly dressed."

"Bring us your C.O. soldier."

"I can't do that, sir. I have my orders."

"Son, you're trying to keep these field troopers from getting one day off to see Bob Hope. You get to stay in this luxury base damn near every night. They get one night a month out of the boonies if they're lucky. Now either get me your C.O. or let us pass."

"I'll call Major Zabrieski. Wait here, sir."

Ten minutes later a jeep screeches to a halt. An MP major jumps out, dressed to the nines, crisply starched fatigues, mirror spitshined, no, patent leather jump boots—no jump wings to show he's earned them, though—patent leather cop gear, holster, etc., very fancy.

He strides over and says to us, "Get that raggedy ass jeep and these raggedy ass troops outta here!"

"On what grounds—sir?" I ask, my back up.

"You're a disgrace to the uniform, ah . . . captain."

"Well, gee, *sir*, I've been fighting the fucking war. So have these *raggedy ass* men. You want to give me a D.R. for fighting the fucking war, *Sir*?"

"I'll D.R. your ass to the brig, each of you." Incredibly his hand is on his holster. He has unsnapped the flap in preparation for drawing the weapon. "We're not going to let yardbirds like you show up on television and disgrace the Big Red One."

By now Johnny is trying to get me back into the jeep.

"Let's go, Jerry. Fuck him, fuck Bob Hope. It ain't worth it."

I start to protest, then he catches me just right.

"Yeah. You're right. Fuck the Big Red One and all the MPs ever whelped."

So we spend Christmas at Lam Son. The turkey is okay, and no one complains about our raggedy ass uniforms there. Another truckload of E.M. is turned back, too.

Fortunately we don't have to stand inspection to use the pool at Lam Son.

Merry Christmas, advisors.

Peace on earth, good will toward men.

My Dearest Darling,

You'll be getting this around Christmas. I hope and pray you'll be happy and well at Christmas.

Your grandmother has been moved back to the hospital from the nursing home. She suffers from emphysema and congestive heart failure. It will get worse. How long it will take they cannot say. Please try to come home while she can still see you.

Love Always and All ways,

Carole

26 December 1969 — 1 February 1970

I'm back on that accursed Dong Xoai — Song Be road. I'm at FSB Mary at first, with one company of infantry and one troop of Fourteenth ARVN Armored Cav. and a U.S. artillery company and the headquarters for an infantry battalion, both from First Cav. I get a small bunker to myself between the U.S. command bunker and Trung Uy Tuy's bunker. We do the same work as before, set up road security along the road every day and protect convoys. But now we have a much greater load of bullshit to haul around because of the American unit.

Problem one: The ARVN troops realize that there are a lot of horny G.I.s on the FSB. They also realize that they have wives and girlfriends of their own. Then Tien tells them that since they're in a static location after much combat, they can bring up their families if they like.

Shortly thereafter the VD rate in the U.S. units goes sky high. The ARVNs have brought their wives and girlfriends and rented them out to G.I.s.

I find myself standing before the infantry lieutenant colonel and artillery captain and getting the third degree.

"Why in God's name did you allow those women on base?"

"I'm neither the base commander or the unit commander. I have no control over the ARVN women. Try asking the battalion commander, sir."

"I'll ask your commander, captain, unless you get these straightened out immediately, you insurbordinate twerp."

"Well, sir, his name is Major Andrews. His call sign is Tiny Guano Six, and he's on forty-four-seventy-five. If he can get those women out of here, more power to him."

"They're your troops," said the captain.

"It's your troops who are getting VD, captain. If you can't control them, how on earth do you expect me to control the wives of troops I have no command authority over?"

"Captain Harris, if I told my men that they would have a one hundred percent certainty of going to the LBJ for getting a piece of ass, they would still go right ahead and get it."

"Outstanding troops, captain. True models of American youth. But what the hell do you think I can do to ARVN troops if you can't even command American troops?"

"That's enough, Harris. I'll speak to your commanding officer. I'm sure he'll straighten you out."

He sure does. He can't get the women moved, either. The ARVN battalion commander tells him to get fucked. So Lieutenant Colonel Pride gets involved and goes to the regimental C.O., who tells him to get fucked.

The problem, of course, is that the ARVNs, their wives/girlfriends, and the G.I.s just want to get fucked.

The U.S. lieutenant colonel has another solution. He sends his troops searching the ARVN bunkers looking for Americans. This does not rank as one of the great military decisions of all time. I live in an ARVN bunker. One of his men bursts into my bunker at oh-two hundred one morning with a flashlight in his hand. I sleep with a .45 under my pillow, hammer down, safety off, and it comes out before I awake, cocked by instinct. Two feet at instinct shooting range, and I point it at the light, thinking it is a VC attack. The ARVNs know to call to me from outside the bunker. Then when I grunt something, they come in. I don't go into Tuy's bunker without getting his attention first. The .45 is aimed at the center of the trooper's chest. The only thing that keeps him alive is that he says, "What the fuck!"

Now I know he's an American. Till now I was just scared shitless. Now I'm terrified.

"Get outta here!"

"What! An American in here? What did you do? Come with me! You're not supposed to be here!"

"Troop, I'm Captain Harris. This is my bunker. I just nearly shot you. Consider yourself the luckiest man in the world and get out of here."

Now I'm shaking like a leaf.

I sit there and get my wits about me. I realize I've almost killed an American, the worst possible thing that could befall me, worse than getting killed, captured, or crippled. I'm so shaken I vomit outside the bunker. I realize that if I've nearly shot one of them, the ARVNs probably will. Tuy intercepts me on the way to the U.S. command bunker.

"Dai-Uy, Dai-Uy. You must stop. Americans coming my bunkers! Very dangerous."

"I know, Trung Uy. I know. I'll take care of it."

I go into the command bunker, pushing aside the guard and waking the lieutenant colonel.

"Colonel, if you don't call your troops off, one of my ARVNs is likely to kill one of them."

"What the hell are you doing in here, Captain?"

"I'm trying to save your men's lives, keep us from having an incident that'll destroy your career."

"If your troops shoot any of mine, I'll—"

"It'll be too late then. Now, goddamn it, Colonel, I nearly shot one myself when one of them burst in on me. I'm no more trigger-happy than the troops are."

A burst of M-16 fire punctuates my words. The lieutenant colonel runs outside. I follow. We run to where the firing took place. An ARVN is holding an M-16 on a G.I. I don't see any bodies.

The ARVN tells me in Vietnamese that the G.I. came into his hooch, and he fired a burst over his head. At least that's what I think he tells me. He could be telling me what a fine weapon the M-16 is. He's talking very fast, and I listen very slowly. But no one is lying in a pool of blood.

"We lucked out, Colonel. Call 'em off."

"I'll call 'em off, Captain. But I want you to transfer to my unit."

"Why, sir?"

"So I can write your efficiency report and fuck up your career."

"You know, sir, I'd take an adverse OER to command a U.S. unit. I'd take worse."

"Really?"

"Really, and sir."

"Yes."

"I really don't give a shit about OERs. This is not my career."

"That's good, Captain, because you're lousy at it."

"Yes sir, I know. Nothing I ever encountered prepared me for living with these people. I can't get them to do what I advise for shit. I don't understand them no matter how hard I try. I have to trust my life to people I couldn't possibly trust with my wallet. I'm terrified that these incompetents are going to kill me or one of my advisors by accident or in a fit of rage. If you want to see me punished, just watch me in this job. I don't think there's a worse job in the U.S. Army."

Problem two: Tanks. I find the artillery C.O. firing the 105 at minimum elevation, hitting stuff three hundred meters away.

"Whatcha doin'?"

"Sighting in armor piercing at point-blank range. We heard there are NVA tanks in the area. We want to be ready for them."

"Great. But they won't come here."

"Why not?"

" 'Cause we've got tanks and artillery. If you only had a few tanks where would you hit?"

"Some place without antitank defenses."

"In other words, anyplace but here."

"Right."

"I wish they would come here with tanks. They make nice big targets. It's the sappers I hate."

No tanks hit us.

Problem three: malaria, FUO, or whatever.

I get a fever and the runs. We have artillery going off making earthshaking noises every so often, and I have rats in my bunker. I hallucinate giant rats. The noises reverberate in my brain. I have horrible hallucinations/nightmares/whatever. I really feel terrible. After a couple of days I stagger to the U.S. medic's hooch, and he puts me on a helicopter to Song Be. While I'm there the fever breaks, and I recover in twenty-four hours, not sure what it is. One doctor thinks malaria, one thinks FUO.

A helicopter brings in a load of wounded. One is an ARVN shot in the head. It's interesting. An AK hit him in the helmet. The round went through the helmet, skimmed the top of his skull, and went out the back. He's holding the helmet as though it's a long-lost child. One of the doctors thinks his skull may be fractured, so they do X-rays.

Problem four: Nightly briefings. Every night the lieutenant colonel has to have his staff brief him. I glean such gems as:

"The sniping team made contact last night at thirteen-thirty. Three targets were sighted. SP-four Harver fired twenty rounds. Results were unknown. A search revealed no blood trails, no bodies.

"A real Annie Oakley, is he?" says a captain in the back row.

Every night one captain's sole function seems to be to tell the lieutenant colonel how much moon was out

168

the night before and will be out tonight. In true military form it's classified in percentages: one hundred percent, ninety-seven percent, zero percent, etc.

Apparently the lieutenant colonel can't tell if the moon's out by looking.

Problem five: The latrines. FSB Mary is U.S. built, so it has U.S.-style latrines, about like old-style outdoor toilets. ARVNs don't sit down, they squat over a hole in the ones they build. So they squat over the holes in the U.S.-built one — and miss. So when we G.I.s go in to use it, shit is all over the latrine. It gives one a great love for ARVNs. Some of the G.I.s threaten to shoot any ARVNs squatting on the toilet seat. I don't blame them. I agree — myself having cleaned up one time too many. But none of us catches an ARVN in the latrines.

Problem six: American G.I.s call ARVNs gooks, which they understand and take offense to. This causes problems when I tell G.I.s not to call them gooks. Two G.I.s are about to see how many teeth they can knock out one night because there's no rank on my T-shirt (of course).

Fortunately I explain that such an action, no matter how justified, will bring adverse consequences.

What the ARVNs call the Americans, the G.I.s don't understand. *Du ma* means motherfucker. I hear it a lot. I do not offer to translate.

2 – 13 February 1970

I take two companies out on a CA into a clearing in single canopy jungle. Two other companies stay on the goddamned road. I'm the only advisor with the two companies in the deep shit, of course. Why Andrews needs two sergeants with him and no one with me I don't know. Maybe he's lonely. Needless to say my pucker factor is high. If I'm hit no one with me speaks any English, so I won't be medevaced. I can barely converse in Vietnamese, so it's not a whole lot of fun.

One of these bastards has stolen my parachute knife and my Swiss Army knife. The Swiss Army knife was tied to a belt loop on my left side with thirty-six inch-long bootlace from an RSP pack, and the parachute knife was similarly tied to my right side. I'm convinced they could steal a rubber from a man during intercourse.

Our fantastically efficient point man walks into an ambush, and rounds start coming into my area. I hit the dirt and roll behind a tree. John Wayne I will not try to be.

It's all over after twenty or thirty incoming rounds and three or four hundred outgoing. Then we check the area.

There's one blood trail, and seven of my troops are hit. Three, the first three, are dead. I'm fairly convinced the other four were hit with M-16s.

I call for a medevac and a hunter-killer team. It's a difficult medevac because we have to hump the stretchers a couple of clicks to a clearing.

The medevac arrives with a heavy fire team for escort and picks up the wounded without a hitch. We throw the dead in, being sensible enough not to call them in as dead but as wounded. Medevacs pick up wounded, not dead and I don't want the ARVNs to have to carry the dead for three days.

The hunger-killer team searches till their fuel gets low and finds nothing.

At oh-three hundred I'm awakened from a mosquito-infested semi-sleep by a loud bang. Then comes automatic weapons fire.

As things quiet down, I ask Tuy what the hell's going on.

"No sweat. Claymores go off. Back sleep, *Dai-Uy.*"

My back is killing me from sleeping on the ground—no hammocks in this operation.

The next morning we find a bear killed by the claymore. They cut it up and carry it with them. When we get on the helicopters the chopper crew is amazed to see one guy with a bear's head, another with a leg, etc.

The choppers move us to another LZ and drop us. We recon the area, spend the night, and do it again the next day. My pucker factor is at the max. I'm exceedingly tired of being the only American with Trung Uy Tuy's merry band. Of course, Major Andrews doesn't agree, sitting fat, dumb, and happy at battalion HQ.

Now we're doing two CAs a day, coming into an LZ as soon as the morning fog lifts, patrolling all day, and doing another CA an hour before dark, humping like mad for an hour and setting up ambushes just after dark.

I'm a zombie, so damn tired from it it's pathetic.

But I hear myself saying to Tuy, "Let me go with an ambush team tonight."

Why am I doing that?

He says sure, not realizing at first he will be without his radio pipeline to the Seventh Air Force and helicopters all night. My radio stays with him. It's really silly. Dumb. Stupid.

So I sit against a tree, three grenades beside my left hand, the pins opened up so I can pull them easily, my M-16 across my lap, and my big knife at ready. I don't know whether to feel like John Wayne or Woody Allen.

This is ludicrous.

Two ARVNs are with me, equally armed. One controls two claymores.

I hope they can stay awake better than I. I'm freezing cold from the late afternoon's rain.

I doze and awake with a start, a grenade in hand, the pin in my right hand.

173

Something is moving.

My night vision is pretty good.

It is a small deer.

Now I have a live grenade with the pin pulled.

Simple, put the pin back in. But I try and realize the ends of the pin have spread and won't go back without pinching.

Simple, I just pinch them together—

And drop the pin.

Oh shit! I can't move much, or I give away my position from the noise. The two ARVNs might kill me if I do.

I try to feel around for the pin.

Now I'm sweating. I have a fucking live grenade and no pin. Jesus H. Christ.

Where the hell is it?

I think I look for it for an hour.

My left hand is cramping.

If I release the spoon I must throw the grenade. After an hour of sweating tension I wonder if I can throw it twenty feet.

Dare I switch hands?

I decide I must or my fingers will open up in a spasm.

I manage to change hands without killing myself.

I relax my left hand. Jesus it hurts.

I search some more, blind, desperate.

Then I think of the smoke grenade pin stuck in my bush hat. People do that with used pins for some reason. Now I'm beginning to see a reason for it. Frantically I feel for it.

It's there.

It works.

I stick it in and spread the pin ends, shaking and sweating.

Finally I lay the grenade down and relax.

I'm sure the VC can hear my heart beat for ten clicks.

14 February — 7 March 1970

We're back at LZ O'Keefe. It would be semi-dull if it weren't for the pucker factor. I'm going on R and R on 8 March, and every night my nightmares get worse and worse. Tuy and I have a bunker with the cav. C.O., Trung-Uy Huong, a really fine ARVN officer. He and Tuy and I get along fine considering. The cav. advisors have their own bunker. The bunker has rats in it. I jokingly say I sleep with a .45 to protect myself from them. But I'm scared of them. Occasionally one'll get inside my mosquito netting, which I tuck in around my bunk. This sends me into an absolute frenzy. All I need is for one of the little bastards to bite me, causing me to have to get rabies shots for fourteen days and miss R and R. Worse if one bites me, and I don't notice it among the normal jungle sores and boils and such, I could die of rabies, not the best way to go. It happens to too many G.I.s. That sort of thing doesn't even make the papers, not a combat death.

The cav. S.A. is a West Point captain named Darryl Kinsey. His sergeant is Armand Spignatelli, from

New York City. Spignatelli I like. He gets care packages of cheese and sausage and strong Italian wine. He shares.

I get a sergeant, Sergeant First Class Andrew Lincoln, a big black man, overweight, from Vernon, Texas, my mother's hometown. His wife and he are getting a divorce. His R and R is coming up, and he is taking it with his kids to Hawaii. He moves into the rat-infested underground bunker.

Kinsey, in discussing this filthy war says, "I'll make major out of this war. I hope there's another little war like it when I'm up for lieutenant colonel."

This impresses me only negatively. After hearing it I try not to treat him like a pariah, but I can't forget he said it.

8 – 14 March 1970

R and R

The flight to Hawaii via Guam is the happiest bunch of people you'd ever see. The stewardesses are volunteers who have asked for these flights. Their aprons have every imaginable pin of the armed forces, ranks from private, first class to stars, battalion crests, MACV crests, wings, CIBs, you name it. They are very friendly. They think they are doing their patriotic duty.

We are fed steaks, a refreshing change from Cs.

The Hawaii flight is for married men seeing their wives. Other choices, for the bachelors, include Australia, Hong Kong, and Bangkok. The bachelors get maps to the approved whorehouses, and we get our wives. The stop at Guam, ostensibly to refuel, and I'm sure they refuel the bird, is so we can get booze cheaply. I buy a bottle of Jack Daniels and one of champagne. Carole flew over on an R and R discount flight and is waiting for me.

The military can't just let their troops go and enjoy themselves. We are bussed from the airfield to Fort

DeRussey, and the wives meet us there. I'm coming off the bus into a sea of women. I don't see Carole in the sea, but since we come off the bus one man at a time, she sure sees me. I am grabbed from out of nowhere, and she has her arms around me giving me a passionate kiss. She looks fantastic.

A chaplain breaks up all the couples to prevent copulation in the briefing room, and gives us a briefing. I have no idea what he says. I am not paying any attention at all. I doubt anyone is.

We take a courtesy bus to our hotel. Carole has already checked us in.

Her hair is too short, but it's blond, and she's down to fighting weight. Also there's absolutely nothing about her that's Oriental.

Our first order of business leaves our clothes strung between the door and the bed. Fortunately the phrase "use it or lose it" doesn't apply for a man who has done without for eight months. Her body is every bit as warm and lush and desirable as I remembered it on those wet, mosquito-ridden nights in the bush. She is also as passionate and horny and demanding as I remembered. I last longer than I expect, and she leaves claw marks on my back when she comes screaming.

She didn't use to scream.

Then, lying there luxuriating in the splendor of the room, cool air-conditioning, soft bed, soft woman cooing in my ear, a goddamn bar in the room for Christ's sake, a patio with a view of Honolulu, I feel a clock ticking in my head already. It'll all be over in a minute. I'll be back in the mud and the blood and the cordite.

She says something.

"Huh?"

"I said, you're awfully fit. Your back's like iron. I can see and feel every muscle. You working out?"

"Every day."

"You must be in the sun a lot. Your neck's brown."

"Yep. The pool between one and two every day."

I get up and run a bath. I fix a drink while it's filling.

"You didn't use to drink Jack Daniels and water."

"Can't find any good mixers, so I got used to it. Want a bath?"

"Sure. Where are we going to eat tonight?"

"Someplace that sells big steaks—no Chinese food, no Polynesian food."

"Darn. I want some poi. We're going to a luau sometime while we're here, aren't we?"

"No, we're not."

"Jerry! This is our vacation. We can't miss anything. They'll all ask about it at the office."

"Lie to 'em. Bath's ready." I climb in and leave her room to join me. I sit back and sip the Jack Daniels. I close my eyes. There's no sound of artillery in the background. The water's hot. It's heaven. She walks in and steps into the hot water.

"Ooh, it's hot."

"I don't get too many hot baths."

I soap and rinse, then repeat, even lathering up the short hair on my head.

"Good grief, Jerry. You act like Lady MacBeth but with blood over your whole body."

I stop scrubbing and start to blurt out something, knowing she's right, then calm down, saying, "No, dirt, not blood. Red Vietnam dirt. The whole country is dirt and mud."

Before we go out I've bathed twice and showered once. I finally feel clean enough to go out.

I put on the R and R tourist uniform: luau shirt, shorts, sandals. Combined with short hair, sun-weathered skin, and a dogtag chain you're pretty identifiable as a G.I. in this outfit. The smarter shopkeepers think I'm a flier from the Rolex GMT, but the rest think I'm an E-4 because I look nineteen or so, and Carole looks about the same. I retrieve my wedding and college rings from Carole and wear them. They feel funny.

We walk to the International Market Place, only a block from our hotel. It's pure tourist trap, ersatz thatched huts selling souvenirs from the legitimate to T-shirts with "Vietnam, the Edsel of foreign policy" on them. I love it.

I find Don Ho is out of town. To Carole this is an international tragedy. I wonder who the hell is Don Ho. I note that the Colonel's Plantation sells N.Y.-cut steaks by the ounce, so we go in there. The minimum is ten ounces. Carole orders that. I order a twenty ounce N.Y. cut.

"Jerry! You can't eat a twenty ounce steak!"

"Watch me! I haven't had any decent food in months, certainly not a good steak."

Wine is complimentary, a liter at each table, with unlimited refills. The waiter is a bit surprised to have to bring a refill very soon. So is Carole. I have inhaled it.

She's even more surprised when I devour the steak and a huge baked potato before she's half done. I end up finishing hers.

She thinks I've gone food mad.

We walk around the market for a while, in and out of touristy shops. It seems to be open quite late. We have a couple of tropical-type drinks in a nice spot, and two hours later I'm hungry again. I get a hamburger, and Carole wonders aloud who I am. The Jerry she knew never ate this much. But then I've done a lot of things the Jerry she knew never did.

In the semidarkness of the room after more sex I hold her. Her long blond hair drapes over my chest, and the smell of her perfume and her clean hair, blended gently with the smells of after sex, takes me far from the smell of gunpowder and *nuoc mam* and dead bodies decaying in the sun. But why can't I forget them?

The next morning I'm up with the dawn, taking pictures of the sunrise. We have breakfast at a little restaurant on Waikiki that serves such things as papaya juice and exotic fruits. Then we rent a little Toyota, so small it's comical, for the rest of R and R on a fifty-nine dollar, ninety-five cent R and R special. It's dirty, and the last renter smoked too much.

We go from beach to beach, to Hanauma Bay, the most beautiful beach I've ever seen. The water's cold there.

One day we go to Pearl Harbor for the tour to the Arizona Memorial. It depresses Carole to hear about death in another war. I want to go to the Punchbowl Cemetery, but Carole vetoes it, making a scene in the tour bus.

We go to every tourist place and trap except the

Polynesian Village because I want nothing to do with any kind of native villages.

The worst trap seems to be Robert Louis Stevenson's grass hut. That's all it is, a hut. Big deal.

At Paradise Park I balk at the walk through the bamboo forest but do it to keep from alarming Carole. She notices I'm sweating halfway through it and wonders why aloud. A bird bites the hell out of my ring finger in the bird sanctuary because I couldn't get my college ring off before we went in. It's all innocent tourist stuff—sorely needed.

I also need some things to take back to Nam, so we go to the Ala Moana Shopping Center, supposedly the world's largest. I see a knife shop and try to get Carole to go into another shop while I get something there, but she comes in while I'm talking to the clerk and hears an exchange I don't want her to hear.

By the time she comes in behind me unobserved I've picked out a Swiss Army knife with all the bells and whistles on it. But that isn't all I need.

"I need a fighting knife, similar to an army parachute knife."

"I'm not familiar with that knife, sir. We have this parachute knife."

He hands me a knife with a hook blade for cutting lines, but it has no switchblade component.

"Not quite. The one I'm looking for is a switchblade about yea long, hook blade on one end, switchblade fighting blade on the other."

"Sir! Switchblade knives are illegal. What on earth do you need one for?'

"What do you think, asshole? Think I'm planning on purse snatching? I need one to kill small dark men

184

in black pajamas before they kill me."

"Sir?" His eyes are as big as coasters.

"I'm a soldier. I'm going back to Nam in a few days. There's a war on there."

"Well—ah—we, ah, don't sell anything like that here. We have big hunting knives, but no, ah, fighting knives. Do you actually *fight* with knives? Don't they issue you guns?"

"Yes. I carry two. I'm not a hunter. I need the Swiss Army knife for a tool and a defensive knife."

"Well, how about something like this?"

He points to a collection of what I would call fighting knives, but labeled Hunting; bowies and Fairbairnes-Sykes Commando knives, even a Gurka Kukri. None of them will do anything my Camillus won't, but I notice a small boot knife with a three-inch blade and a boot scabbard that is concealable. I buy it and the big Swiss Army knife.

Then I turn around and see Carole. Her eyes are bigger than his. She appears to be in shock. I pay for the knives and go outside, taking her by the arm.

Outside she says, "What in God's name do you need with a—a dagger like that? You've always had a Swiss Army knife, but that's a killer's knife. Tell the truth. You don't have a desk job, do you? You're in perfect shape, tanned, hard as a rock, and you don't relax even in your sleep."

"No, I don't have a desk job."

"Do you kill people with a knife?"

"Not yet."

"Not—but you have killed people."

"There's a war on, darling."

"I know that. Don't get flip. I didn't know I

married a killer. Are you in tanks again?"

"No."

"No. Infantry? Is that why the dirty envelopes? Your letters look filthy half the time."

"Yes. I live in the bush with Vietnamese. I get to the rear every couple of months. I had a desk job but couldn't hack it."

"You—you—you lying son of a bitch. You said you were a G something or other in the rear."

I say nothing. I just walk toward the elevator. She walks along berating me for not telling her, for writing cheerful letters. She's still at it when we get to the top and step off at the revolving restaurant.

"Do you want to talk about it?" she asks. For a girl in Mensa she's not too bright at times.

"Yes. I flew all the way from Saigon after a day's traveling to get there just so I can talk about the goddamned war and killing dinks. I live for the day I can stand up in front of the auditorium at Texas City High School and tell 'em all how it feels to fight for your fuckin' life."

A patron in the next booth, a man in his forties, leans over and says, "Sonny, we don' use language like that in here."

In my best command voice I say, in a cold rage, "Get back in your seat and mind your own fuckin' business or I'll teach you how I feel about a fuckin' civilian calling me sonny after I've spent eight months in a fucking jungle fighting for you so you're not there yourself, so you can watch us get our asses shot off on the six o'clock news. Got it, motherfucker? Or would you like for me to show you the way?"

He gulps and sits back in his booth. Then he and

his companion leave, their drinks unfinished. He is still very white.

"That was barbaric. You're mad at me and took it out on that poor man."

"Fuck him. I haven't been in a Rotary Club picnic, you know, and nobody who wasn't there gives a shit or even knows what the fuck's going on. That asshole will go home, watch Walter Cronkite talk about the light casualties we had today, and when some G.I. comes into his store, he'll charge him double and tell him he should have gone to Canada, or tell him he was in a real war, not this stinking mess."

Lunch, a very fresh seafood salad, is delicious despite a lack of conversation from Carole. Finally she starts talking about the view from the revolving restaurant, which in fantastic.

She avoids the subject of what I do until, unfortunately, late that night after the sex is done with and I'm lying on my back in semidarkness sipping Black Jack and ice, with one arm around her. She says, "What's killing like? Do you enjoy it?"

What the fuck kind of question is that? "Much more than the alternative."

"What alternative?"

"Dying."

Some places offer R and R discounts. Some overcharge soldiers. Some blatantly don't want our business. I hear comments about "crude, rude soldiers need to get back on some army post where the Military Police can control them." Just what I need to hear.

Every third man on the streets and in the shops is obviously on R and R, but when I ask for an R and R discount at one place the girl says, "R and R? What's that?"

Three banks won't cash my Vietnam-issued money orders, a common brand. Finally I give up and sign them over to Carole, letting her take them home with her to deposit in our bank, using Master Charge and her traveler's checks. They take them everywhere. It's ridiculous.

One day we take the sunset cruise on the pink catamaran, *Ali Ali Kai*. The meal on the boat is chicken and rice. I'm almost sick. Carole doesn't understand why. I shut up and eat.

I manage, one evening, from Fort De Russy Beach, a telephoto shot of a 707 cutting through the setting sun. I tell Carole to send me a copy of that photo when I see the slide of it at the six hour photo store the next day.

"Why?"

"For the same reason I want the pictures of you. So I can dream."

The Kodak Hula Show, basically one picture-taking opportunity after another, especially for those of us with telephoto lenses, is a high point for a while. Then the emcee mentions a lot of the audience is men on R and R and asks us to stand up.

We do, several thin, tanned young men with short hair, usually urged up by our wives. Several blacks are standing, too.

There is light applause. Then it grows. Then we sit down.

The man next to me, seeing two Pentaxes and five

lenses, says, "Are you a professional photographer in Vietnam?"

"Yes," I say, eyeing him levelly. "I shoot the enemy."

Finally the six days and five nights draw to a close. I'm convinced it was six minutes, not six days.

For the last night I buy a tie and make reservations at Michels, a fancy restaurant on the water between Diamond Head and Waikiki.

The maitre d' pays no attention to me. I have to get his attention almost violently to get in, despite the reservations. Then we're shunted to the bar long enough for us to enrich the bartender before we're shown to a nice table by the water's edge.

Next to us is a foursome celebrating the birthday of a black-haired woman in her thirties. I look around. I am, by far, the youngest man there. Thirty-five must be the normal minimum age of admission; or maybe it just takes that long to make enough money to afford the place. Of course the women range from eighteen up, from spectacular to awful.

Carole is the most spectacular, in a low-cut dress with a pushup bra, giving her enough cleavage to lose me in for minutes at a time.

I order the most expensive thing on the menu for two: steaks, of course, no chicken, and a good (expensive) wine, a Chateauneuf du Pape.

The foursome seems to be eyeing us. Finally they have a birthday cake over for the black-haired woman. They invite us to join them. Then I discover why they've been eyeing us.

"Are you on vacation?" they ask.

"R and R."

"What's R and R?"

"Rest and Relaxation, also known as I and I, Intercourse and Intoxication. Five nights and six days out of the war."

"War? What war?"

"Vietnam. Don't they talk about it at home? I thought it was in all the papers."

"Oh. Yes. My Lai. Tet. Napalming kids. War crimes against Vietnamese," says the birthday lady.

"That's the one," I say coldly. "I'm going back tomorrow. I'll try to napalm a kid for you."

"How does a soldier pay for R and R?" asks the man who invited us to join them.

That's it. They couldn't figure out how someone as young as I can pay for this.

"We get R and R discounts."

"But still. Isn't combat pay just sixty-five dollars a month?"

"Yes, but bullets are free. I have to pay for my own napalm, though. That's 'cause it's so much fun makin' crispy critters out of little kids. Anyway, a captain makes about twelve thou a year for napalming kids — before expenses," I say.

"Blood money," says birthday lady.

"You're a captain? But you're so young!"

"Yeah, there aren't too many old captains left."

I can hear birthday bitch's teeth clamp shut.

"Is it dangerous what you do?"

"Yeah, those kids carry AK-forty-sevens."

The waiter comes by with our bill. The guy asks if he's going to give us an R and R discount.

He says, "No, sir. Usually we give a couple of free drinks, though."

"Fine we'll take two *Mai Tais*."

The waiter calls the maitre d'. We get two *Mai Tais*.

I hold Carole tight all night. I don't want to let her go.

We dress in near silence, breakfast in near silence, and drive to the airport in near silence. Tears fill Carole's eyes, and she breaks into tears whenever she talks.

I'm not much better. Talking is difficult.

I'm scared.

She starts to talk then. "You be careful. I want you to come back. Come back any way you can. Don't try to be a hero. You'll be my hero if you just come home."

The steps up to the door of the 707 are higher than any hill in ranger school. Going aboard takes more courage than assaulting a machine gun nest.

I stare at her all the way up. I get a window seat and stare out the window at her. She watches the plane pull away till I can't see her anymore. Getting on that plane is the bravest thing I've ever done. I know I'll never see her again. I am a prisoner who has just walked up the gallows steps.

15 – 16 March 1970

We land at TSN in late afternoon. The liaison sergeant for Team Seventy picks me up in a Jeep. He has another captain leaving on R and R tomorrow. He knows the last chopper has left for Lai Khe (the team moved there in February). So I'll have to spend the night.

"Fine, MACV BOQ is okay," I say.

"Ah, you don't want to stay there, sir. Filthy place. Got roaches. I'll put you in a nice hotel and pick you up in the morning." He gives me a conspiratorial wink.

"Fine, but no whorehouses."

He gives me a strange look. He turns to Captain Yates, the captain going on R and R in the morning.

"Wherever. I don't care as long as I get on the plane in the morning," he says.

So he takes us to the Star Hill. It's next to BOQ number two, and the sergeant mentions American food is for sale in the snack bar at BOQ number two. Since I'm unarmed, I don't want to go very far anyway.

When we pull up to the Star Hill ten young women come to meet us.

"Sergeant, this is quite obviously a whorehouse."

"All the hotels have whores, sir."

"Thrill."

"You got somethin' against women, sir?"

"Not a thing, just whores."

The girl who takes my B-4 bag says, "Tonight, I be your gi'l."

"You'll never get rich that way."

God, she's ugly.

The first floor has a bar. It's full of drunken helicopter pilots and whores. I let the girl put my bag in my room and shoe her away.

At dusk I go over to BOQ number two. They have a bar and grill upstairs. I get a burger and fries and a beer.

Then I see Maj. George Kronsen come in. Major Kronsen is an Air Force intelligence major I knew in England. He sees me and joins me, smiling.

Kronsen is on his third Vietnam tour. He takes a tour in Nam, one away, and volunteers to come back. All three tours were voluntary. Of course, were I he, working as he does, I would stay here till the war ended. He works in Seventh Air Force HQ behind a desk in an air-conditioned room. Kronsen is gay, so he has no family to leave.

We discuss old times, old friends, and old acquaintances. He asks what I do and says, "You're not on one of those LRRP teams, are you?"

"No."

"Good. I saw 'em bring one of those teams in to TSN after a long time in the bush. They acted like

194

animals, smelled, wolfed down steaks."

"They don't have a nice, civilized job. What do you do?"

"Targeting. Same as in Europe. It's useless, though. Every time I come up with a decent target, they veto it. You can't hit that, you'll kill somebody. It's pathetic. They've competely emasculated us. When I was here before, at least, I could target some real targets. It's pathetic now. Too afraid of world opinion. The anti-war people. I tell you. I don't want to go home now. They tie our hands and cut our throats and call us murderers."

"Yeah."

"Where are you staying?"

"Star Hill next door."

His eyes grow wide. "That's a—a brothel, you know."

It's not often I hear someone say the word "brothel."

"No, George, it's a whorehouse."

"Oh. W-what's it like wi—with a prostitute?"

"I don't know. I'm unlikely to find out. I just had enough sex for three men for a month. Now if I were not just coming back from R and R I might find out."

We talk till curfew, and I return to the Star Hill.

The ugly whore meets me on the stairs. I guess she didn't get lucky in the bar, or maybe she got lucky thirteen times, and they're all passed out with smiles on their faces all over the hotel, I don't know. "I be you' gi'l now? Sho't time, long time, much boom-boom."

"No, thanks."

"You no like Ly? You wan' 'notha gi'l? I get 'notha gi'l."

"No, thanks. I don't want a girl."

"No? Oh you wan' boy? I get boy."

"No! No boy!"

"What you wan' then?"

"How about a horse?"

While she figures that out I get inside and lock the door.

I soon hear in the next room noises that indicate that Yates couldn't wait to meet his wife. I wonder how he'll explain giving her VD.

The next morning I fly to Lai Khe. Fortunately I miss the work chopper to FSB Mary, so I have to spend the night in Lai Khe.

Pride is there and sees me at the O club that night when he comes in to get his toddy.

I suppose Pride could be a human being if he loosened up thirty thousand percent. He talks about his R and R to Australia, the women he met and the pubs he crawled. I'm quietly stunned. Then he mentions he's ordered a Boss 302 Mustang from the PX for delivery when he returns to the U.S. This floors me. His clone, Major Andrews berated me for reading *Road & Track* because it's immature to be a car nut.

"Too bad you missed it, Harris."

"What, sir?"

"The big firefight."

"What happened?"

"Body count of a hundred and twenty-five!"

"How many did we lose?"

"A few. Doesn't matter. Caught 'em ambushing a

convoy at the intersection near Bunard. Napalmed the bastards. Lost ten semis, though. Several truck drivers."

"Jesus Christ!"

"You shoulda been there."

I'm awfully glad I wasn't.

Dearest Jerry,

I guess you'll be getting this after R and R. I'm so looking forward to it. It keeps me going when I'm down to know we'll be together soon. I see the war every evening on the six o'clock news, and it's so awful. I don't know how those men can do it, go out and hunt for human beings like they were animals. I'm so glad you have an honorable job behind a desk.

All my love,
Carole

17 March 1970

The road has six destroyed semis along it with the loads unattended to, boxes of .50 cal. ammo strewn about, burned-out cabs.

The hundred and twenty-five NVA are being buried with a bulldozer when I get back. The smell is unbelievable.

Lieutenant Colonel Pride accompanies me to Bunard. Then he tells me to take the chopper to Song Be to pick up a body. I grab Sergeant Binh, the interpreter, and we go.

One of our ARVN troops died in the Song Be ARVN Hospital.

We stop there and ask for the body. A Vietnamese nurse takes us to a building behind the hot, stinking hospitals.

It is a building of nightmares. Bodies lie on stretchers covered with ponchos. Flies buzz, and the smell is of putrification.

The nurse won't go in. She says it's the third one on the left. The interpreter balks. He won't go in either.

He says, "It's haunted."

"Orders, Trung Chi. We must."

"No, *Dai-Uy*. Haunted."

"Trung Chi. We must bring this body back, and I can't carry it myself. You must help. You knew that when you came."

"No! I no carry."

I unsnap the .45 and pull it out, leveling it at him.

"Inside, Trung Chi."

I hold the door open for him.

He curses violently in Vietnamese and shakes his head, but he goes in. Inside he says, "No," again.

"Trung Chi, if I can't carry the body back, I'll have to blame someone. I'll blame you and leave your body with his."

I'm bluffing, of course, but he picks it up. We carry it to the chopper and put it on.

When the chopper gets airborne the stretcher shifts, and I have to grab it to keep it from falling out. The poncho blows open, revealing decomposing, distended guts about three inches from my nose. I close it frantically and gag. The world swims for a few minutes, and I'm near to vomiting.

Finally we land, and two ARVNs take the body.

I walk to Pride.

"Sir, don't ever tell me to escort a body like that again."

"You giving me orders now, Harris?"

"Please."

"That's better."

Later Andrews asks me why I said that.

"If he does I'll blow his fuckin' head off."

18 March — 5 April 1970

I move back to FSB Mary, Tuy's company is there, along with a squadron of Fourteenth ARVN Cav. Spignatelli and Kinsey are there. The U.S. units have gone.

Spignatelli, Kinsey, and their interpreter have the old U.S. command bunker to themselves. I move in with them.

The command bunker is T-shaped with the entrance at the left side of the top bar. A fence surrounds the bunker, with a bit of a maze to get in. You have to go to your right, find a gap in the overlapping fence, go left, and go right again, then go left into the bunker, through a blackout blanket, and right again. Now you're inside the old briefing room. It has a door on each far side. Each leads into the main room. Spignatelli and Kinsey are bunking opposite the first door. I go to the bottom of the T and set up a cot and mosquito netting. The right side of the T-bar, the old lieutenant colonel quarters, houses the interpreter, a little friendly Vietamese named Phuoc. Yes, it's pronounced close to fuck.

A small, high window is just down the wall from that room, providing the only outside light.

Behind the bunker is an outhouse that I can keep ARVNs away from. They don't come into the inner fence unless we want them to.

FSB Mary is, in short, heaven for an advisor. I'm getting very tired of the road, though. Every day we put out road security. Then once a week or so we do a CA looking for the NVA. Of course, the NVA find us when they want to, not vice versa.

On some nights we have surprise Mad Minute. Sixty seconds of firing every weapon on a three hundred sixty degree basis, just in case someone's sneaking around. It usually scares the shit out of me.

I'm approaching one hundred hours CA time in helicopters and not the least anxious to try for two hundred. At one hundred hours you get an air medal. At two hundred they give your widow your posthumous second award.

Andrews goes on R and R. During the eight days he's gone I spend twenty-three hours in C and C choppers. When a convoy comes, I go up in a loach and try to locate trouble spots.

When the shit hits the fan, I have Casper Milquetoast for a pilot.

B-40s hit two trucks, and I tell him to head for the spot. He pulls up to four thousand feet. I cannot control from four thousand feet, but I can't get him to go any lower. We're above the F-100s, for Christ's sake.

The F-100s napalm three NVA into crispy critter condition. The transportation company loses two trucks and three men. Hell of a trade.

I complain to the helicopter company about their pilot.

The C.O., a Major Zariecki, comes down the next day to see me.

"I received your complaint, Captain. What you have charged usually results in a court-martial. Do you want that?"

"No, sir. I just want a helicopter pilot that will help me do my job. If I can't do it because I can't see, men die. From four thousand feet I can't do my job. I can't make excuses to my C.O. for failing. You know that, though. I'm sure you don't take any excuses. It doesn't matter, though. When we get ambushed, people die."

"I understand. You're one of those gung-ho, aggressive grandstand types, Harris. But Lieutenant Hebb is very short. He's going home next week. He has stopped being aggressive. You can understand that, can't you?"

"No problem, sir, and nobody's ever called me a gung-ho, aggressive grandstand type before — or probably ever will again, but I take those convoys seriously."

"Okay, so do I. I'll make sure your unit gets an aggressive pilot next time. Okay?"

"Fine, sir."

"Is that enough for you to drop this matter?"

"More than enough."

Of course, he sends a WO-1 whose mission is obviously to scare the living hell out of me. He zooms from zero feet to two thousand feet, dives back, circles, rocks. The chopper isn't stable the entire time I'm in it. I manage to avoid losing my lunch, but not

203

by much.

When Major Andrews returns, they send him the same stick jockey, and Andrews barfs all over the cockpit.

One day Andrews sends for Hatten and me to come to his location at Bunard for a special assignment.

We take the jeep and drive down. When we get there, I say, "Okay, sir, what's the big assignment?"

"Well, I'm by myself for the rest of the week, and that half-barrel needs burning." He points to the half-fifty-five gallon drum in the latrine. It is full of shit and maggots. Really lovely, it's indescribable.

"There's the diesel fuel. Take it outside the berm and go to it."

"Are you serious, sir?"

"That's right, Captain. In an advisory team officers have to work like everybody else. Take the shit out of the berm and burn it. Then bring it back here. Got that, Captain?"

"Yes, sir," I say, the anger at a danger level. "Got it."

The half-fifty-five gallon drum is heavy for two, and the contents smell horrible and swim with maggots. Flies engulf us. We get the disgusting package outside the berm and pour diesel fuel on it. We can't get it to light. We try matches, then we stick in lighted pieces of paper. Nothing works. Then Andrews comes by and says, casually, "Pour some gasoline on top. Everybody knows you can't get diesel to light easily."

"Sorry, I'm not an expert at burning shit," I say where he can hear me. When he gets out of earshot, under my breath, I add, "I'd give my right nut to be

204

able to stuff his face in this barrel."

Finally we get it lit and go inside Andrews' squad tent to watch the smoke rise. Andrews is drinking a beer while we work. The smell from the burning is as unforgettable as it is unbelievable.

"Why don't you two take the jeep and drive down the road to O'Keefe and check the deployment of the troops?"

"Yes, sir."

As soon as we get out of sight, I say, trying to calm myself down, "We'll go on to Dong Xoai, get a couple of Beer thirty-threes and a block of ice."

"Hey, great, but won't that piss off the major?"

"If so, he'll be pissed at me. That's the advantage of being a SP-four when there's a captain along."

"Right."

"Anyway, I'm pretty pissed off myself at him. Fuck it. It don't mean nothin'."

We drive fairly quickly, but still slow enough to check on the deployment of the troops, most of whom seem to be on a church picnic.

We get a couple of quick beers in Dong Xoai and dicker with the icehouse over the price of a block of ice. It ends up costing five dollars. I'm sure an ARVN would've gotten it for two, assuming he didn't just stick an M-16 in the guy's mouth and take the ice. We throw it in the back of the jeep and start driving back.

"My girl's started writing me again, Captain. Got three letters last bundle."

"Great. Why'd she stop?"

"Said she was bored waiting for me and not going out. Said she went out a couple of times and felt guilty, me being ten thousand miles away and suffering for my country. She didn't once call me a baby killer."

"You're lucky. Half the mail to A.P.O.s starts out, 'Dear John.' "

"Yeah, I guess so. I'm glad she's waiting, but I don't know if I'm just horny, or if I love her."

"Well, I wouldn't get married the day I return, then, if I were you. I'd just shack up a while."

"Did you do that?"

"Fuck, no. Carole was a good Catholic girl, or at least her mother thought she was. We'd been to bed together, but we couldn't live together. That was a no-no. Her mother wouldn't allow it. She didn't even want me to marry her daughter because I wasn't Catholic."

"Well, I've been saving my money. I think I'll extend for six months, save the money, and I'll be short enough then for an early out. Then I'll find me a nicely restored fifty-seven T-bird, grab Connie away from her parents for a week or two and disappear away to a little white beach. I'll worry about marriage later."

"Sounds good to me. But you couldn't get me to extend for this place for a month with the Dallas Cowboys Cheerleaders."

"I can understand that. Look at that. There's a snake in the road."

"Big sucker. Run over it."

"Ah, Captain, it's just a harmless ol' snake. I can't hurt it." He dodges to the right and slows down drastically. The snake is crossing from left to right. When we get close to it, it rears up and arches its head. It's a cobra. In a split second, faster than I can believe, it strikes in panic at the jeep and digs into Hatten's exposed shoulder. He screams and loses control of the jeep. It slides off the road into the ditch, tips, but doesn't roll over. In total panic I grab the hand brake and turn off the ignition. The snake is in the goddamned jeep! It's stuck for a while to Hatten's shoulder by its fangs, then strikes Hatten again and again, totally freaked out.

I'm fairly freaked out, too. I roll out of the jeep on the right side, frantically trying to get away from that big motherfucker.

"Sir! Help! The snake's got me!"

"What the fuck can I do?"

"Help! He's bit me! The son of a bitch bit me!"

In blind panic I pull Hatten's arm, pulling him out of the jeep from the passenger's side. The cobra goes out the driver's side. I empty my M-16 at the fleeing snake without a hit. I'm in a total panic, completely freaked out.

I turn to Hatten, who is already having trouble breathing.

"Where'd he bite you?"

"My . . . my shoulder . . . my neck . . . I don't know where else."

"Oh, my God! My God! Jesus, shit, I can't put a fuckin' tournequit on your neck. I — I'll call for a medevac." I go to the radio and frantically call Andrews.

"Alpha, K-Kilo. I n-need an urgent m-medevac. Urgent. Romeo's been bitten by a c-cobra. He needs anti-v-venom ASAP. Over."

"Kilo, Alpha. What the fuck's goin on there. I

want an explanation. Over."

"Get me the goddamn medevac! Now! Immediately! Urgent! I'll explain later. I've got to give first aid, coordinates, ah . . . er Kilo Tango five-six-three-four-eight-seven. Urgent. Do you copy? Over."

"Solid copy. Over."

"Roger, out."

I try. I strip off Hatten's shirt, cut the fang marks and try to suck out the poison even though that's not the army-approved treatment because most guys, in panic, cut the snake-bite victim too badly. I do, too, but I have nothing to lose. I'm shaking like a leaf, and it's hopeless, but I have to do something. I can't just let the boy die.

"C-can't breathe."

"Hang on. The chopper's on the way. You'll be okay."

"C-can't breathe . . ." He chokes. "Dyin' . . . ain't I?"

"No, Mike. I'll keep you alive. Hang on."

"D . . . I don't . . . wanna . . ." The next word is just an exhalation of air. "Die . . ."

His eyes roll back. His chest muscles are rigid. He can't breathe. I breathe for him with artificial respiration. I'm in a complete panic, crying like a baby and barely able to control myself enough to breathe into Hatten's drooling mouth.

It takes seventeen minutes for the chopper to call in.

"Hershey Three Kilo, This is Medevac Three. Over."

"Three, Kilo, over."

"Hershey Three Kilo, this is Medevac Three. I'm

enroute to your location. Is the position secure? Over."

"Roger. Secure. Hurry and have anti-venom ready. Situation critical. Need artificial respiration and anti-venom ASAP. Over."

"Roger. Medic is standing by with anti-venom. Pop smoke. Over."

"Roger. Wait. Smoke out. Over."

"Roger. I identify violet. Over."

"Roger. That is correct. Over."

"Okay, we're coming in. Over."

"Roger."

The chopper lands downwind, in the smoke but dispersing it. Two men run out of the chopper, one with a syringe in his hand. They get to Hatten. The one with the syringe pulls back one of Hatten's eyelids and says, "Too late. This man's dead."

"What! Give him the anti-venom!" I scream.

"Hey, man, he's dead!" he said, looking into my eyes. Then he sees the terror in these and says, "Okay. Okay, I'll do it." He injects Hatten, while the other man gives artificial respiration. They put him on the Huey, giving mouth-to-mouth respiration and CPR as it lifts off, trying to bring a dead man back to life. Hatten is pronounced DOA at Song Be. He had been bitten five times, including once on the neck.

Standing in front of a fuming Lieutenant Colonel Pride, I listen silently at attention.

"You let your man get bitten by a fucking snake. You fucked up, Captain. Can you give me one reason why I shouldn't have you court-martialled?"

209

"Go ahead, sir," I say quietly, almost crying. I have been, when alone, like a child.

"I might. I might, captain. I don't understand you, captain. You're unlucky. You have a little black cloud over you. People die around you. Good people. Why?"

"I don't know, sir."

"I don't know either. But I don't want you in my team. It'll take me a couple of weeks, but I will talk to Colonel Norman. You've done nothing but fuck up since the day you got here. You're nothing but a second lieutenant with two years' active duty. If you did one thing competently, I'd change my mind, but I know that won't happen. Try not to kill anyone else on our side, captain."

"Sir, I didn't kill Hatten." I think of Andrews, off scott free. When I'm not blaming myself, I blame him. But then I know that it doesn't matter. It was just Hatten's turn to die. War makes fatalists of us all."

"You were responsible. Get out of here."

On April 5 Tuy wants to have a party. Kinsey has just left for R and R, and I provide two cases of Cokes, one of beer, and one bottle of Johnny Walker and one of Jack Daniels for the officers and NCOs of both units. Tuy provides the ice.

As usual, the ARVNs want me to drink along with them, and I try to drink Coke, but they keep pouring either J.W. and J.D. in it, so by twenty-three thirty I have a good buzz and toddle off to bed.

The walk from the underground former medic

bunker to mine is twenty feet. I'm not quite to the staggering stage.

I take off my boots and shirt for a change and sleep in pants and T-shirt.

Spignatelli is snoring in the bunk across the way. His interpreter is having a wet dream in the next room.

6 April 1970

At oh-one hundred all hell breaks loose.

Lives well established for a number of years end suddenly and violently. Survival becomes more than difficult.

Fifteen sappers have penetrated the wire and booby traps to reach the berm. Then a mortar attack commenced to give them cover as they went over the berm and led their buddies through the paths they have made through our wire, boobytraps, and mines. They and their buddies are storming bunkers, shooting everything that moves, and throwing satchel charges into every bunker they run past.

One, Tengh Kao Dong, a tall, muscular youth of nineteen, a three year veteran of attacks like these, throws a satchel charge into a bunker and runs past it, throws another into another bunker, and sees the big bunker with the fence around it. He has run out of satchel charges, but he still has a grenade and his AK-47. He runs around the fence till he finds the entrance and starts through the maze.

It's almost light inside the bunker from explosions

outside even though there's only one window.

I sit up to put on my boots.

"Incoming," says Spignatelli.

"You sure? Sounds like a Mad Minute."

"Nah, can't you hear the mortars coming in, cap'n?"

"I sure don't. It sounds like a Mad Minute to me."

Tengh has found his way into the bunker. He hears voices in the darkness and arms a grenade and throws it toward one of the voices.

Nothing happens. It is a dud.

He aims his AK-47 at the voice.

I bend over to tie my shoelaces and start to say something. The thought is forever lost when the mosquito netting erupts, and my eyes are filled with flame.

I hit the ground and roll toward the back door to the conference room.

What the fuck is going on?

I do a rapid inventory.

One. An automatic weapon, aimed at my head, has just fired a burst and missed because I bent over to tie my shoe.

Two. The weapon is now raking the room. It is quite likely that the shooter is blind from the muzzle flash. I hope so, anyway.

Three. Spignatelli is probably dead.

Four. My .45 is out of reach under my pillow.

Five. My M-16 is out of reach on the far wall rack.

Six. My big survival knife is out of reach beneath my cot, ditto the boot knife.

Seven. I am now fully sober and awake.

Eight. I think I have wet my pants.

Nine. I am scared to death. I snap.

From the conference room I run to the other door and tackle the guy doing the shooting. I'm not sure what happens for the next few seconds.

"C-captain? That you?"

I vaguely remember a flashlight going on and off almost like a flashbulb.

"Captain?"

The light again.

"Ah, sir. I — I think you can stop now."

"Huh?"

"Sir, you can stop."

"Stop what?"

The light goes on again. I look down. I've been stomping on the NVA's head. It looks pretty grim with brains and blood. I stop. My heart is pounding out my ears. I take the light.

Mrs. Harris, your little boy Jerry just beat a man to death.

He is dressed in khaki shorts and Ho Chi Minh sandals, with a khaki bag slung from one shoulder and an AK-47. His back is obviously broken, and blood is running from his mouth in a steady stream.

I lean up against the wall and flick the flashlight off. I'm shaking like a leaf.

"You okay, Cap'n?"

"Y-yeah. You?"

"Yeah. The sucker missed me."

"How?"

"The good Lord looks after drunks and fools."

"Jesus. We're being overrun."

215

"Sappers."

I grab my M-16 and pistol belt and harness, helmet, and PRC-25 radio and start out the door.

"Get HQ on the net, order a heavy fire team and a flare bird while I talk to Tuy and Huong."

"Rog."

"And shoot anything without a helmet."

I come out of the blackout curtain into an eerie world of shifting shadows from descending flares, streamers of tracers going out, and blossoming mortar rounds around.

An APC is on fire.

I start to the medic bunker.

"*Toi la Co-Van my,*" I say to the guard. At other times I've been kept out of places because the guard was told not to admit anyone who didn't know the password. If this is the case this time, I'm in trouble.

He shouts at me for the password. "*Toi la Co-Van my. Dai-Uy* Harris. *Co-Van.*"

He motions me in, muttering "*Du ma.*"

Then an AK-47 erupts to my right.

The guard at the door to the bunker crumples and falls down the stairs of the underground bunker. I whirl, flip off the safety, point by instinct at the muzzle flash, fire the M-16 from the hip, full auto three rounds, and am rewarded to see a short NVA blown backward by the impact, arms outstretched, AK flung away. His body sprouts guts and blood from a solid, multiple round belly hit.

When I turn away he is still alive, but doomed to a few seconds to minutes of unbelievable agony. This bugs me, and I turn back and pop a round into his face. I do not dwell over the results. A switch has been thrown in my head, and morality decisions no longer interfere with survival decisions. Mrs. Harris's little boy Jerry has grown up into a mean son of a bitch who would like to go home. Mrs. Harris's little boy Jerry will never go home again, not after tonight.

"Trung-Uy! Trung-Uy Tuy! It's *Dai-Uy* Harris. I come in. Okay?"

"*Dai-Uy*! Come in! Quick!" I hear from down in the bunker.

I come down the stairs. Two ARVNs are bent over the broken figure of the guard, who is still moving, clutching one shoulder and emitting animal noises.

On what is normally Tuy's dining table is another wounded ARVN, blood glistening in the dim light of hand-held lanterns. Two men are working on him. He is obviously groaning and squirming in agony. I glimpse intestines and look away.

Tuy is by his radios along with his exec. "*Dai-Uy*! You get helicopters! VC inside base!"

"I know. I've ordered a heavy-fire team. How bad? How many inside? Must tell HQ."

He turns to his exec, and they exchange guesses.

"Fifty, seventy. Many. I have casualties. We may lose. Much damage."

"Roger."

I turn on the radio and call in.

Andrews answers, "Where the hell have you been?"

I ignore the stupid question. "We have NVA inside perimeter, estimated five-zero to company size, plus incoming eighty-two mike-mike and Sierra Alpha. We have casualties already, over."

217

"We know. We can hear and see it on the horizon. Forney Hustler One Alpha already called. I have a heavy fire team on the way and a medevac coming. Over."

"We're not secure for a medevac. Over."

"Roger. I know. I'm going to have them sit down here till you're secure. Over."

"Roger. Good thinking. What is load of heavy fire team? Over."

"Guns and forty Mike-Mike. Over."

"Request another heavy fire team, this one with ARA, also a Shadow, a FAC, and some napalm-equipped close air support. Got that so far? Over."

"Roger copy. Call sign of first fire team is Cobra Two, they'll call you on this push. Lima on Black-horse push is calling for rest. Over."

"Roger. Also bring Sierra Bravo eight inch in to points Bruce and Cadillac, the one-five-fives from Bunard onto Gladys. Over."

This is a quick and dirty code. Bruce is a boy's name. A certain map coordinate has been coded Boy. Next time I could call George and get arty on the same point. Another point is coded Girl, another Car. Map coordinates take too long when the shit is hitting the fan.

Tuy says, "*Dai-Uy*, we go to command track."

"Right."

The radio crackles: "Roger. I'll need a sitrep ASAP. Over."

"You know what I know. Counterpart is going to perimeter. I'm going with him. Can't fight a war in a bunker. Over."

"Roger, waiting out."

218

We go topside and make a dash for the command track. Spignatelli is going to the exec's track one hundred eighty degrees from the one Tuy and Huong, the cav. C.O. and I run for.

I adjust the eight-inch artillery. Just the time I get it where I want it, the FAC calls in and asks me to stop it. His F-100s are almost on station. He needs more illumination.

Fortunately, Moonshine Six, the flareship shows up.

"I have a four hour flare supply. Can I be of assistance? Over."

Moonshine Six, this is Six-Six Yankee, affirmative. We're low on mortar flares. How about one high center continuously and more on call. We've got bad guys all over the place. Over."

"Roger. We can do a low pass to shake up the bad guys. Over."

"Roger. Go to it. Over." I turn to Tuy. "Heads down, Trung-Uy. They're going to make a low pass."

"*Ya, fi!*"

The helicopter flies over at about one hundred knots just above our antennas, M-60 machine guns in the doors firing continuously, not hurting the NVA much, but making the beleagured ARVNs cheer.

The mortar attacks are the first target for the F-100s. We can't napalm our own troops, but we still have NVA popping up inside the perimeter. So we stop the mortars first with napalm where Tuy thinks they're shooting from.

The track next to ours is hit by a B-40, and flames shoot into the air.

The gasoline tank blows. The ammo from the track starts going off. Tracer bullets are flying, and 40 mm grenades bloop out a few yards and fall harmlessly to the ground, unarmed. The heat is intense. Huong orders our track to move.

Too late!

Wham!

Oh, shit! Not again! I'm on my ass, and the world's very bright. I stagger up. It wasn't as bad this time, at least this APC isn't on fire. I see blood about my chest, arms, and left leg, but not much. I wipe my hand over it. It isn't mine.

Tuy is on his hands and knees, shaking his head. He turns to me. "B-forty," he says.

Then I realize the .50 caliber in the track next door is firing an uninterrupted stream.

Oh, my God! The gunner is standing in the middle of the flames, hands reflexively on the triggers, and .50 cal. bullets are going into bunkers down the line.

Finally he slumps and the gun shoots upward, tracers erupting from the orange flames.

Huong is hurt. His right arm is almost torn off.

"*Bac Si! Bac Si!*" I yell. A medic runs from another track and goes to work on him.

Huong, like Tuy, is one of the few real soldiers in the ARVN, so it's more tragic that he is hit.

They're dragging the driver out of our APC. He's still alive but filled with schrapnel.

Tuy and I crawl to the next track, and I work with the FAC till the F-100s are empty of ordnance. At least they let me use the napalm in close. When we start taking fire from our own bunkers, resulting in more casualties on the tracks, I call for the ARA.

"Cobra Two, this is Swarthy Matron Six-Six Yankee. Over."

"Yankee, This Cobra Two. Over."

"Cobra Two, Yankee. What is your armament? Over."

"Forty Mike-Mike and mini-guns. Over."

"Roger. I desperately need some ARA. Over."

"Rog. Cobra Four is on the way with ARA. Meanwhile can I help. Over."

"Roger. Believe me, I need your help, but the timing is off. I'm getting fire from my own bunkers because the bad guys have taken them over. Give me some minimum safe distance runs on the Sierra Whiskey of the perimeter, really close, guns only. That'll keep their heads down. I don't know what else to do. Over."

One of our tanks moves to fire on the bunker we're getting fire from, and a B-40 blows a hole in the cupola and disables the gun. Luckily no one is killed, and the ammunition doesn't catch fire. It's a fluke.

"Six-Six Yankee, this is Cobra Four. Over."

"Cobra Four, Six-Six Yankee, you're just what I need. We're taking fire from one of our bunkers. I'm going to fire a fifty cal. at it. I need you to rocket where the tracers hit. Break. Moonshine, three more flares would be nice. Over."

"Yankee, Moonshine. Wilco. Over."

"Trung-Uy, fire on that bunker with the fifty caliber. Use it to mark for the helicopter."

"Okay, *Dai-Uy*."

The .50 cal. fires a stream into the bunker, tracers

221

pointing to it accurately.

"Six-Six Yankee, Cobra Four. Be advised, your target is within fifty yards of friendlies, and fifty yards is below our minimum safe distance. Over."

"Roger, Cobra four. My initials are Juliet Hotel. I say again, hit that bunker. Over."

That's it, asshole, pass the buck. If you hit a bunch of ARVNs I'm the one who gets the court-martial.

The first Cobra screams in low, firing a rocket seemingly over my head. It is very hairy. If that son of a bitch sneezes, he can take out my track or a bunch of my troops, and if I'm still alive, it'll be my fault. The 2.75 inch rockets pack quite a wallop.

The first Cobra blows the bunker to bits.

"Cobra Four, good shooting. Now—"

Green tracers converge on my track just below me. I dive inside as they rake the top of the track. The gunner is killed.

"Cobra Four. I have another target. Did you see the source of the green tracers? Over."

"Negative Yankee. Over."

"Roger, Cobra Four. Wait one. We'll shoot at the new target. It's another bunker. Over."

We can't fire .50 cal. from our track till we get the dead gunner out, so we use a .30 cal. and .50s from other tracks.

"Got it. The bunker on the Sierra getting all the fire, over three from the other. Over."

"You got it. Hit it. Over."

"That's within minimum safe distance. Over."

"Okay, okay, you've got my fuckin' initials. Hit the goddamned bunker. Over."

222

"Roger, Six-Six Yankee, next bird is going in now. Adjust. Over."

"Roger. Over."

The next bird accelerates in its dive and fires two rockets. They miss short.

"Cobra Four, Six-Six Yankee, short five yards. Over."

"Roger. I'll get it. Over."

He dives in. I feel very naked. I'm on a direct line to his target. I know how the other side feels when those things dive in.

The pucker factor is definitely high.

The bunker explodes in an orange ball, and all is quiet inside the perimeter.

Two NVA run from another bunker. Orange tracers converge on them, and they fall in sprawled heaps.

I direct Cobra Four at other targets, outside the compound, and Spignatelli has some targets for Cobra Two. We divide the FSB on a north-south line, with Spignatelli going on our alternate frequency and working cobra Two on his side while I work Cobra Four on my side. I order another heavy fire team to replace these when they run out of ammo or gas.

Shadow is on station. Shadow is a C-119 with three 7.62 mm mini-guns which fire two thousand rounds per minute, each.

They fire all tracers. The NVA hate them.

All flares are allowed to burn out, and the place goes black. Shadow drops flares below it to illuminate the target and block their presence, and a stream of red fire comes out of nowhere onto the treeline in likely places. I see NVA moving, trying to get away

223

from them. They fail. Every square yard around the perimeter takes a bullet. The word awesome comes to mind.

A foo gas container in the perimeter explodes, adding to the fireworks, as if all the powers of hell are at my command.

Some NVA are still at large inside the compound, trying to get out. Green tracers scare me back into the track.

I talk to Tuy, then we spread the word to button up, and I have Shadow shoot up FSB Mary. God help any of our people who aren't under cover.

As the bullets clatter on the lid of this tin can I hope none of them are armor piercing.

Spignatelli is on the radio as soon as we unbutton and climb up onto the flare-lit scenario of hell.

"Six-Six Yankee, Forney Hustler One Alpha, we've got gas over here, sir."

"Gas? What kind? Over."

I look over and see the cloud of white gas enveloping the far side of the perimeter.

Spignatelli coughs and sputters.

"CS."

"CS? Where'd they get CS?"

"I don't know, but they're choking us."

"That's our stuff. Wait a minute. The U.S. had CS canisters in the wire. I'll bet the Shadow blew one away. Over."

"That's great. It still burns like hell. Over."

"Rog. Un-ass the area till the cloud passes, over."

Then a strange voice comes over the radio.

"Swarthy Matron Six-Six Yankee, this is Blackhorse Mike, over."

Who the fuck is Blackhorse Mike? I frantically page through my SOI. It's got to be someone high up from First Cav. I can't find it and don't have time to keep looking. Mike . . . the way those guys keep using the same call signs for months, probably maneuvers, operations, G-3? At three A.M. it's probably an assistant G-3, some light colonel or major with a hard-on for "action." Deliver me from field grade R.E.M.F.s.

"Go ahead, Mike."

"Swarthy Matron Six Six-Mike, this is Blackhorse Mike. Be advised your radio procedure is incorrect. Over."

"Mike, this is Six-Six Mike. This is a combat push. If you merely want to critique our etiquette, do it later. I have troops in contact. Out."

"Don't out me. Do you know who this is? Over."

"You're not in my SOI, so you're not in my chain of command. Frankly, I don't care if you're CGU-SARV. I've been overrun, and I can't waste radio time. Get off my push! Out."

"Swarthy Matron Six-Six Yankee, this is Blackhorse Mike. You alerted my eight inch over two hours ago then stopped using them. I direct you to use them. Over."

"Negative. I have half the TAC air and rotary wing in Vietnam over me. Trajectory interferes with firing passes of alpha Charlies. Over."

"Swarthy Matron Six-Six Yankee, this is Blackhorse Mike. If you were at all competent, you could keep them out of my eight inch trajectories. Over."

225

"Roger. I'm not. Get off this push. I'm too heavily engaged for this bullshit. Out."

I'm taking sniper fire from the trees dead west, an occasional small arms' round and a mortar round every now and then. It's degenerated into harassment, but it's working. It has our full attention.

Tuy tugs my sleeve. "*Dai-Uy*. We have fourteen wounded — bad — must get out."

"I know, Trung-Uy. One's Huong. I've got —"

Over the radio comes the FAC. "Blackhorse Mike, this is Nightrider Three. If you fire eight inch, I'll cancel the next flight. I have a flight of four coming in with all napalm. I'll not risk it with your artillery. Over."

"Nightrider Tha-ree, this is Blackhorse Mike. I want your initials and serial number. I'll have you court-martialed along with Swarthy Matron Six-Six Yankee. Over."

"My initials are Charlie Romeo. I won't give my serial number over a clear net, but my call sign will be enough for your purposes. Out. Break. Matron Six-Six Yankee, this is Nightrider Three. I have a flight of four Fox one hundreds. Where do you want them? Over."

I consult the map and Tuy and tell him. One by one the F-100s come in and drop their eggs of pure flame, right where I want them. After all this practice, it's as if I were dropping them myself. Of course, if I make a mistake, the court-martial will act as though I was.

As the last one makes its last pass, I look at my watch. It's oh-four hundred. I've been fighting for three hours.

"Trung-Uy, are there any VC loose inside the wire now?"

"No, *Dai-Uy*. All dead. You get medevac copter now?"

"*Ya, fi*." I talk into the handset. "Six-Six Mike, this is Yankee. Over."

"Go ahead, Yankee."

"Let's crank up the medevac. I have fourteen urgents. Eight are litter. Over."

"Roger. Pilot was right beside me waiting. He's on his way out to the bird. Over."

"Roger, out."

"Matron Six-Six Yankee, this is Medevac One-two. Over."

"Go One-two."

"We're enroute to your location. I need max illum. Put up every flare you can, and shut off all artillery and all outgoing Sierra Alpha. I'll need a strobe on the target. We'll come in blackened out and out of the Whiskey at Tango Tango Lima. Got that? Over."

"Roger. Moonshine, do you copy? Over."

"Roger. Solid. I'll put out four in the air at once. Over."

"Describe the LZ, over," says One-two.

"Big red cross north-west center of LZ. I'll be there with a strobe in my hand. I can give you a Cobra escort. Cobra Two is on my alternate push. I'll get him onto this push. Over."

"Roger. LZ secure? Over."

"Negative. We're still taking Sierra Alpha fire. But some of these guys won't last till dawn. Over."

"Roger. Give us the Cobras, and we'll go in. Over."

"Wait out." I switch down to alternate to get the Cobras back up to my primary frequency. They've been under Spignatelli's control. I'm back on primary in thirty seconds.

"Swarthy Matron Six-Six Yankee, this is Blackhorse Mike. Over."

"Go."

"Swarthy Matron Six-Six Yankee, this is Blackhorse Mike. Negative on that medevac. Do not risk that bird to save your little people line twos. Wait till dawn. Over."

"Blackhorse Mike, this is Yankee. It's not up to you, it's up to Medevac One-two. My men are dying. Over."

"Swarthy Matron Six-Six Yankee, this is Blackhorse Mike. Are you aware of what constitutes an urgent medevac? Over."

"Mike, Yankee, of course. I've been doing this a while. Do you have anything constructive? Or do you just want to fuck up a combat push? Over."

"Swarthy Matron Six-Six Yankee, this is Blackhorse Mike. This is a direct order. Under no circumstances are you to bring in that medevac without my permission. Over."

"Oh, fuck off. Break. One-two, Yankee. Over."

"This is One-two. I'm ready to come in. Over."

"Roger. Out. Break. Blackhorse Mike, this is Yankee, order refused. Initials Juliet Hotel. You are not in my SOI, so you are not in my chain of command. Out."

"Don't out me, you son of a bitch. I out you. Out."

Jesus Christ. The motherfucker's worried about

228

who says out and who says over, as if it matters.

Now I'm the one who's calm, discussing plumbing fixtures over drinks. I haven't gotten excited all night. Where is Mrs. Harris's little boy Jerry?

Tuy and I move the the medevac pad.

The wounded are brought up from the underground bunker.

Medevac One-two briefs Cobra Two. Spignatelli will control them so I can concentrate on the medevac.

I tell Tuy just the litters first, but I know the ambulatory wounded will storm the chopper.

"Trung-Uy, if one ambulatory wounded gets on board, nobody leaves. Understand?"

"*Ya, fi*. Okay."

Right. We'll see.

Four flares are out. All the shooting stops. It's quiet and very unreal under the flarelight.

I unsnap the strobe from its case on my harness and flip it on.

Thwap-thwap-thwap-thwap. I hear the chopper.

The strobe is going *pop-pop-pop*. I'm holding it up in my right hand as high as I can.

I see nothing. All is black outside the perimeter. The shadows climb as the flares float down.

Then a small black helicopter silhouette appears and grows as if by magic. All depth perception is gone because of the ever-changing flarelight.

The rotor blast hits me, and I put my rifle down to grab the whip antenna so it doesn't get into the rotor.

The strobe light I let dangle. My right hand has my handset, the left the antenna.

Crash!

There's a stinging, ringing sensation in my right ear, and my right hand stings.

I look at it. The handset is shattered. My hand is bleeding. Oh, shit! I've been shot at.

But I can't go far. The chopper is touching down.

I turn around. All the ARVN troops with the wounded are gone. The ambulatory crowd on the chopper.

"NO! Goddamn it! Get off!"

I'm motioning and screaming. The crew chief helps me shove them off. Then he and I put the first six stretchers on, and the worst two ambulatory.

The chopper lifts off. Then it shrinks and disappears above the flares.

I turn around to pick up my rifle. It's gone.

"Trung-Uy. I need a radio and my rifle."

He turns to one of his men and barks an order in Vietnamese. The man runs off. He returns with a radio quickly.

"Tomorrow we find rifle."

"No, Trung-Uy," I say, as I tune his radio to my frequency. Mine has a destroyed handset and took a round in the radio, which would've been in my back. The sniper's pretty good. "I bring no more medevacs till my rifle's returned."

I turn to the radio. I get Song Be artillery. "Fire mission." I call in eight inch on the side where the sniper is shooting. The Cobras have left with the medevac bird. Cobra Four will return with a medevac.

An ARVN sergeant hands me my rifle. It's taken less than two minutes.

A medevac calls back in a few minutes. He's on his way back.

Now comes the fun part. I think the sniper's still there. I have to do it again.

Try not to think about it, Harris.

Strobe on, arm up. Try not to shake. Surprisingly it's easy. I'm kind of numb.

Ah, there is strobe light. Drop three feet. Fire for effect.

Mother.

It's the same show again, four flares, eerie, shifting light as the flares float down.

I still have no depth perception. A black dot grows into a miniature Huey which grows into a real one, but black.

Thuck-thuck-thuck. Holes appear in the chopper's side as I slide a stretcher in. I run back for the other one.

The pilots are sitting calmly as they take hits. I'm impressed.

Finally we get the other stretcher in, and it lifts off. Of course the amublatory wounded have already climbed aboard.

It gets away. I radio thanks to the pilot. I want to cry and laugh simultaneously.

It gets quiet and dark.

I start the artillery again, and Spignatelli adjusts it while I prepare a spot report.

"*Dai-Uy*. Prisoner," says Tuy. "Live VC in bunker. Wounded."

We go in the direction of the bunker. I hear a gunshot across the compound. Two ARVNs with .45s in their right hands have a slumped body between them.

"So sorry, *Dai-Uy*. He die of wounds."

Yeah, he sure did. There's a .45 hole right between his eyes.

"Damn. A prisoner would be very useful."

"Sorry, *Dai-Uy*. He die."

"Yeah. Trung-Uy, I need ammo resupply requests, and we need to talk."

"*Ya, fi.* Take little time. No first sergeant."

"Oh? What happened to Binh?"

"Come here. You see. Look."

By another bunker is the body of Binh, rifle still in his hands. He is surrounded by three sprawled NVA bodies.

I bend over and pick up his M-16. There is blood on the buttplate. A round has failed to eject. The bolt is halfway forward, stuck trying to chamber the next round. It's a class two malfunction, requiring a cleaning rod to clear, sometimes with partial disassembly of the rifle. He killed two NVA, then his gun jammed. He killed one with the butt of the rifle. The butt is cracked from the impact. It wasn't even a good club. Then four AK slugs stitched across his chest.

"I'm sorry, Trung-Uy. Very sorry. Binh was a good soldier."

"The best. Numbah One. Twenty-two years in the army."

I call in the spot report. The reply should have been predictable.

"Matron Six-Six Yankee, this is Six-Six Hotel, have you personally counted the enemy bodies? Over."

232

"Negative. ARVN count. Over."

"Not acceptable. Must have senior advisor count. Over."

"Roger. As soon as I send the resupply request, I'll take a walk and count them. Over."

"Negative. We need a count now! Over."

"Well, you're not going to get it. I'm going to send the resupply request, first, because I want an early resupply in case we get hit again. Over."

"Headquarters needs a count now. Over."

"Fuck headquarters. We need resupply. Are you prepared to copy? Over."

"Roger. Go," says Andrews, obviously fuming.

I give him the numbers and sign off.

"*Dai-Uy*. We do sweeps at dawn," says Tuy.

"Roger. Sergeant, you want to go?" I ask Spignatelli.

"Sure, sir."

"Good. I'll count the bodies while you do the sweep."

He starts to walk away. I think of something. "Sergeant."

"Yes, sir?"

"If you take any prisoners, I'd like them alive."

"Yes, sir."

I call for a hunter-killer team to work with Spignatelli.

I start out to walk the perimeter and count bodies. The sun is coming up. I've survived the night.

My head's down. I'm thinking about something as I walk. I still haven't tied my bootlaces or put on a shirt. I've taken off my pistol belt and Y-harness, but

I have my M-16 in my right hand.

All thoughts end when I almost step on the scalp. First I see a four inch by three inch patch of skull and hair, then brains, more pieces of skull, then an NVA with his head blown off. His tongue is hanging out as is one eye.

That's one.

Several of them were hit in the head. An M-16 blows up a head like a melon. I begin, from the corpses, to piece together what happened.

First sappers carefully came through the south wire, cutting wires to trip flares, opening a path. Three of them died on the berm. Under the cover of mortars others came through their paths and killed the inhabitants of the nearby bunkers. Then they took them over and fired on us.

One man threw satchel charges in three bunkers in a straight line from the first one to mine. Inside he must've been out of charges. He died there.

Four men were armed with B-40s. They blew two APCs and failed to torch a tank before killing everyone in a bunker, and, in various ways, dying themselves.

The burning APC .50 cal. gunner killed four of my men. FSB Mary was not designed as a cav. base. It was a leg infantry and artillery base. So no provisions were made for APCs, no inverted U-shaped outcroppings to allow an APC an uninterrupted field of fire. Poor design, not the dying gunner, killed my men.

Dead NVA are everywhere in grotesque positions. Gut-shot NVA have guts hanging out, even from small holes. Apparently the little .223 M-16 bullet goes in and forces intestine out the entry hole.

Arms and legs are missing. Some men were killed with rockets and are blown to chunks. M-16s blow off arms when they hit them just right. One dead man was castrated by an M-16 bullet and died. He has no other wounds.

The ARVNs begin to move the dead to one place, lining them up in a grisly trophy collection. They are not mutilated or defiled, neither are they treated as former human beings, but just as disgusting, heavy burdens which contaminate those who handle them.

Finally I am sure there are, indeed, fifty-five NVA dead. ARVN dead are on stretchers, with ponchos over them. Bare feet stick out.

Tuy does something I have not seen an ARVN do. He goes quietly and squats by the corpses of his men for four minutes, as if he is talking to them. Then he stands up. From fifty feet away I can see the sadness on his face.

I call in the fifty-five figure as confirmed. Congratulations are relayed back from Colonel Norman.

Spignatelli calls me to say he has a prisoner, lightly wounded. He is bringing him in. I report it to headquarters immediately.

When Spignatelli's track comes back through the gate, I run to reach it.

Tuy does too. He has his .45 out. I run to beat him.

"Trung-Uy. What are you going to do with that forty-five?"

"I kill him, *Dai-Uy*. He VC. Kill all VC."

"Trung-Uy! No! We need prisoners. We need information. He will be more useful if he talks."

We've reached him now, a dazed youth with a bandage on his head. He has not been hurt bad.

"No, *Dai-Uy*! I kill him. VC kill my parents, my sister. Rape my sister—cut open—I kill VC! Kill all VC!"

"I've reported a P.O.W., Trung-Uy. It's too late."

He points the .45 at my sternum.

The intensity of his feelings are now quite apparent to me.

I do a deep inhaling.

The trigger of his .45 takes about seven pounds to trip the sear and cause the hammer to fall, which, in this instance, will blow a half inch hole in my sternum and a three or four inch hole out my back. I'll take two, three minutes to die, less if I'm lucky.

It's fish or cut bait time, Jerry. How important is it to you to follow the rules? Good guys don't kill prisoners. If he kills him, it won't be as if I killed him. Anyway, a few hours ago I would have killed him. So what's the difference? I won't have blood on my hands.

The hell I won't.

"I must kill him, *Dai-Uy*. VC kill my parents, my sister, my friends, my first sergeant," he says, his eyes on fire.

"Don't do it, Trung-Uy. I agree with you. I know how you feel. But don't do it." I switch to Vietnamese. "Question him. If he does not talk, then shoot him." I turn to the prisoner. "Answer our questions, or he will shoot you." I turn back to Tuy. "Okay?"

"Okay, *Dai-Uy*." He holsters his .45. I walk away, my knees weak, a hollow feeling below my sternum.

236

The P.O.W. talks up a storm. I'm very glad my fatigue pants cover up my shaking legs.

Spignatelli boils eggs for breakfast. I break mine open. It's soft-boiled, gooey yellow. I see brains and scalp and nearly puke. I give it back to him.

Colonel Norman arrives first. By now word has reached all the way to Saigon, and ghouls will be enroute.

He brings a case of beer!

I meet him at the helipad. He walks with me to my bunker for a briefing.

He bumps over the dead NVA. I'd forgotten about it. I call Tuy to have it dragged out and put with the others.

Flies converge on the bloody spot. The interpreter goes to work cleaning it without being asked. ARVNs never do something without being asked, so I'm surprised.

"Okay, captain. I have your request for ammunition resupply. Do you have anything to add?"

"I need another PRC-twenty-five. One was a combat loss."

"How?"

"Small-arms fire."

"Oh," he says, an eyebrow going up. "Use the one I brought. I'll get another at Lai Khe." He turns to his Nung bodyguard and tells him to get it out of the chopper. The Nung puts down his Swedish K and leaves the bunker.

Using the big plastic-covered situation map I describe the battle to him.

"At oh-one hundred a company of the Two hundred seventy-fifth NVA Regiment under the command of a Lieutenant Linh, with a strength of sixty-two men made an attack using sappers who came in here, here, here, and here, surprising our troops rather effectively, neutralizing our mines and booby-traps in paths they marked with cloth strips, and turning the claymores on our troops. A mortar attack commenced, and this allowed several troops to penetrate the wire. Fifteen died outside the berm, but forty got inside. They captured, temporarily, this, this, and this bunker, and destroyed this one. At this point my company first sergeant, Binh, killed three NVA in close combat before being killed. These three carried unexploded satchel charges so his effort probably saved our command bunkers from satchel charges. I'm recommending him for an impact Bronze Star."

"I'll see it's approved."

"B-forty attacks at these tracks succeeded here and here, wounding Second Squadron's C.O. seriously. He was one of the fourteen wounded medevaced."

"How many wounded total?"

"Just fourteen. If any were lightly wounded, they didn't bother to report it. Another B-forty attack on this tank failed to destroy the tank.

"We utilized four heavy-fire teams, eight sorties of F-one hundreds, two flare ships, one FAC, one Shadow, and one hunter-killer team at daybreak. It's still out. Medevac One-two made two sorties. I have six KIA. Cav. has eight. There are fifty-five NVA bodies, and one P.O.W. The P.O.W. is a seventeen-year-old private, and he has told us probably all he knows, which isn't much."

He nods and smiles. "Very good, Captain. My congratulations. You surprised me. Major Andrews and Lietuenant Colonel Pride said you were dead calm on the radio. Colonel Thuong thinks you're the greatest thing since sliced bread, as does Lieutenant Tuy and Captain Tranh. They say you and Sergeant Spignatelli saved their bacon."

I don't know what to say. I mumble something. He congratulates Spignatelli and leaves the beer.

The next visitor is a major from First Cav. I find him standing on one of the NVA dead with one foot as if the NVA were a goddamned lion while a lieutenant takes his pictures.

"Sir, get off that man. Lieutenant, no more pictures." I grab the camera.

"Why not?" asks the lieutenant.

"It's a crime, lieutenant."

"Who do you think you are?" storms the major.

"I'm Captain Harris, sir. This is my firebase. No photos of war dead."

"Like hell it is. We'll take any goddamned pictures we want," says the major.

"Not on this firebase — sir." By now I've gotten the film rewound and half out of the camera. It's still intact, though.

"What the fuck? What makes you think you can order me around like that?"

"Well, for one thing, I killed the man you're standing over. For another thing I'm aware of the

239

MACV regulations and Geneva conventions concerning war dead. If you don't want my ARVNs to escort you off the base, then get away from these dead and point your camera in another direction."

The major starts walking toward me. "I want your name and serial number, Captain. Do you know who I am?"

"I don't care if you're General Abrams, Major. No photos of dead. Harris, oh-five-four-three-one-nine-one-four."

"You—you're Six-Six Yankee! You insubordinate ass!"

"And you must be Blackhorse Mike."

"That's right, and I'm gonna court-martial your ass for last night. I'll just add this to it."

"Now we both have something to file charges on."

"What do you mean?"

"I've got the camera and film. Photos of war dead with you standing over them. I believe that's a crime, is it not?"

"I'll have your ass for this."

"Sir, I just spent the night fighting NVA hand-to hand. Do you think I'm afraid of you?" Of course I am.

"What the hell's going on here?" comes a booming voice from behind me.

I turn. It's General Garry, CG First Cav. the major is on his staff.

I salute. He returns it.

"You might want to get these developed, sir."

"George," he says, looking at the major. "Are you taking body pictures again? Haven't I told you about that once? Give me that film, son. I'd overlook body pictures by combat troops, but not operations personnel."

I hand him the film. He pulls out the tab and spoils it.

"Go back to Song Be, George," he says. Then he turns to me. "Fine show here last night, son. What can First Cav. do for you?"

I think I've just been pulled off the hook.

"Thank you, sir. I don't think we need anything. Our resupply should be sufficient unless they're short something. Nothing's arrived yet."

He turns to his aide. "Billy, send them a pallet load of small arms and mortar ammo anyway." He turns back to me. "I can tell you're tired, son, but are you up to giving me a tour of the perimeter."

"Certainly, sir."

After he leaves Lieutenant Colonel Pride arrives. I'm very ragged then from total exhaustion. Things begin to get confused in my mind from fatigue. He questions me incessantly, and when we walk the berm he asks why 40 mm grenades from the burned-out APC aren't picked up. It's pretty obvious the entire unit is rebuilding bunkers and wire and such, but I promise to get it done before dark.

Then he finds the hand. It is lying on the berm near an APC.

"What's this hand doing here?"

"I guess it's just lying here," I say with a firm grasp of the obvious.

"That's not what I meant, captain."

"Sir, there was a lot of fighting here. They'll get it

picked up."

"Is it friendly or enemy?"

In my entire life I have never heard a dumber question.

"Sir, it's just a hand now."

"Well, find out."

"Yes sir."

"Now."

"Yes sir." I run to Tuy, ask him to get the hand picked up, and return. "It's NVA, sir. It'll be gone as soon as they get to it."

"Why not now?"

"Everybody we can spare is rebuilding bunkers. We might get hit again tonight. It will be handled, sir." Jesus, you dork, I want to say, we got fucking overrun, and you're worried about a goddamn hand? Do you think it's haunted like the old Peter Lorre movie?

He continues to nitpick, to ask questions, and to interrupt the answers with more questions. No "well done," no "you fucked up kid," just nitpicking.

Finally he leaves. I'm really exhausted by then.

Johnny East is on the second one with a bottle of Jack Daniels for appropriate future use. He mentions that we're the talk of Lai Khe. When the NVA hit Chanh Tanh last week they overran it, killed eighty-seven ARVNs and Captain Steele, the S.A., and blew up most of the base. Only twelve NVA bodies were found. Turning the tables on them has made us fair-haired boys.

Later I find the grenade under the bed.

Dear Jerry,

I got a letter from Kim and Ron. Kim is worried about you, as much about what it'll do to you afterward as the danger. She's afraid you'll be changed, asking what it'll do to you to kill people. She brings up the immorality of killing, for whatever the reason. Ron has a good job in San Francisco. He's working for a wine distributing company. He managed to avoid the draft after college, now that they've got that lottery system.

She got me to thinking a lot. How can you justify killing people, for whatever the reason? You don't have to actually kill anyone yourself, do you? Don't enlisted men do that?

What will you be like when you come home? Will you be the high-principled, fun-loving young man I married? Or will you be burned out? Will you be like you were at R and R? Sometimes you scared me then. I hope you were just that way because of the strain of the war.

One of the women at the N.O.W. meeting told me about an article in one of the women's magazines which says you're all unexploded bombs ready to happen when you come home. I read it. It gave histories of men who had come home and acted crazy. It told women not to have anything to do with Vietnam vets. I don't want you to be like that. I don't want you to change.

Love,
Carole

7 April—1 May 1970

On 8 April we find another NVA, wounded. He was a mortarman. He says his lieutenant was killed and the rest of the mortar crew wounded. They split up, and no one made the next rendezvous point but him. In other words, out of sixty-two, we killed sixty, captured two.

Then who mortared us on the night of 9 April?

An 82 mm round is in my door, unexploded.

I'm beginning to think this cat has used up more than nine lives.

On 10 April I'm told to catch a log bird for Lai Khe.

There Lieutenant Colonel Pride says I'll relieve Major Babcock. He'll become G-4 Advisor. I get ready to meet the chopper, and I'm called back. Major Babcock has gone to Colonel Norman requesting more command time instead of a staff position. He has been passed over for lieutenant colonel once, and only command time will save his career. Norman grants his request.

I get to stay in Lai Khe overnight while they

reconsider my future.

I see the dentist. He'll pull a wisdom tooth on the morning of 11 April.

I catch Johnny in the Officer's Club and buy a few rounds. We get fairly well loaded, and he says, "Wanna pizza?"

"D-don' tal' about pizza. Had no pizza in nine months. No pizza. No pussy since R and R. All th' pussy 'round here slant-eyed pussy. N-need round-eyed pussy . . . 'n' pizza. Round-eyed pizza."

"No. No shit, there's a Pizza Hut at Eleventh ACR."

"Ah, c'mon. A Pizza Hut?"

"Yeah. Come on. Let's go get a pizza."

"No? It's late."

"No sweat. I gotta jeep."

So we stagger out to his jeep. Neither of us is fit to drive, but that doesn't stop us. The gate guard is skeptical.

"We're goin' to the Pizza Hut. Wanna piece?" says Johnny.

"You sure it's okay, sir?"

"Yeah, it's okay. I'll bring you back a piece," says Johnny.

"Okay, sir. It's your funeral."

We keep it between the ditches from Team Seventy to a strip beside the airfield. It's all inside the perimeter fence at Lai Khe. Neither of us is drunk enough to go outside the fence. There, in all its ammo box glory, is a Pizza Hut.

Ahead of us in line a guy orders ten large with everything to go.

"It be a while," says the Vietnamese counterman.

"Fine. Two beers while we wait."

We sit at a table waiting.

"Jerry, you know why that guy ordered ten?"

"Party? Got some for th' whole unit?"

"Pizza chopper."

"Huh?"

"Pizza chopper. They gotta chopper that delivers pizza to the field."

"Nah! You're shitting me."

"Nope. Thirty-four point fifty-five. Call sign Pizza Hut. Call 'em some time. For an order of ten or more, they deliver. Day or night, no sweat. It's a project of the av. company."

"Jesus. Thirty-four point fifty-five? Day or night? Amazing. I still think you're shittin' me."

The guy takes the ten pizzas into a jeep and drives off. Then we get ours. We sit there BSing about women and the army till we're done.

"I don't get it. Carole's writing about the morality of the war. Some organization I never heard of. Ever hear of the N.O.W.? What the fuck is that?"

"National Organization for Women or something like that? Fenimist—ah, feminist shit. What they saying?"

"We're unexploded bombs. Stay away from Vietnam vets. That sort of thing."

"Shit. With your job she should be praying she has someone to stay away from. You're on a one-way trip to Arlington if you don't get out of the fuckin' field."

"I would if I could. But I'd just get into some kind of trouble here. I had a sergeant one time, Garner. You probably know him. Spent seven years in the field. Trying to stay in the field till he retires. Just gets into trouble in the rear. I guess I'm the same way. I can't go to the rear. I know what it's like in the boonies, so I can't put up with the bullshit with the REMFs. I don't know how you do. You don't act like a R.E.M.F."

"I don't either. But a quartermaster type has no place to go into the boonies. No quartermaster boonierats. We're all R.E.M.F.s by definition."

"Yeah. I'd a been all right if I'd been in a combat support branch. But no, I had to ask for Armor, the combat arm of, ah, ah, decision."

"Why'd you get into Armor?"

"I couldn't decide."

"Tha's funny. Funny. I spent a year in Armor. Goddamned tough duty. Th' only tough stuff here is puttin' up with th' bullshit. Bullshit, bullshit, and more bullshit."

"Have another beer."

The drive back is memorable. I just wish I could remember it.

The next morning I have the tooth pulled. Then I see Colonel Norman.

"Captain, I'm giving you to Lieutenant Colonel Rains in Ninth Regiment. He's got an opening in One—Nine. You've earned your own team."

"Yes sir."

"You don't look pleased."

"Sorry, sir. My looks are probably the dentist's fault. But I admit I'd rather stay in Eighth Regiment under Lieutenant Colonel Pride."

"Why? I thought you hated his guts."

"Well, sir, he's not my favorite person, but that doesn't matter. When I'm in contact he gives me the ordnance I need. I can trust him when the shit hits the fan. That's all that counts."

"Well, I understand. None of us are in a popularity contest, are we? Unfortunately we don't have any jobs for you in Eighth Regiment. You deserve your own team, and we need experienced, proficient team leaders like yourself."

"I understand, sir. I'll go wherever I'm pointed."

"Good, good. I know you'll do a fine job there. Their AO is the roughest of the three."

"Sir, you could have talked all day without saying that."

"It's not too late to extend," he says laughing.

Lieutenant Colonel Rains is a kindly looking grey-haired man with glasses. He seems a bit confused. Much to my chagrin I find he has not commanded any unit since he was a captain. He's a Saigon staff type trying to get his command ticket punched.

His staff advisor is tall and old, a Captain Follett. Follett was a legend at Armor school. He was an E-7 when he took OCS. He knew everything there is to know about tanks. He used to stand up and correct lecturers about minutiae. He graduated with very high honors, and they grabbed him as an instructor for two years. Then he came to Nam as a captain in an infantry unit. He is as new as Rains. Neither has any combat experience.

Thrill.

Follett briefs me. Rains says something about my wealth of experience being sorely needed. I spend the night in An Loc with HQ and go to my unit the next day.

I decide they're in deep trouble at Ninth Regiment HQ if I am helpful.

My counterpart is a tall, thin *Dai-Uy* Quan. Quan is part of a politically active family which is currently on the winning side in Saigon politics, hence his success in the military. He is dour and suspicious. I am too young. His exec is a *Dai-Uy* Vinh. Vinh is friendly, outgoing, and speaks good English. Naturally he is also gay. Just what I want to go into the jungle with: a homosexual Vietnamese. My interpreter's name is Dong, a sergeant who was an MP in Saigon till he deserted. He spent five years with One—Nine as an LCDB. When his sentence was completed he got back his former rank, but he can't be an MP again. He wishes he was. He's five feet seven inches, speaks *very* good English, including a complete command of slang obscenities.

My team consists of LT. Robert Simmons, SP-4 Larry "Duke" Wendell, and SP-4 John T. "Wyatt" Booker.

All I get out of the first meetings are the nicknames.

Simmons is surly. He has been in Nam almost as long as I, all with One-Nine, and wanted the team himself. He has been de facto S.A. for three weeks.

He's a good-looking, tall, blond kid from Oklahoma, a pre-law student who got drafted between graduation and law school. He was on the wrestling team in college, a fraternity type, and married while a second lieutenant. The girl was socially acceptable to his parents and a cheerleader in college. She was not the great love of his life, I discover, but Oklahoma

250

lawyers with visions of a political career don't marry Jewish girls. A photo of a large-breasted, black-haired Jewish girl still inhabits his wallet. However, he has a new love, one he hasn't seen: a new baby daughter, Betty Ann. He looks at pictures of her often. She was born after his R and R in Hawaii.

Duke is nineteen, fat, with a whiny voice. His sole desire is to be back in New Jersey at his mother's Tastee Freeze. He has had the clap twice, so he thinks he's a great lover. I fail to see the connection. His MOS is interpreter. He speaks almost as much Vietnamese as I do.

Wyatt is so named because he wears a six inch barreled Smith and Wesson .357 Magnum revolver in a western-style holster on his right hip. The bottom of the holster is strapped to his leg.

He's a thirty-three-year-old, six foot two inch-tall, thin black man from New York City. He joined the marines at age sixteen and was found to be underaged while on overseas duty. He was thus barred from reenlisting in the Marine Corps, so he joined the army. He spent six years in and left. In civilian life as a night club manager in New York City he was shot twice, had other personal problems, and reenlisted at age thirty-one. His MOS is commo.

Both men, despite their training, are in infantry sergeant's jobs.

We're in a nameless little firebase with deep bunkers and large rats. Companies go out on individual operations. I send Simmons and Duke the first time. Now I know the real reason Simmons wanted to be S.A. It wasn't ambition. The S.A. stays at headquarters while the assistant humps in the boonies.

My main excitement while they're out is a battle with an oversized rat in the bunker. If someone had ever told me I'd someday be killing rats with a four battery flashlight, I'd have laughed in his face.

After two days Simmons asks for Wyatt, saying Duke's whining is driving him crazy.

Thrill.

One—Nine is not the greatest fighting unit of the ARVN.

Simmons's company gets hit, and they run, panic, and shoot indiscriminantly. Simmons and Wyatt do a good job keeping reasonably calm while under fire from their own troops as well as the NVA. Third Company finally gets their perimeter stabilized, and Simmons calls for gunships. They work over the enemy for a while, but soon Third Company runs out of smoke grenades. Helicopters need smoke in heavy jungle to mark friendly boundaries. This means they're in trouble.

I'm in the C and C chopper with Quan. We go back to base and get a sandbag full of smoke grenades and return.

We hover over a hole in the jungle, and I lay down and lean out, holding to a seat belt with one hand, and the bag of grenades with the other. I have on headphones so I can talk to Simmons.

I see him, and he's directing me back and forth for the drop. I drop.

Then the chopper lurches, rolls sideways, and catches.

I pop out like a rubber ball on a rubber band, my grip on the seatbelt the only thing holding me.

Then I'm hit hard just below the midsection. The

pain is unbelievable.

Harris, *do not* let go of the seatbelt.

My vision blurs and goes dark around the edges.

I realize my arms are wrapped around something hard and cylindrical.

Jesus! It's the skid!

I'm outside the chopper hanging onto the fucking skid!

I look up. The right gunner is firing past me.

He can't get me back up.

I look down.

I wish I hadn't looked down.

We're climbing.

Memo: Don't let go of the skid, Harris.

I wrap my legs around it. The pain from hitting the skid with my middle is pretty solid.

Oh, Jesus, we're four thousand feet up!

I look up again.

The gunner is reaching for me. He's strapped in at least.

I don't want to let go of the skid to try and climb up.

I'm absolutely paralyzed. I've never been so scared in my life. By comparison hand-to-hand combat is a picnic.

I can't move.

He's yelling at me to take his hand. But I can't stand to let go with one hand. I'm scared.

Oh, God, don't let me fall.

I wrap the right arm around tighter and reach up with my left.

He grabs my wrist.

He pulls, but I don't let go with my right hand.

He's yelling at me to let go so he can pull me up. I would if I had any control over my body whatsoever. I can't because I'm paralyzed with fear.

Finally I release my right hand and reach his left arm and hold with a vise grip.

I'm over the edge, then inside. Both gunners were pulling me, though I only saw one.

I start to turn toward the pilots and ask what the fuck's going on.

Then I see the pilot. His head's been blown off. There's a gaping hole in the Plexiglas with an eighty mile per hour wind coming through it. The copilot is flying. He is bloody. I can't tell at first whether it's just gore from the pilot or whether he's been hit. Then I realize he took a round through his right shoulder. I don't know how he manages to fly with his left hand. I certainly don't know how he managed to keep from crashing when we were hit. One of the gunners goes up and starts giving him first aid. I throw up out the right side of the chopper, then sit back down and look at Quan.

My God, he's smiling. He didn't lift a finger to help.

I actually reach for my .45 to shoot him. That's when I realize my .45 is missing. It fell out sometime, I guess.

At Lai Khe they pull out the dead pilot and put the wounded pilot and me into a jeep and carry us to the medics. The pilot gets worked on first, of course. Then they carry him on to Long Binh in another chopper after they stabilize him.

Me they X-ray and poke. Amazingly enough, I'm just bruised. I can't move very much for a couple of days, though.

I also can't sleep. I'm still scared. I get so scared sometimes I vomit — when nothing's happening. Heartburn is chronic. I drink Maalox by the bottle. I just can't get over it. Flying in helicopters is impossible. I shake and sweat and have to close my eyes. I am terrified.

Two days later I'm looking for another .45. I mention it to a liaison sergeant who's short.

"I don't have a .45, sir, but I got this."

He holds up a CAR-15. It's a chopped and channeled M-16, designed for cramped spaces such as the inside of tanks or FAC planes, or for airborne troops. It has a good telescoping collapsable buttstock, ten and a half inch barrel with a long, heavy muzzle brake/flashhider on the front, better foregrip than a 16.

Where it should say M-16 on the receiver it says Colt Commando.

"Oh, Christ! Now I'm a commando. Does this cocksucker shoot?"

"Does a bear shit in the woods? Shoot it."

I have four magazines with me at the time, one in my 16, and three in a pouch. I take the three and fire off one in three-round bursts, one in one long twenty-round burst, and one single fire, all at stuff floating down a stream nearby. It's nice. It does shoot.

"It shoots. How much?"

"Eighty dollars."

I hand it back. "Sorry."

Well, make me an offer."

"Forty."

"Ah, come on, cap'n. Where else'll you get one?"

"Where else'll you sell one?"

"Sixty."

"Sold."

Best investment I ever made.

2 – 10 May 1970

Cambodia has been the main topic of discussion on AFVN radio and, of course, among the troops. U.S. units have been in Cambodia for a while with some success, or at least we hear about successes. In the States, though, National Guard troops have shot and killed college students at Kent State University for rioting in protest of the invasion of Cambodia. I haven't heard all the details yet, but I'm sick. Americans wearing the same uniform I wear with some pride have, either through panic or terrible leadership, shot against our own kids. No National Guardsmen were killed or wounded, so it wasn't self-defense. Bob and I discuss it. He thinks the college students got what they deserved.

"They were throwing rocks and garbage at the Guardsmen. You'd shoot at 'em, too."

In my mind I see Van shooting the kid.

"No, you don't shoot M-14s at kids for throwing things at you."

"You think these great troopers from Eleventh ACR you think so much of wouldn't waste 'em if they saw them chargin' 'em? You know damn well they would."

"God, I hope not. If they would, there's no hope. The National Guard is mostly draft dodgers and rich kids. They're second-rate, and they oughta be court-martialed for murdering those kids."

"Nah, they shoulda killed 'em all. Anti-American little shits."

We're called to a big briefing with regiment at An Loc. As I've feared, there's a map of Cambodia on the wall. One — Nine is shown CAing into an open area surrounded by jungle, then the familiar arrows and hieroglyphics we're used to indicating booniehumping.

"Motherfucker," says Simmons.

"What would your mother in Oklahoma City say, Bob?"

"I shoulda gone to Canada."

"Too cold. Girls have blue legs. Speak French. I guess you don't want to fight in Cambodia any more than those Kent State kids."

"You son of a bitch."

Lieutenant Colonel Rains, Simmons, and I go on a helicopter recon.

We don't even get close when the chopper does weird gyrations and heads for the trees, flying away from the area. I try to keep from screaming or throwing up.

"What's up?"

"A fifty-one cal. was locking in on us by radar. My ECM buzzed," says the pilot.

Fifty-one cal.? Radar controlled? Don't those things need a couple of trucks and a whole lot of crap? Sounds like an ideal TAC air target to me. Also sounds quite unlikely.

Later Colonel Norman asks me if I thought we were in danger from a .51 cal.

"Yes sir, I do. But then I believe in the Easter Bunny."

"Right." He laughs. "Let's walk out to the berm, Captain Harris."

As we walk over he says, "Where'd you get the CAR-fifteen?"

"Don't ask, sir. I won't ask you where you got a Browning Hi-Power."

"Does it shoot?"

"I've put, ah, three hundred odd rounds through it without a bobble. Still I'm keeping it squeaky clean inside."

"I've used them. I like them for heavy jungle. Colonel Pride would never approve, though."

"It's my skin, sir."

"Yeah. I agree. Jerry, I've got a proposition for you. Extend for six months, and I'll make you a TOC duty officer, guaranteed safe duty, and with my pull and another efficiency report like Colonel Pride just wrote on you, I'll guarantee you the career course when you return. You'll make major at minimum time in grade."

"I'll have to think about it, sir. Anyway, isn't it too late for me to extend?"

He laughs. "When I leave here they're going to pin a star on me. If I recommend approval, it'll be approved, deadline or no deadline."

"Tempting, sir, but I think I'd rather go home. I'm not in this for my career."

"Then why are you here?"

259

"Because while fat, dumb, and happy on a dream assignment in England some clown sent me orders for Nam."

"Okay, okay. You can still change your mind till I leave."

Lieutenant Colonel Rains doesn't want to go back. Norman gives him a written order to recon the area, and a Major Veneris is sent along to make sure he goes.

Fortunately the chopper pilot orbits the wrong clearing. I can see ours off to the west. Bob and I check the real LZ against our maps while Rains and Veneris talk about this one as if they had good sense. I want the NVA to think we're coming here.

Then I realize Four—Nine is coming here.

The next morning we wait for the fog to lift on the side of the road just inside Vietnam near the border. I've got the team pretty well stripped for action, packs with three days' rations, nine full twenty-round magazines, two smoke grenades each, two frags each, one radio battery each for Bob and me. Duke and Wyatt have radios.

My big knife is on my left side now, and the little CAR-15 is a dream, lighter and smaller than the 16 and a hell of a lot handier.

We have on steel pots and boonie hats in our packs, the pots on Norman's direct orders. I'm not impressed. I saw how easily that 7.62 Russian round went through that ARVN's helmet at Song Be. It's just weight.

Wyatt has his .357 Magnum. As we wait Duke is playing with it and drops it, breaking the spring which rotates the cylinder. Now Wyatt has three

260

pounds of dead weight.

He is not pleased with Duke. Neither am I. I elucidate what will happen to him should I ever again catch him playing with a weapon.

Inside our packs are our VC hammocks and ponchos with which to make shelter—and lots of bootlaces. Sewing kits, first aid kits, and writing material add a little weight. We also carry all the water we can stand.

We are prepared to stay a while.

Colonel Norman's chopper comes in. He has with him a CBS News camera crew and prima donna reporter Eric Masterfield. I'm not impressed by anyone in a tiger suit who didn't earn it, and he and his crew have them on, neatly starched—over low quarter shoes.

Norman tells me to take care of him and to make sure he gets to photograph anything interesting. I offer to put him on the lead chopper.

"Ah, er, do you, ah, think that's wise?" says Masterfield. He's overweight, with coiffed black hair with maybe just a touch of Grecian formula, perfect tan.

"Well, my lieutenant's on the lead chopper, and he'll have to take care of you. I'm in the C and C chopper and the last one in."

Norman says, "How about the second chopper. Can't you move Simmons into it without losing too much?"

Great, we're going into the most important LZ of my war, and I'm having to change up plans in order to please a fucking TV reporter.

"Sure, sir. That'll be fine. Bob, move to the second

chopper. Clear it with your counterpart."

"Swell," he says, happy as a lark to be with a CBS reporter and, likely, to be on TV soon.

Masterfield asks me questions.

"Now, you're C.O., right?"

"No, I'm senior advisor. *Dai-Uy* Quan is the C.O."

"Oh? A Vietnamese in command?"

"Right. It's a Vietnamese unit."

"Oh. Then he's Colonel Quan?"

"Captain."

"A captain is in command of a battalion?"

"Right. Captains and majors command battalions. Three battalions per regiment with a lieutenant colonel or colonel in command. It's the French system."

"Oh. French, huh?"

"You remember. Dien Bien Phu, 1953."

"Oh, yeah. How many men do you have?"

"Four seventy-five." We had five ninety before word came out we were going to Cambodia. One — Nine is a really gung-ho unit.

I ask him, "How long will you be with us?"

"Oh, this stuff'll be on the six o'clock news tonight."

"Good. We don't have supplies for you to overnight."

"I never stay out overnight. It's cold scotch and warm bar girls."

"How long you been in Nam?"

"Five years."

Five years? And you didn't know the ARVNs used the French system, or that captains commanded battalions in ARVN units, or that ARVNs commanded their own troops?

"That's a long time. You here all that time by choice?"

Of course, with an expense account, warm bar girls, and cold scotch, I might stay five years.

"Well, you gotta do it if you want the ol' career to go anywhere. The bureau chief says he needs a man here full time, and I'm it. Beats being police reporter in Cleveland."

"Yeah. I bet."

He asks me, "How big is your body count?"

"We just started the operation."

"No, I mean yours personally. Colonel Norman says you're a hotshot. Told me to ignore your child's face, that you're a cool head under fire. Says he's trying to get you to extend. You're wearing a big knife and carrying a CAR-fifteen like LRRPs. You must be a killer."

Simmons is laughing. "Him? He's never fired a shot in anger."

"Is that true?"

"Against my religion. I'm just a pacifist too scared to run to Canada. I tried to claim conscientious objector status, but they didn't recognize my religion."

"What religion?"

"I'm a devout coward."

"I should have seen that coming. You'll never get on the six o'clock news that way."

"Good. I don't want on it."

"Why not?" asks Simmons. He sure does.

"My mother watches the six o'clock news."

"So?" asks Masterfield.

"So she'd see me going on the scariest operation I

ever went on. She thinks I run a desk in Lai Khe. As far as you're concerned, I'm Captain Smith from New York, and I don't want any pictures. Take Simmons's picture. He wants people at home to see him."

"Okay, if that's the way you want it."

The fog lifts, and I take off in the C and C ship. Yes, I am still terrified of being in helicopters. I strap in and hold on so tight it's pathetic. I don' t know how I keep my voice from showing how scared I am. I'm not sure I do.

I have eight Cobras to give ARA prep of the area. I brief the Cobra C.O., Cobra Six, that I might need something after everybody's on the ground, to either save some or have his first shooters refuel and rearm. He tells me it's a superfluous request.

I have a major as pilot. It's his squadron of Hueys.

The Cobras go in and prep the perimeter of the LZ pretty thoroughly.

Then the first load of troops—eight choppers at a time—sixty-four troopers on the ground.

It's a cold LZ, thank God. Someday, someday it won't be.

"Victor, this is Kilo." It's Simmons.

"Kilo, Victor, go," I answer.

"We've got a bunker complex down here. Over."

"Inhabited? Over."

"Negatory, at least so far. Over."

"Roger. Beware of boobytraps. No souvenirs. Over."

"Hell, there's a nice pith helmet in one. You can see it from the outside. It'd be a great addition to my Ho Chi Minh sandals. Over."

"Negative, for Christ's sake. No souvenirs. Over."

"Roger."

Simmons has Wyatt with him. Wyatt'll keep him out of trouble. Wyatt's the one I want with me when the shit hits the fan.

The eight choppers pick up sixty-four more troops and come back. It's still a cold LZ, but I hear over the radio bits and pieces on the division net.

Four—Nine has a very hot LZ. Four choppers were blown out of the sky. Some of the troops in the other four wouldn't come out of the choppers. The chopper crews pushed some out. Then an ARVN turned his M-16 on a chopper crewman and killed him. The machine gunner killed the ARVN, and all the choppers pulled out, one dropping a couple of ARVNs out from two hundred feet. The fifteen or twenty troops on the ground are being cut to pieces. My reserve Cobras are taken to that LZ.

Masterfield wants transportation to go with them. Colonel Norman's chopper picks him up as my third load comes in.

Good riddance.

Simmons is semi-pissed. Masterfield had him in front of a bunker, filming him as he asked him questions about the bunker complex: "Ah, we call this complex New York City 'cause it's so big. Must be a hundred heavy-duty bunkers here, a hospital, a training center, a prison."

After the fourth load we refuel in Song Be. Then we bring in four more loads uneventfully. I'm the last one on the ground with Quan, his radio operators, and Duke. Simmons has been calling for me to get to his location as soon as I get down. When I get there, in the midst of a large, camouflaged bunker complex, he's white as a sheet. Wyatt is almost as white. On him it's an accomplishment.

"What's up?"

"This." He turns and points.

I drop my rifle and fall to my knees. It is a revelation, like finding God, a discovery that changes me forever. Whatever I was before, I will never be the same. Mrs. Harris's nice little boy Jerry just disappeared off the face of the earth, never to return. The man who will return in his place, if he returns at all, will be taken as an imposter immediately. Jerry Harris never understood the war. The imposter understands completely, for it is all explained here.

Tied to a tree by a big bunker is — was — an American soldier.

The man — boy — nineteen, twenty, twenty-one, was tied to the tree, his clothes cut or ripped off. Then, and I'm not sure what order these were carried out, his toenails and fingernails were pulled out, the bottoms of his feet sliced to hamburger, his knees crushed with rifle butts, his balls and penis cut off, his belly slit open and his intestines pulled out on the ground to be chopped to pieces, his eyes gouged out, his ears and nose cut off, and his throat cut with his balls stuck in his gaping cut-open throat. His penis hanging out of his mouth like an obscene cigarette.

I throw up. Then I throw up again. Then I gag dryly. The ARVNs are acting as if nothing has happened. I'm sure I've lost much face. I don't care. Jerry Harris died here, too, along with his innocence and all his sense of values. His replacement has no innocence and only one value. He has seen the essence of this war and understands it deep in the marrow of his bones.

I finally manage to talk. I get on the radio and call for Colonel Norman. He's still in range over Four—Nine's fiasco.

"I have the body of a Uniform Sierra Papa Oscar Whiskey. I need it extracted soonest. Over."

"Victor, this is Hanover Six. I'll pick it—him up. Things are getting calm over here. We had a hell of a fight goin' for a few minutes. Any details? Over."

"Nothing I want to give over the air. Over."

There's something cut on his chest. I turn to the interpreter. "What does that say?"

"Do not follow us."

"Jesus!" I key the mike. "They have more, more P.O.W.s!" I reach over and touch the disgusting, pitiful object, the body of the boy that could be me. He's still warm. "They have more, and they don't want us to follow them. This boy's still warm. They're not very far ahead of us. Over."

"Roger. I've gotten reports. There are—oh hell, I'll tell you on the ground. But we know there are more. Over."

Then they've got them. And we're close. God what I'd give for a Mike Strike force or a company of American infantry.

"Lieutenant Simmons, get some of the ARVNs to get this man into a body bag, and get him to the LZ. *Dai-Uy*, which way did they go? Do you know?"

He speaks Vietnamese to his exec, who answers, then he says, "Northeast."

"We follow. Yes?"

"*Ya, fi.* Soon."

"*Ya, fi.* Now."

"Okay. We not done checking bunkers. We finish

first."

"*Dai-Uy*, they have more P.O.W.s. We must catch them."

"American P.O.W.s?"

"Yes."

"We check bunkers, then go."

"*Dai-Uy*, either we go now, or I pull my advisors. The chopper is coming for him. We'll get on it."

This is not good advisor tactics. If he does what I want now, he loses face. If he does not, he loses us, because I'm not bluffing. I'll probably be court-martialed, but I don't give a damn. I have no time. I am not going to wait around.

"I send one company ahead, okay?"

"Okay," I say, taking the face-saving compromise. It'll work.

"Lieutenant Simmons, you and Duke stay with headquarters group. Wyatt, come with me. We're going to the First Company."

ARVNs are loading the mutilated corpse into a body bag. Simmons is watching. He nods, obviously near to retching himself.

But Quan says, "*Dai-Uy*. You stay with me. Send Trung-Uy ahead. You my advisor."

"*Dai-Uy*, I would ordinarily. I can't now. I must be with the lead company. If something like this," I say pointing to the boy being put into the body bag, "happens to someone else because I didn't do my job better than I ever have before, I couldn't live with myself. Please, take no offense."

"Okay, *Dai-Uy*. But I no like. You my advisor."

"Come on, Wyatt."

I move out toward the lead company. Wyatt easily

268

keeps up. I talk on his radio to Norman.

"I'm moving to the lead company. We're going after them. He is still warm. They aren't more than an hour ahead. I need a hunter-killer team. Over."

"Roger, Victor. I'll get you one somehow. Every helicopter in Vietnam is engaged today. I don't know where I'll get the blade time. I've been trying to get a Mike Force to block, but they're engaged, too. I think you'll be on your own. Over."

"Roger, Six. I hope I can get this mob to move out fast enough. Over."

"Roger. Out."

I catch up to the lead company commander, Tu-Uy Nguygen. He's gotten his orders by radio and is moving out.

I tell him in pidgin Vietnamese, "Quickly, quickly, we must catch them."

"We catch them, *Dai-Uy*. Boy, you made *Dai-Uy* Quan *beaucoup* mad." He's speaking English while I speak Vietnamese. What a mess.

"Sorry."

"Sorry? No sorry. You numbah one! We kill VC."

He and I are with the lead platoon. We're moving very quickly. I'm in a sweat and hurting, but I don't grumble or bobble. The vision of that P.O.W. consumes me.

The hunter-killer team calls in. They're enroute and want me to pop smoke. I explain we'll move through our own smoke, to search ahead a click.

Then there's firing ahead. First Company stops and takes cover. Nugygen, Wyatt, and I run cautiously to the line.

Two men lie dead, one gut-shot, one with the top of

269

his head blown off. Everyone is on line returning fire.

The hunter-killer team is too late. Maybe we're not.

I pop smoke and tell them to cut off the retreat lines but not to shoot any P.O.W.s.

The jungle is too thick. They can't see the smoke.

I hear a woman scream and some ARVNs scramble ahead on the right. We run with them.

A woman in black pajamas runs toward us through the thick jungle, hands up yelling, *"Chieu Hoi! Chieu Hoi!"*

Somehow nobody shoots her.

She is pregnant and maybe eighteen, maybe younger.

One ARVN grabs her and searches her yelling, "It's all right! It's all right! No one will hurt you." He finishes searching her and turns to Nguygen. "She's okay."

She's speaking too fast. She's saying, I think, that she was their prisoner, that she's no VC. She tells the village she was taken from.

I keep moving.

Then I'm ahead of the others and the bushes clear out, and I can see. In the clearing a black-clad figure is standing over a kneeling, crying, head-down American boy. The black-clad figure is about to shoot the boy with a K-54 pistol.

It's all slow motion. He turns and starts to point the pistol at me.

The clock is running.

My CAR-15 is at my hip. I can't spray from the hip, or I'm likely to hit the boy.

I pull it to my shoulder and try to get the NVA's face in the sights.

But he gets the shot off first. I see the muzzle flash. I

know in that split second the clock has run out, and he has beaten it.

I get a terrific blow in the forehead, and it knocks me backward.

The world goes out. I do not see my life pass before me. I do not desire to recount my sins. I do feel regret.

When it comes back I feel pain. My head is a timpani. *Boom*-boom, *Boom*-boom, *Boom*-boom. Oh, Jesus it hurts. I hear Vietnamese voices and feel a tugging at my feet. I open my eyes. ARVNs are pulling my boots and belt off.

Am I dead?

No, because as I start to speak I hear Wyatt.

"Hey, muthafucka!"

I turn. He pops the one at my right boot with the butt of his M-16 across the side of his head.

"Leave 'im alone, muthafucka!"

I sit up, nearly retching.

"The boy!" I croack. "Wyatt! The boy! What happened?"

"I'm okay, sir. This man shot the VC lieutenant." It's the boy. He's pointing to Wyatt. I can see now. The young GI is standing now, close to me, hands behind him, still tied up I guess. I reach for my big knife and cut him loose. His hands are blue.

I look around. There's a black-clad body twenty feet away. I stand up, look around, and an ARVN hands me my CAR-15. They were stripping my body. I feel for my wallet. It's gone. One of them hands it to me. Gee, they were fast. Not fast enough; the money's still there, what little's in it. One doesn't need much on an infantry operation in a hostile jungle.

Wait! Why am I not dead? I feel my forehead, which

seems to be the center of the pain, and look myself over.

Then an ARVN hands me my helmet. There's a hole where the captain's bars are inked on the camouflage cover. There's an exit hole in the back. This makes no sense, as there's no hole in my head. I actually feel for one, feeling stupid.

I pull the liner out. It has no hole in it, just a groove. The round penetrated the helmet but not the liner. Thank goodness for low-powered pistol rounds. A .45 would have killed me.

I think I'm crying now. I'm not sure. I put the helmet on and stagger over to the black pile of rags twenty feet away. He's missing the top of his head. Brains are in the grass behind him in chunks, with clumps of black hair behind that. That doesn't bother me, as the sight of enemy dead will never bother me again, but he's also missing his K-54.

It'd be a great souvenir.

The kid is standing behind me, rubbing his hands together. They must hurt like holy hell right now.

"Damn, did you see who got the pistol?"

"No, sir." He's got a First Cav. patch on and no rank. I realize his right leg is bloodied. It's an old wound.

"I'll get you out of here real quick. How many P.O.W.s were with you?"

"Seventeen in all, sir. One they cut up in front of us. He was wounded and couldn't have made the trip. They were showing us what would happen if we couldn't keep up. It was awful—"

"I know. I saw him. You and fifteen others moved out."

"Yes, sir. I was last because of my leg. The others are

pretty far ahead. They stuck me with the rear guard. When you caught up with us they were going to shoot me—"

"I know."

Wyatt says, "We got eleven bodies, sir. Two of our men are dead, one wounded."

"Rog," I say, taking the handset to call in medevac.

"Hanover Six, this is Millet Three Victor. Over."

"Go Three."

"I have a medevac—urgent, one Uniform Sierra ambulatory, one ARVN, ah, er, Wyatt, is that litter? Litter. Over."

"Roger. I'll pick 'em up myself. One of 'em your team? What's going on? Over."

"Negative. A Papa Oscar Whiskey. We caught up with the rear guard. One-one November Victor Alpha KIA, ah, one-zero AKs, two line ones, one line two. We got one Uniform Sierra Papa Oscar Whiskey. Over."

"Outstanding! Over."

"I'm not so sure. There were more. This was a rear guard. The rest got away. Over."

"Roger. Wait over."

"Roger."

"Pop smoke. Over."

"Roger, smoke—out. Over."

He is orbiting nearly a click away, so the smoke gets pretty high before they see it.

"I identify violet. Over."

"That is correct. Over."

Then Nguygen points to the girl.

"Six, Victor. I almost forgot. We got one more. Female Vietnamese, says she was prisoner of NVA. Very pregnant. Can you take her? Over."

"Negative. We have room for only two more. Over."

"Roger. It'll be the resupply chopper for her. Sorry."

The chopper comes in, flinging smoke away, and I put the kid on it. ARVNs carry the litter and try to put on the two dead, but the crew waves them off. We'll have to hump dead till we get resupplied.

We never catch the rest of the unit with the prisoners. I can't get Quan to move fast enough. After all, they're just American prisoners.

I didn't get the kid's name.

We move on till dusk and set up an NDP. About then it really sinks in that the NVA have won. They delayed us with a squad of eleven and got away with fifteen P.O.W.s — fifteen Americans who'll be tortured, starved, and exploited for propaganda purposes. This was the most important operation of my life, and I've blown it. In the darkness of the hammock under my poncho spread out like a roof and tied with bootlaces I cry silently because the hurt is too much to take like a man. The phrase goes through my mind, "You have been tried and found wanting."

We cross Four—Nine's path. We talk with the advisors. They're all still alive miraculously, but Sergeant First Class Collingsworth was in the lead chopper. He escaped the crash with a singed uniform and managed to stay alive in the hour and a half they couldn't get any reinforcements on the ground. Out of twenty ARVNs on the ground who survived the landings, three and Collingsworth are still alive and unwounded. Collingsworth is a third tour veteran, with previous tours in the First Infantry Division and MACV. He controlled helicopters, jets, and a Shadow from the prone position. The fighting went from small-arms to hand-to-hand. He says he killed one NVA with a Ka-Bar knife. One hundred fifty-six NVA bodies are still there. A chinook carried off two 51 cal. machine guns, fifteen RPG-2s, and a hundred and twenty AKs. Four—Nine had fifty-six casualties, including twenty-seven killed. The aviation company lost seventeen killed, five wounded. It was a fiasco in other words.

The NVA dead included women. This I haven't

encountered before. I ask if they're like our girl prisoners.

"I doubt it, sir," says Collingsworth. "We found weapons on the bodies, and I saw one of them shooting at us. Besides, how do you know yours isn' VC?"

"I don't, but she says she's going to kill the bab because it's a Communist's baby."

"Oh."

We hump through the boonies at a pretty rapi pace, moving all day and setting up an NDP an ambushes at night. It's hell on those doing th ambushes.

The next morning we find more bunkers. This tim they're occupied. The souvenirs coming from then are 7.62 mm rounds.

Simmons and Wyatt are with the lead company.

"Victor, Kilo. Over."

"Go Kilo."

"We're taking fire from a bunker here. Sierra Al pha. Over."

He's pretty excited, judging by his voice.

"Roger, Kilo. Can you use any ARA or TAC air Over."

"Negative. The motherfuckers are twenty yard away, under heavy trees. Will have to take 'em out Over."

"Roger. Over."

"We have a line two, will need a medevac. Over.

"Roger. I'll call it in, but you'll have to get secured Over."

"Roger."

I get regiment. They're set up at our original LZ

now.

"Millet Six, this is Three Victor. Over."

"Frothy Millet Tha-ree Victor, this is Frothy Millet Six Romeo Tango. Over." They always have proper radio procedure in the rear.

"Six, this is Three. I have troops in contact. I'll need a medevac, urgent, whenever things get secure. Over."

"Frothy Millet tha-ree Victor, this is Frothy Millet Six Romeo Tango. Do you want me to request a medevac now, or are you just making conversation? Over."

Some SP-4 in the rear is fucking with my mind, secure in the knowledge that whoever is on the other end of the radio is a long, long way from him. No senior NCOs or officers must be near.

"Six Romeo Tango, get Six Actual or Alpha on the phone. Over." Jesus, what a smartass.

"Frothy Millet Tha-ree Victor, this is Frothy Millet Six Romeo Tango. Negative on that request. Six Actual is eating and Six Alpha is doing a report. Over."

"Six Romeo Tango, Three Victor. If you don't get one of those Oscars on the phone in thirty seconds, I'll file charges for insubordination in a combat situation and endangering lives and government property. Then when I return on the next chopper that lands here, I'll ring your fuckin' neck. Over."

"Three Victor, this is Six. Over." Aha, Lieutenant Colonel Rains's voice. Good.

"Six, Three, you've got a real problem with that RT. I have troops in contact, and I don't need smartasses. I'm in heavy vegetation, so I can't use Alpha Sierra, but I have one line two already, urgent. I request you scramble a medevac to your location, with a Cobra escort, and then I'll call 'em in when it's secure. Over."

"Roger, Three. Good plan. Wait out."

Simmons calls. "We've taken two more line twos, one line one. We've dropped grenades in the bunkers. They should be — oh, shit. They're shooting again! Over."

They pour everything into the two bunkers, small arms, a LAW into one. Nothing works.

They call for the people to *Chieu Hoi,* but one calls back, "No! You'll kill me!"

"No! *Chieu Hoi! Chieu Hoi!* We will treat you like a brother."

"I don't believe you! You take no prisoners."

"No! *Chieu Hoi! Chieu Hoi!*"

"No! You will kill me."

The ARVNs start chanting *"Chieu Hoi! Chieu Hoi! Chieu Hoi!"*

Shooting comes out of the bunker.

Finally the first sergeant grabs four stickers of C-4, ties them together to a grenade, and puts them on a string. He ties one end of the string to a stake. He repeats this; then he runs to the bunkers under a heavy volume of covering fire.

He gets on one bunker, pounds the stake in, pulls the pin, and throws the explosive inside a firing port.

Then he runs to the other and repeats. The first blows and collapses the bunker. The second blows as he runs back to safety.

When they dig into the bunkers they pull out two bodies. One guy is obviously dead with large pieces missing from his anatomy. The other guy has only a gash on his left buttock.

The medic pours peroxide in the gash, and the guy comes to.

I call in the prisoner on the radio. Six has been unable to get a medevac because U.S. units are in contact, but the ARVNs send an ancient CH-34 for the prisoner, and it takes our wounded, too.

Two guys with an AK-47 each held off a battalion for two hours. Simmons sums it up. "In the U.S. Army a guy woulda got the Medal of Honor for that."

We find a cache of weapons in another bunker, a .51 cal. MG, an AK-47 with a folding stock, and 28 with wooden stocks, an 82 mm mortar, and a broken SKS with no stock. Too bad, SKSs can be taken home and are the second most desirable souvenir behind the K-54 pistol. I still want to know who got that one. I've put the word out that I'll buy it, but no one's offered it for sale. He probably thinks, rightfully so, that I'll shoot him with it.

In the rear the prisoner is put into a tiger cage and questioned. He says nothing. They torture him — nothing. It won't be till two days later when a rocket explodes behind him and he doesn't flinch that an advisor says, "He's deaf." Of course he is, from all the explosives. To written questions he gives quick answers.

Duke is driving me batty. He never shuts up. He bitches about the heat, the humidity, the bugs, the snakes, the thorns, the vines, the weeds, the trees, the puddles, the ants, the food (C-rations), the speed of the march (fast and unrelenting), the infrequency of breaks from said march, the taste of the water after one adds one iodine tablet for a canteen of clear water or two tablets for a canteen of muddy water, the weight of his pack (admittedly heavy as are they all), water, ammo, M-16, grenades, helmet, uniform, and boots. He complains about the leadership in regiment, Lai Khe, Saigon, and Washington, not to mention mine and Quan's, which he does. He complains about getting VD the last time he had leave, not getting VD lately, and being horny. He complains about being dirty and sweaty. He wants to be back at the Tastee Freeze his mother owns in New Jersey. It's then that I remember that were there no war, he'd be a teenaged soda jerk. He says he'll *Chieu Hoi* if we're overrun because he doesn't trust the ARVNs to defend themselves and us. Then he says he wants a chance to shoot a dink. I offer him the chance to walk point, though it'd be hard to explain to Lieutenant Colonel Rains if he got zapped.

I try everything but shooting him to shut him up. Direct orders, indirect orders, requests, and suggestions don't work for more than five minutes. Then he starts over. After a couple of days I'm approaching the point of slitting his throat with my survival knife. After another day I want to do it with the Swiss Army knife because it'll take longer and hurt more.

We move from dawn till dusk. It's heavy undergrowth with little light getting through from the sun.

Men with machetes cut paths, but not much of one, understandably tiring of cutting large paths. So we go under long, thin, thorny vines. I'll pick up one with the back of my hand and slide under it. It'll fall off my helmet and hit the back of my neck. So there are thorns in the back of my hands and the back of my neck. They get infected. The hands are swollen. My neck is uncomfortable.

Water is a problem. We drink copious amounts. Our uniforms are white with salt. We take salt tablets and malaria tablets, a little daily orange one for one type of malaria, and a weekly horse pill for another. Some guys try to not take one or the other claiming it causes diarrhea, but after eating so much rice and C-rations, that's not a problem with me. I'm constipated most of the time, with bloody hemorrhoids a consequence of several months in Nam. Shitting in the woods from a squat is not a common skill to city boys. Duke falls over backward once and gets shit all over himself. This makes him even less popular with the rest of us till he gets clean in a bomb crater full of semi-dirty water.

Wyatt doesn't complain. When he talks, he talks of New York City and pimps and hoods. He doesn't seem to miss it. I think he's gone from one combat zone to another. The way he talks he's more afraid of New York hoods than the NVA. He also talks of his wife who is giving him trouble in her letters. This I understand. I haven't been exactly getting the best letters ever. They haven't quite started "Dear Murderer," but that's the idea. "How can you do such things?" In Wyatt's case he suspects his wife is getting fucked by a white man, their landlord. This makes him occasionally edgy toward the rest of us, me in particular as the symbol of white authority. I think I could be walking a tightrope soon.

Bob is also bothered by his letters from home. He gets pictures of the daughter he's never seen, born after his R and R.

His talk is about college, the college wrestling team, and OCS.

We get five minute breaks every hour and a half hour at lunch when we can take off our damn packs and sit or lie down. My shoulders and back are pure fire by then. I find I can lie down, drink heavily, and be fast asleep by the time the signal is given in five minutes.

Three C-rations a day to a man in a static situation is too much. I'd eat two at FSB Mary. Now it's not enough. There's no waste, and we're hungry all the time. I have two sticks of C-4, so we can heat the meat courses with a small square of C-4. Duke is trying to trade his for something else—as if we liked pork any more than he does.

On the third day the resupply helicopter has no food on it.

This is semi-serious.

I call to Six.

"We received no rations today. This is a problem. Over."

"Roger. What is that? Over."

Jesus. What is he smoking?

"We're out of food. Over."

"What did you do with the food I sent three days ago? Over."

"We ate it. Over."

"Well, you'll have to do without till you're resupplied."

"When are we getting resupplied? Over."

"In three days, of course, as per SOP. Over."

"Well, we don't have rations to last three days.

Over."

"Oh, don't you get ARVN rations? Over."

"Negative. Over."

"Well, I suggest you talk with counterpart and get some of their surplus. We have no rations for you and no plans to resupply you for three more days. You should have carried more. Over."

I'm nearly to the point of screaming incoherently in the radio. There is a long pause before I answer. I'm trying to calm down, and I do check with Quan. He certainly has no surplus of rations. He gives us a few bags of rice each and a couple of cans of apricots and a noxious tuna concoction.

"Six, this is Three Victor. I don't know what's going on back there, but we're humping flat out here, and we can't do it without rations. We can only carry three days' worth, and anyway, that's all we were given. The plan was to resupply every three days. We need rations ASAP. Over."

"Roger, Three Victor, but, ah, er, my Sierra didn't requisition any. Over." Swell, so Captain Follett is incompetent. So fire him. "I can have some by next scheduled resupply. Over."

"What are we supposed to do in the meantime? Over."

"You're soldiers in a combat unit. Quit whining and suffer a little. Out."

I never had these problems with Lieutenant Colonel Pride.

The next resupply has no water. When I call about it, Follett asks, as though he's in a total fog, why I want any. "Aren't there bomb craters around?"

I give up.

At night we find trees and tie the VC hammocks between them, tie the poncho over it like a tent with the indispensable bootlaces, and carefully arrange things so when it rains, and it always rains, as little as possible gets wet. Of course, we alway get wet. Sleep is a true luxury.

It's semi-bright one night. We're around a bomb crater, and the moon's out. All is jungle-quiet, meaning the normal jungle sounds, when I hear, "Fuck you."

What? I think. It is an Oriental voice. Have the NVA found us? Are they taunting us?

"Fuck you."

I wonder where it is coming from. It sounds like a hundred and eighty degrees from the last time.

"Fuck you."

"Fuck you."

Jesus. There are two of them. Have they got us surrounded? Are we about to be killed, overrun, knifed in our hammocks?

"Fuck you."

"Fuck you."

I have my CAR-15 in my hands.

"Fuck you, fuck you."

"Fuck you, fuck you."

"Fuck you, too," says Dong.

"What the hell is that, Dong?" I ask him finally. He seems merely annoyed by the noise.

"Fuck-you lizards."

"What?" I whisper.

"Fuck-you lizards, about four, three feet long. Their mating call sounds like 'fuck you' to American ears."

"Jesus. They scared the shit outta me."

Duke pipes up, "They never scared me. I knowed it all along."

"Duke?"

"Yeah?"

"Fuck you."

The lizards echo, "Fuck you, fuck you, fuck you."

18 — 24 May, 1970

Eight UH1Hs pick us up, sixty-four men at a time and move us to a clearing on the edge of a swamp. The hieroglyphs on the map run us through a section marked blue and green — swamp.

I know we'll find nothing there, and so does Simmons, but there's no telling that to anyone at regiment.

The NVA aren't stupid. They won't headquarters in a swamp.

Follett is proving semi-useless. Lieutenant Colonel Rains had to scrounge C-rations himself last time, and Follett can't send helicopters to the right coordinates. Three — Nine had a very hairy situation because Follett sent choppers to three-nine-six-eight-four-five-seven-zero instead of four-five-seven-zero-three-nine-six-eight.

Water is no problem in the swamp as it was in the higher ground. We ran out and had a chopper bring some, but it was a UH1D instead of an H, and it couldn't hover over our small clearing in the hundred and ten degree heat/ninety percent humidity. It made passes at eighty knots, dropping the water out in artillery tubes with little accuracy and losing most of the water containers in the deep woods. Dodging one in head-high weeds I lost my famous helmet with the hole in it. I'm still pissed. I had intended to smuggle that home somehow and put it on my mantle.

Now we've got water. It gets deeper as we go further, first puddles, then over our ankles in low spots, then all the time, then to our waists and eventually armpit high in places. Leeches bite us unmercifully. I'm lucky. My legs get a few. Duke gets one under his foreskin. He wants me to medevac him.

"No, Duke, I'm not going to call in that one of my men has a leech up his dick."

Wyatt says, "Fuck," and sticks a lit cigarette at it. Duke pulls away squealing.

"Look, muthafucka, I'm not gonna burn your dick, I'm gonna burn the leech so he'll let go."

"No! No! I'll—I'll pull him off."

"Fuck! Don't you ever want use your dick for fuckin' again, suckah?"

"What do you mean?"

"If you do that, you'll leave the head in, an' it'll get infected, and your dick won' get hard again. I burn the leech off, you'll be okay."

"Oh Jesus. Oh, Jesus. Fuck, shit, piss, come, God. Motherfucker, goddamn motherfucker," says Duke, almost crying, definitely whining.

"Well, what'll it be?" says Wyatt.

"Okay, goddamn. Do it." He squeezes his eyes shut and holds both hands on his penis so only the head and the leech protrude.

Wyatt puffs hard on the cigarette and aims it

expertly at the leech. It releases and falls off.

"Gee, that was a real cocksucka," Wyatt says.

We spend three days in the swamp with leeches and snakes and such. Bob sums it up. "This is a perfect description of hell."

Finally we begin to come out of it toward high ground. We find a bunker complex—inhabited. We lose our point man and one more discovering that. I call for air support as we dig in fifty yards from the bunkers. There can't be more than a few guys in the bunkers, judging from their volume of fire.

A FAC shows up in an OV10 push-pull Cessna.

"Victor, this is Skypilot, I have four Fox Fives with seven hundred fifty pound bombs enroute. Over."

"Roger, Skypilot. We have a bunker complex ahead. I'll pop smoke at our front lined. I need hits on the bunkers fifty yards to the Whiskey, two-seven-zero degrees. Over."

"Roger, Victor. Are your troops protected? Over."

"What's he mean?" says Wyatt. "That we got rubbers on?"

"What the fuck? Over," says Bob.

"Negative. Over," I say, almost laughing into the mike.

"Be advised that the minimum safe distance for troops in the open is three hundred meters. Over."

"Roger." I turn to Quan. "We need to back up some. We're too close."

"They get away."

"I tend to agree, but the fighters won't drop unless we do. They're afraid they'll hit us."

289

"*Du ma!* Okay, *Dai-Uy.* We back up. *Dinky dau du ma.*"

So we move maybe a hundred yards. Quan just won't move more than that. We lose all contact if we do.

We pop smoke.

The first F-5 comes in and drops—too far away.

"Skypilot, Victor, right five zero your direction, that's five-zero meters to the echo, ninety degrees. Over."

"Roger, five-zero meters to the echo. Over."

The next one drops closer, but not close enough. Then the FAC decides he's too close to us.

Quan doesn't want to move anymore. He reports two more KIA from the company in contact.

"Skypilot, Victor. Right five-zero, that's echo five-zero, initials Juliet Hotel. Over."

"Victor, Skypilot, negative. That's too close to your troops. Over."

"Skypilot, this is Victor. The maximum effective range of an AK-forty-seven is three hundred meters. In this jungle the max range is about a hundred fifty meters, maybe a hundred. We're taking casualties from AKs, and your bombs aren't stopping it. I've given you my initials so I've taken responsibility. I'd rather risk shrapnel than more men killed by AKs. Now drop the fucking bombs where I told you. Over."

"Victor, this is Skypilot, negative, negative, too dangerous, we're going home unless you move back. Over."

I turn to Quan. "He wants us to move back more, or he won't drop any more bombs. What do you want to do?"

290

"We move back, they shoot us when we do. In these trees we safe from bombs unless real close. I no move back."

"He's going home with his bombs, then, *Dai-Uy*."

"Fuck him. We here to kill VC."

"Skypilot, Victor. If you leave now, I'll report it to my Charlie Oscar as deserting troops in contact. I may never get outta this fuckin' place, but if I do, I'll press the case till hell freezes over. Now your inaction is getting my troops killed. Drop the fuckin' bombs. Over."

"Negative, Victor, we're goin' home. Out."

We spend another three hours taking the bunkers, losing three more men to take three dead bodies in the bunker.

My complaint never gets past Lieutenant Colonel Rains.

So much for close air support from F-5s.

We find a nice spot for resupply, a clearing up a hill a bit from a cold, clear stream.

Rains comes in the log bird. We unload it, and I ask Rains if he'd like to talk in the coolness of the "HQ" area.

"Is it secure?"

"Well, more or less. There's nobody here but us and the NVA."

"You have security out?"

He's looking around a bit frantically. I forget he's never been under fire. I'm perfectly comfortable here. This is a rest situation for me. For him it's the front.

"You have security out?"

"Yes sir."

Usually at this time the S.A. asks what one needs and gives one slight hell for one's transgressions. Not Rains. He tells me his problems—as if I wanted to know. I have a very provincial view of the war.

"I have a problem with Follett."

"You noticed."

"I've got to replace him with someone who can get the job done. He can't seem to do anything right."

"Well, don't look at me, sir," I say before he has a chance to ask me—if he intends to.

"You don't want the job?"

"No sir. Till my tour's over this is the job I want. No more changes."

"Okay. I'll bring in Captain Hill."

"Excellent choice, sir. He's second tour. Should know what our problems are out here."

"That means giving Three—Nine to Captain Follett."

"Poor Three—Nine."

"Captain!"

"Sorry, sir. On the next resupply here's a list of stuff we're low of or out of, if you could, sir."

"Oh, yeah. Well. Here's the op plan for the next week."

I start copying it on my map with a grease pencil on the encased map.

I hear Duke complaining as they stow away C-rats. "Goddamn! Ham and motherfuckers! Shit! Them's older than we are."

I look up. That gets my attention. Ham and lima beans haven't been current C-rations for a while. They're totally inedible by everyone I've ever met.

"Having trouble getting C-rations, sir?" I ask Rains.

"Had to buy them. Advisors are on separate rations. Advisors are supposed to live off the local economy. We aren't authorized Cs."

"Jesus. Don't you have any scroungers?"

"No place to scrounge, Captain. The U.S. units are all leaving, and we're not in exactly the best position to go scrounging."

"When it's my turn in the rear, sir. I bet I can come up with something."

"Don't be a smartass, Captain. You don't know what it's like."

"Yes sir. On the other hand, we've been humping pretty hard and have done without food at all some days, and we get —" I say, picking up one C-rat, "1960 vintage Cs."

"I had to buy them, Captain. That'll be twenty-four dollars."

"Jesus." I hand him twenty-four dollars. "That's the last fuckin' straw. Now I'm broke. If your people can't scrounge them, give me a chopper and one hour's blade time, and I'll come up with a pallet load for the whole unit."

"Don't make silly boasts, captain. I'm not about to request or waste an hour's blade time on a wild goose chase."

"Yes sir. Meanwhile we eat 1960 C-rations while on a hell of a hump."

"We all have to accept a few sacrifices, Captain. There's a war on."

"Right. Sir?"

"What's that?"

"The local economy sucks."

When he goes back to his chopper, it won't start. The battery's dead.

The crew calls on the radio till they reach a Chinook flying over. The pilot says he'll come down and jump start the Huey.

Jump start a Huey?

The chopper crew throws out a smoke grenade — into the chest-high dry grass.

When the other chopper lands its blades fan up a really roaring fire.

We cut off bushes and beat the fire out. I take so much smoke I'm wheezing and weak. The chopper makes it off safely.

Come again, Lieutenant Colonel Rains. Maybe you can burn us all up.

We're late leaving the LZ, and we're making a mad dash for our NDP in heavy bush. Since we've had trouble getting decent trees to hang our hammocks to because the ARVNs take the good ones, Duke sprints ahead to secure some. Duke, first in hammocks, last in war.

From out of behind a tree pops an NVA in khaki shorts and Ho Chi Minh sandals. He tosses a grenade at Duke's feet and runs. Duke panics.

He fires wildly into the air, backing up and staring at the grenade. Of course, safety would be behind a tree a couple of paces on either side, but he's panicked out.

I'm eight paces behind him and out of sight because of the trees. I hear shooting close to home and panic, too.

I dive behind the biggest, closest tree and land in six inches of mud and water, drenching myself and blinding myself with mud on my glasses.

I frantically get my weapon into position and try to flip off the safety.

Jesus! It's frozen!

The motherfucking safety won't move!

I take my left hand and push on the lever.

I hear more firing, now silence.

The grenade didn't go off, but at this time, I don't know what the hell's going off.

The NVA got clean away.

Finally the safety comes off and slides to Auto.

"You can get up now, Captain," says Simmons derisively.

I look up. He's standing and walking forward. The ARVNs are staring at me. I'm a mess.

In their eyes I'm also a coward. I hear the words *"dinky dau"* in the noise.

"Big help you were, Captain," says Simmons, putting a certain negative, sarcastic emphasis on the word *captain* that makes me want to punch him.

Duke walks back, very white, babbling.

"What happened, Duke?" I ask.

"If you'd been standing up you'd have seen, Captain," says Simmons.

"Okay, okay. What happened, Duke?"

"VC. Little guy, tan shorts, Ho Chi Minh sandals, jumped out from behind a tree and threw a grenade at me. Landed between my feet!"

"A dud?"

"Yeah. Ah, yes sir!"

"Did you get him?"

"No. I—I shot at him. I just backed up—in shock—and shot at him—wildly. Didn't hit him."

"Next time, Duke, jump behind a tree," I say. "The grenade might go off."

"God, Cap'n! I thought I was dead. I never been so scared in my life."

"That's okay, Cap'n Harris was scared, too," says Simmons, a chuckle in his voice.

I start to say something but bite my tongue.

We walk forward to the tree from where the NVA jumped. An ARVN is looking at the grenade. It is a Chinese copy of the old U.S. pineapple with a spoon and a pin. The pin has been pulled, but the spoon hasn't opened.

The ARVN is probing it with a stick. I move on quickly to get out of range.

When we set up that night I spend an hour detail cleaning the CAR-15 in the dark. The safety works now that it's oiled. The swamp had done it in— almost did me in.

Simmons has gotten a long, thick letter from home with a bunch of pictures of his baby. Maybe it's the moonlight, but he looks awfully grey.

I sleep with the CAR-15 cradled in my arms and my Camillus knife stuck in the tree for easy reach. But I dream of the P.O.W. all cut and mutilated.

25 — 31 May, 1970

We hump through drier and drier terrain, tall trees, hostile undergrowth, lots of bomb craters. On the next resupply we get new uniforms, "sterile" meaning no insignias. We bathe in a bomb crater and feel a little bit better.

Then it's more humping. We've stopped for lunch. I start to sit down. I've pulled the pack straps off my shoulders with my thumbs and I'm halfway down, overbalanced.

"No! *Dai-Uy*! No sit!" It's Dong.

I stop. What is it? A mine? I'm overbalanced. I fall forward. At least I won't hit the mine.

It's not a mine. It's a blue-grey snake, a krait, the "Asian two-step," more deadly than a cobra, and I almost sat on him. He strikes at my foot, gets the sole of my boot, and scampers away.

He's as afraid of me as I am of him. I think, Gee, live through ten months of combat to get killed by a fucking snake?

I thank Dong profusely. I sit down shaking now and take out a marvelous C-ration meal of spaghetti and meatballs and a square of C-4, build a little stove out of rocks, and light the C-4. Then I cut open the C-ration can and set it on the stove.

Simmons says, "Too bad you didn't get that snake. Great souvenir."

I'm pondering this when I look up and see the NVA. He's wearing khaki and Ho Chi Minh sandals, no helmet, no hat. What's more important, he has a shiny new AK-47 at port arms. Ten feet behind him is another NVA.

I pick up my CAR-15, flip off the safety to Auto and fire as I dive behind a log screaming, "VC!"

Several other guys are doing the same thing, and neither guy gets his weapon into firing position before taking hits. The lead guy is lifted off his feet and thrown to the ground, his chest spouting red before he knows what hit him.

I look around. Every American is prone behind cover except Wyatt. He's standing against a tree, his M-16 sighted in on the two fallen NVA.

"Wyatt! Get down!"

"They ain't hurtin' nobody!"

"I know! I don't want you hit by an ARVN! Anyway, there may be more." He gets down behind the tree.

"How the fuck'd they get there?"

"Don't know. Just walked into the center of our unit fat, dumb, and happy and undetected, I guess."

I hear Quan yelling cease fire in Vietnamese. The firing stops. We were sure putting out a lot of rounds.

I go over to the first guy, thinking, here's my chance to get souvenirs—Ho Chi Minh sandals. It'll shut Bob up.

I pick one off his right foot.

"Grenade!" yells Wyatt.

The second NVA wasn't dead.

I dive behind the nearest tree. "Oh shit, killed picking up a fuckin' souvenir. How dumb can you get?"

Boom!

Much firing ensues. Finally the cease-fire comes again.

I get out from behind the tree feeling sheepish and walk over to the first one. I reach down to pick up the other sandal and discover his foot and the sandal are missing. The grenade must have done it. His buddy was trying to throw the grenade at me, figuring this one was dead. He didn't do a very good job.

I look down at the body and see a face looking back at me. He blinks.

"Bac Si! This one's alive." I doubt he will be for long. He has lost his right elbow. He'll lose the entire arm if his other wounds don't kill him. He has a sucking chest wound that might. He's losing surprisingly little blood from the foot wound. Shrapnel must have chopped the foot off neatly. I wonder where it went.

I join a crowd looking at the other one. He must have thrown the grenade left-handed, because his right arm took one just below the shoulder. Another shattered his pelvis. Then, while he sat up to throw the grenade, his chest took several solid hits, and his expression belongs to the afterlife. I'm no longer bothered by seeing dead enemy. Now I hate them enough that it feels good. I wonder if he was with the group that cut up that poor boy.

I go back to the first one. Bac Si looks at me. "*Dai-Uy*, if I try to save him, it a waste. He dead soon."

"Try, Bac Si. Try anyway. Dong, ask him if he wants to go to a hospital. American doctors work on him."

Dong looks at Quan, who nods. Dong asks him. He says, weakly, "*Ya, fi.*"

"Tell him if he tells me where his unit is, I'll get a helicopter and send him to a hospital."

Dong translates, and the NVA starts talking quickly.

Quan looks up at me. He whips out a map and shows it to the wounded NVA. He points weakly and says something.

I'm already on the radio calling for a medevac. He's keeping his part of the bargain, so I am, too.

Quan looks up. "Right here, *Dai-Uy*!" He's pointing to a heavily wooded area across from a clearing we've almost reached. "A battalion! A training battalion. Green troops with a cadre of only fifteen experienced soldiers."

"Jesus! We can surprise 'em."

Simmons says, "A dream! Surprisin' the NVA!"

"*Dai-Uy!* You get Cobras. I get Spads," says Quan.

Great idea—the F-5s haven't worked because of their FAC's timidness. Quan will call VNAF Skyraiders, old Korean War vintage prop jobs that carry a tremendous amount of ordnance and drop it with extreme accuracy. Some of the VNAF pilots have been flying the same plane for years and years in combat and have become some of the most adept dive-bombers in the world.

I call for Cobras, two heavy-fire teams.

The NVA dies just as the medevac pilot gets on station.

We go over to the edge of the clearing. We keep a three hundred and sixty degree security, so only the lead edge of the battalion is at the clearing, maybe thirty to fifty men. Between us and the supposed location of the NVA battalion is a football field-sized but oval-shaped clearing. It's our intended resupply point. We pull up to the edge of it and get behind trees. The Spads go in first.

They're dropping five hundred pound bombs thirty to fifty meters away. Large pieces of shrapnel come flying into the trees. One hits a tree forty feet up and falls harmlessly onto Duke's pack.

"I'm hit! I'm hit!"

"Shaddup, mothafucka!" says Wyatt.

I position the Cobras so that if there are NVA in that bush, they have only one place to go — toward us.

The Cobra pilots start calling, "I'm getting running figures," as they make their runs. They start calling in hits. They're using their 7.62 mm mini-guns and 40 mm grenades on the running troops. One Cobra has 2.75 inch rockets with "nails," fléchettes. The nail description is appropriately accurate.

Then we get the rest running in our direction to get away from the bombs and rockets.

It's a charge. They're yelling, screaming, running toward us and shooting — hundreds of them.

Suddenly I'm no longer an advisor watching the war. It's aimed directly at me, and I'm on the front line lying behind a tree. Quan leans into a firing position with an M-16 beside me. I flip the safety off on my CAR-15 onto Semi and extend the collapsable buttstock. I put my cheek down onto the stock and look through the sight. I sight in on a running figure's head and squeeze the trigger.

His head explodes and he drops. I sight in on the one next to him. Thirty meters, nearly pistol range. I sight and squeeze again. Sight picture, trigger squeeze. This is what it was all about, all those hours on the ranges at Ft. Sill and Knox. They're targets, just pop-up targets. But these targets torture and castrate and kill. Sight picture, trigger squeeze. Aim for the head, in the center. Sight picture, trigger squeeze. I aim for the head because I like to see it explode. Sight picture, trigger squeeze. It's easy. Sight picture, trigger squeeze. They tortured that poor kid to death in the most horrible of ways. Sight picture, trigger squeeze. If they get to us, they'll do the same to me, or kill me. Sight picture, trigger squeeze. Basic marksmanship, breathe, relax, aim, slack, squeeze. Put the front sight on his nose and squeeze. Front sight, squeeze the trigger. Targets. Front sight, squeeze the trigger. It takes half a second to a second to go from one to another. Front sight, squeeze the trigger. I'm supposed to be an expert marksman. This is the test. Front sight, squeeze the trigger.

I miss once. He's bobbing up and down too much. I aim again lower, sight picture, trigger squeeze. He drops, a center chest hit. The one next to him I hit in the head. I look around. Wyatt is standing behind a tree shooting rapidly and accurately in semiautomatic. Duke is nowhere in sight. He has run back somewhere. I can't see Simmons, either. I keep shooting till I've emptied the magazine of ammunition. I reload and chamber a round. Now the Cobras are shooting into the clearing.

But they're almost on us, the survivors. I shoot rapidly, sight picture, trigger squeeze, semiautomatic. Only hits count. In ten seconds or less I've emptied another magazine. Frantically I reload. They're right *here*. I flip to Auto and spray upward, lying on my back. For God's sake, one's right on top of me. He's wild-eyed, panicked. His AK is spraying high. He lowers it, and a loud *thuck* erupts from the tree by my left ear. I pull the trigger back and hold it, hitting him in the guts and letting it ride up under recoil. It cuts up a red swath, and his wild-eyed expression becomes permanent. I'm empty again. I must've fired most of a magazine into him. I grab for another magazine and shove it home. It's harder this time. I'm shaking too much. *My God, I'm going to die!* I think, totally panicked.

Something moves. I whirl, shooting. I've killed a branch from a tree. I look around. I realize I'm standing up, and only Wyatt is standing with me. I look into the clearing, wild-eyed. It looks like a very messy meat market. I see a little movement on the field and fire at it. I reload and keep firing. Others are too. We've gone berserk. There is no thought of saving the wounded. If it moves, kill it. It's a threat. Then there is nothing alive out there. There are NVA bodies inside our line, but no NVA remain alive. I hear, my ears ringing, "Bac Si! Bac Si!" and I realize we didn't get off scott free.

But almost. This has been a full-fledged, fur-lined class A success.

Wyatt says, "Hey, cap'n, is it just you an' me?"

I look around. Simmons is nowhere to be seen.

Neither is Duke. "Son of a bitch," I mutter.

Wyatt says, "Hey, cap'n. You okay for a honkie lifer."

"Don't say that too loud. Somebody'll call you an Oreo."

Quan is standing now. "Numbah one! Numbah fuckin' one!"

His M-16 is empty. So is mine. His LCDB gives him a magazine. Quan tosses it to me and takes another. I reload. I was completely out of ammunition. Had there been a few more . . .

We're laughing maniacally now. This is what it's all about. There's a high to it. That's what they never tell the folks about back home. Killing someone who's trying to kill you gives you a high because you know he's dead and you're alive. You've cheated God and the devil. It's an unbelievable feeling of power. I couldn't describe this feeling if my life depended on it. I want to do it again, to scream, to dance, to cry. I'm alive.

Wyatt understands. He's got a grin on his face I've never seen. I wonder if I have the same grin, part little boy in the cookie jar, part Satan and pure evil. Probably.

"*Dai-Uy*, we need medevac."

"How many, *Dai-Uy*?"

"Fourteen. Ten dead."

"Jesus." I grab the handset on Wyatt's radio. I realize Duke and Simmons have returned from their run to the rear. I also realize I'm resting my rifle on a dead NVA and move it.

"We've had a little shooting gallery down here. Over," I tell Six, a smartassed quality in my voice.

"I'll need two medevacs. Fourteen urgent. *Dai-Uy*, how many stretcher?"

"Ten. Bad hurt, *Dai-Uy*."

"Gotcha. Ten litter, four ambulatory."

"Roger. I need a spot report. Over."

I give him one. He doesn't believe it.

"I need a body count. Over."

"Situation not secure enough yet. Over."

"Now. Over."

"Trust me. It's not secure. Over."

"I can't use your estimate, Three, I must have a count. Over."

"I'm not dying to give it to you. Out."

I call out two hunter-killer teams and handle the two medevac choppers. We also will need a chopper for the friendly dead, but, of course, that's less forthcoming.

We occupy the enemy headquarters very carefully, but not carefully enough. Two survivors shoot at our people in separate instances, killing one LCDB and wounding a grunt. They don't do a great job of sniping, because our guys kill them both very quickly.

"Amateurs. We're fighting amateurs with amateurs," says Wyatt.

I call in still another medevac and put some of the bodies on it with the trooper with his shoulder shattered.

Then Six calls back. "You never gave me a count on the bodies. Over."

"Roger. We're still finding them. They're nailed to trees, lying in blown-up bunkers, pieces of them in tree branches. Not all of them are dead. They're still shooting occasionally. How do you think we got those last casualties? Over."

"Count 'em — yourself. That's an order — now. Then call me back. Out."

So I count bodies. Four hundred seventy-two. Four hundred six have brand new AK-47s. None has a pistol or a machine gun, or at least if they did the ARVNs hid them from the Co-Vans. I find it strange. Maybe the survivors ran off with the RPDs, RPGs, and K-50s. I think one body is outside our perimeter as I scare the shit out of a trooper and myself. I think briefly of Mickey Marcus, making it through World War Two and some awful battles in the '48 Israeli war of independence only to get shot by a nervous sentry while taking a leak. God, it's so dangerous here you're lucky if your friends don't kill you, much less your enemies. Christ, we lose twenty percent of our casualties to jeep and truck accidents, A.D.s, and the like. I've been scared so long I'm just numb. Fuck it. It don't mean nothin'. That's the motto of the Vietnam War. If I live, I'll have it tatooed on my dick. If I die, I can have it put on my grave.

"Six, this is Three. We have four hundred seventy-two November Victor Alpha Kilo India Alpha. Over."

"Roger. That's hard to believe. Did you count them yourself? Over."

"That's affirmative. I counted feet and divided by two. Over."

"Roger. How about weapons? It'll sound like a massacre to the press. I hope they're all fighting age. Over."

Jesus, what an asshole. "This isn't My Lai. These motherfuckers were shooting at us. I have four hundred six Alpha Kilo four-sevens. Over."

"Did you count them yourself? Over."

"Affirmative. Over."

"Good, good. Still, I won't report them on till we've brought them back."

"Why the hell not? Over."

"Because Four Kilo reported two tons of weapons, and they fit in one Huey, and the report went all the way to Nixon."

"Roger. I understand." Follett. Mr. Cool. That asshole could fuck up a wet dream. "I need some Hueys for these weapons. Over."

"Roger. I'll get some. Out."

We move on after we've searched the area thoroughly. No one questions the fact that we have four hundred seventy-two enemy KIA and no prisoners. I'm not in the mood for prisoners, though. I sure wouldn't try to keep an ARVN from shooting one.

We spend the night not too far from the firefight.

The next day we go through a terrible draw, heavy with insects and nearly impossible vegetation, vines with thorns, deep undergrowth. Then on the other side we start finding bags of rice, not little bags of rice, big hundred kilo bags, stacked in camouflaged stacks. We find, eventually, twenty stacks of ten bags. At two point two pounds per kilo, that's forty-four thousand pounds of rice. I get conservative and report twenty tons of rice. In reality, I'm two tons short.

"Three, this is Six. That's impossible. Have you counted it yourself? Over."

Here we go with the count bit again.

"Negative. Still unsecure. Over."

"You know the rules. All counts must be personally made by the Sierra Alpha. Over."

"Roger. As soon as it's secure I'll count every bag myself. Over."

"Negative. Immediately. Over."

"Nah, you'd never get the letter right. Over."

"What letter?"

"The one to my wife explaining that you got me killed counting rice bags. Over."

"Okay, okay. As soon as it's secure. Out."

When we've finally made three interlocking company-sized sweeps and secured the area I count the rice bags.

"Six. Three. Count completed. Over."

"Good. Good. How about the rice? Over."

"It's still twenty tons. Over."

"Did you count the bags yourself? Over."

"Affirm. Over."

"Not even your lieutenant counts. Must be you personally. Over."

"Jesus H. Christ! I went out and lay my fuckin' hands on every fuckin' bag. There are two hundred bags marked one hundred kilos each. You figure it out. Over."

"Ah, er, roger. Out."

Then he calls me back. The supply chopper is on the way. "Put your Echo Mikes on it. There's a promotion board meeting for Echo Five tomorrow. Over."

"I'd like to see them promoted, but doesn't the promotion board know there's a war on? I can't do without my Echo Mikes in a combat situation. Over."

"I'm sending you an experienced Echo Six, third tour, very good man, till they're back. Over."

"Jesus. Okay. They're good men, so I don't want to see them miss a promotion. Over."

"Roger. Out."

I tell them. They're ecstatic. I take Duke aside and tell him, "Duke. You need to find a job in the rear."

"I'd sure like to, sir."

"I mean it. I'm not going to say anything about your actions under fire today, I don't even blame you. But if I saw you deserting me under fire again, I'd blow your fuckin' head off. You find a job in the rear, got it?"

"Y-yes sir," he says, locked in a gaze I didn't know I had in me.

I tell Wyatt to come back at all costs. One of the misfortunes of war is that only the best can stay at the front. You can't trust the rest. Wyatt I can trust, no matter how much he hates honkies.

They get on the chopper, and a short, black E-6 with a CIB on his chest gets off. He salutes. I return it and shake hands. His nametag reads Powers. We offload C-rations for four and some water and, thank heaven, some mail. The Cokes and beer I asked for aren't on it. I'm ready to shoot either the chopper pilot or Six. I call him about it. He says they were put on the chopper. I hope the chopper crew enjoyed our drinks. We've been on rancid water for three weeks.

Then Quan says, "*Dai-Uy*, you want CKC?"

CKC—an SKS. I don't know why ARVNs call them CKCs, but yes, I want one. I can see it over my mantle when I tell the grandkids, "Yes, kiddies, there I was, deep in enemy territory. . . .

"*Ya, Fi!*"

"Come with me."

309

He takes Powers and me to a hole in the ground, an underground bunker. One of his troops is handing out AK-47s, one by one. Quan says something to him too fast for me to catch it, and the guy comes out, smiling.

"*Dai-Uy*. They all down there. A hunnerd seventy-five. You go down, pick out four for you an' you men."

Swell. Just what I always wanted to do, go into an enemy bunker full of booby traps and pull up rifles.

Why do you think they call them booby traps?

I crawl in, taking a flashlight.

It's a big bunker, five feet high, eight feet on a side. Stacked floor to ceiling are weapons and ammunition and mines. One side has a big stack of Russian TMN-46 antitank mines.

Next to that is a stack of SKSs and AK-47s. On top is one cherry SKS, pretty polished wood stock, all the bluing intact, Chinese spike bayonet folded up. It's a really nice souvenir. I reach for it.

Why do you think they call them boobytraps?

I stop with my hand on it.

Dumbshit! Dumbshit! Dumbshit!

I examine it with the flashlight. Why is it on top with so many others, all of which are normal military arms, that is to say worn, wood stocks from an orange crate, bluing half gone, some with, some without bayonets?

When I see the string I don't even panic. I follow it down. It's slack, so I cut it loose from the weapon with my Swiss Army knife. Then I panic. The other end of the string is attached to the boobytrap detonator of the bottommost antitank mine. I sit down a minute and just shake.

I look up and see two ARVNs and Powers staring down. The ARVNs are laughing. Powers looks confused.

Dumbshit! Dumbshit! Dumbshit!

Lord, if I live through the day I promise never to be a dumbshit again.

I bring up that SKS and the best two of the fifty down there. Quan's men can bring up the rest. I give one to Simmons, one to Powers.

"Sergeant, you're double lucky."

"I know I'm lucky to get this, but why double lucky?"

" 'Cause if that stack of antitank mines had gone off, pieces of you would be found half a click away."

Simmons says, "Boy, are Duke and Wyatt going to be mad when they hear."

"Tough shit. There's a war on."

"Can we get a couple of them?" says Powers.

"Want to carry them?" I ask. "We'll have to hump these till one of us goes to the rear."

"Right, sir. Forget I said it."

I call in the report of the count of weapons. Six doesn't believe it again, of course.

When things calm down I talk to Powers.

"I understand you have a wealth of experience in Nam."

"You got that right. This is my third tour."

"My God, third tour and in the bush? Who did you fuck?"

"I asked for this job."

"What makes you keep coming back?"

"Well, I volunteered th' first time to make E-five.

311

Came over with the Big Red One. First of the second in '65. Then my wife had another baby. Needed money. Came back to make E-six in late '67 to the third of the Eighth Infantry, Fourth division. Now I need ta make E-seven."

"Christ, what timing. They just centralized E-seven promotions."

"Yeah, suh, but they's one more board before it goes army wide."

"Well, I'll see if I can get you in it. Do you have enough time in grade?"

"Three months short."

"Swell. I'll see what I can do. Probably not much. I need your experience here meantime. You're replacin' two men who did one and a half men's work. So you'll need to do one and a half. Don't play John Wayne. Just stay cool. Competence and accuracy at controlling fire support are what counts here. Done any fire support — calling in Cobras, jets, and artillery?"

"Yes sir. I spent both tours in the field."

"Both tours? Jesus. You need a nice job in the TOC in Lai Khe."

"Can't get promoted there."

"Sure you can. All the asslickers and brownnosers get promoted there."

"Yeah suh, but I ain't enough a bownnoser."

Perfect.

I brief him on the idiosyncrasies of calling in fire in our AO.

Then I get with Simmons alone and tell him he needs to get a job in the rear.

"You're gonna say somethin' about the firefight,

312

aren't ya?"

"No. You've been in the field eight months. It's time you got a job in the rear."

"Well, it wasn't my fault. I—"

"I said I wasn't gonna talk about it. I don't want to hear any excuses. You've been a good officer for eight months. You need a job in the rear. I'm gonna tell Rains that. No mention of the firefight. Be prepared to go with the next supply chopper."

"Ah—ah, thanks."

In my sleep I fall out of the hammock in a nightmare of close combat in which I'm shooting ghostly VC who don't fall and keep coming.

1 – 5 June 1970

We send the weapons out on Hueys and start loading rice on Hueys. It works on the weapons but not with the rice. At the rate of five bags per Huey it'll take forever. We're told to cut a bigger LZ so a Chinook can land.

I put Simmons and the SKSs on the last Huey instead of one bag of rice. Now it's just Powers and me. Each of us carries a radio.

The Ninth's regimental commander has counted weapons by then and realizes he's three SKSs short. This would be no big deal except he's selling the captured weapons on the black market, and this shortage will cost him money.

When the chopper lands in An Loc Ninth Recon surrounds the chopper with automatic weapons and demands the SKSs. They search the chopper and find nothing. The regimental C.O. is near to slapping Simmons, screaming at him an inch from Simmon's face. Simmons shows admirable restraint. Finally the chopper is released. They fly to Lai Khe where the chopper crew opens the locked storage compartment accessible only from outside the chopper. They had landed on HWY fourteen and loaded the weapons into it.

At Lai Khe Simmons locks them in a Conex and begins the paperwork necessary to take the war souvenirs back to the world.

While he's gone the ARVNs start cutting a big LZ out of a small one, cutting down trees. ARVN engineers arrive by Huey to assist. But they have very little explosives with them. They empty the antitank mines of explosives and use them.

I notice they are putting the explosives on the wrong side of a monster mahogany tree.

"*Dai-Uy*," I ask Quan, "doesn't this need to be on that side?"

"No, *Dai-Uy*. They engineers. They know business."

So much for advice. I *di-di* the area. Unfortunately, I get distracted by another problem on the far side of the LZ and don't mention it to Powers.

When the tree goes it falls a hundred eighty degrees off target, and Powers is hit by a falling branch and luckily only scratched and cut. Had it been five feet over, he would've been killed.

I say nothing to Quan. The ARVNs think it's hilarious that the engineers dropped a big mahogany tree a hundred eighty degrees off course.

I hope the engineers have lost enough face to commit hara-kiri, but no such luck; wrong people. Vietnamese don't commit suicide, unfortunately.

Simmons comes back on the supply chopper. He

couldn't find a job in the rear. The dog robbers and REMFs have all the cushy jobs sewed up. There aren't any lieutenants' slots back at Team Seventy HQ. He looks awfully dejected. We haven't moved. We're still widening the LZ. Once a day a Chinook comes over and the pilot says, "No, too small."

We keep cutting and clearing.

The NVA realize we've been in their supply cache for three days. They start probing us. We get hit at dusk by a small probing attack. We're well deployed with LPs and ambushes out over a two by one click area, so at the CP we merely hear fairly distant firing.

"Dai-Uy," says Quan. "I have two men wounded. You get helicopter."

"Bring them here. I call medevac."

"No. From LP. Too far out. Take medevac there."

"Dai-Uy, you know I must look at wounded to see how bad."

"No way. Too far. Bad hurt."

"Litter, or ambulatory."

"One litter, chest wound. One ambulatory. Arm. Bad hurt. Bleeding bad. Need medevac now."

"Jesus." I shake my head. I pick up the handset looking at Simmons and Powers as though they were gods who could guide me. Of course, they aren't, and they don't. Whatever I do will be wrong. If I don't call the medevac, the ARVNs will have my head, especially if they die. I'll probably get a court-martial out of it. If I call a medevac—a night medevac—without looking at them and they aren't badly hurt, maybe even if they are, I can get a court-martial.

"Six, this is Three. Over."

"Sharper Millet Tha-ree, this is Sharper Millet Six

317

Romeo Tango. Over." It's the smartassed E-4 again. He needs to be humping a radio with one of the line battalions.

"Six, Three, medevac request, urgent, one ambulatory, one litter. I need a jungle penetrator. Over."

"Sharper Millet Tha-ree, this is Sharper Millet Six Romeo Tango. Roger your request. Is it absolutely necessary? Over."

"Six Romeo Tango, if you don't get that fuckin' medevac ASAP I'm gonna get your ass into my unit. Ever hump eighty-five pounds on your back through a swamp? Roger? Over."

"Roger. Wait out."

"Dai-Uy. This is very dangerous. Can those men last till morning?"

"No. They die."

"You sure.?"

"Ya, fi! They die! Must have medevac!"

"Okay, I was afraid you were going to say that."

"Sharper Millet Three, this is Sharper Millet Six. Over." It's Lieutenant Colonel Rains.

"Six, Three, over."

"Three, Six. A night medevac is awfully hairy. Have you examined the wounded? Over."

"Negative. They're a click away or more. Over."

"Well, move 'em to your location."

"Not possible. Very bad terrain. Over."

"Then go to their location. Over."

"I'd love to, but it'd take all night in the dark in this stuff. Then it'd be a daylight medevac, and we wouldn't need this conversation. Over."

"Roger. Wait out."

I wait and hear, "Medevac One-two is enroute.

Push thirty-five point thirty-five. Cobra Two escort. Over."

"Roger. Going to thirty-five point thirty-five. Out." I switch frequencies.

"Dai-Uy, is the area secure?"

"Ya, fi." Ya, fi. Ya, fi. I guess I'd lie like that if it was my men dying, but I doubt it. I don't feel secure in the CP.

"Did you kill any NVA?"

"Ya. We get bodies tomorrow."

Right. If there are any out there now, they won't be in the morning. They never are. We don't leave our dead on the battlefield. Why should they?

"Anyone over there have a strobe?"

"No."

"Course not. Tell them to build a fire."

"Build a fire?" says Simmons.

"Know a better way? It's dark! Smoke bombs don't do much!"

"God Almighty! A fire! You tryin' to get us all killed? We're bound to be mortared."

I get my back up. "Lieutenant, the trees are fifty feet tall. How the hell do we signal the Huey if not with a fire? Wave our arms?"

"Let the cocksuckers die. Don't get us killed."

Quan gives him a dirty look and mutters *"Du ma."*

"Shut up, Lieutenant," I say.

Fortunately Medevac One-two calls in, defusing the situation. He's too far away for my meager antenna. I can hear him, but I can't reach him. I keep trying. Eventually I get through and get him pointed toward us.

Quan, Powers, and I stand in the middle of our

319

LZ. I have my strobe out and held as high as I can hold it. Simmons won't come out of the trees. He thinks I'm nuts for using the strobe. Powers, on the other hand, won't leave my side. Medevac One-two can't find us. I plan to point him on a seventy degree azimuth when/if he finds us.

The Cobras haven't shown up yet.

For fifteen minutes we give him directions and he searches, click by click for us. We can hear his rotor blades. He manages to go from our west to our east without crossing over us.

Finally he flies over us and sees us. But it still takes ten more minutes to find the fire from the platoon with the wounded. Finding a small fire in a heavy double canopy jungle in the dark is no picnic. The fact that they find them at all is proof the crew's good, very good.

His fuel is getting low, and the Cobras haven't even come on the frequency yet.

"How bad are they wounded?" he asks me.

"I don't know. We can't get there. Counterpart says they'll die before morning without treatment. Over."

He decides to come in without the Cobra escort.

He hovers over the fire and lowers the jungle penetrator. First up must be the less wounded. They extract him easily and get him into the chopper, announcing same on the radio.

They drop the penetrator for the next man.

They never get him into the penetrator.

The sky lights up.

A B-40 rocket hits the Huey and turns it into a roman candle.

From my position I see the light, the flash, realize

four or five good men have just died for me, and I fall to my knees saying "no, no, no," softly.

There is small-arms fire off where the wounded were, mostly AKs.

Then, insanely I call for Medevac One-two over and over again until Powers takes the handset from my limp hand. I'm crying softly and without control.

Medevac One-two doesn't answer. All aboard are dead. The wreckage will be found tomorrow in a thick growth of fifty-foot trees. Five badly burned bodies will be located, each no larger than a big dog, charred black. We will put them in body bags and into another Huey from the same squadron.

But tonight I weep for the crew of Medevac One-two. I, in my incompetence, have killed them.

The next day I see the man with the chest wound who would not last the night. He is not chipper, but he is alive and able to talk. His "chest" wound is in his shoulder and not terribly severe. Quan lied. He fooled me after all these months. I am a fool who has learned nothing in ten months living with the Vietnamese.

Of course we do not find any NVA bodies. Somewhere some B-40 operator is getting a medal for shooting down an American helicopter. Somewhere else a young wife is seeing two green uniformed men walk up her front walk to announce her husband's death in combat, and she goes noisily berserk, screaming at the men, "You've killed him! You've killed him!" when she should be screaming at me. I can hear her, so maybe she is.

For three days I am catatonic. I go through the motions, but I cannot think except of these men whom I have not seen, who have so many times come to my aid, all our aid, regardless of danger to themselves. I've killed them by bringing them into a trap.

Simmons realizes I have done nothing worthwhile, retreating into my shell. I hear him say to Powers, "Look at him sittin' there. The shell's there, but there's nobody home."

6 June 1970

Rains sends me to Lai Khe, leaving Simmons in charge. Colonel Norman's leaving, and his replacement, Colonel Shaw, is here, so there's a change of command ceremony of sorts and a hail and farewell so Norman can say good-bye to his friends, and Shaw can meet his officers. Rains says Norman asked him to make sure I'm there.

I'm still numb. I make the trip on the log bird. Rains sees me at regiment and tells me to get a fancy-clean set of fatigues for the rear. I go to the supply sergeant first, get another set of fatigues and boots, get with *mamasan* and her fantastic sewing machine, and she sews on all the patches. Johnny has warned me to make sure they're all put on, the CIB, airborne wings, ranger tab. I stifle an urge to have them all put on my skivvies especially the CIB, just received in the last mail after ten months of paper foulups. I feel like a real dufus in a new, clean uniform with all that stuff on. At least I don't look totally like an FNG because of the patches. You can usually tell an FNG by the color of his fatigues. They fade quickly and become workable instead of stiff. Old fatigues are like an old dog. They look like shit, but they don't let you down, and they go everywhere with you. I feel almost ill when I throw the old ones away. If I tried to save them, they'd be all patches.

I see the local MO, a stocky drafted M.D. from Denver who has a goddamned air conditioner. He agrees I have hemorrhoids and hookworms and recommends sending me to Japan. I tell him, stupidly, that I'm too short. Anyway you can't take an SKS to Japan. I also feel somewhere along the way I'd get waylaid in Saigon and get the operation done there and be back in the field feeling worse. This guy is appropriately anti-war and tends to send everyone as far from the war as he can. He doesn't know that this can be counter-productive. He has sent a guy to Japan for something before the guy had ten months and five days in the country, and the guy didn't get credit for a completed tour, so he was sent back to Nam for a new tour as soon as he recovered. I do take some medicine back for the worms.

The hail and farewell for Norman and Shaw is at the O Club at seventeen hundred. By then I've had three showers, used a real sit-down latrine, and gotten my hair cut. I may be human again soon. Every S.A. is there. If there's a major NVA offensive tonight Fifth Division is in trouble.

Capt. Alvarez, the admin officer, and a typical R.E.M.F., says, "Take off that CIB."

"Why?"

"Your orders were rescinded. It was issued by mistake. You don't deserve it."

"I've been in an infantry job for eight fuckin'

324

months. I've been shot at so fuckin' many times I can't count it. I've met the requirements eight times over, for Christ's sake. What the fuck do you want?"

"One signature was missing on the application. It'll have to be resubmitted."

"Fine, resubmit it and quit fuckin' with the combat troops."

"Don't talk to me like that. Take it off."

"Fine, later. Go back to your air conditioning and hot and cold running C.O.s and leave me alone."

But he persists until I take out my Swiss Army knife and cut it off.

Colonel Norman says nice things about me, saying the OER Pride did on me before he left was one I should be proud of. I couldn't care less about my OER. I'd turn them all in to be able to step off the plane at Travis in one piece. The agonizing part is that I'm getting short enough to think it might happen.

In any case I hate to see Norman go. I can trust him. Shaw looks about fifty-five, lean, wrinkled, like a farmer, white haired. He shakes my hand like a man trying to prove something. This scares me. He's trying to scare me, but not the way he does. He wants to be thought of as a hard-assed motherfucker. I see something in his eyes that scares me. I wish I could figure out just what it is.

"S.A. One—Nine, huh?" he says to me. "You're too young for that."

"I'll be happy to take a job for a younger man in the rear, sir. I've been in the field for ten months."

"How long'd it take you to make captain?"

"Two years, sir, just like all the other junior captains around."

"Shit. Took me seven years. You young pups sure are lucky."

"I've been lucky, all right, but I'd rather be a lieutenant in a safe desk job."

"Don't be flip with me, boy. Can you handle a man's job?"

Before I can really put my foot in it by telling the old bastard off, his ASA, Lieutenant Colonel Langly, says, "Captain Harris has been doing an exemplary job. He's one of the most experienced infantry advisors we have. Unfortunately we're losing him. He's leaving us in July. Going home."

"In the Korean War," says Shaw, "the guys who stayed in the field so long were the duds." I don't understand why he's baiting me. I notice the patch on his right shoulder is a Second Division patch. Korea. Christ, he hasn't been in combat since he was a lieutenant!

Again Langly comes to my rescue. "Captain Harris had a job here. He volunteered for the field."

Shaw finds another S.A. to bait, and I leave the hail and farewell for supper. Afterwards Johnny and I return to the club to talk and drink Jack Daniels. He's just had his second R and R.

"How'd you get two?"

"Five days' leave. Was on standby to Sydney, but didn't make it. Decided to just stay in Saigon for a week. Picked up a cute little whore for the whole week—well, four days. Got one the first day, but got tired of her after one night. Same as all the others I'd had. Could've been doing the laundry. But the second one! She taught me some things I didn't know. I haven't fucked so much in a week since I was nineteen. Didn't know I had it in me."

"What was her secret?"

"Mainly I think she liked it. She'd get all worked up about it, eyes roll back in her head, start groaning and moaning, then little screams, then a shriek. Really went berserk when she came. My wife never acted like she enjoyed it like that."

I keep my thoughts to myself.

"You don't play with the whores, do you?"

"Haven't yet. Would've had I stayed in the rear much longer."

"Why not?"

"Fear of VD, a promise to my wife I'd be faithful. Afraid I'd find Suzy the slasher."

"Suzy the slasher?"

"Saigon Suzy, a whore in Saigon who's castrated several hundred GIs, usually along with disemboweling them, since 1967. They've never caught her."

"Castrates 'em and leaves 'em alive?"

"No, she kills them, too."

"Well, I didn't know about her. Glad I didn't. Probably couldn't have gotten a hard-on if I'd have known that."

"Sorry I told you. I wonder what their C.O.s told their parents on the death reports. I also don't know if I could even make it with a paid whore. I like to think the girl's getting something out of it."

"She was. Twenty dollars a day."

"That's the point."

"Your wife enjoy it?"

"Yeah. I guess so. She sure acts like she does. Why?"

"I don't think mine ever did much till R and R. Maybe we just did it so much, I don't know. She started asking for it. She never did before. We did it so much it started taking me a long time, and she really got off. Maybe I just never took enough time before."

"Maybe so."

"Your wife get off?"

"Yeah. I guess. Says she does. Acts like she does. Like your little whore she kinda goes berserk."

"Ready to go home to her?"

"Is the Pope Catholic?"

"What are—" Someone walks in. It's a SP-4 Cortez.

"Captain East?"

"Oh, no, what is it?"

"Seventh Regiment has a unit in contact. Need an urgent resupply."

"Shit. Sorry, Jerry, there goes tonight's episode of the *Playboy* advisor."

"Good luck."

"Yeah."

He leaves, and I'm alone with my Jack Daniels.

Aha, in comes young Lieutenant McKee. I invite the young silver bar to sit with me and note that the left chest area of his sharply pressed and starched fatigues is decorated with the coveted Combat Infantry Badge.

Now this on the surface is not surprising. Tens of thousands of these badges have been awarded to men who had set themselves apart from most soldiers by being in infantry combat, the worst kind, for a sustained period of time. However I know that Lieutenant McKee had been an assistant advisor to Three—Nine for only two weeks before being sent to the rear because (a) he was useless and, (b) he had a skin rash. His C.O. had allowed his relocation for medical treatment of a severe skin rash mainly because he thought he would be better off without him than with him. I had never heard Lieutenant McKee called by name in Ninth Regiment, just his nickname, the whiner.

When he got to the rear he talked the doctor into a permanent restriction to the rear (!) Perhaps knowing the good lieutenant's total lack of command skills, the doctor had the army's best wishes at heart. I don't know. I suspected he wanted to get us all out of combat when he tried to send me to Japan for hemorrhoids. I couldn't see telling my grandchildren I'd gotten out of combat because Vietnam gave me a pain in the ass.

Unfortunately Advisory Team Seventy's T.O. and E. does not allow for lieutenants in the rear. Lieutenants are staff advisors to infantry units, intelligence advisors, and armored cav. advisors, all proper combat jobs. The rear is for support troops. The HQ Co. C.O. is a captain with a distinguished combat record and enough wounds for a temporary profile. Lieutenants are being phased in as TOC duty officers because of a shortage of captains, but only very good ones. That wouldn't do for Lieutenant McKee. He'd probably call in a Cobra strike on BOQ number one with his knowledge of map reading. So an enterprising field grade type created the non-T.O. and E. job of XO, HQ Company. Since this wasn't an authorized position, he was still officially listed as staff advisor to Three—Nine, and Three—Nine does without a lieutenant so Lieutenant McKee can sleep in a cot with maid service, hot meals, and rum and Coke.

Now Lieutenant McKee doesn't know me from Adam, and I am wearing R.E.M.F. garb, starched fatigues with all the R.E.M.F. badges, no regimental crest on my pocket, and spit-shined everything, so maybe he thinks I am a fellow R.E.M.F.

I buy the good lieutenant a drink, and when it arrives, ask him, "How did you get a CIB, lieutenant?"

"I was an advisor at an infantry regiment."

"Oh? But weren't you just there for two weeks?"

He's not just a little slow on the uptake, but he begins to realize I have some knowledge of his situation. "Well, yes, but I was medavaced."

"Medavaced? You were never under fire and merely sat on a hill for two weeks."

He looks at me as if I am an idiot, totally unaware of the facts in the case. "But I was medavaced," he says again as if that explains everything.

"Medavaced? For what?"

"A skin rash," he says disgustedly, realizing he can't lie to me about it.

"A skin rash?"

"Yes, a very bad skin rash. The doctor told me I could die if I stayed in the field."

The dumb son of a bitch doesn't realize what he just said, I think, laughing in my Jack Daniels. We could all die in the field.

"Correct me if I'm wrong, Lieutenant. A coveted CIB is given to those brave heroes who have been under fire in an infantry assignment for more than one month unless wounded first. I know this because I have been in an infantry unit long enough to have impregnated one of these lovely C.O.s like the bartendress here and still be here to name the baby were I so lucky as to get lucky with one of these innocent lasses. And I still don't have one through the screw-ups of R.E.M.F. S-one types uncounted."

Now this goes right past him like a fastball that the batter didn't even see. I am not a R.E.M.F. but he hasn't figured that out. "MACV Regulation (he quotes a number, for Christ's sake!) states that a soldier is eligible for a CIB if medevaced from an infantry assignment."

"Christ, McKee, you went back on the log bird!"

The fat young lieutenant straightens at this. His expression clearly indicates that he thinks I am a drunken idiot with no knowledge of regulations and life in the rear echelon.

"It was a medevac!"

"Now I was told by a reliable source, the S.A. of Three—Nine, that you got on the log bird after days of whining about a skin rash."

This gets his back up. "Officially it was a medevac! We called for a medevac, and the log bird just got there first."

"Oh, I see."

About then I realize that, of course, awards and decorations would go through an office next to his, so of course he has a CIB. The awards and decorations officer probably got a favor from him in return. His R and R will come on time, and he'll probably get a thirty day "drop" at the end of his tour. Such is the life of a rear echelon "soldier." The terms R.E.M.F.

and RAP certainly come to mind.

I also realize that Lieutenant McKee is dumb as a post. He certainly doesn't realize he is talking, not to an R.E.M.F., but to a guy who has just spent the better part of a year being the duck in the shooting gallery. In my light Jack Daniels haze I am waxing eloquent, not to mention sarcastic.

"Good Lord. Did you perchance get anything else? A Medal of Honor? A virgin sacrifice? Maybe a Purple Heart for the rash? Was it a VC rash?"

"No, but I do have a Purple Heart."

By now Brother Jack is having some effect, so I ask, "How, pray tell?"

"One of my many duties," he begins, very officially, "as executive officer for Headquarters Company, is Rabies Control Officer. This means I have to get rid of all the stray dogs on base—"

"Dogcatcher. I've heard of dog robbers, but—"

"Rabies Control Officer! I shot one with my M-16 once and caused a general alert on base, so I was ordered not to shoot them anymore. Shooting is not allowed on base. So I took a bayonet after one, and he bit me."

"You don't get Purple Hearts for that, do you? If so, I have some leech bites I'll turn in."

"No, silly. But they sent me to Cam Rahn Bay for two weeks for rabies shots—"

"Really? Are there any more dogs around? Let me get the next one. Will they send me there if one bites me?"

"Those shots hurt!"

"So do AKs, shrapnel, mines—"

At this point an intelligent individual would realize

that he is not talking to a R.E.M.F. FNG, despite my uniform, but McKee has half the IQ of a mahogany tree. He must be regular army. He puffs up as though a stupid child has interrupted him. "May I continue?"

"Oh, sorry. Certainly."

"While I was at Cam Rahn Bay we had a sapper attack. When running to the bunker in my shower shoes I fell and broke my big toe on my right foot —"

"For that they give Purple Hearts?"

"Yes. MACV Regulation (there he goes, quoting another regulation) states that injuries caused by enemy action —"

"Spare me. Okay. You have a Purple Heart. You're a hero."

He is indignant, angrily turning red in the face. He feels he is a hero. I think of Norton and Baker getting the same Purple Heart for their terrible, terrible wounds. He continues excitedly. "That's not all. When I got to the bunker none of the medics could make the fifty caliber fire. So I cocked it for 'em and fired it. The next morning they found a dead VC in front of my bunker, so they gave me a Bronze Star with V device." He is proud of that. No doubt the terrified medics probably did think that anyone who could work the mysterious cocking mechanism of a .50 caliber M2 machine gun is a hero. Even most grunts don't remember that it takes two tugs at the cocking handle, not one. Also many commands give medals for every enemy body found, not this one, of course. Certainly a bunch of medics would not be aware of what standards are normally used to define "Valor in Ground Combat" as the Bronze Star citations say. For a frightened, untrained medic to grab an M2 Browning and kill a few sappers is an act of valor. For a trained infantry officer, it is basic duty. So McKee, with no combat experience, thinks he really is a hero.

Stunned, I order another round of drinks. "Gee, Lieutenant. I really misjudged you. You're really a hero. For that you deserve a drink." So I pour it on him.

7 June 1970

I return to LZ "Mutha," named by Powers for the fact that cutting it out is a "mutha." Wyatt is with me. Duke has a job at regiment. Both are E-5s now. Wyatt asks me why I got rid of Duke and not the lieutenant. "I tried, Wyatt. There's no room at the inn. The R.E.M.F.s have the place locked up. There's without a doubt the most useless lieutenant in the U.S. Army getting fat and decorated back there. No room for a war-weary combat veteran who's burned out."

"If'n I fuck up, bitch a lot, an' run away, will you send me to the rear?"

"No, Wyatt, you're doomed to end your tour out here in the earth's asshole just as I am."

I have most of an RS pack, lots of mail, and six beers with me along with LRRP rations for several days. Reluctantly I leave six cases of LRRP rations at regiment with orders to send them to us at three day intervals. But I haven't even left before I see the smartasssed SP-4 eating a beef stew unit.

In three days they'll be gone. Scrounging them was a snap, too. The guys at regiment must be total dorks. If they have to buy rations they're idiots or the laziest motherfuckers ever put into the U.S. Army.

Simmons looks haggard. The stack of mail cheers him slightly, the LRRPs more.

The LZ is still not Shithook sized. Since I also brought fifty pounds of C-4 and some det. cord the work goes faster. It was also easy to scrounge, but then I have no trouble getting anything from engineers.

Some day I'll put "scrounger" on my resume, no doubt.

It's a hundred ten degrees with ninety plus percent humidity. We basically sit around the edge of the LZ in T-shirts reading or writing letters until dark.

Simmons has moved his hammock into the trees. The CP is on the edge of the LZ.

"Why'd you do that?" I ask.

"So that when they mortar the LZ, they won't get me."

"Sounds reasonable, but doesn't that make it difficult to get to Quan when the shit hits the fan?"

"Fuck him. Let him get to me."

"Tonight stay with the rest of us."

"I don't want to."

"That's not a request. You can stay far enough away that one round won't get us all just as usual, but you're too far away."

He gives me a look akin to seeing a bug in your hamburger, shakes his head, and mutters something I can't hear. Then he moves his hammock.

Regiment is closer now, so they're giving us eight inch artillery support. Since our presence here is known to the enemy, we have H and I fire all night. It makes sleeping more difficult.

"This is incredibly boring work," I say to Wyatt as we watch them cut more and more trees.

"Yeah, but bettern' humpin' through th' boonies."

"A-men. I don't guess anyone ever died of boredom."

"Can't say much for LRRPs, though."

"You rather have Cs?"

"Nah, shit's shit."

Things quiet down after dark, and I lie in my hammock dreaming lurid dreams of a warm, soft blonde with lush breasts.

Wham!

I'm blown out of the hammock, or I roll out reflexively onto the ground between two logs in a nearly natural foxhole.

Wham! Wham!

The world's lighting up. We're taking incoming. I hear Vietnamese screaming and talking rapidly.

Then I realize Quan is yelling, "Cease fire" in Vietnamese into the radio.

Wham! Wham!

Shrapnel and tree limbs are raining on us. I'm on my belly, helmet on, tight, low position.

"Bac, Si! Bac Si!" God, what a horrible, plaintive cry that is, no matter what the language.

My left leg is on fire. It feels like a couple of fire ants have hit the calf. I lie on the ground still, though, not daring to raise my head. Someone is screaming and crying.

Quan says, "Okay, Cease fire! Cease fire! *Dai-Uy.* You get helicopter. Wounded."

"Why are you saying cease fire, *Dai-Uy*?.

"Our artillery — short rounds."

"Oh, Jesus. Jesus God. Short rounds. Why? Why?"

"*Dai-Uy*, come quick!" It's Dong.

Then, "Cap'n Harris! Over here!" from Powers.

I run toward his voice. They're both yelling about the same thing.

Powers has a flashlight turned on.

The screaming is coming from there. He points the light at a writhing, horrible, unforgettable figure of bloody stumps, feet missing, blood and glistening muscle visible to the crotch. There's blood where sex organs should be.

It's Simmons. The medic is trying to hold him down. Simmons is screaming uncontrollably.

I grab the handset of Powers's radio. "Six, this is Three, over."

"Station using incorrect procedure, this is Sharper Millet Six Romeo Tango. Over."

"Cut the crap, asshole, this is Three. I need an urgent medevac. Over."

"Sharper Millet Three, this is Sharper Millet Six Romeo Tango. Are you addressing this station? Over."

"Six, Three, get me a goddamn urgent medevac, Uniform Sierra personnel. Over."

"Sharper Millet Three, this is Sharper Millet Six Romeo Tango. Do you request a night medevac? Over."

I'm in a cold sweat of panic.

"Affirmative," I scream into the mike. "Urgent! Uniform Sierra personnel. Do you understand me, you idiot? I have an American with his legs blown off

338

bleeding to death. Quit fucking with me, or so help me, I'll cut your fuckin' balls off and stuff them down your throat! Over."

"Sharper Millet Three, this is Sharper Millet Six Romeo Tango. Roger. If you insist, I'll call for a medevac for tonight. Do you need a Cobra escort? Over."

"Yes! Yes! Affirmative! Get them here now! My lieutenant's hit bad. Get someone here, for God's sake, and quit fucking around. Over."

Tears are streaming down my cheeks. I'm totally out of control. If that kid were in sight, I really would cut off his balls and stuff them down his throat. I've never been in such a state of rage in my life.

"Sharper Millet Three, this is Sharper Millet—" There are fumbling noises, squelch breaking, then Rains's voice, "Three, Six. I'll get something fast as I can. Hold on. Wait out."

My heartbeats, probably at one-sixty a minute, must take thirty seconds each. I feel like it's an hour before he calls back, but meantime the medic can only give him a shot and unwrap a couple of pressure bandages, so it must be only a minute. I wind up holding pressure on one spot while he continues to work. Powers is holding one, too. Both of us are praying—aloud, even though neither is religious, and I'm actively anti-religion.

I make the mistake of looking at Simmons's face. He's got the face of a dog with his leg in a bear trap. He's saying "no, no, no!" Then he fixes his glassy-eyed gaze on me. His eyes clear up, and he says, "You son of a bitch! You son of a bitch!"

I turn away unable to face him, my hand clenching

on the bandage.

"Three, this is Six. Over."

"Go, Six."

"Medevac One-one enroute with Cobra Four Escort. Will contact you this push. ETA two zero minutes, over."

"Roger, Six, this push, Medevac One-one. Over."

"If you get time, I need a spot report. Over."

"Nothing much to tell, just five short eight inch rounds, One Uniform Sierrra, two ARVN casualties. Over."

"You mean friendly fire? Over."

"Roger. Over."

"How bad is your Lima hurt? Over."

Give me a break, idiot. He can hear me. I ignore the question. "Later. Out."

I look at Simmons. "You'll be okay. You'll be going home. You'll be okay." My mind goes back to the training. *Tell him he'll be okay. If it doesn't show on your face, he won't know.* Swell. If I'm ever shot in the face and some guy says I'll be okay, I'll know my jaw's blown off, and I'll die of the shock. Only it isn't his jaw.

Whatever the doc gave him takes effect, and he passes out, that, or he loses consciousness from loss of blood. Bac Si has put a needle into his arm, and a bottle is dripping into it, blood expander, I guess. He's tied off the stumps, and the bleeding is almost under control. I realize his testicles are hanging by little bits of flesh. Bac Si puts pressure bandages on the spots and does not cut the little bits of flesh, thinking, as I do, that even though it's inevitable, he will not be the one to do it.

340

Finally I hear, "Sharper Millet Three, this is Medevac One-one. Over."

"Medevac One-one, Three. Over."

"I'm enroute to your location. I think I've been there. Is this where we extracted Medevac One-two? Over."

"Affirmative. Over."

"Roger. Can you mark your position? Over."

"Roger. I have a strobe. I'll position myself and the strobe in the middle of the LZ. Over."

"Roger. Is the position secure? Over."

"Affirmative, casualties caused by friendly fire. Over."

"Roger. How many, and what description? Over."

"Rog. I have two ARVN ambulatory, one Uniform Sierra litter." I turn away and speak softly. "Traumatic amputation, both legs. He's most urgent . . ." Then I add, for some reason, "He's my lieutenant. Over."

I stand in the LZ. Simmons wouldn't have liked it, Harris making a target of himself again. No sweat. They don't go after targets. They hit bystanders, guys with kids, guys whose guts have been chewed up so bad they can't act like the brave young boys they were ever again. You don't have to be brave to get killed in this war, I think, adding, in an insane parody of an old saying, but it helps.

I stand there thinking of Simmons singing, as we walked in the swamp, the tune of "Walking My Baby Back Home": "Gee but it's great, after raping your date, dragging her body back home . . ." I see him looking at the pictures of his kid, thinking of all the war movies my generation grew up with. The guy with a kid always got killed.

341

Insanely I think of McKee, fat and clean in the rear, eating steaks and drinking good whiskey while men with balls lay their lives on the line out here in muck and mud, insects, disease, snakes, and the most vicious, competent enemy ever faced by American soldiers. He gets the same combat pay. He has been decorated. He'll go home a hero in his own mind. I could cheerfully shoot him if he were here. If it would put Simmons back together, I would.

Finally, they see me, and the chopper comes in under mortar flares, blowing up dust and leaves, a growing black apparition in the eerie, shifting light. Wyatt and Powers carry the stretcher on board as the ARVNs jump on.

Then the chopper lifts and disappears into the darkness outside the flarelight.

8 June 1970

The doctor is probing my leg with only a local spray. I am not pleased.

"Don't be such a baby, troop. These are just pinpricks. Bits of shrapnel the size of your pinky nail."

"Mother. That's easy for you to say. You're doing the poking."

"There's a war on. Things are tough all over. You should have gotten this done at a forward aid station. You don't need a trained surgeon to get a few bits of metal out of your leg."

"My lieutenant's here. This is the only way I could get to see him."

"He have a few bits of metal in his legs?"

"No. He no longer has any legs."

"Oh, too bad. He the young blond with his testicles blown off, too?"

"Unless there are more unlucky bastards like him in this war."

"Too bad."

"Ouch. Christ. Did you pull the wings off flies as a

343

kid?"

"Quit complaining. You'll get a Purple Heart out of this. Won't that make it worth the pain?"

"I've got a Purple Heart. I just want a Band-Aid. Old joke. Bill Mauldin 1944. Anyway, no Purple Heart for this. Friendly fire. Though I don't know why they call it friendly. Most of my friends never shot at me at home."

"We get a lot of it. Can't any of you bastards shoot straight?"

"Personally, I shoot better than you cut. I can't vouch for the ARVN artillery."

"Sometimes it's artillery. Sometimes it's bombs. Sometimes it's grenades. Sometimes it's jeeps. If the VC don't get you, you get each other. One third of our business is vehicle accidents. There. I'm done. Keep it dry for a while. I'll give you a temporary profile."

"Fuck the profile, just give me a pocket full of bandages so I can change 'em often."

"Are you going back to the field?"

"Of course. I thought you said it was just a scratch."

"Well, it can get infected easily."

"Then give me some pills."

"Okay, but you could spend a week in the rear."

"Too many assholes in the rear."

One of the nurses chuckles under her mask.

"Okay, okay. Lieutenant Banks, give him a lot of bandages and a week's supply of tetracycline two hundred fifty Q.I.D. Go and get yourself killed, troop. You're crazy."

"Write that down, doc. Write that down."

"Another 1944 joke?"

"Probably older than that."

I put my pants back on and go looking for Simmons.

The Ninety-third Evac is arranged in plus-shaped wards, with nurses' stations in the center of the cross. I walk by some really groaty buildings with field latrines marked Hepatitis. The other buildings have modern plumbing. I go to the wrong buildings about four times and ask sixteen dead-eyed nurses directions along the way. Each gives me the look of a woman inspecting a fish her husband has just given her to clean. I feel bad till I see they do it to everyone, not just semi-groaty field troopies. Their eyes are even deader than the whores. I guess it's a reaction to the pain and suffering.

The sweet angels of mercy of the movies seem to be missing. They probably died the first time they got a nineteen-year-old kid with his balls stuffed down his throat.

He's lying with tubes in both his arms and his nose, a tent over his body so you don't notice parts are missing. He's in a private room near the nurses' station.

"He'll be going to Zama on the next plane," says a semi-friendly nurse before I go in. "He's survived the surgery, and he's stable."

"How much did he lose?"

"Huh?"

"When I put him on the chopper he had lost both feet, and his sex organs looked done for. How much did he lose? The doctor said he had his balls blown off. Did he lose them?"

"Oh, I couldn't tell you."

"Lieuten—miss. This is my lieutenant—my friend, my charge. I need to know."

A senior nurse, a captain, has been sitting at the next desk listening to our whispered conversation. She leans over and says, "He lost both legs, Captain, one below the knee, one above. His penis and testicles could not be saved. He also lost three fingers and a lot of blood. He's very lucky to be alive."

I turn white, I'm sure. "Tha—that's not my definition of lucky. He's twenty-five. His life doesn't look too rosy."

"Are you this solicitous of all your troops, Captain?"

"This is the first American I've—I've lost."

"American?"

"My troops are ARVNs."

"Oh. How lucky. Some officers have lost hundreds like this."

"You can see him, but just for a minute—I mean that captain, one minute."

I go over to his bed. He sees me. "Y-you," he says, his eyes those of a wounded dog. His voice is a rasp and the most chilling sound I've ever heard. "Get out you son of a bitch! Get out! No! Look! Look what you've done!"

I back away, horror struck, feebly saying, "Me? N-no! No!"

"You did this!"

"No! No!"

"Look at this! Why? Why did you save me for this?"

The older nurse has me by the arm and is pulling

me away.

"No, no!"

"Come on, Captain. Get out of here," she says, not too gently.

I walk the gauntlet of Vietnamese patients who are by now jeering. My head is turned toward the door with the pitiful figure of Simmons framed in it till the door slams behind me.

The nurse shoves me against the wall with surprising force.

I look at her for the first time. She is a thirtyish captain with her black hair in a severe bun, wearing fatigues as they all do, looking as unfeminine as possible.

"How dare you upset my patient like that."

"He — he's my friend, I —"

"Friend? Can't you see he hates you?"

"But —"

"Don't you see what you've done to him? You idiot! You —" She is obviously in a rage and at a loss for words. She turns away and walks back into the ward, closing the door behind her.

There is nothing to do but break down into a complete puddle or walk away. I come close to breaking down, but I walk away, shaky, limping, tears streaming down my face, totally broken. I wander for I don't know how long then kind of come to and go to the chopper pad and wait at the helicopter company O Club for the next bird to Lai Khe.

"Fuck it, it don't mean nothin'."

But it does, of course.

9 — 27 June 1970

We finally get all the rice extracted with no further casualties. I'm not much help. I just sit quietly when I'm not needed. I don't make any suggestions. Powers does most of the talking on the radio except when Six asks for me. Six doesn't ask why I'm not doing my job. Perhaps he understands. Then we move on. In a four day move we walk to regimental HQ and become palace guards while Two — Nine humps some. We need the rest.

There's little food at headquarters, and the LRRPs I left are, of course, gone. This makes me mad and I begin to snap out of it.

I take a three-quarter ton truck and Powers and go two clicks away to a Eleventh ACR unit on a scrounging mission. The ASA said there was just no food to be had. I refuse to believe it. You just have to know how to scrounge.

The drive is semi-scary since I'm not too sure of the security of the area, but regiment has had no activity at all, so we're just locked and loaded, CAR-15, M-16, and an M-79 cut into a pistol with a shot round in it.

I start at the CP, while Powers finds the mess sergeant. I don't necessarily intend to ask the C.O. for the rats unless he seems friendly. If he doesn't say no, then Powers can back door them.

I don't get to the C.O. Sitting in a deck chair in a T-shirt, fatigue pants, and shower clogs, is Jim Burton, now First Lieutenant Burton, a 1968 graduate of the University of Houston ROTC department and old Scabbard and Blade brother. I was one of his sponsors, in fact.

"Goddamn, they'll let anybody int' this war, won't they? Where th' hell'd you come from?"

"ARVN unit down the road."

"Fantastic. Gawd, you're decked out for bear, Matty Mattel, bowie knife, and ah—shit, what's that?"

"M-79."

"Not like any I ever saw."

"Turned up in an NVA cache. We thought we'd use it a while before we turn it back in."

"Was it cut up like that?"

"Officially, yes."

"You been in shit where you'd need somethin' like that?"

"Nah, I just carry it to impress the whores and R.E.M.F.s. What'chu doin' here?"

"F.O. to this here cav. unit. What're you doin' here?"

"I'm on a scroungin' mission. They cut off C-rations to advisors. Said we should eat off the local economy. You're it."

"Whatcha need?"

"Whatcha got? Cs, LRRPs, any kind of rations. Food in general."

"Hell, that's easy. I'll need the C.O.'s okay, but we got Cs comin' out our ears. Come with me." He leads me to an older lieutenant colonel who's smoking a pipe before the situation map. "Sir, this is an old college buddy, Capt. Jerry Harris. With the ARVNs next door. Can we spare 'em some Cs?"

"I should say so. We've got 'em coming out our ears. Some nut keeps sending three a day per man, and Cookie's got a field kitchen for two meals a day. See Cookie. Take what you want. Tell you what. A chopper's due at fourteen hundred with a pallet. I'll have it unload over your place. I don't want any more around here. We've got enough."

"Good grief. That's more'n I expected."

"Well, can you use 'em?"

"Of course, sir."

"Good. Fill up your truck, and I'll divert the next load. Anything else we can do for you?"

"Got any blondes hidden away in the bunkers?"

"Sorry."

Burton and I walk over to the mess tent where Powers has already talked Cookie out of a truckload of Cs, two bushels of oranges, a crate of apples, and three jerry cans of gasoline.

"Heard from any of the others from U of H?" he asks.

"Mike Clarendon was at Ft. Lewis with me. Then he went north. That's all I know."

"You heard about Roger Stimpson, didn't you?"

"No."

"Rented a plane coming home from helicopter

flight school. He, his wife, and Joe Burke and his wife. Hit a storm. Crashed and killed 'em all."

"No shit? Gee, I'd forgotten people died except in combat."

"Benny Karnes, the guy who terrorized you so much in your junior year?"

"Yeah?"

"Damn near flunked out of Infantry O.B.C. Graduated last in his class. Lieutenant Colonel Tolbert had to RBI. Big stink."

"God, how could anybody be so dumb? Anyone with an IQ of sixteen can pass Infantry O.B.C."

"You know about Frank Oaks?"

"Yeah. Tank knocked over on its side by a mine. Fractured his spine."

"Yeah. But he's okay, now. At UH taking law when I left. A civilian."

"He's lucky. Could be in a wheel chair."

"Yeah."

We have everything loaded pretty quick and head back to our unit.

A loaded three-quarter ton truck full of rations makes us popular with everyone except the ASA who looks like a fool. The arrival of a pallet load of Cs makes me a legend in my own regiment.

My orders for DEROS come in for July 1, a twenty-five day drop. I'm ecstatic.

We finally leave Cambodia, marching across the border and setting up a FSB on the SVN side.

My turtle, Andrew Key arrives for OJT. All is quiet except the troops bring their wives/girlfriends in on

352

the bus to the nearest road, then to camp. At oh-one hundred one morning Dong bursts into the advisors' hooch.

"*Dai-Uy, Dai-Uy*! Come quick! Need helicopter. Sojer real sick!"

"Show me," I say.

He leads me to a hooch. "It—it not sojer," he says.

"Not soldier? What is it?"

"His wipe. His wipe—he real sick."

Before I can decipher this we reach the hooch with the lights on in it.

Wipe equals wife, I think. And Dong has gender problems in English. "He" is in obvious labor.

I call a medevac, but they won't come till morning.

"*Dai-Uy*, you must help," says Dong.

"Get Bac Si."

"Bac Si need you help."

"My help?"

"He never deliver baby."

"Neither have I."

"You help. You know how."

"What makes you think I know how to deliver a baby?"

"Do you?"

"Yes, but that's not the point. What makes you think that?"

"You help. Bac Si pass out."

"Why?"

"It his baby. His wipe."

So I get to deliver not one baby, but two, identical twins. Neither is named after me.

28 June 1970

I go to Lai Khe to process out, the happiest I've ever been. I've made it. I've survived my tour. Jerry Harris is alive and well on his way home from Vietnam.

I start at admin and get the little form with a page of blank spaces which must have initials in each space before one can leave. At least as an officer I can sign most of them myself. I get as far as the supply sergeant and am turning in much of my stuff when the admin officer Captain Alvarez finds me.

"Colonel Shaw wants to see you in his office right now."

"What the fuck for? I thought I was to have dinner with him tonight."

"Tomorrow night. You're here too early. You goddamn field troops are all alike, trying to get out of work. The rule is you leave the field thirty-six hours before your flight. Not before. Colonel Shaw has a mission for you."

"Mission? I'm too short for a mission. Fuck off. It's not funny."

"No joke, Harris. Now. Bring your field gear. You'll need it."

"Oh, shit." I follow him. Shaw pulls one of the "I'm in power" ploys. He reads something on his desk for about five minutes before he returns my salute.

"You're supposed to be the fair-haired boy of Ninth Regiment, Harris."

"News to me, sir."

"Yeah, I don't know what they see in you, either. What the hell are you doing in Lai Khe?"

"Processing out, sir."

"You're too early. You should still be in the field. It's only a six month tour. Not fair to cut it short."

"I've been in the field the whole year, sir."

"Doesn't matter. I fired Captain Follett this morning — incompetence. Unfortunately his battalion has a company-sized insertion at fourteen hundred hours today. I need someone experienced in CAs. You're it. You'll have to run it. Then you'll stay with his battalion at Chan Tanh till you have only thirty-six hours left in country. Then you can come here and process out."

"Sir, can't you get someone else? I've done enough CAs for a lifetime."

"Harris, are you refusing a direct order? If so, I'll send your ass to Bien Hoa for a general court so fast it'll make your head spin."

"Sir, I'm not refusing. I'm just requesting you get someone else. I'm burned out. I've done my part.

356

I—"

"Shut up, captain. That's a direct order. You will replace Captain Follett as S.A. of Four—Nine temporarily and you will fly C and C for their insertion at fourteen hundred hours today. Any questions, captain?"

"Yes sir. Why me?"

"Get out there and do it, smartass."

"Yes sir."

So I wind up on a Huey for Chan Tanh, in old jungle fatigues, harness with two smoke grenades and only three magazines for the CAR-15, a map, and an SOI. I get the PRC-25 radio from the two black sergeants who currently make up the entire advisory team at Chan Tanh.

The radio battery is dead. "Sergeant, get me a battery that works."

The chopper is ready to take off. The ARVNs are aboard, Major Hung, the C.O., Sergeant Major Tranh, an LCDB who carried radios, and Captain Truong, C.O. of Tenth Company, the one we are to insert.

"Ain't got no more, Cap'n."

"Get the one from the CP."

"Cain't. We need it."

"Just get the fuckin' battery, Sergeant. You can get another. I can't."

Cursing and kicking, he goes and gets it. It works. We take off.

The insertion is so far from friendly troops preparation it consists solely of ARA from two Cobra heavy-fire teams. The plan is that they work over the area with rockets, killing all the NVA in the area (fat chance). Then we come in southeast to northwest, mark the spot for the lead chopper with red smoke, and circle above while four choppers bring sixty-four men in two loads, thirty-two each, eight per chopper.

The first lieutenant piloting the Huey asks me, "You done this before?"

"All I ever want to, and more."

"Oh, good, this is my first time as mission commander. Give me any pointers you can."

"I've got one."

"What is it?"

"Don't get me killed."

"Right."

When we arrive the HFT is working over the jungle surrounding this convenient four chopper-sized clearing. The puffs of smoke are coming from the ground dully, not at all like you see on TV. I can't hear them, of course. We take a couple of passes over the area then go in to drop smoke.

I'm wishing I was already in that freedom bird on the way to Travis, or already on Galveston beach, getting my ass sunburned, or anywhere but here. I have a particularly bad feeling about this operation.

"Cobras, this is Bigshot," says the twenty-one-year old kid in the pilot's seat. The pilot's a kid, the co-pilot's a kid, the gunners are kids. I can't see the Cobra crews, but I know they're kids. I'm an old man at twenty-four.

"Go."

"I'm going in to drop smoke. I'll bank right. Give me covering mini-gun fire. Over."

"Roger."

We go in, flanked by four of the most lethal helicopters ever designed. They're firing a steady stream of mini-gun fire.

The co-pilot drops a smoke grenade out the left window, then we bank left—

Straight in front of the stuck and still firing runaway mini-gun of Cobra Two. Bullets rake the side of the chopper just aft of the door gunner.

Jesus Christ!"

"Motherfucker!"

"Momma!" I hear over the radio. I add "Son of a bitch!" Real creative am I in a crisis.

The marvelous turbine which powered this particular UH1H does what you'd do if six 7.62 mm mini-gun slugs went into you. It dies.

So does the LCDB. He falls out of the lurching beast a hundred and twenty feet to the jungle. I see him slide out. I can't hear him scream, but I can see his mouth open briefly before he disappears from view. I'm strapped in. Mrs. Harris didn't raise that big a fool.

A Huey without motive force will auto-rotate down. That's what they tell you at Tan Son Nhut during inprocessing.

They're right.

Up front, the two kids are frantically trying to make this collection of non-working parts reach the clearing.

I'm reassessing my previous statement that I've survived my tour.

Lieutenant Frazier and WO2 Darryl Cunningham are earning the singular honor of being the only helicopter pilots to be shot down by a friendly Cobra helicopter during the Vietnam War.

They almost reach the clearing. The only thing that stops them is a fifty foot tall tree. Almost doesn't count except in horseshoes and hand grenades.

They just barely clip the tree—hard enough to throw us down on the left side of the nose.

Cunningham sees the earth rush up and no more.

The left door gunner, SP-4 Joshua Myerson, is trapped when the chopper rolls down. I hear him screaming as the crashing sounds die in my ears.

I have no wind. I am seeing stars. I can't breathe.

I'm alive.

Oh, shit, what a mess.

Fire. Oh, God, don't let there be fire.

I hear moaning.

Now the pain from the seatbelt injuries has started. Damn I'm glad to have them. The alternative would've been the LCDB's plunge.

I unstrap.

The Vietnamese unstrap. They climb out of the chopper, ignoring the dead and injured. Like the rest of us they want to avoid the fire that hasn't happened but will. They didn't call these bastard choppers Zippos for nothing.

I'm disoriented. When I more or less .get my bearings, I go for Myerson, reacting to his screaming by instinct, not realizing the abject danger of staying in this future firebomb. His right leg is crushed under the chopper, and the machine gun had flailed around his middle. He's in a total panic, screaming at the top of his lungs.

"Okay, son, I'll get you out."

How, I don't know. I start digging around his leg. Finally I can get it free. It's a bloody mess, almost cut off below the knee, and soon will have to be for sure. I must be hyperventilating. I think I'm going to pass out I'm so scared. I can hear the chopper bursting into flames in my mind. I can see myself screaming as I burn. I use his belt as a tourniquet.

I hear the pilot.

"Oh, Jesus, oh Jesus! Darryl's dead! Darryl's dead!"

So what else is new. I've seen so many die now I don't think I'd get excited no matter who it was.

"Get your ass over here, lieutenant, or we all will be. Anybody else able to help?"

"Yeah," I hear. I turn and look. It's the other door gunner.

Outside I hear staccato popping — small-arms fire! Oh, shit!

We pull Myerson out of his little pocket, then up across the chopper — left to right now being down to up. Frazier looks out.

A shot rings out, something big, 12.7 mm I think, commonly called .51 caliber — equal to our .50 caliber, and definitely bad news. His head explodes. Brains, bone, and blood goes everywhere.

I keep my head down and turn to the right gunner. He's pretty big. "Carry this guy to that log over there," I say. "I'll cover you."

He's pretty stunned. He stands there not moving for too many seconds. I feel silly slapping a two hundred twenty pound potential Oiler linebacker, but I do, oblivious to the fact the big son of a bitch could knock me into the next province.

"I'll cover you! Now!" I stick the CAR-15 out and loose off fourteen-fifteen rounds in short bursts, then say, "Go!"

He runs for the big thirty-eight inch mahogany log—and makes it. I fire five more rounds—at nothing, just bluffing fire, pop in another magazine, and run for the log, my radio on my back. I hear the big machine gun open up.

I almost make it. The chopper blows up so violently I go head over heels.

I lay on the ground a minute, motionless, wiggling fingers and toes to see if they work. A man doesn't feel pain at a time like that—later, but not then.

Nearly everything works. My knees hurt after a minute. That is a good sign.

I crawl to behind the log, prop myself into firing position, and loose off a round in the general direction of the 12.7 mm fire we were getting. Then I try the radio.

"Cobra One, this is Flapjack Six. Over."

"Go, Six."

"Rog. You can see the Sierra has hit the fan. We need some ARA about fifty yards southwest of the urning chopper. Bunker 50-51 caliber fire. Over."

"We're all out of ARA. All we have are some mini-gun rounds left. Over."

"Roger. Use them. Over."

Gee, he's so calm. I'm trying to sound equally calm and bored, but I feel like the pig discussing breakfast with the hen who suggested he provide the bacon, and she provide the eggs. "Bacon and eggs is a breakfast to you, but it's a real commitment to me."

"Six. One. I have four Cobras from Song Be, with ARA and nails. Over."

"Roger."

"Meanwhile we have the four slicks full of little people. Want to land then? Over."

"I'll leave that up to the slick's C.O. I'd judge it to be hairy. Over."

"Rog. Break, Bigshot Five, wanna go in? Over."

"Okeydokey. On the way. Over."

I watch in awed horror as the idiot brings the four choppers in to a hot LZ with God knows how many more 12.7 mm machine guns, how many neatly camouflaged bunkers, with no ARA, no artillery, no jets. Another kid playing John Wayne?

They come in diamond formation. They hover low, and the damn ARVNs won't come out.

I've forgotten. Where are Hung and company? I look around. There he is, sprawled in the clearing, his guts trailing out for three yards. The expression on his face is not happy. He is still alive, too weak to scream. He is moaning a horrible moan, though. Tranh is sprawled over a large area because he is cut

363

in half at the groin. Truong is in a heap with his leg
almost detached. Welcome to the wonderful world o
war, boys and girls.

"Cobra One, this is Flapjack Six. The ARVN C.O
and all his crew are dead. They're probably waiting
orders up there. I guess you'll have to—"

But my words are interrupted by 12.7 mm fire
which signals rocket fire.

The lead chopper is hit with 12.7 mm fire and fall
heavily, bursting into flames. ARVNs run out, o
fire, only to be hit by 12.7 mm fire on the left side—
the gun that'd gotten our guys. On the right side
hear AK fire and imagine a similar fate.

The next two choppers are hit with B-40 rocket
and explode. The tail-end Huey pulls up, spilling
three or four ARVNs as it climbs. I can imagine th
crew is not happy with the ARVNs for not getting ou
on schedule, making the choppers sitting ducks.

Two B-40 rockets narrowly miss the climbing Huey

Now I have a little problem. Instead of being safel
in the rear I'm on the ground with two guys, on
wounded, one armed with a .38 revolver.

Against us are:

One—12.7 mm heavy machine gun in a well-buil
bunker.

Two—RPG-2 rocket launchers.

One—or more AK-47 rifle.

Let's see, the 12.7 mm takes two to three men, th
RPGs one to two, one rifleman, minimum. That'
five to seven minimum. Great. I have fifteen t
eighteen rounds left. All those times I carried six t

ten magazines and never needed them, and now I have fifteen to eighteen rounds left. Story of my life. Fucked up again, Harris. Of course, Alvin York could've killed 'em all with that many. Unfortunately, Alvin York I'm not.

"Six, Cobra One. I see where the rockets came from. Making a run."

The Cobras come over, firing short bursts, conserving ammo.

"Got you, cocksucker," says one of the Cobra gunners.

"There's a tunnel. I saw one go in a hole."

"Watch out for rockets."

No rocket fire from the bad guys — which might mean they're out of B-40s.

The 12.7 mm fires at the Cobras. The lead Cobra follows the tracers back and puts accurate fire down the goddamn hole.

I hear screaming from the bunker, and the firing stops. The screaming continues. Somebody is gut-shot.

"You got the son of a bitch."

Then 12.7 mm rounds plunk into the log I'm behind.

Oh, shit.

"Somebody's still alive in there, but good shooting."

I see movement to my right, spin, and fire three rounds on quick semi. An NVA pops out of the bushes, flops on his back, and lies still.

The big future Oiler linebacker/right door gunner,

nametag Washington, is huddled in the fetal position.

"Oh, shit," I say. "Just what I need. You hurt, Washington?"

No answer.

"Washington! Are you hurt?"

"VC. They're gonna get us."

"They sure as hell will if you don't get up and fight."

"Give up. No rifle."

He isn't exactly a portrait of courage. Of course courage doesn't apply in such a situation. I'm fighting for my life. It doesn't take any courage to fight rather than to die. A housecat will fight like a tiger if cornered.

"We can't give up. They don't take prisoners. Your only chance is to fight."

He crawled out of the fetal position and lay by the log.

"No rifle. Just this thirty-eight."

I look around. Hung had carried a .45, and so had Truong. Tranh had an M-16.

"I'll get you one." I picked up the handset. "Cobra, this is Six."

"Go."

"I need covering fire. One of the dead ARVNs in front of us has a rifle. We need it. Over."

"Okay, we'll make a couple of harassing passes with mini-guns while you grab it. Over."

"Roger."

I wait till the Cobras are popping out mini-gun rounds and making a lot of noise overhead and run for Tranh. His rifle is under his body. I grab it and go for his harness with its magazines. It won't come off, of course. I'm shaking and pulling. A 12.7 mm round hits his body, blowing off a chunk, and I take off, 12.7 mm rounds chasing me. I dive over the log at flank.

"Here, Washington. You've got a fucking rifle now. Kill somebody."

"Y-yeah."

"Six, this is Cobra One."

"Go."

"We've got a problem. Over."

"Go ahead."

"That expended our mini-gun arms. Two of our birds have reached fuel bingo. Over."

"Roger. How long can the other two stay? Over."

"They left Song Be fifteen minutes ago. I can't reach them by radio. Over."

"Are they overdue? Over."

"Roger. Over."

"Scramble some more. Something. Even some slicks with door guns. We're naked down here. Over."

"Roger. Wait. Out."

I know he's on another frequency talking to base. I feel physically ill and want to throw up. He can't stay more than five minutes. As soon as he leaves, they'll move in.

Two Cobras peel off and head for Song Be.

"Six, One. They won't scramble more choppers. Someone's got his head up his ass there. Something about blade time. The other fire teams are lost.

367

Either I gave them the wrong coordinates, or the TOC did. Cobra Two's at bingo. I'm sending him on. Over."

"And what's the bad news? Over."

"What can I say? I'll stay here as long as I can. Over."

"How come you're not at bingo? Over."

"More conservative flying. Over."

"Rog. Sure. You're at bingo, aren't you? Over."

"Roger. I can stay ten more minutes if I land at Xuan Diap. Over."

"There's nothing there, is there? Over."

"R.F.P.F. Company. They can bring me some fuel there. Over."

"That's playing the odds pretty close. Over."

"How long can you last when I leave? Over."

"Oh, long time, ten, fifteen minutes. Over."

"What's your status? I'll relay it to your TOC and try again for another fire team. Over."

"Line one—U.S.—two. ARVNs—four. Line two— one. We have two M-16s, thirty rounds five point five six, one thirty-eight revolver, five rounds, one smoke grenade. Over."

"Roger. Oh, Jesus Christ. Wait out."

"Yea, though I walk through the valley of the shadow of death, I will fear no evil . . ."

The 12.7 mm is silent, but AKs start popping off rounds from the bunker and another spot. We're surrounded.

I hear a rustling to my right. A grenade comes out and hits in front of the log. We lay down behind it. It goes off harmlessly. Most of the grenades I've encountered were harmless anyway, except to the thrower. I pop the CAR up quick enough to hit the guy who threw the grenade. He was, of course, charging after it. Two AK rounds hit the log just below my face. I love mahogany. If I live, I'll decorate my entire house with it. "Short, add three inches, fire for effect," I say as I get as low behind the log as possible.

Then I take a deep breath and almost break up when I say over the radio, "Cobra, Six. Make one low pass to keep their heads down, then get the hell outta here before you run outta gas. Over."

I wonder if the chopper pilot ever saw *The Bridges of Toko-Ri*.

"Roger on the low pass. I'll stay a while, though. Those guys are on their way, soon."

"Hell, you must be on fumes. Over."

"Pretty close. Over."

"Then scat. Over."

"You going to be there when I get back? Over."

"That's affirm. I'll dance with them that brung me. Over."

"Roger. Good luck. Over."

"Thanks. Out."

He makes two passes, then I can see both crewmen salute as they peel off and go south.

"Now the shit has hit the fan, truly and thoroughly. Come on, motherfuckers. I'll just pretend you're Colonel Shaw."

AK fire is in single, careful shots. There is no 12.7

369

mm fire. Perhaps they're as low on ammo as we are

My faithful companion is a total wreck. I keep kicking him to try to get him to fight. Myerson is unconscious, in shock.

Things could be worse, I think, but I can't guess how.

Finally Washington starts acting like a soldier, though not very well. He sticks his head up too far over the log and takes an AK round in the left eye. His head explodes, showering me with blood and brains.

The NVA charge. I manage to shoot up the rest of my ammo. I hit one at the waist. Two others dive back into the jungle.

They are wearing khaki, ragged, with Ho Chi Minh sandels, no pith helmets, no packs. They are ragged, worn uniforms, like their wearers. Tough little motherfuckers, I think.

It is quiet for a while. Then there are a couple of feints. I use up all the 5.56 mm ammo to keep them back. Eventually I'm down to the .38, realizing I've never fired a revolver in my life. Oh well, sight picture, trigger squeeze. This is why I was trained so long in marksmanship. How different can a revolver be? Think of the cap pistols you shot as a kid, Jerry.

Another grenade comes, a Chicom pineapple type. It lands right beside me. I scoop it up and throw it over the log. It doesn't go off.

"Goddamn lousy grenades."

Then, apparently they decide to charge. Yelling insanely seven of them appear, running at full tilt,

370

bayonets charged.

"God Almighty, not bayonets!" I'm shaking frantically as I fire the .38 as fast as I can. I have little presence of mind, but enough to aim for head shots because the puny little .38 round can't stop a charging armadillo. God, for a .45.

"This is it! Goddamn Shaw!"

One throws a satchel charge. They must be out of ammo and grenades.

I grab it in midair and throw it back.

It goes off. I remember the flash, red going to white, and being thrown backward, then nothing.

Then comes the pain. My head is throbbing. I'm retching my guts out. I'm blind. I hurt everywhere.

Son of a bitch. I must be alive, I think.

I hear Vietnamese voices around me.

I can taste blood through the vomit. I'm trying to get onto all fours.

I feel an awful blow to my side, a kick. It knocks me over. I groan reflexively. That brings me another kick.

I lie there groaning and hear two Vietnamese voices. I think I can understand them. I think it translates to:

Voice one: "Lieutenant, don't kill him."

Voice two: "The motherfucking American (*Du ma My*—the same thing the ARVNs call us) killed half my troops! Cut off his balls and stuff them down his throat!"

371

Voice one: "Wait! There's a bounty on American prisoners. This one's an advisor, a captain. Look at his patches. MACV—advisors. Two black bars. Captain. He'll be worth a lot!"

I can now see light out of my right eye. Tears are coming from the pain and washing the blood out of it. The left one is swelled shut.

Someone grabs me by the hair and pulls me erect. I collapse. I feel hands picking me up. I am slammed against the nearest tree.

Voice two: "Motherfucking American butcher! War criminal! I think I'll cut your balls and prick off and make you eat them!"

Obviously this guy never went to Dale Carnagie.

I am not terribly thrilled by this news, but at this point, I am not surprised. Maybe, if I'm lucky, they'll do it quickly.

Then, to punctuate his remarks, he hits me in the balls with something. I double over and vomit some more. The pain is unbelievable, indescribable. I still can't see, but now I can't see white stars.

Voice one: "Turn him in. You'll make captain. I'll make warrant. You'll get a medal for capturing a prisoner. You already have medals for killing Americans. Headquarters wants prisoners. You'll hurt him more by taking him prisoner. Death is nothing. Prison is torture."

Voice two: "Pull him up." Someone does. "Motherfucking American! Motherfucker!"

He kicks or hits me in the balls again. Tears are streaming down my cheeks. I have nothing left to retch. I know he'll beat me to death. The tears clean out my right eye enough to see him. My glasses are gone. I have twenty-one hundred without them. But I can see his angry, ugly young face now, inches from me.

He has smallpox scars and a broken nose. His hair has patches missing. I think he has scabies.

"Kill me, you cocksucker," I say in English. Hoping he will. He knees me, but I twist enough to protect myself.

"He killed six good men. His helicopters killed seven more. He must die."

"Lieutenant," says voice one, "he wants to die. Prison will degrade and destroy him. You will be promoted and decorated. You can go home as a hero. Isn't that better?"

I look around. I can see voice one. He is a very tough-looking guy, large for a Vietnamese, maybe five feet eleven inches. His face and chest are scarred. He is missing his two front teeth. He wears only tattered khaki pants and Ho Chi Minh sandals.

He is a fool. The lieutenant, while insanely angry, is right. I have to die. They can't take me back to the North. If I'd taken a prisoner while deep in enemy territory with only a few men and no support, I wouldn't try to take him back.

In that case, what's the difference between that and shooting a twelve-year-old kid caught with foot mines? Why am I moralizing while this motherfucker tries to kill me?

The lieutenant picks up the .38 revolver and opens

it. I can't tell how many rounds are left. He spins the cylinder and laughs. Then he sticks the barrel roughly against my forehead and pulls the trigger.

I know I'm going to die. It won't hurt. It won't hurt. It won't hurt. God, please, don't let it hurt.

Snap.

He found at least one empty cylinder. They might all be empty. I lost count in the assault.

"All right," says the lieutenant. "We will take him with us." This surprises me more than a little.

I look around and count only six NVA. They are a scraggly lot. A couple have bloody bandages from minor wounds.

Then I see Myerson. He is against another tree. His throat has been cut, and in the slit are stuffed his balls. His penis hangs from his mouth like a cigarette.

They tie my hands behind my back and tie a rope around my waist and one around my neck. Voice number one takes both ropes, jerks the one around my neck hard enough to get my attention, nearly strangling me, then motions me to follow.

I follow.

I'm dragged and kicked and pushed along at a quick pace. Everything hurts: my head, my face where the eye is closed, my arms from the ropes tying my hands, my neck from the rope, my chest, legs and feet from the exertion, my guts from the vomiting, my groin from the beating. A rib feels broken. I think the appropriate word is agony, but misery might suffice.

I really want to die. I also want to get my hands

around Shaw's neck before I die. Then it comes to me someone else would have had to do the mission, as stupid and useless as it was, if I hadn't. If it had gone well, it would've accomplished nothing. The war wouldn't have ended any sooner, and no Americans would've gone home any sooner. In other words, this is a waste. Myerson, Washington, all the others, a waste.

We go all night at a relentless pace. I fall several times. When I do one of them screams in my face, slaps me, and pulls me up.

Just before dawn, I am so exhausted I decide when I collapse next time I'll just let them beat me to death. At least it'll be over. One of them throws me down, in the crotch of a tree and covers me up with brush.

I pass out or fall asleep, hoping never to wake again.

DAILY REPORT, 28 JUNE 1970

To: Senior Advisor 5th ARVN Division

Subject: Extra recon.

1. At approximately 1645 hours my unit arrived at insertion point for 10th Company, 4/9. Utilizing two HF Teams, we inserted 48 troops in one wave without incident.

2. At the location we found 28 ARVN bodies, 10 NVA bodies, and 16 US bodies, all 1st Aviation Bde. personnel. Report of same to 5th ARVN resulted in request for search for one US personnel, Harris, Jerry A. 05431914.

3. Secondary search resulted in find of buried US and NVA weapons, but no more bodies.

4. US bodies were evacuated to Long Binh. ARVN bodies were evacuated to Lai Khe.

5. Be advised that atrocities had been committed on some US bodies, specifically castration.

6. Unit extracted at 1850 hours.

Robert A. Senders,
MAJ, Inf. USA

29 June – 1 July 1970

I dream of hell, of pain and heat and sweat. I see myself as they cut off my balls and prick, as they cut my throat and stuff my balls down my throat and put my prick in my mouth.

I awake in sweating heat, needing to piss, cramped, unable to move. Eventually, after two or three hours I piss in my pants. It isn't much. I am dehydrating and know it. An American drinks a gallon a day in the hundred degree weather with one hundred percent humidity of the jungles in the central highlands. I've had nothing to drink for twenty to twenty-four hours. I won't last long.

It rains in the afternoon. I try to drink rainwater but can't. Soon I'm shivering cold and soaked.

At dusk one of them picks me up, a grunt I begin to call number three, with the lieutenant number one, the ambitious sergeant number two, a short guy with a wounded arm number four, a near toothless one number five, and a young kid number six. Number six has a slight head wound and a lot of pimples. It is a scraggly group.

Number three is five feet six inches tall, stringy, with sores on his neck and a cauliflower ear. He gives me some water, not enough, for I am badly dehydrated. Somehow he's gotten hold of a C-ration can of pork, and he feeds it to me with chopsticks. Some rice he more or less pours down my throat. I realize he's taken rations from dead ARVNs. Then I realize the sergeant is telling him that Americans can't eat their food, but need G.I. food, and to make sure I eat it.

The fatted calf . . .

I ask for more water—in English. No way would they learn I understand Vietnamese.

He tries more rice. I shake my head. He points to the empty green can. I shake my head. He picks up the canteen. I nod.

"Water."

"*Nuoc.*"

"*Nuoc,*" I say. I know it's *nuoc,* asshole.

He gives me some.

The lieutenant says something about not letting me drink it all, and number three stops.

Then they pull me up and begin marching north again. I try to watch the stars and moon from beneath the jungle canopy. In places it is possible. In others it isn't.

We are going northwest. The angle I know only by the stars. The lieutenant has a compass. I file this away with other possibly useful information, such as:

Number one carries a captured M-16, a captured .45, and his AK-47.

Number two carries two captured M-16s and his AK-47, along with a knife, a big American-looking survival knife.

Everyone's AK-47 is out of ammunition.

Apparently they buried the 12.7 mm MG and RPGs and any captured weapons they can't carry.

Number three carries three M-16s.

Number four carries one and an AK.

Number five carries two and no AK.

Number six carries my CAR-15 and an AK.

The U.S. weapons, from dead ARVNs, have full magazines and spares.

We go at the same relentless pace all night. I think I'm going to die from it. Bamboo vines and other jungle garbage cut my face and neck over and over. When I went through the jungle before, I could use my arms to fend them off — and I had a helmet. Now I'm bareheaded.

Unfortunately I can't turn off my brain. It occurs to me that soon I will be questioned and tortured. What can I do? I toss that about a good long time. Finally I decide to answer their questions when I'm questioned. I don't know anything important, and they'll get it anyway sooner or later. Superman I'm not. Then it occurs to me that they'll parade me in front of a camera and have Captain Harris admit to war crimes and atrocities and poor dental habits, etc. It won't be a case of answering questions or not.

This leaves me one solution: Do something that'll

get me killed. I don't think I have much to lose. I won't survive this, and I might save some pain.

I wait for my chance. Trussed up like a Christmas turkey I can't do much, even toward suicide.

What fools the NVA are. They treat prisoners with calculated cruelty. If they treated them nice, they'd have to take reservations at the Hanoi Hilton. We have so many disaffected G.I.s that would find a way to defect. Then the NVA would have one thousand to two thousand screwed-up G.I.s to parade before Swedish TV cameras or Jane Fonda. But no, they break bones, pull out fingernails, crush testicles, whip, freeze, and broil our unfortunate pilots and grunts, stiffening the resolve of those fighting to die rather than be taken prisoner. Ol' luckless Harris couldn't even manage that.

I fall once too often. Number one doesn't like that. He slaps me and yells in my face, his face two inches from mine. Then he takes the .38 and puts it to my forehead. Very slowly he pulls the trigger.

Click

"Oh, shit."

It is not the reaction he wanted.

They all laugh.

Number one and number three jerk me up. I go along as best I can. They don't seem to push me as hard as they had.

At dawn the situation is like the night before except number three feeds me some rice and an ARVN issue can of tuna. They'd robbed the ARVN bodies for food as well as rifles. Then I realize the E.M. are carrying ARVN packs. ARVNs carrying packs and two or three rifles each couldn't maintain the marching pace of these guys.

I sleep a bit until it gets really hot during the day. Lying there awake I try to work the ropes loose, with no luck. Just to prevent that they've wrapped the rope connecting my feet to my hands around my feet till it is as tight as I can stand it, feet touching hands. My hands are swollen and numb. I fear losing them. There has to be some way to get loose, to escape or make them kill me.

It's raining again. They start moving in the rain. I hear one say it won't be far now.

I begin to put pieces together. They'd started on patrol, I gather, a one hundred and sixty man company, with a captain in charge. After six months fighting only these six remain, with the lieutenant the sole surviving officer. They're going to a staging area to be reassigned to a new unit.

These must be a tough bunch of cocksuckers, I think.

We march at a killing pace till midnight or so. It is a dark, cloudy night. I can see no stars.

Then we come to a deserted bunker complex under heavy canopy above, making them invisible from the air.

Number one grabs the chain from around my neck that holds my dog tags and jerks it off. Then he goes into one of the bunkers and starts talking, either on a radio or a field telephone. He is reporting my capture. "Harris, Jerry A., zero-five-four-three-one-nine-one-four, A pos, Protestant." He has trouble getting that out. He spells everything but the ASN.

Apparently he is told to wait there, that someone will come and fetch me. He comes out and gives a speech after twenty minutes on the radio. I think he's congratulating the troops on behalf of their beloved division C.O. He says they've done damage far in excess of their numbers, that their actions of the last six months will become legend.

While he is talking, I'm sitting, legs out, hands on the ground, not trussed up too bad. My hands are stinging like hell. They're stinging because number three retied them a bit looser. I'm flexing my fingers and rotating my wrists to get the circulation back.

"You are true liberators of the people. We fight for a just cause, and we are winning. Your sacrifices are not in vain."

Jesus, give a guy a little rank and he makes speeches. Then he passes out drinks from a bottle in the bunker. They eat and drink, toasting and laughing.

Number one and number two talk about the results of my capture. Number one is to accompany me to North Vietnam as his reward. Number two will get a platoon of his own. They're quite happy with themselves.

They manage to get fairly drunk. I hope they have ten bottles of whatever it is. They're drinking like ARVNs, passing the bottle and the cap. The guy whose turn it is will fill the cap and drink it, then pass the bottle to the next guy.

While they're not particularly alert, and while I have some use of my hands, I reach into my right boot and extract the little boot knife. I'd hate to fight a battle with it, but I can cut myself loose, and I proceed to do so. I figure all I'll be able to do is to get myself killed and perhaps take one or two of them with me, but it beats ten years in a prison camp being tortured slowly to death.

Unfortunately the bottle empties, and they are still awake.

The party breaks up, and they go off to sleep, the lieutenant in the bunker, the others outside. Great!

Then, oh, shit, they put number six on guard duty, right in front of me. Number six is sixteen or seventeen, probably strong as an ox despite his size. I am as strong as an enraged canary. I figure he'll hear my heartbeat and check my ropes at any moment, but no, he sits and hums tunelessly, staring at me.

I wait — and wait. I pretend sleep.

Everything is dead quiet. The other five are sound asleep. Then number six turns around, trying to sit more comfortably.

I can't waste any time.

I spring. My right hand goes to his mouth. I remember dimly that if I pull his head back too far, I'll cause the jugular and carotids to retract behind some muscle tissue. If I had a long enough knife, it wouldn't matter. But it does. I pull back pretty hard anyway. My left hand goes to his throat, slashing the knife across his throat as deep as I can cut. I want his windpipe cut, too. He grabs at my hands, but I press harder on his mouth. Within thirty seconds his brain dies, and he lets go and slumps. I hold on until he stops twitching. His sphincters relax. Somehow they never mention this in the movies. I put him down carefully and look around. I expect to see the other five with fixed bayonets, but no, just silence.

Number two has a big knife. He is my next target, even though I feel he will be the toughest. I need the knife, though. I have number six's AK, now reloaded from a bunker cache, but I don't even pick it up. If I make noise I'm dead. It is still five to one. I wish they were more drunk.

Very slowly I creep to number two's sleeping area and watch him carefully. I can see from only one eye. It is hard to see the necessary details: He is on his back, good; hands to his rifle at his right side, bad.

I breathe deeply a couple of times and try to stop shaking. I am shaking like a leaf and have a strong urge to throw up.

"Yea, though I walk through the valley of the shadow of death I will fear no evil . . ."

Like hell, I'm scared shitless, I think, hopefully not aloud.

"Oh well, they can kill me, but they can't eat me."

I use the same technique. I grab his mouth with my right hand and slash quickly with the edge of the knife in my left hand, except quickly this time, from above his head. Then I grab his arms to keep his finger from the trigger, dropping my knee to his face. He dies as silently as the other, though not without kicking and struggling.

I take his knife, a marine issue Ka-Bar. He has kept it clean, rust free, and sharp. It is a huge killing knife. Marines swear by it.

I am covered in blood. My arms, legs, and chest are all wet. It's about to get worse.

Number three is sleeping on his stomach. I bypass him and go to number four. He is on his side. I put my hand over his mouth and stick the knife in above the kidneys, moving it back and forth to get the arteries. I use so much force that I sever his spine. The legs kick and go limp.

It is as if there are two of me, one killing like some goddamned machine, and another watching dispassionately wondering what has happened to Mrs. Harris's nice little boy, the weak, underweight one who used to run away from fights.

Number three rolls over and groans. I can't afford his waking up. I dive at him, trying to silence him and stick the big knife in just under his rib cage at the same time. The knife hits into mark, his heart, but he lets out a loud grunt. I have blood all over me.

I hear number five waking up and go for him before he is fully awake. He is sitting up and fends off my clumsy attack with his forearm, throwing me to the ground.

Oh, shit.

He grabs for his AK, and I lunge and slash, ripping open his left shoulder. He ignores this. He has the AK pointed at me now, and I have less than a second.

With my right arm I knock the rifle off aim as I lunge with my left, go in under his right arm and rip open his chest from armpit to sternum. He screams, but the scream ends in bubbles.

Then the lieutenant's AK goes off, a full automatic burst of ten to fifteen rounds.

I hit the ground and roll. He is in front of the bunker. I am five to ten paces from a rifle—a lifetime—if I try to get it.

I don't. Even if I live, then if I fire it, I'll be as blind as he must be after firing that AK in the dark.

"That's it. He's blinder than I am."

I scoop up a rock and throw it right and go left. He fires at the rock.

I reach him. He slams my shoulder with the rifle, too close to fire. I fall—hard.

I hit on my back.

He is in control now.

I'm dead.

All he has to do is to fire—six to twelve inches from my face.

He does.

Click. The AK is empty. The AK-47 has two fatal flaws. The safety goes *clack* quite loudly, and it has no bolt-hold open mechanism when it fires the last round so that the firer will know he is holding an empty weapon.

I react.

He reacts. He tries to use the rifle as a club.

I dodge left and down, then go up at his feet with all my strength. The knife goes between his legs into his groin to the hilt. He screams.

I pull the knife up, seeing Myerson the whole time.

I split open his abdomen to the sternum and pull the knife left, so his intestines fall out onto the ground.

Even in the dark I can see the look of astonishment on his face. He stumbles forward trying to catch them. But by then the initial thrust, which severs the inferior vena cava and inferior aorta, has killed him. I will hear the sound he makes in my mind, forever, I think.

He falls in a writhing heap.

Then all is silent.

While I still have my wits I check each body. Then I throw up and shake for a while, sitting on the bunker, completely out of control.

Now what?

I'm fifty to seventy-five miles into enemy territory, alone, hurt, lost, soon to be hunted by some angry NVA, in other words in deep shit. What do I do now?

That thought makes my mind flash back to all those training exercises when the TAC officer, who has put you into an impossible situation, turns to you and says, "What are you going to do now, Lieutenant?"

"Well, I don't stay here. I grab food, a rifle, ammo, and the lieutenant's compass and go south — fast."

So I do. I find two bags of cooked ARVN rice, a C-ration spaghetti, canned bread, chocolate, a can of beans and wieners, one of beef, one pork, one apricot, a can of peaches, and a candy bar, stuff they had scrounged from the battlefield and were saving for me. Searching the mess that was the lieutenant, I find my Swiss Army knife — complete with can

389

opener. I can't bite all those cans open. I also find my watch on the lieutenant's arm.

I also find the compass — worth more than the food, rifles, and ammo.

I can only guess where we are. The bunkers are old and well built, and there is a radio with a permanent antenna in the trees. From the stars the one night I knew we'd gone at about an azimuth of three hundred and ten. That meant a hundred and thirty degrees for my return. At least I hope so. They could have just gone three hundred and ten degrees that night and turned in a different direction from then on.

We'd crossed a river on the way. That is my first target. I take my CAR-15 and ten magazines. I also take the .45 the lieutenant had stolen from the ARVN. In my physical condition I am pretty heavily loaded.

Then I stop. CAR-15s sound much different from AKs. I put down the CAR-15 and pick up the lieutenant's folding stock AK. I take seven thirty-round magazines of AK ammo and leave on an azimuth of a hundred and thirty.

If I fire on NVA, I want them to think it's other NVA firing by mistake. If they think that for a second, it'll help. I take only one canteen. Unfortunately NVA have no iodine tablets for water purification. I am risking dysentery and dengue, but I have no choice. I will refill the canteen from the river and from bomb craters.

I don't know how far away are the guys coming to get me. I know by dawn I'd better be across that river.

I remember from all those old western movies that they can't track you across a river. You just walk, wade, or swim down the river a ways.

My heart is still a hundred and twenty beats a minute. This isn't really going as planned. I'd expected to die in the escape attempt. After all, weak, hurt, little me against six tough, battle-hardened NVA, it is ludicrous.

I feel as though I'm making enough noise to be heard a kilometer away, and I know anyone who hears me will not be friendly.

The night belongs to the NVA.

But I have to move. When they find their six buddies, I will be a much wanted prize.

I trip and fall once or twice. Then I calm down. This is just like a night compass problem at Ft. Benning. Take a reading. Find a target. Walk to it. Then take another reading.

Of course, I did lousy on those courses, barely passing. Here barely passing is probably a failing grade.

I've gotten this far. I just keep putting one exhausted, shaking foot in front of the other — very carefully.

I can hear and smell the river before I can see it. The bank is steep, too steep to climb. I walk downstream looking for a safe crossing place.

I find a thirty-inch diameter mahogany tree across the span and almost get on it to walk across.

Then I think: Did Mrs. Harris raise that dumb a child? I take a wide swing around it. Very carefully.

If, I think, this had happened to me the first month or so I was here, where would I be now? Answer: in a body bag, having died shortly after the helicopter crash. In that case, I think, it's best it happens now, when I know how to handle it—if indeed I'm handling it.

I walk as quietly as possible downstream about twenty yards from the riverbank, nearly a full click. When it gets lower, where I can walk to the water, I do. Then I walk to the middle, where the water comes to my chest, and wade downstream for maybe a click and a half. Then I come out the other side, not at a particularly easy crossing point, but at one where I have to climb a bit. Ambushes I don't need—by either side.

It has occurred to me I have no friends in this area. If there is an ARVN or U.S. patrol or ambush out I'll be just as dead as from an NVA ambush.

But then, in times of crisis one never has any friends. You're always alone. You're born alone, and you die alone.

I hear something, but then I've been hearing things all night. I freeze.

Four dark shapes pass twenty or thirty yards away, silent, unidentified. It could be four NVA or a U.S. LRRP team, ARVNs, anyone. In the dark they're my enemy unless they say something in English, preferably with a southern accent. Vietnamese can speak English, but you have to be born in Georgia to have a Georgia accent.

No such luck. Only an idiot would talk at night on

a long range recon patrol, and I'm not sure I want to be rescued by an idiot.

I know no one will rescue Harris except Harris, which means Harris is in deep trouble.

Trouble? Fifty miles in enemy territory, hurt, half blind, alone, lost, scared half to death; you call that trouble?

By comparison Custer was in no danger.

Sitting Bull was a pussycat.

The four strangers keep going. I don't know which side they are on. I stay where I am a while. Then I move on. The sun is coming up. I am tempted to keep going, but I am nothing but a target in the daytime. I eat and camouflage myself into some bushes and try to sleep. The adrenaline has worn off, and I sleep till the afternoon heat wakes me. Then it starts to rain. In rain I can move on. Noises are masked in rain and vision is reduced. Rain is better for me than night.

I move on. A hundred and thirty degrees. Take a reading, pick a point. Walk to it. Take another reading.

I get into swampland. The water is up to my ankles first, then, as I go further, to my chest. I get tired of holding my rifle and pack over my head and detour toward higher ground.

When I get to firm, if soggy ground again, I stop to get rid of the leeches. Of course I have no cigarettes to burn them off. I have to think for a while. How do I make the little bloodsuckers to let go? If I just pull them off, they'll make infected sores, and I have a lot of sores already. I don't think I want more on my legs and buttocks. But I have nothing, so I scrape them off with the Ka-Bar. Leeches inject an anticoagulant into their bite. The bites bleed freely after I kill the leeches, running down my legs.

I go all night, as hard as I can. In my mind the NVA are right behind me. In reality I don't know how far behind they are, or even if they're behind. I don't know how hard an American is to track for an experienced NVA. I don't know if I have a smell that makes me easy to track or not. I heard all the stories about NVA tracking Americans by their aftershave or their cigarette smoke. I haven't used aftershave or smoked or any of the other dumb tricks.

"Fuck you."

Oh, shit, does that scare the hell out of me. Of course, it's just a Fuck You lizard. I resist the urge to yell "Fuck you," back.

Come morning I move for a while, but when the fog burns off, I cover myself with bushes and sleep in the crotch of a tree, totally invisible to anyone more than ten meters away.

I awake in the heat of the day. My water is gone. I am as dry as a bone. I didn't dare fill the canteen with swamp water, of course. My lips are splitting open. I am dehydrating. I find a bomb crater with more or less clear water in it and wait till dark before going out into the open to fill my canteen. There is no question of boiling it for cleanliness. I am desperate. I don't dare light a fire. Better to risk dysentery or worse than to guarantee certain death from a fire.

I know you can see a match for miles, perhaps not

in this thick jungle, but you can see far enough.

I stay there till dark, eat some of the Cs and rice and start out for the night's compass course. One hundred and thirty degrees. Take a reading, walk to that point. Take another reading, pick out another landmark, walk to it. Sometimes I have to take a reading every fifteen paces, the trees are so thick. I make only three or four clicks because of fatigue, bad terrain, and bad water. I stop before dawn, exhausted by diarrhea.

I am dehydrating more that way. I figure I'll be dead within thirty-six hours, or at least too weak to survive alone, unless I get some safe water. I can't eat. I have food, but if I eat, it'll just go through me. I can't waste it like that. I need the nourishment.

I have to search for water, but I am so exhausted and in so much pain from the dehydration and accompanying loss of potassium and calcium and such, I can hardly move. The pain is exquisite.

This is where the battle is lost, where the unsung hero dies alone and unrecorded, his bones lost forever in a cruel, deep jungle.

July 1, 1970, Texas City, Texas

The phone rings at the Harris house. Forty-eight-year-old Wanda Sue Harris, on her way out the door, late to work on the three-thirty to eleven-thirty shift at Texas City's Monsanto Chemical Company, runs back to the phone and picks it up.

"Hello."

"Mrs. Harris?"

"Which one? And who wants her?"

"Mrs. Jerry A. Harris. This is Western Union. We have a telegram for her, ma'am."

"She's not here. But go ahead. Give it to me."

"Yes, ma'am. From Department of the Army, Washington, D.C. to Mrs. Jerry A. Harris:

"We regret to inform you Capt. Jerry A. Harris was reported missing in action 28 June 1970. Further details will follow when available—"

Mrs. Harris angrily slams the phone down. "Another damned crank call!"

She has been getting crank calls ever since it came out in the newspapers that Jerry was in Nam. Anti-war sentiment is high in Texas City. The patriotic types keep quiet, and the anti-war types make noise. The lunatic fringe has been shooting at recruiting offices, setting fire to a recruiter's car, and harassing relatives of servicemen, that sort of thing. Eventually four will be arrested with a crude bomb meant for a recruiting officer.

Mrs. Harris remembers her son's letter.

"If I am killed, two army personnel will inform you in person. If I am wounded or missing you will receive a telegram. These telegrams are marked 'Hand deliver. Do not telephone.' "

So she knows this is a hoax.

She does not know a new Western Union operator is more worried about her pregnancy test than reading every special instruction on a telegram.

That operator marks the telegram Delivered by Telephone and files it.

Mrs. Harris never tells her daughter-in-law about the call. They've had a fight, and they aren't talking much.

2 — 12 July 1970

When I find a clear, running stream, I can only crawl. I drink heavily and eat some of the rations I have with me, hoping some of the nutrition will stay with me.

I would give my left nut for some Lomotil.

I just lay there near the stream trying to regain my strength for a day and a night.

The next morning I feel well enough to move a bit. I am still as weak as a kitten. I camouflage myself into some bushes and sleep.

When I awake, I know immediately something is wrong.

Ten meters away a NVA is taking a shit.

How many of them are there?

He wipes himself with some leaves and starts pulling his pants up. Then he looks right at me, or maybe the .45.

He dives for his AK.

This tells me something in a split second.

One: If he had a lot of men with him, he would yell out instead of reaching for his AK.

Two: He's about to kill me.

I stick my arm out straight with the .45 in my left hand, braced with my right, put his diving head on the front sight, and fire. The gun bucks in my hand, and I fire again. The NVA takes a hit in the neck, and one in his side and dies without crying out or getting his pants up.

Now, how many more of them are there?

I can run and find out, or I can stay camouflaged and wonder.

Then two guys walk over to their buddy, with quizzical looks on their faces. As soon as I see them I flip the AK safety off and fire. They've each turned in my direction, hearing the *clack* from the safety, when the rounds hit them. Both go sprawling.

Now everything's quiet. I crawl away from my position as low as I can, waiting for the crack of an AK, maybe, if I'm lucky, preceded by a *clack*.

But I hear nothing. I keep on crawling.

I must crawl a mile. I'm so covered in scratches from the thorn vines blood is running into my good eye, and I taste blood. I find a good spot and camouflage myself in and sleep.

Come night I trudge on, sleep all day, and trudge on at night, running out of clean water again, and eventually running out of food. Food I can live without for a while. Water, however, is critical.

I am in a drier area than before. There are no streams. I finally find a mass of bomb craters and fill my canteen from a clear pool in one.

I hear a helicopter while sleeping one day. I get up and run to the nearest clearing. I can see a Huey overhead now. I run to the middle of the clearing, waving my arms in the air.

They don't see me at first. Then the chopper banks. They have seen me.

Saved!

Then I see the flashes from the right-hand-door gun and see the bullet impacts to my right.

"The motherfucker's shooting at me!"

I run left knowing he is leading me too much. He'll figure it out in a minute.

"You motherfucker! I'm an American!"

I run for the deepest bushes. The chopper follows.

I run into stuff I'd normally avoid, deep thorn bushes and vines. I cut my face and arms to ribbons.

But I lose them. They circle a while and go on.

"Harris, you have no friends."

I would give a year's pay for the I.D. number of that chopper.

I move out of the area quickly in case they bring in an equally myopic hunter-killer team.

That night the runs come back. I've had nothing to eat all day and have nothing now. I'll lose strength fast.

I hurt so much I have to lie down and try to sleep.

My dreams are even more of a nightmare than reality. Rats eat my guts out. Vietnamese scream in my face and cut on my abdomen and hit and beat me. Colonel Shaw laughs hysterically as I writhe in pain.

I awake sweating and shaking, my abdomen on fire with terrible cramps. I have caught something, some FUO.

I have to move on, I think, and I move as best I can, staggering, falling, wandering. I am totally lost. I try to use the compass, but I know I am wandering from fatigue and delirium.

I sleep in the open somewhere. When I wake up, I have no idea where I am or how long I've slept.

My head is splitting. I drink the last of my water. I can hardly move from pain.

Then I realize the fever is gone.

I find a bomb crater and fill my canteens and drink my fill.

"Harris, this is it. You've no food. The water's killing you. You're one dead son of a bitch."

I can't walk. I lay against a tree, exhausted, broken, delirious. I can see Carole's face. She is crying. She is wearing a black mourning dress, but it comes below her ample breasts, framing them and accentuating them. They are quite luscious with erect nipples. They seem almost real enough to touch and only about six inches from my face. She is wearing a .45 in a strap holster on an army issue pistol belt. I know I'll never see her again. I know I'm dead.

No I'm not. I sit up. I'll get back — to her. I'll do anything to get to her. She makes my life worthwhile and worth saving. There are grubs crawling around the log in front of me. They aren't appetizing, but I remember they are pure protein. I grab and eat one before I can think about it too much.

I gag, but it stays down, washed down with much water. I eat another.

"Just close your eyes, turkey, it's protein."

I keep down enough to fell full.

I go on. Now I am less cautious. I begin to lose sanity. I am talking aloud to myself, singing, moving in daylight, sleeping a lot.

I hallucinate Carole fucking with an NVA in full

lack pajama uniform and pith helmet. She seems to
ave slanted eyes. She is naked except for jump boots.
he is laughing at me. Then she is panting and
roaning, then screaming in orgasm. I see Lieutenant
'olonel Pomeo, his horrible expression when the
ack of his head was opened. He is saying, "What are
ou going to do now, Lieutenant?" Lieutenant? Didn't
  make captain last year? Why is he calling me
eutenant? Why is he talking when he is obviously
ead? Then my grandfather says, "I never thought
ou was gonna be worth nothin' nohow. Such a
nartasssed kid. No guts."

"Granddaddy, you've been dead for three years."

"You're dead, too, son. Dead and unburied. They
houlda buried you, son. You're beginning to stink."

One of my high school teachers appears leaning
gainst a tree, Mr. Litton, a thin, effete homosexual.
I'm disappointed in you, Jerry. You were such a
mart boy, with such drive. You could have stayed
ome, avoided this. All you had to do was spend the
eekend with me. The army wouldn't have had you
hen. You're dying alone in a godforsaken jungle ten
housand miles from home, and nobody gives a
amn. You poor, stupid bastard."

Once I fire my AK at what turns out to be a bush.
I kill a small python and cut off strips of raw meat
nd eat it. I find an orangelike slightly sour fruit. I
void berries.

I hallucinate Colonel Shaw, Carole, dead Myerson
alking with his prick in his mouth. "You're dead,
aptain. They'll cut off your prick, too. Maybe they'll
ive it to Simmons. He needs one. Give him your
rick. You won't be needing one anymore. You're

dead . . . dead . . . dead . . . Captain . . . Captai
. . . Captain . . .

Diarrhea starts again. I lose all strength and li
against a tree. I pass out, thinking, *Too bad, Carole
You'll be a beautiful widow. Your late husband di
love you. Spend the insurance money in good health*

The white sun becomes a tunnel, and it has
bright, bright white center. It has stairs. I'm climbin
the stairs. At the top a woman is standing, her leg
apart, feet spread. She is a backlighted silhouette, bu
obviously naked, the curve of her breasts outlined b
the bright light flaring across them, the pubic hai
glinting in the white light. She wears a beret. She
carrying an M-16 and is beckoning. She is Madam
Death in Battle. Does this count? Is this battle? O
merely war? It must. She is beckoning me, and she
quite desirable. She is the most desirable woman i
the world. I think she is Carole. I climb up the stairs
I almost reach her, but she recedes as I get higher u
the stairs to the light. It is incredibly hot.

Vietnamese voices:

"He is dead."

"Careful. He may be boobytrapped."

"Are you sure he's dead?"

"Smells like it."

I rouse, see two Vietnamese in front of me, and g
for my AK.

"No! ARVN! Friend!"

I shake my head to clear it. Madame Death i
Battle disappears. They are in dark green fatigues
with steel pots. They carry M-2 carbines, which ar
aimed at me.

I start crying. They are ARVNs.

"ARVN?"

"R.R.P.F." Ruff Puffs, local militia.

"Bac Si. Sick. Help."

"We take you to our camp."

They help me up, supporting me with their shoulders. They walk, virtually carrying me no more than five hundred yards before an R.F.P.F. compound comes into sight.

I've almost died five hundred yards from help.

In the compound they give me soup and rice and tea. I ask them to get their advisor. He is with another company. After half an hour he arrives.

He is a young, dark-haired, tall captain named Owen. He smokes a small cigar.

"What unit?"

"Team Seventy, Fifth ARVN, Lai Khe."

"I'll call them. They'll send a medevac. Bac Si says you're in pretty bad shape. Dysentery, fever."

We wait for an hour and a half. Then finally we hear a chopper. By then I've passed out again off and on, hallucinating and dreaming. I think I talk with Owen, but I don't know for sure.

Then everything fades to black.

I am back in the hands of the NVA. But they speak English. That white tunnel returns, with the naked Madame Death in Battle, but now I can see her face. She has an Oriental face, but blond hair, long and straight, like Carole's. She is no longer gesturing. She is guarding the opening to the blinding white tunnel. She is naked except for the beret and a bandolier of M-16 magazines. Her M-16 is pointed at my crotch. Now a VC flag is a loincloth. She seems to be talking in a masculine voice and answering herself in a feminine voice.

"Put this in his right arm. I'll put the other I.V. in his left," says the masculine voice.

"Jesus, is he skinny. Look at those ribs stick out," says the feminine voice.

"He weighed ninety-five pounds when checked in," says the masculine voice.

"Amazing how they can be in such bad condition as this and have a hard-on."

"Men are born with a hard-on and die with a hard-on."

"Unless they bleed to death."

"Yes. Amazing, he's so dehydrated, too. You'd think that'd stop it."

"Or the one hundred twelve pulse and eighty over forty B.P."

They are putting needles in my arms! "Torture!" I say. "Truth serum!" I fight them. They are going to cut my prick off and stuff it down my throat. No, not after all this, not now!

I hear "Thorazine! Hold his arms!" I feel a jab in my right arm. Then I begin to swim in a dark pool and eventually to float. The pool has bodies floating in it, bloated like fish. On shore white-bodied naked women with black triangles of pubic hair contrasting their white bodies are standing, pointing at me. "That one's alive," says one.

"Which one?" says another.

"The one with the hard-on."

Then they fade away and all is black and calm.

I wake ravenously hungry. My nose itches. I try to scratch. I can't move my arms! My eyes open to a view of pure white. I hear muffled voices. I turn my head. A bottle is hanging on each side of me. I follow the tubes down to each arm with my eyes.

Nothing happens for an hour or so, then a woman in fatigues, her hair tied in a bun, walks by and notices I'm awake. She walks over.

"Good morning," she says.

"Good morning. Would it be too much to ask where I am, and what the hell's going on?"

"Yes. You're in the prison ward of the Ninety-third Evac in Long Binh. You were violent when brought in. But, let's see, you're dehydrated. You suffer from malnutrition. You test positive for malaria falciparum, dengue fever, and hookworms. You weigh ninety-five pounds. You have several semi-healed cuts and sores all over your body. Most are infected, but we're giving you antibiotics for that. We took shrapnel out of your forehead, just over your left eye, embedded in your skull, your left elbow, and your left forearm. Three ribs are broken. There are a lot of small pieces still in you, above the waist, none in a dangerous spot, just big enough to show up on the x-rays. They'll work themselves out. We had to sedate you when you were brought in. That's why you're strapped down."

"I thought you were NVA. Fever."

"What are NVA?"

"North Vietnamese Army. You know. The enemy. There's a war on out there. They're the bad guys. We're the good guys. That's why I'm being treated as such a hero after I escaped from them."

"Right. Just when I thought you were being lucid. No one escapes from the enemy in this war. I guess we'll have to keep you tied up."

"Well, that's okay, but it does create one problem."

"What's that?"

"I have to take a piss something terrible."

"I'll get you a bed pan urinal."

"Are you going to hold it?"

"If necessary. If I release your arm will you behave?"

"Yes. By the way, if I didn't escape from the NVA and wander through the jungle till rescued, why am I in such terrible physical condition?"

"It says on your chart you were AWOL for thirteen days."

"AWOL! That's ridiculous! I was missing in action. Where do you get this AWOL shit?"

"That's what it says on your chart. Your unit reported you were AWOL when we called and told them we had you."

"Ah, yes. If it's on paper, it must be true."

"Is it?"

"No, it's bullshit. My helicopter was shot down. I was captured. I escaped. I was held by six NVA regulars, and I killed them and escaped. Thirteen days? I guess so. It could've been longer. I lost track of time. An R.F.P.F. company found me nearly dead."

"Killed six men? How horrible."

"Would you prefer that they killed me?"

"No, but killing is a sin. Couldn't you have escaped without killing them? I know you call them gooks, but they're human beings."

"No. I couldn't. Are you going to keep me tied up? I can't be too dangerous in this condition."

"All right. I'll let you loose. I don't believe a word

of it, but if you can think up a cock and bull story like that, you must be semi-lucid. If you give me any trouble it's the sedative again. You're a prisoner here, not just a patient. We can do barbed needles and proctoscopes, wake you every hour, all kinds of things to make you miserable."

"Ah, yes, a true angel of mercy. But one thing, as a prisoner I was kicked in the balls, had ribs broken, and was almost castrated. A revolver was stuck in my forehead and the trigger pulled. Don't threaten me. Don't ever threaten me, even in jest. Write that on my chart, and tell everyone who'll do anything with me, because, by God, nobody's ever gonna threaten me again!"

"Okay. Okay. But drop that silly story. You'll get out of here faster."

"You can kill me, but you can't eat me."

"Captain, we're here to save lives, even of criminals!"

"Well, lady, you see, I almost died. I think I came about that close. That's why I won't be scared of dying again, because you know what?"

"What?"

"Dying is a lot more pleasant than surviving."

"Then why did you survive?" It's obvious that she doesn't care that I did.

"For a lady — for a lady."

The JAG type wears glasses, has hair too long for a captain, and is nervous.

"You are charged with being absent without leave for a period of thirteen days. You did not return voluntarily but were apprehended. That makes it worse. You missed a scheduled military flight. You were found in possession of stolen U.S. government property, specifically, one Model 1911A1 forty-five caliber pistol, serial number 095467. Your dog tags were missing, and several uniform items were missing. You were also in possession of an enemy weapon."

"Bullshit."

"Which part?"

"The charges, asshole. I was on a fuckin' mission. I was shot down, captured, and escaped. How the fuck did that become AWOL?"

"Your unit's morning report listed you as being AWOL. It's an official government document."

"So what? It's bullshit."

"Look, in view of your status, being overdue for a trip home, if you'll accept an article fifteen, take a month's loss in pay, you can be on the next plane after you recover."

"Forget it. I'm not guilty."

"What is your defense? I have the affadavits and depositions here. How are you going to counter them?"

"I wasn't AWOL. I was shot down. I was ordered by Colonel Shaw to fly C and C on a company insertion. I was shot down and captured. I escaped and walked back from Cambodia."

"That's ridiculous. The records of your unit show you as AWOL as of 28 June."

"I was on a goddamned mission!"

"According to your unit, since you were assigned to a helicopter, and you were not on or near that

410

helicopter when it was extracted, you are considered AWOL."

"Is that army logic? Everybody on that chopper is dead but me."

"Harris, if you persist in this fantastic story, I'll have trouble defending you."

"Who claims I'm AWOL? Where did the charges originate?"

"Captain Alvarez, your admin officer. He signed the morning report."

"This is insane. I wish Colonel Norman were here to see what happened to his crack unit."

"Colonel Norman? You mean General Norman?"

"That's him."

"He's in MACV HQ. General Brassey died of a heart attack. He's taken over for him temporarily till a replacement comes from the world."

"Get a hold of him. Tell him I'm here. I need to see him."

"I can't tell a brigadier general some captain wants to see him."

"You tell him I want to see him or get me a lawyer who can tell him. Is that so goddamned much to ask?"

"Okay, okay, I'll tell him."

"Don't just humor me. Tell him. If he's the officer I think he is, he'll come."

13 — 24 July 1970

I realize the fever is back. I sleep the afternoon away in painful, frightening dreams. Madame Death in Battle returns, but she is covered in maggots, and her skin is the blue of death. She beckons me with her M-16, but I shake my head no. She turns her back and walks away. One leg is a bloody stump, ending above the knee. I realize I have seen at least one stump like that.

I awake to a meal of Jello and bullion and tea. I wolf it ravenously, my appetite back, the fever gone for a while. A nurse comes by and tells me they'll put me on a regular menu after twenty-four hours without fever or the runs. Since I have everything normally caught by G.I.s except gonorrhea or hepatitis, they want to get my G.I. tract back to normal.

"What, no gonorrhea after all the screwing the army's done to me?"

"Everybody uses that line."

General Norman comes by.

"Evening, Captain."

"Evening, sir."

"How do you feel?"

"Like shit. But I'm getting better."

"What happened?"

I tell him in some detail, leaving out Madame Death In Battle. He's impressed by the hand-to-hand combat parts. I'm not. It scared the hell out of me. He likes war stories.

"Harris, this time you *will* get a Purple Heart."

"I don't want a Purple Heart. I want these silly charges dropped."

"I'm working on it. Your lawyer came by, scared to death of talking to a one star. When I finally got the story out of him and that it was you, I sent a couple of my people to Lai Khe. I looked over the charges and knew something was wrong. Captain Alvarez has rotated, so he can't be questioned easily. He put AWOL on the morning report for 29 June, saying you were AWOL since sixteen hundred 28 June. But he authorized the standard MIA telegram to your family on 30 June. I'm guessing it was just a mistake on the morning report, but he's not here to question. Then there are the collateral charges, the stolen property charge and the destruction of government property charge. Since you were reported as AWOL by your unit, the MPs checked the serial number of that .45 you were found with, and since it came from Four—Nine, it was quote, *stolen*, unquote. The destruction of government property charge is ridiculous, because your dog tags and other issue items were missing. They should have been just marked down as combat losses, but I think an overzealous

414

MP lieutenant wanted some charges to plea bargain away so he could have something stick. I've talked to your C.O. If you'll accept a verbal reprimand, he'll just give you an article fifteen, and you can go home."

"Nothing doing. That idiot C.O. knows I was on a mission. He sent me kicking and screaming on it. Let him court-martial me."

"He will. You know it won't work, Jerry. You'll have to stay here a long time for the court-martial."

"Fuck it. I don't deserve a fucking article fifteen, and you know it."

"I know, I'll work on it. Get some rest. We'll work it out. Not the first fuckup of the army, though. While I was with Project Delta, I was bringing choppers into a hairy LZ. A general who didn't know how to spell Delta came over and said, 'Dumbshit, I'm in command now,' and took over trying to direct them in from his chopper. The next two crashed. Then the asshole tried to fry me for it. I got out of it and got him fired. I'll get you out of this. Oh, Jerry?"

"Yes sir."

"It's not too late to extend."

"Sir, have you had a mere captain tell you go fuck yourself since you made general?"

The next day General Norman comes back. He carries a folder with him and pulls a sheet of paper from it. "Jerry, this is a translation of this," he said, handing me the first sheet of paper and pointing to a light tan, wrinkled, dog-eared piece of paper.

"Reward — 50,000 piastres reward. Wanted, American war criminal: Harris, Jerry A. 05431914, Protestant, blood Type A Positive, murdered 6 liberators of the people and escaped confinement for war crimes. 50,000 piastres will be paid for proof of his death. Harris, Jerry A. is extremely dangerous.

"Team Seventy's intelligence advisor, Lieutenant, Shapiro, gave me this. It is proof you were where you say you were."

"Swell. Does that get me a ticket home?"

"No, but I can arrange that. Colonel Shaw agreed to drop the AWOL charge, but not the stolen property or destruction of government property charge. Those will be dropped, and he will give you a written reprimand which will stay with your field two-oh-one file until you leave his unit, BFD, if you sign a letter apologizing for stealing the .45 and losing your dog tags. That way everyone saves face, except you. Of course, Colonel Shaw won't give you any medals. I would have, if I were S.A. for Team Seventy, and I suggested one, but he says only posthumous medals should be given, that we give away too many."

"I don't give a shit about medals, General. I just want to go home. I also think it's pretty asinine to have to sign an apology for stealing a .45 back from the enemy and losing my dog tags while captured."

"So do I, but since he's my replacement, and I'm not in his chain of command, I can't do what I want to, which is to shove the .45 down his throat. Here, read this. You may change your mind."

To: Senior Advisor, Combat Assistance Team 70
Subject: Apology
1. I humbly apologize for stealing a Model 1911A1 .45 cal. pistol from a North Vietnamese Regular Army soldier who had previously stolen it from the late Major Le Tuan Hung, commanding officer of 4th Battalion 9th Regiment, Army of the Republic of Vietnam. I promise never to steal any U.S. Army equipment from a North Vietnamese soldier again.
2. I humbly apologize for losing my dog tags and other issued equipment while a prisoner of war in Cambodia. I promise never to lose U.S. Army equipment while a prisoner of war again.
Jerry A. Harris
Cpt, Armor, USAR

I laugh for maybe ten minutes uncontrollably. Then I take the general's offered pen and sign it, still laughing.

"Now. When can I get out of this motherfucker and get back to the world?"

"The day after they release you from this hospital. Good luck, Jerry."

"Thank you very much, sir. I now owe you my freedom as well as my maturity."

"You oughta stay. I could get you a job. A U.S. unit."

"I just want a job as a survivor."

I've never seen a female bird colonel before. But

there she is. She has an entourage as bird colonels are wont to have, and she comes to my bed.

"Captain Harris?"

"Yes, ma'am."

"I'm Colonel Russell, director of nursing. The hospital commander has just ordered me to personally see that you're moved to a regular ward at General Norman's request. He said that you were put here by mistake."

"Fantastic. First thing that has gone right for me in months."

She supervises as they put me in a wheel chair and moves me, tubes and bottles and all, to a ward with prettier nurses and no guards.

But make no mistake. Nurses in a ward in an evac hospital full of broken, bent, and mending men and boys have all the warmth of a frozen daiquiri. They hide their femininity under fatigues. They don't do small talk. It matters not that most of these boys would give them their G.I. insurance to hold their hands or talk for half an hour. The nurses can't afford to. They have had an ice water transfusion. It is definitely *not* like this in the movies. The lightly wounded are treated as malingerers, and the severely wounded are treated as laboratory animals whose survival is needed to complete a project. Their eyes are dead, and their expressions are masks of fatigue, pain, disgust, and distrust. Without exception, they are much older than their years. But then, my eyes are dead, and my expression is one of fatigue, pain, disgust, and distrust. And I am much older than my years.

Colonel Russell gives instructions I am to be

treated super well. I immediately feel guilty.

Next to me is a guy with bandages all over his body, with his head and one arm wrapped, too. Tubes are all over him, too, with bottles filling and draining. I think of the soldier in white in *Catch 22*.

A boy, for that is what one must call a twenty-year-old, even if he is in a tiger suit and wearing lieutenant's bars, sits beside the soldier in white.

"It wasn't my fault. We did everything right. We'd been on LRRPs for four months. We weren't green. They managed to hit us anyway. Jake, Lewis, Rodriguez all got killed on the spot. Frenchy, Perry—this is Perry, and I got out of the kill zone. We killed three of them. The rest ran off."

He stops and lights a cigarette with shaking hands. "I called a Dustoff. When we went for the chopper we got hit again. Perry got hit by a grenade. Frenchy was killed. I wasn't touched. A Mike strike force came in and extracted the bodies. It wasn't my fault."

I don't know what to say. "No, it wasn't your fault. Sometimes you can do everything right and get killed. That's why they call it a war."

"Yeah?"

"Yeah."

Maybe it helps. At least he doesn't keep saying, "It wasn't my fault."

I get new glasses the first day I'm able to walk, and when I'm released I have to go back to Lai Khe to finish checking out and to get my personal gear, especially the dress uniform required for military airline rates in the U.S. and my SKS.

While there I call Carole from a MARS station. Since radios are used for the link between Nam and the U.S., with a radio-telephone patch from a ham station in the U.S. connecting to the phone system, we have to talk using "over," so the radio operators can switch from transmit to receive, and vice versa.

Mom answers the phone. The ham operator in the U.S. explains how to talk to her then tells me to go ahead.

"Hello, Mom. Over."

"Son! Are you all right? Over."

"I'm fine. I'm fine. I'm not missing anymore. I'll be home in a few days. Is Carole there? Over."

"N-no, son. Didn't you get her letter? O-over."

"No. I've been away from my unit. What letter?"

"Say over, Captain," says the radio operator.

"Over."

"Oh, God, I—I don't want to—to tell you this. Oh, God, I wish you'd gotten her letter." There's a long silence. "Son, Jerry, she left. She left last week. O-over."

"Why? Over."

"I—does it matter ? Ah, she said that the demonstrators are right, that you're, you're all m-murderers. I don't want to be the one to tell you this, son. She doesn't understand that you have to fight, son, to serve your country. I understand. Our whole family fought in World War Two, Wesley in Korea. I understand. But . . . she said she couldn't live with a—a murderer. There isn't anyone else, at least I don't think so. Her . . . her girlfriends. They're all antiwar, and—and they kept talking about how immoral it is to fight the war. You don't know how bad it is here against the war, son. I get harassed. Phone calls about how I raised a killer. Letters without any signatures. It's awful. She isn't cheating on you. She . . . she just left. Took the cats and your car. Don't know where she went. Over."

"Captain, your three minutes are up. Say good-bye," says the radio operator.

I'm crying now. The radio operator is almost crying, too. "Good-bye, Mom. I'll be home in a few days. Over."

"Good-bye, son. That's the best news I could get. I'll be waiting. Ah, come—come on home soon, son. Your grandmother's taken a turn for the worst. Don't—don't waste any time. Over."

"I'll be there as soon as I can get there, Mom. Good-bye. Out."

I try to have dinner with Johnny, but Colonel Shaw demands my presence at his table. He pins a Bronze Star on my chest, the one all officers get for completing a tour without fucking up too badly. It must hurt him immensely to do it, judging by his expression and comments. "This, ah, is for, ah, er, doing a good job, I guess."

Then after dinner he demands my presence in his quarters.

"Well, Harris, I need this little going-away talk in order to endorse your efficiency report before you leave."

"You already have, sir."

"Oh? What'd I give you?"

"Ninety-six, sir, same as Colonel Rains."

"Oh, must've had an aide do it."

"Yes sir."

"Well, what are you going to tell the folks back home?"

"That I'm glad to be home."

"I mean about the war."

"The war sucks."

"Think you did any good here? Think you contributed to the war effort?"

"No, sir. I think I wasted a year of my life trying to advise people who didn't want my advice, who were fighting only for Honda motorcycles and Sony tape recorders."

"You don't think you were helping keep Communism out of South Vietnam?"

"No, sir."

"What do you think will happen when we leave?"

"In a month the NVA will plant a flag in Saigon."

"Well, with an attitude like that what would you say if I said I thought you set the advisory effort in your unit back five years by feeling that way and not having the right attitude?"

"I wouldn't say very much."

"Why not?"

"Because I don't care."

"About what?"

"About what I did to the advisory effort. The advisory effort sucks."

"Are you going to tell that to the folks back home?"

"No, sir. I'm not going to tell them anything. They don't give a damn about us poor, dumb bastards who went off to fight their war for them. They've made heroes out of the cocksuckers who ran away to

Canada or Sweden. They won't want to hear from me. My folks will just be glad I survived so they didn't have to go to a funeral. They won't want to hear how their little boy called in napalm to make 'crispy critters' out of human beings, or how their little boy threw up when he saw a a kid from home with his balls stuffed down his throat. I'll pretend that I don't want to talk about it like vets have since the Trojan Wars."

"What good do you think that'll do for the war effort here?"

"What do you want me to do? Make recruiting speeches? Do you really think we're doing any good? The ARVNs I've seen couldn't fight their way out of a paper bag. Their officers are more interested in harvesting bamboo from a fire base than setting up good fields of fire. They're corrupt. They're lousy fighters, and they're not dedicated. The NVA are very dedicated. They fight to the death regardless of their own suffering. They're tough little motherfuckers."

"What am I going to do to change your opinion?"

"You won't, sir. My opinion has been forged in a year of pain."

"You pompous ass! You've been in the jungle with one unit, and you think you know about the war. You fail to see the big picture. You don't even know what's happening in this big war. How dare you presume to even have an opinion."

"I think I've earned one."

"I don't, Captain. I think you're an immature, smartassed kid who should still be a second lieutenant. I spent seven years before I made captain. You think that because you led troops in combat and

423

called in fire that you're a mature officer?"

"No, sir. I'm a civilian in uniform. I thought we were talking about the war and what I'm going to say about it. If you want me to mouth the official line in order to end this interview, I'll do so. Our Vietnamization program is working. Our wonderful Vietnamese allies are great fighters, and they'll surely be able to beat the NVA on their own if we just supply them with napalm and bullets. Does that help, sir?"

"Get out of here, Captain, before I charge you with insubordination. Go home."

"Thank you, sir. I will. And sir?"

"Yes."

"I hope you get the Silver Star for your work here."

"Ah, er, thank you, Harris."

He apparently never figures out I meant by his rules — posthumously.

Johnny and I talk and drink in the bar till it closes and in his hooch later, promising to meet in the U.S. when he comes back. I know we won't. We'll want to forget about this place, the Colonel Shaws of the world especially. I'm so numb from the phone call the Jack Daniels doesn't have much effect. I can't imagine a life without Carole. Johnny is solicitous. I imagine hearing me tell of it scares him, too. He's got a wife to lose, and he can imagine it happening to him.

"I've heard of Dear John letters over here, but due to the marvels of modern technology you can get a Dear John phone call direct from home ten thousand miles away," he says.

Despite the liquor I hardly sleep.

The next morning I take a helicopter to Saigon.

424

The chopper pilot flies over the Star Hill. Two of the girls are on the roof sunning themselves naked. He flies low and hovers. They wave. He must do this every day.

Hell of a war.

25 July 1970

I'm in Tan Son Nhut waiting for my flight, my long-awaited and once-missed freedom bird. I don't dare say, "I've survived," because I know someone, somewhere, will grab me off the plane and send me back to the bush. When I went through customs they found the Ka-Bar. The young MP held it up and said, "Sir, this is government property."

"Specialist, they sell those in mail-order places."

"Sir, this is government property. It says U.S.M.C. on it. If you want to try and keep it, you'll be charged with stealing government property and court-martialled. You can still throw it in the amnesty box."

So I threw it in the amnesty box and said, "*Du ma,*" under my breath. At least I got the SKS through. Of course it was a registered war trophy. I never thought of needing to register a Ka-Bar since they sell them in mail-order places.

Now I'm in the men's room taking a piss. The graffiti over the urinal says, "Vietnam, love it or leave it."

I think I will.

Spending a year like this does one thing for you, it makes you numb. It provides a local anesthetic for the mind. They can cut and stitch, and you don't feel it at all now. All year I survived because I had something to go home to. Now I don't. Carole's gone. I survived to be with her. Now she's absorbed the anti-war, anti-soldier propaganda, and I don't have her anymore. Maybe I can get her back. A man who could survive all this should be able to win back the woman he loves. Of course, she could be right. I could be the monster murderer she thinks I am. I guess I won't know till I get back into the world, away from green uniforms, Vietnamese, and M-16s. I pull out the lighter General Norman gave me the last time I saw him. It has a MACV crest on one side, and on the other, "Yea, though I walk though the valley of the shadow of death, I will fear no evil, for I am the meanest son of a bitch in the valley."

Maybe, General, but I doubt it. I don't feel like a mean son of a bitch. I don't know who I am. I'm not the kid who came here last year. I'm at least a hundred years older, though probably not any wiser.

I remember a plaque at the SF B Team bar at An Loc.

> You haven't lived,
> till you've almost died.
> For those who fight for it,
> Life has a flavor
> the protected will never know.

Maybe. I sure don't taste any flavor now. I'm just

428

numb.

The motto of the Vietnam War jumps out in my mind. Fuck it. It don't mean nothin'. Just continue to march.

Finally they call my flight. I walk out into the hot sun and onto the plane, finding an aisle seat because my left leg is still a little stiff from the infected leech bites and such, and my ribs throb unmercifully, and I'll get to stretch it out a bit there. Next to me is a sergeant with a CIB, jump wings, and three rows of medals. We don't say much to each other. I don't really want to sit by a R.E.M.F., so he's fine. Field troops have something in common, no matter what the rank.

Finally the big 707 gets its turn, and the thrust pushes us back in our seats. When the wheels leave the ground there's a big cheer. It's the happiest plane in the air right now. I'm cheering, but I think I'm crying. "Leavin' on a Jet Plane" runs through my mind. I'm finally leaving on a jet plane. It's about time, my twelve month dream. I look around at the happy faces in line with me. They all have dead eyes and very old expressions for such young men.

I might make it home after all. Of course, I have no idea what I'll do when I get there.

VIETNAM GLOSSARY

A—Alpha (in the military phonetic alphabet)

ACAV—Armored cavalry vehicle: modified APC with shields added to the gunners' positions. The U.S. Army forgot the lessons of Vietnam, and current APCs don't have the shields. Should there be another war with U.S. troops involved, the position of the APC gunner will not be a coveted one.

ACR—Armored Cavalry Regiment. No, they don't have horses with armor; they have tanks and APCs full of infantry.

A.D.—Accidental discharge of a firearm.

AFVN—Armed Forces Vietnam, the radio and TV network. The six o'clock news on AFVN was called, with some reason, the six o'clock follies.

A.G. — Adjutant Generals Corps. Paper pushing pussies.

Alpha Sierra — Air support.

AK — AK-47 — the Russian, or Chinese supplied assault rifle used by the Communist forces, one of the finest rifle designs in history. A = assault, K = Kalashnikov, after the Russian sergeant given credit for designing it after examining a captured German assault rifle. Forty-seven was the year it first appeared in service. It fired a 7.62 mm x 39 mm cartridge which produced terrible wounds and penetrated jungle growth better than the little 5.56 mm U.S. round.

AO — Area of operations

AOBC — Armored Officers' Basic Course; nine fantastic weeks at beautiful Fort Knox either freezing or frying in the mud and the crud with a bunch of really swell assholes, for ROTC graduates and holders of direct commissions. West Point grads only had to have a 6 week cram course.

APC — Armored Personnel Carrier: a big box with tracks on it and a V-8 in the nose, made from "armored" aluminum. Basically not worth a shit against obsolete hand-held five dollar antitank weapons. M-113s used gasoline engines and richly earned

432

the name Zippos. These were given to ARVNs in the belief that the ARVNs weren't worth a shit anyway. U.S. units got diesel engines and much fewer barbecued troops.

A.P.O. — Armed Forces Post Office

ARA — Aerial Rocket Artillery: armament of helicopters, 2.75 " rockets were equivalent to 105 mm guns and a lot more accurate. Good stuff.

Article 15 — A section of the Uniform Code of Military Justice; a form of nonjudicial punishment.

ARVN — Army of the Republic of Vietnam, also called Marvin, little people, and counterparts. Some of the most inept soldiers since Sergeant Bilko was cancelled.

ASA — Army Security Agency.

ASAP — As soon as possible

Asian Two Step — a krait, a deadly poisonous snake indigenous to South East Asia, so venomous the locals said if one was bitten, one would go two steps and die.

AWOL — Absent Without Leave.

B — Bravo

B.A.R. — Browning automatic rifle: A fine automatic rifle firing .30 caliber rounds in twenty round magazines. It was great if you were a two hundred fifty pound linebacker because it was heavy. ARVNs couldn't lift the mother.

Beehive — Artillery or cannon (tank) rounds filled with hundreds of small metal darts.

Bingo — The point at which an aircraft has just enough fuel to reach home base.

Bird Dog — A light fixed-wing observation aircraft. Designated O-1A or O-1E.

Bivouac — Set up camp

Blackhorse — Call signs for First Cav. (U.S.), from their shoulder patch; a large yellow patch with a black horse and a diagonal bar across it. Ask a cav. trooper what the patch stood for, and he would tell you, "The horse we never rode, the line we never crossed, and yellow is the reason why." But it is not advisable that nonmembers say such things to First Cav. veterans.

Blade time — Used when referring to available helicopter support. Units were allocated a specific amount of blade time daily.

Boc Chi — Vietnamese for medic or doctor. Hearing
Boc Chi!" in a combat situation was akin to hearing
Medic!" with a U.S. unit. I.e. bad news.

Boonies — Also boondocks, bush, Indian country,
jungle or any remote area away from a base camp or
city.

Boonierat — A soldier who lives in the boonies, i.e. a
combat soldier, not a R.E.M.F.

BOQ — Bachelor Officers' Quarters, not nearly as
much fun as the Star Hill.

Butterbar — Second lieutenant, O-1, the lowest form
of life. The most dangerous soldier in the world is a
second lieutenant with a map in one hand and a
compass in the other.

C — Charlie

CA — Combat assault. In this context it means air
assault, i.e. jumping out of a perfectly good helicopter, or rappeling down from one into a hostile landing
zone. If one wanted an Air Medal, one had to spend
one hundred hours in aerial flight, but one hour of
CA equaled four hours toward the Air Medal.
Twenty-five CAs earned one an Air Medal therefore,
if one survived.

Cadre — Headquarters personnel. In a company, the

C.O., XO, and first sergeant would be the cadre.

C and C (chopper)—Command and control. Th[e]
man in the C and C chopper was in command of th[e]
operation on the ground, ostensibly including th[e]
choppers, though the chopper pilots did pretty muc[h]
what the hell they wanted to. If one wanted an A[ir]
Medal, one had to spend one hundred hours in aeria[l]
flight, but C and C time counted as two hours fo[r]
every hour actually spent.

CPT—Captain, 0h-3: "a second lieutenant with tw[o]
years' active duty."

CGUSARV—Commanding general U.S. Army Vie[t]
nam, the head motherfucker in charge.

Chieu Hoi—Literally, "Open Arms," an amnesty pro[-]
gram for VC. Eventually it became a synonym fo[r]
surrender. One didn't shoot at someone yellin[g]
"*Chieu Hoi*," unless one thought he might be fakin[g]
or carrying a boobytrap, or unless he'd just shot on[e]
of your friends, etc. etc.

Chinook—CH-47 helicopter, big banana-shaped twi[n]
rotor A/C. Called "Shithook" with some reason.

CIB—Combat Infantry Badge. Blue and silver badg[e]
with Springfield rifle on a blue field with a silve[r]
wreath around it. Given only to troops in an Infantr[y]
MOS for an extended time, in infantry combat. Th[e]

other badges, airborne wings, marksmanship badges, ranger tabs, etc. were given out in schools in the U.S. This one you earned the hard way.

Claymore — A fan-shaped lane mine which, when detonated, propelled small steel bits in a sixty degree fan-shaped pattern.

Click — Kilometer. A military map is divided into grid squares of one kilometer, one thousand meters.

Close Air Support — Air action against hostile targets that are close to friendly forces requiring close coordination between the air and ground elements. Since grunts and air force types speak different languages, a translator, or forward air controller, FAC, is required. Then if you're lucky, you don't drop a bomb on your own troops.

C.O. — Commanding officer

Cobra — AH-1G attack helicopter: a streamlined two-man craft with immense firepower.

Col. — Colonel, O-6.

Commo — Communications or signal equipment, such as radios or telephones.

CORDS — Civil Operations and Rural Development: winning the hearts and minds of the Vietnamese.

Co-Van — Advisor in Vietnamese, or it might translate asshole, I'm not sure.

CP — Command post

CPO — Chief petty officer, a Navy N.C.O.

C-ration — Combat rations, as if anyone eats in combat. Really good stuff if you're going on a diet. One gets a really swell main course such as rancid pork, a can of apricots or peaches or fruit salad (I used to love fruit salad) or pears, a "bread" or crackers tin, a candy bar, peanut butter or jelly with massive doses of preservatives, coffee, chocolate drink, "cream,'" sugar, toilet paper and cigarettes, so old that Luckies are in some of them. Nine C-rats in your pack will make you really stand tall.

Crispy Critter — Anyone hit with napalm, named after a cereal popular at the time. It helped one forget that one was burning people to death. A certain grisly humor was required to stand the horror of it all. Napalm has a smell unique in the world and can trigger the gag reflex of a veteran to this day.

Crunchies — Infantry troops, also called grunts. The word crunchy comes from the sound an infantryman makes when run over by a tank.

CS (gas) — A nonlethal gas issued to U.S. troops.

438

D—Delta

Dai-Uy — Vietnamese for captain.

Deputy CG — Deputy commanding general. A U.S. division had two, one for maneuvers, one for supplies.

DEROS — Date eligible for return from overseas. The date estimated one would be going home, if one survived.

DFC — Distinguished Flying Cross, given for heroism in operations involving aerial flight.

Di-di mau — Get the hell out in Vietnamese.

Dink — enemy soldier. Vietnamese called the enemy dinks and objected when Americans called them gooks. Consequently advisors had to be careful in their speech.

Dinky dau — Crazy in Vietnamese.

Dog robbers — Rear area types, originally generals' aides who would "rob the goddamned dogs" to keep the generals happy.

D.R. — Delinquency report, i.e. a ticket.

DSC—Distinguished Service Cross, the highest award given by the U.S. Army for conspicuous gallantry. Most gallantry was inconspicuous.

Du-ma—Vietnamese for motherfucker.

Dustoff—Medical evacuation helicopters, called medevacs in some areas.

E—Echo

ECM—Electronic counter-measures. Your car's radar detector keeps you from getting tickets because the military needed to know when radar was being trained on them, so don't say nothing good came out of the war.

E.M.—Enlisted men.

Escort—Armed helicopter escort: Cobras.

F—Foxtrot

FAC—Forward air controller—an air force fighter pilot stuck flying a little bitty prop driven A/C with only six W.P. rockets for armament and thin aluminum for armor.

Fire base—Artillery firing position secured by infantry.

Fire fight — Skirmish between opposing units. It's a battle if you're involved, a skirmish if someone else is involved.

Firefly — Call sign for some flareships, also mission name for armed UH-1 helicopters with searchlights looking for targets of opportunity at night.

Flare ship — Any aircraft, fixed wing or helicopter, used to drop illumination flares.

FNG — Fucking new guy, anyone with any less time in Nam than you.

Foo Gas — Drums of jellied gasoline fired defensively as a mine. Also spelled phougas.

Freedom Bird — The plane which took survivors of their tours back to "the world."

Freq — "Freak" also. Slang for frequency. See also Push.

FSB — Fire support base, same-same as a fire base.

FUO — Fever of unknown origin. If the medics don't know why you're puking your guts up with a one hundred and five fever, it's FUO.

G — Golf

G.I. — Government issue, slang for soldier, from World War Two

Green Beanies — Slang for another slang term, "Green Berets," referring to Special Forces troops, used by those who did not think all Special Forces troops were John Wayne.

Grunt — Infantryman, same-same crunchie

Gung-ho — Very enthusiastic

Gunship — Armed helicopter. By 1969, this meant Cobras.

Ground Pounder — Infantryman

H — Hotel

H and I (fire) — Harassment and interdiction fire. Artillery fire preset to known approaches to a friendly location to harass any enemy snooping around and interdict his movements. Generally it kept friendlies awake and wasted ammunition.

HE — High explosive

Hoan Hoi — Vietnamese drinking game which would be at home in a second-class college fraternity in the U.S. where the man of the minute gets to empty a highball glass in competition with another sucker while the surrounding drunks shout *"Hoan Hoi."*

Hot — A dangerous situation, such as a hot LZ.

HQ — Headquarters

Huey — UH series helicopter, the workhorse choppers of the Vietnam War. UH1D and UH1H were current in 1969. The D model had trouble on hot, humid days. The H, with more power, didn't.

Hump — To carry on one's back.

I — India

Illum — Illumination flares or searchlights.

Impact Award — An award for valor given as soon as possible after an action.

Incoming — Receiving enemy fire.

J — Juliet

Jungle penetrator — Device lowered and raised by cable from a helicopter used for extracting a person (usually wounded) from heavy jungle.

K — Kilo

Ka-Bar — A marine-issue fighting knife: a big, ugly,

bowie knife derivative.

KIA—Killed In Action, the second worst thing that could happen to a soldier in Vietnam.

L—Lima

Laager—Dutch term from the Boer War, all around defensive position by mechanized vehicles, the modern equivalent of circling the wagons.

LAW—Light anti-tank weapon, M-72: an expendable rocket launcher, also useful against bunkers.

LBJ—Long Binh Jail

LCDB—*Lau Cau Dau Binh*: ARVN soldiers who committed a crime, such as deserting, or punching out an officer, were sentenced to a term of being a slave of the unit, carrying heavy burdens, but no weapon, at twenty-six dollars a month, which was insufficient to buy food, much less clothing. At the end of the term, the unfortunate soldier got back all his old rank and position. However, "elite" soldiers, such as armor or recon went to an infantry unit.

Lifer—Career soldier, a term of derision by draftees and other non-lifers.

Little people—Slang for Vietnamese people. Vietnamese objected to this term, too.

Log Bird — Logistical resupply helicopter

LOH — Light observation helicopter, also LOACH.

Lomotil — An anti-diarrhea medicine.

LP — Listening post. Two or three poor bastards spending the night outside their own lines listening for enemy troop movements, trying not to fall asleep, and, hopefully, not getting killed.

LRRP — Long Range Recon Patrols. LRRP rations were freeze-dried goodies such as beef stew or spaghetti with a candy bar and some of the accessories of C-rats. Lighter in weight and much superior to C-rats. Advisors seldom saw them unless they scrounged them. A good scrounger was worth his weight in platinum. Also called LRPs and Lurps.

1LT. — First lieutenant,   O-2.

2LT. — Second lieutenant,   O-1.

LT.C. — Lieutenant colonel,   O-5.

LZ — Landing zone. There are two types of landing zones: hot, meaning someone shoots at you, or potentially hot. It's like playing Russian Roulette. Sooner or later you get a hot motherfucker and people die in the LZ.

M — Mike

MACV — Military Assistance Command, Vietnam

Mad Minute — Concentrated fire of all weapons from a base for a brief period of time, usually at a good attacking time in order to scare the hell out of the enemy, not to mention anyone who's asleep on guard duty.

Maj. — Major, O-4.

MARS — Military Affiliate Radio System. Radios in Vietnam linked to ham radios in the U.S. One could call home with a MARS radio occasionally, paying for only the call from the ham's location to one's destination. Radio procedure was required, though, with the use of "over," which was sometimes difficult for the folks at home.

MATS — Military Air Transportation Service.

Medevac — Medical evacuation by helicopter. Also called "Dustoff," depending on the AO.

Mensa — An organization for geniuses and other assholes. It has little to do with Vietnam, as most people with brains avoided Vietnam.

MG — Machine gun.

MIA—Missing In Action.

Mike Force—Also Mike Strike Force: mobile strike force operated by Special Forces composed of indigenous personnel and used as a reaction or reinforcing unit. I.e. when you needed rescuing by ground units, you got these guys.

MO—Medical officer.

Moonshine—Call sign for a flare ship, a helicopter with a four hour supply of aerial flares.

MOS—Military occupational specialty; what you were trained to do in the army.

MP—Military Police

MPC—Military payment certificates: the monopoly money used to pay us with so we wouldn't do anything immoral such as currency manipulations while we did such fine, upstanding things as killing and maiming.

M-16—Standard U.S.-issue rifle, fired .223 ammunition (5.56 mm NATO), semi-automatically, or automatically at the flip of a switch, weighed about six and a half pounds, used twenty round magazines though thirty round magazines were available on the civilian market. Called "Matty Mattel" (though so was the M-60 MG) because of its looks. It was all black, with a flimsy plastic stock. The ones issued to ARVNs were early issue, usually worn out, and as reliable as a two dollar watch. Later ones had the bugs worked out and became a good assault rifle.

M1911A1 — Colt .45 caliber automatic pistol, designed by John Moses Browning to meet U.S. Army requirements at the turn of the century. Used a seven round magazine. It possessed great stopping power and reliability under adverse conditions, but was hard to teach to non-gung-ho troops and without the most modern safety systems, so dumbassed troops were occasionally shooting themselves or their buddies with them. However, in a trained hand, it is the greatest military sidearm ever designed. The U.S. Army has been trying to replace it without success since 1954.

M-60 — A 7.62 mm machine gun, bipod or tripod mounted, very reliable but heavy for ARVNs to carry.

M-79 — Single-shot 40 mm grenade launcher. Broke open like a single-shot shotgun.

My Lai — Site of a "massacre" of Vietnamese "civilians" by a platoon of the Eleventh Infantry Brigade. As horrible and senseless as it was, it was blown all out of proportion by the U.S. press, who concentrated on it and ignored the VC massacres at Hue (four thousand people murdered) and other places.

After that, all anti-war reporters seemed to be looking for another My Lai, and many of the people at home thought all soldiers in Nam massacred everything that moved.

N — November

NATO — North Atlantic Treaty Organization. A 7.62 Nato is the designation of the standard machine gun round.

NCO — Noncommissioned officer. In the army this meant E-5, sergeant, and above. PVTs., PFCs, and SP-4s were just enlisted men and couldn't go to the NCO club.

NCOIC — Noncommissioned officer in charge.

NDP — Night defensive position. The Cong owned the night, so we went into defensive mode at night.

Net — Radio network: the sum of the units working together on the same frequency.

Nung — A Chinese sect, usually large guys with warrior instinct. Generally much better fighters than ARVNs.

Nuoc mam — An unbelievable sauce made from fish and salt. The Vietnamese lay fish strips, then salt, then fish strips, then salt, etc. on a board and put it out in the hot sun and let the oil which comes out collect in a bottle. They use it on everything. It is not called armpit sauce for nothing. AFVN used to define "numbah ten" as a *Nuoc Mam* meal. Sometimes they add hot peppers, to make it even more unbelievable.

NVA—North Vietnamese army. The really bad dudes. November Victor Alpha. Officially called PAVN: Peoples Army of Vietnam, but none of us called them that or even knew it.

O—Oscar

OCS—Officers' candidate school: a training course for those who haven't been to West Point or ROTC. Graduates are commissioned second lieutenants.

O.D.—Officer of the day; also olive drab, sometimes interchangeable

OER—Officer efficiency report: the little piece of paper upon which an officer's career depends.

OIC—Noncommissioned officer in charge

Out—Radio procedure. "I am finished talking and the conversation is over." When talking to a senior officer, one could not say "out." Only he could. Sometimes this got very Michael Mouse and petty.

Over — Radio procedure. "I am finished talking. It is your turn to talk." One did not say "over and out" except in old movies.

P — Papa

P-38 — Small can opener usually carried on the chain with one's dog tag or in one's pocket on a key ring. Anyone relying on one for a long time will want to use an electric can opener forever back in the world.

PBR — Navy-ese for patrol boat, river

PCOD — Pussy cut off date: Approximately three weeks before going home one stopped fucking around in order to allow VD's wonderful symptoms to show if they were going to in time for treatment before one infected one's wife, girlfriend, boyfriend, or doberman.

Peace — What we were fighting for. "Fighting for peace is like fucking for chastity."

PFC — Private first class, just above private E-2. Everyone in Vietnam was at least PFC unless one fucked up royally.

Piaster — South Vietnamese currency, one hundred of which was worth about one dollar and fifteen cents in 1970.

P.O.W. — Prisoner of war.

PRC — 25 — "Prick twenty-five: a personal radio backpack sized, big enough to be bitch to carry a long time along with normal field gear and a rifle

Prep — Preparation or pre-strike by air force, artillery or Cobras firing on an LZ prior to landing. The grunts always wanted more prep, the planners, who weren't getting shot at, less.

PSG — Military-ese for platoon sergeant.

Pucker factor — Fear. When you're so scared your asshole puckers up real tight, you have a high pucker factor.

Push — Slang for radio frequency. I have no idea how push became a slang for this.

PX — Post exchange

Q — Quebec

R — Romeo

R and R — Rest and recreation vacation taken during one's tour in Vietnam, also called I and I for intercourse and intoxication. All personnel in a combat zone, even R.E.M.F.s, earned one R and R per twelve month tour or six month extension.

452

RAF—Royal Air Force. How the RAF got in a book about Vietnam, I'll never know.

RAP—Rear area pussy. See R.E.M.F.

RBI—Reply by indorsement. "I/my troop(s) fucked up because . . ."

Recon—Reconnaissance

Regiment—Four ARVN battalions (of approximately five hundred men) and one recon company made up one ARVN Infantry regiment.

R.E.M.F.—Rear Echelon Motherfucker. Self-explanatory and appropriate. The hard-corps criteria will be used here, because I have heard middle-echelon RE-MFs call anyone further from the front than them R.E.M.F.s. If one lived in the field with a combat unit, armor, artillery, or infantry, one usually was not a R.E.M.F. But some artillery units lived pretty plush. "Anybody without a CIB is a civilian."

R.F.P.F.—Regional and popular forces of Vietnam: sort of the National Guard working near their own homes; not the best ARVN troops.

Roger—Radio procedure for, "I receive and understand your transmission." One did not say, contrary to Hollywood, "Roger Wilco." See Wilco.

453

Rome Plows — big bulldozers built by the Rome Plow Company. Used for clearing jungle.

ROTC — Reserve Officers' Training Corps.

RPD — Russian built light machine gun.

RPG — Russian manufactured anti-tank grenade launcher. An RPG-2 fired a B-40 rocket.

RSP — Ration Supplement Pack: a big box of goodies; cartons of cigarettes for trading with the natives or smoking, pipe tobacco, cigars, bootlaces; the single most useful commodity in Vietnam, candy on which many advisors lived for many days when the menu at the ARVN mess read rice and cat or rice and putrid fish or rice and bear's brains, etc. You get the picture.

RT — Radio-telephone (operator)

RVN — Republic of Vietnam

S — Sierra

S.A. — Senior advisor

Saigon-Warrior — The ultimate R.E.M.F.

Same-Same — Pidgin English for the same as.

Sappers — Specially trained enemy trained to infiltrate heavily defended positions, blaze a trail through wire and boobytraps, and deactivate some.

SFC — Sergeant, first class; E-7, equal to PSG in an administrative position.

Shadow — AC119 fitted with three mini-guns for aerial fire support. Fired six thousand rounds a minute of tracers from a blacked out A/C.

Short — Also shortimer: someone who had little time left in Vietnam. In any particular group, the one with the least time remaining was short. Elaborate shortimer calendars were kept on a daily basis. A popular one was a pornographic drawing of a voluptuous female with the last day in the appropriate spot.

SKS — Semi-automatic ten shot World War Two vintage Russian (or Chinese or North Vietnamese copy) carbine; a fine battle rifle in its day, compared with M-1 Garand in some respects. Most had a vicious-looking spike bayonet which folded up neatly.

SOI — Signal operating instructions: the frequencies and such one needed to talk on the radio.

SOP — Standard operational procedure

Spad—Nickname for an Al Skyraider: an ancient Korean War vintage prop-driven dive bomber which did wonderful things for our side in Vietnam because they carried a *lot* of bombs and hit their targets well. Perfect A/C for close air support missions.

SP-4—E-4. The U.S. Army did not, contrary to popular fiction, have corporals in Vietnam. Specialist, grade four, not fourth class, replaced them.

SSG—Staff sergeant, E-6

Sterile—Unmarked: A sterile uniform had no insignia. A sterile weapon was untraceable as to its source.

Survivor—A Vietnam vet.

T—Tango

TAC—Tactical air command: the nice guys who dropped napalm and bombs on request and occasionally on the enemy.

Tet—Vietnamese new year.

T.F.W.—Tactical fighter wing

Tiger suits—Multicolor striped camouflaged fatigues. They were not authorized for most troops. Green Beanies, LRRPs, and reporters wore them because no one could tell them not to. If a regular trooper wore them, some R.E.M.F. field grade officer would make him take them off. John Wayne wore them.

TOC — Tactical operations center

T.O. and E. — Table of organization and equipment

Tracers — Ammunition which left a glowing, visible trail.

Trip-wires — Fine wires stretched across trails, tunnels, etc., and designed to set off boobytraps.

Trung Chi — Sergeant in Vietnamese

Trung-Uy — First lieutenant in Vietnamese

TSN — Tan Son Nhut

Turtle — One's replacement. He was called a turtle because he took so long in coming. After all, one had been waiting for him for a year.

Tu-Uy — Second lieutenant in Vietnamese

U — Uniform

U.S.A.I.D. — U.S. Agency for International Development. Their decals were on a lot of jeeps driven by madams and ARVNs. I think they were naive civilians giving away our tax dollars to Vietnamese who sold the stuff they were given on the black market. On the other hand, they could have been a CIA front, but the CIA didn't know their ass from a hole in the ground in Nam, so it doesn't matter.

U.S.A.R.—United States Army Reserve, as opposed to Regular Army types, who were known as lifers and other less polite terms.

V—Victor

VC—Viet Cong, or Communist Vietnamese, also called Victor Charlie, after the phonetic alphabet words for VC. The better ones we called Mister Charles. By 1970 most VC were dead, either through the efforts of the U.S./ARVN forces or because the NVA wanted them all dead by the end of the war so they could have all the cookies for themselves.

VNAF—Vietnamese Air Force

VNAV—Vietnamese navy

VOQ—Visiting Officers' Quarters: an Air Force term, as no one would visit an army base.

W—Whiskey

Wilco—Radio procedure for "I receive and understand your transmission and will comply." So, if you ried to sound like John Wayne and said, "Roger wilco," you were being redundant by saying, "I received and understand your transmission, I receive and understand your transmission and will comply." It was most unmacho and unmilitary to say "Roger wilco."

WO-1 — Warrant officer, grade one, usually a helicopter pilot who didn't go to college and didn't qualify for a commission.

World, the — The U.S.

W. P. Rocket — "Willie Peter": white phosporous rocket, made a big white puff of smoke, harmless unless you happened to get touched by the phosporous, which would burn through to the bone.

X — X-ray

XM177E2 — A 5.56mm submachine gun known as Colt Commando or CAR-15, a shorter, handier version of the M-16, short barrel, long flash-hider, noise suppressor, and revised handguard. Early ones jammed as often as early M-16s. Designed as a survival weapon, it was very useful in close-quarter combat such as heavy jungle.

XO — Executive officer

Y — Yankee

Ya, fí — "Yes, surely," in Vietnamese.

Z — Zulu

THE SAIGON COMMANDOS SERIES
by Jonathan Cain

#2: CODE ZERO: SHOTS FIRED   (1329, $2.50)

When a phantom chopper pounces on Sergeant Mark Stryker and his men of the 716th, bloody havoc follows. And the sight of the carnage nearly breaks Stryker's control. He will make the enemy pay; they will face his SAIGON COMMANDOS!

#4: CHERRY-BOY BODY BAG   (1407, $2.50)

Blood flows in the streets of Saigon when Sergeant Mark Stryker's MPs become targets for a deadly sniper. Surrounded by rookies, Stryker must somehow stop a Cong sympathizer from blowing up a commercial airliner—without being blown away by the crazed sniper!

#5: BOONIE-RAT BODY BURNING   (1441, $2.50)

Someone's torching GIs in a hellhole known as Fire Alley and Sergeant Stryker and his MPs are in on the manhunt. To top it all off, Stryker's got to keep the lid on the hustlers, deserters, and Cong sympathizers who make his beat the toughest in the world!

#6: DI DI MAU OR DIE   (1493, $2.50)

The slaughter of a U.S. payroll convoy means it's up to Sergeant Stryker and his men to take on the Vietnamese mercenaries the only way they know how: with no mercy and with M-16s on full automatic!

#7: SAC MAU, VICTOR CHARLIE   (1574, $2.50)

Stryker's war cops, ordered to provide security for a movie being shot on location in Saigon, are suddenly out in the open and easy targets. From that moment on it's Lights! Camera! Bloodshed!